# The Sixes

## ALSO BY KATE WHITE

### FICTION

Hush

Lethally Blond

Over Her Dead Body

'Til Death Do Us Part

A Body to Die For

If Looks Could Kill

### NONFICTION

You on Top

9 Secrets of Women Who Get Everything They Want

Why Good Girls Don't Get Ahead but Gutsy Girls Do

# The Sixes

*a novel*

# Kate White

*An Imprint of HarperCollinsPublishers*

THE SIXES. Copyright © 2011 by Kate White. All rights reserved. Printed in the United States of America. No part of this book may be used or reproduced in any manner whatsoever without written permission except in the case of brief quotations embodied in critical articles and reviews. For information address HarperCollins Publishers, 10 East 53rd Street, New York, NY 10022.

HarperCollins books may be purchased for educational, business, or sales promotional use. For information please write: Special Markets Department, HarperCollins Publishers, 10 East 53rd Street, New York, NY 10022.

FIRST HARPERLUXE EDITION

HarperLuxe™ is a trademark of HarperCollins Publishers

Library of Congress Cataloging-in-Publication Data is available upon request.

ISBN: 978-0-06-208870-3

11 12 13 14  ID/OPM  10 9 8 7 6 5 4 3 2 1

To Seth Holbrook
Stepson Extraordinaire

# The Sixes

# 1

Something wasn't right. She sensed it as soon as she began to walk across the quad that night. The weather was practically balmy, weird for late October, and yet the air carried the pungent smell of wood smoke. But that wasn't the reason things seemed strange to her. It was the deserted pathways. Though Phoebe wasn't really used to the place yet, she expected to find more than just a few people crossing campus at eight o'clock on a Friday night.

She'd veered left, planning to exit through the eastern gate, when with a start she discovered where everyone was. About forty people—both students and faculty—were congregated in front of Curry Hall. In the two months she'd been at Lyle College, she'd noticed that kids often relaxed outside this particular dorm, tossing

Frisbees or lolling on the slope of the balding lawn, but tonight everyone was standing, their arms folded and their backs stiff, as if poised for news.

As she drew closer, she saw what was drawing their attention: two campus police, as well as a local town cop, were speaking to an auburn-haired girl who appeared to be fighting back tears. The dean of students—Tom something—was there, too, head lowered and listening intently to the girl.

Phoebe's first reaction was to just keep moving. There were things she needed to do in Pennsylvania, but getting involved in someone else's drama wasn't one of them.

She started to walk away and then stopped. She knew that ten minutes later she'd regret not finding out what all the fuss was about.

She edged back toward the crowd and sidled up next to two young men on the fringe, who also looked like they'd just stopped to check out the action.

"What's going on?" she asked the one closest to her. He glanced at her and shrugged.

"No idea—I just got here," he said. He turned to the guy to his right, whose blond hair was closely cropped. "Any idea what's up?" he asked.

"Not sure," the other guy said, "but I think it has something to do with this girl named Lily Mack. That's her roommate over there."

Phoebe took a moment to process the name. It wasn't someone in either of the two classes she taught.

"Thanks," she said and snaked toward the front of the crowd, hoping to score more info there. A second later she realized she was now standing directly behind Val Porter, whose long, prematurely gray hair gleamed, even in the dark. Val was a women's studies professor with an office just down the hall from the one Phoebe was squatting in this semester, and though on the surface Val was courteous enough, Phoebe had detected a mild disdain ever since their first encounter. Maybe, Phoebe had thought wryly, Val thinks I set the women's movement back on its ass by my behavior.

Phoebe started to shift positions, not in the mood for a Val moment tonight. But uncannily the woman seemed to sense her presence, and she turned around. The movement stirred the scent of patchouli from Val's skin.

"Hello, Phoebe," Val said. There was a slightly disapproving tone to her voice, as if Phoebe had burst in late for an important meeting.

"Hi, Val," she said pleasantly. Her MO at Lyle was to play nice, not create any unnecessary ripples. She'd had enough of those in her life this past year. "Is there some kind of problem?"

"A student is missing," Val said bluntly. "Lily Mack—a junior. Her roommate reported it to the campus police a little while ago. No one's seen her since last night."

"How awful," Phoebe said. The revelation caught her like the nick from a razor, and she found herself grabbing a breath. "Well, kids this age can be pretty irresponsible at times," she said, recovering. "Is it possible she's just gone off with a new boyfriend?"

Val gave her a withering look, suggesting that Phoebe didn't know a damn thing about "kids this age."

"Anything is possible, of course," Val said dryly. "But according to Tom Stockton, she's not the type to just go AWOL."

"I take it someone's called Glenda?" Phoebe asked, referring to Glenda Johns, the president of the college.

"Of course. This could get very, very messy."

"How do you mean?" Phoebe asked.

"This girl's boyfriend disappeared this past spring. He was a senior here, and he took off without a trace."

"Do they—"

"Will you excuse me?" Val said abruptly. "I better check in with Tom and see if there's anything he'd like me to do."

It was more than a dismissal. It implied that Phoebe's help wouldn't be needed—ever.

"Good luck," Phoebe said, keeping her voice even. "Let me know if I can do anything."

Val started to turn but then looked back, giving Phoebe's outfit the once-over. That's rich, Phoebe thought. Val's fashion style could only be described as high priestess meets seductress—lots of crushed velvet, jangling bracelets, and deeply scooped necklines—and yet she always eyed Phoebe's clothes as if her fairly classic style didn't pass muster.

"Doing something fun tonight?" Val asked in a tone that suggested she hoped the answer was no.

Phoebe was tempted to deliver a zinger, like, "Actually, I have a hot date with the captain of the men's lacrosse team," but that was precisely the kind of ripple-making she needed to avoid.

"Just grabbing a bite to eat," she said instead. "'Night."

Phoebe turned away and continued down the path across the quad, heading east once again. Lyle wasn't exactly a gorgeous college. All the buildings were either nondescript red brick or concrete, without an inch of ivy shooting up their sides. But there were dozens of big maples on campus, planted when the school was built in the 1950s, and at night, illuminated by moonlight and streetlamps, they looked majestic and almost magical.

As Phoebe hurried along the path, she thought about the missing girl. She also considered the impact the situation could have on both the college and Glenda Johns, who was not only the president but also Phoebe's friend. Two and a half years ago Glenda had been recruited by Lyle College to boost its lackluster reputation and flabby endowment, and though she'd been making progress, it had been tough going. A second missing student in a year would hardly help.

Outside East Gate, Phoebe waited for the traffic light to change, crossed the street, and then walked three blocks down the Bridge Street hill to Tony's, a small Italian restaurant she'd discovered after she'd arrived in Lyle in late August. It was one of those land-that-time-forgot kind of restaurants, with an amateurish wall mural of Venice, dust-coated plastic ferns, and platters of shrimp scampi reeking of garlic, but Phoebe found the small, candlelit rooms to be comforting.

She'd already eaten at Tony's earlier this week and hadn't planned to go back so soon, but a psychology professor named Duncan Shaw had more or less forced her hand. The two of them had ended up on an impromptu committee together, and she'd sensed his interest in her from the start. Several days ago, to her dismay, he'd asked if she'd like to join him and a few friends Friday night for dinner. He was attractive, a little mysterious-looking, even, with his dark beard and mustache. Engaging, too—affable without giving too much of himself away—with a wry sense of humor. But she was on a self-imposed sabbatical from anything romantic, so she wasn't going to be stupid and bite. She'd told him sorry, she had plans tonight, but thank you, and prayed he'd taken the hint.

She'd originally planned to eat at the bar of a new restaurant at the edge of town, where the food and ambience were surprisingly upscale, but now she couldn't take the chance of bumping into Duncan there. After her last class she'd picked up the ingredients for a salad with the intention of staying in. But then, feeling too restless to face a night alone in the tiny house she was renting, she decided she'd sneak off to Tony's. She figured it was the last place in the world Duncan and his pals would be welcoming the weekend.

When she reached the restaurant, she paused for a moment outside, trying to shake the twinge of melancholy she felt. Metallic chips in the old sidewalk caught the moonlight and sparkled like crazy. From a few blocks farther downhill, she could pick up the smell of the Winamac River—muddy, fishy, but rousing in a strange, earthy way. Sometimes from outside Tony's she could hear music wafting up from the taverns along River Street, but it was too early right now. Hopefully, she thought, Lily Mack had hooked up with a guy last night and spent the day in bed with him, oblivious to anything but the wild sex she was having.

As Phoebe entered the restaurant, the short, pudgy Tony greeted her with a bear hug, once again declaring her his favorite blonde. After her first dinner there, someone had apparently divulged to him that she was a famous writer from New York City. Obviously, Phoebe thought, the person had failed to reveal the rest of the story, or Tony would be far less jolly about seeing her.

He led her to her usual table at the back of the main dining room, which ran adjacent to the bar area. She slipped off her trench coat and glanced around the restaurant. It was about three-quarters full, and most of tonight's patrons were well into their meals. She'd come to learn that people ate insanely early in small-town Pennsylvania. At moments like these she felt like Alice after she'd slipped down the rabbit hole: everything around her was not only disturbingly unfamiliar, but it made no *sense*. Seven months earlier she'd been living in Manhattan with her partner Alec, just off the tour for her latest book—*Hollywood's Badass Girls*. She'd bought herself a beautiful pair of diamond studs to celebrate the book's sixth week on the *New York Times* list. Things couldn't have been sweeter. And then it all came crashing down.

It had started with Alec. One night after dinner, when she began to clear away the dishes, he'd held up a hand from his seat at the table and asked her to please wait.

"What's up?" she asked, sitting back down again, predicting what was coming. He was probably miffed at how distracted—and absent—she'd been during the last leg of her book tour.

"We need to talk," he said slowly.

"*O-kay,*" she replied, slightly disconcerted now.

"I care about you, Phoebe," he said soberly, "and we've had five great years together."

My God, she thought, is he about to dump me as we sit here with a platter of chicken bones between us? "What's the matter?" she demanded, unable to keep the edge out of her voice.

"I've always known you didn't want to get married. And I accepted that."

"Well Alec, if I remember correctly, you've never wanted to either," she said.

"I guess. I mean, sure. But . . . . I don't know, lately I've wondered if I may have been wrong thinking that."

The comment stunned her but at the same time eased the twinge of anxiety she'd begun to feel. "Are you saying you want to get *married*?" she asked, smiling a little. But then she saw from the panic flashing in his eyes that she had it wrong.

"It's not just marriage," he said quickly. "I think I'd like *kids*, too. And I know that's a deal breaker for you."

"Well, it's a deal breaker *now*, certainly. I'm forty-two, and there's not much chance of me getting pregnant. But let's at least talk this over. If you're feeling different about certain things, I'm happy to listen."

But his decision wasn't open to discussion. He'd made up his mind to move on and move out, to try something new in life. No, there wasn't another woman, he said. Phoebe had just sat there at the table, reeling from the shock. She knew things weren't perfect with them, that their relationship was less than passionate these days, but she cared about Alec and had never seen this coming.

"I actually thought you might be relieved," he said after a few minutes.

"What's that supposed to mean?" she asked angrily.

Alec had shrugged. "You haven't seemed quite . . . I don't know, in the throes of the relationship lately.

Even with all your crusading, you used to still save some energy for me, but not anymore."

Six weeks later he called Phoebe, wanting to let her know—"out of fairness"—that he was seeing a thirty-one-year-old woman at his law firm. No, he swore, nothing had happened while he was still living with Phoebe, but "to be perfectly honest," he realized in hindsight there'd been a certain attraction from the beginning.

Phoebe had set the phone down feeling stung and humbled. So this must be karma, Hollywood style, she had thought. Is this what I get for calling Jennifer Aniston a Needy Nellie on *Entertainment Tonight*?

She buried herself in work-related projects—research, speeches, TV appearances. But in late May that went off the rails, too. Her editor, Dan, the preppiest gay man she'd ever known, had called her at 9:00 a.m., just as she was sitting down at her desk in her home office. A surprise, because he rarely rolled into the office before ten.

"Have you heard?" he demanded breathlessly the second she answered.

"What? That I've been short-listed for the Pulitzer?" Phoebe had asked jokingly. And then, as if her brain was on a two-second delay, she realized his tone had sounded jittery, not gossipy.

"A blogger is saying you plagiarized your last book," Dan told her. "That you lifted some of the stuff on Angelina Jolie from another writer."

"That's totally untrue," Phoebe had said indignantly. "*What* writer? *Where?*"

"Some British chick who writes for a UK Web site. Huffington Post is the one reporting it. But Gawker has already picked it up."

"Well, it's a lie. I've never taken a thing from another writer."

But she had. Not intentionally. Over the next weeks, as the nightmare began to unfold, she discovered that a freelance researcher she'd used for the book had typed up notes from some blogs and stupidly placed them in a file of Phoebe's own typed notes rather than in a research folder. When Phoebe had read the notes months later, it wasn't hard to mistake them for her own work—the writer actually seemed to be aping a blunt style that Phoebe was known for—and she had incorporated them directly into her manuscript.

On the advice of spin doctors at a top PR agency, she'd made a statement explaining everything, but the press coverage had been unmerciful and unrelenting, fueled in large part by the glee of the people who'd come off badly in her books. *See*, one Hollywood agent had declared in an interview, everything Phoebe Hall has ever written is total fabrication.

Thankfully, Phoebe's publisher accepted her version of events—or at least seemed to—after the blubbering researcher had admitted her error in front of a conference room of executives. They said they were committed to working with Phoebe and had every reason to believe things would blow over, just as they had for authors like Doris Kearns Goodwin, who'd been in her position. But they wanted to hold off on the paperback edition of the book until the situation cooled down. Meanwhile, the press—especially papers like the *New York Post* and Web sites like Gawker—kept at it. Reporters had even camped outside her apartment building to hurl questions at her as she came and went, as if she had run a huge Ponzi scheme or stabbed her husband in the heart with an ice pick. Before long her prized gigs—TV appearances on the *Today Show* and *Entertainment Tonight*, her own blog on the Daily Beast—were put on hold or dried up entirely.

Her pit bull agent, Miranda, had been blunt but empathetic. After all, she counted on those big advances and had a stake in Phoebe bouncing back.

"You'll ride this out, Phoebe, don't worry," she said. "You're one of the toughest women I know."

Was that a compliment? Phoebe wondered.

"Why don't you go somewhere where you can just chill for a while?" Miranda continued. "Cabo, for instance. That's where I'd go. And you can finish the proposal for the next book while you're there."

Fat chance on Cabo, Phoebe had thought. Thanks to the increased expenses from carrying her apartment alone and the fact that the paperback was on hold, she'd be lucky to swing a trip to Tijuana. Sure, she had built a nice nest egg over the years, but it would be foolish to tap into it now. And what's more, she hadn't dared tell Miranda: she didn't have a clue what the next book was going to be.

And then her old friend Glenda Johns had called with a plan. She suggested Phoebe teach a couple of nonfiction writing classes in place of a professor who'd decided to delay coming back after the birth of her child. It seemed to make all the sense in the world. Phoebe could sublet her apartment and regroup in a sleepy Pennsylvania town away from the prying eyes of the press. And with a clear head she could focus on what her next book should be.

When the waiter arrived, she ordered the grilled chicken with rosemary, one of the few dishes on Tony's menu that wasn't up to its eyeballs in sauce. During dinner she made some mental notes about her classes the following week. Once or twice her mind found its way back to the missing girl. Just let her be okay, she thought. Later, as she lingered over coffee, Tony sent over a plate of zabaglione with strawberries. It was delicious, and she ate the entire thing, wondering if all the sugar would make her feel less morose—or perhaps even more so.

" 'Night, Tony," she said after she'd paid her bill and rounded the corner of the dining room. He was standing at the host's podium with the reservation book, just to the right of the bar. "The zabaglione was divine."

"For *you*, I use my finest marsala."

"I could tell—thank you."

There were three people at the bar—a middle-aged couple and a solo guy with wavy, dark brown hair, his back directly to her. As she said good-bye to Tony, the guy at the bar turned his head in her direction. She saw recognition in his eyes and didn't understand why. Then she realized: it was Duncan Shaw. He'd shaved off his mustache and beard in the three days since she'd last seen him.

Instinctively she dropped her mouth open in shock—at seeing him there, and at the change in his appearance. She watched his brown eyes flick to the left, just over her shoulder, checking to see who she'd been eating with. A second later his eyes betrayed his realization that she was alone—and that she'd lied to him about having plans. Damn, she thought. I am totally busted.

He smiled ever so slightly. Unsurprising, she thought. He's not the sensitive type who's going to seem wounded.

"Oh, hello," Phoebe said, flustered. She noticed that in front of him were a half-filled pasta bowl and a nearly empty glass of wine. "What—what happened to your friends?"

"They wanted to drive to Bethlehem for dinner, and I realized I wasn't up for that big of a night."

"Look, I feel incredibly awkward," she said, moving a little closer out of Tony's earshot. "I don't want you to think I lied to you."

He smiled again, a little fuller this time so that it made the skin around his eyes crinkle. Though she guessed he was in his mid-forties, his skin was very smooth, perhaps from having had the beard. "Don't worry," he said. "I'm going to have another glass of wine and see if that will take the sting out." The words could have played sarcastically, but his tone didn't let them.

"But it wasn't a lie—really. I had planned to stay in and work, but at the last minute, I ran out to grab a bite."

"No need to explain." Not quite as friendly this time. She wondered if he was one of those dark-eyed guys who sometimes got moody or sullen.

"By the way, I like your new look," she told him, at a loss as to what else to say. But she meant it. She noticed for the first time—without the beard and mustache— that his nose had an appealing beak. More pirate than professor, she thought.

His smile returned. "Thanks. The beard was just an experiment, and it ran its course. Though I haven't stopped jumping each time I look in the mirror."

The bartender sauntered over to them.

"Can I top off your wine for you?" he asked Duncan.

"That'd be great," Duncan said.

"How 'bout you, ma'am? Can I get you something?"

For a split second she thought Duncan would urge her to accept the offer, and to her surprise she realized she'd tell him yes. But Duncan said nothing, his silence nearly palpable. Of course, she realized. She'd made a bit of a fool of him, and he had no desire to have her stay now.

"Um, no, thank you," Phoebe said. She turned back to Duncan. "Well, I'd better get back. Enjoy the rest of your evening."

"You too," he said.

What a dope I am, she thought as she made her way back up Bridge Street. I should have stayed in, eaten the damn salad. Well, at least this would discourage Duncan Shaw from asking her out again. He seemed nice but this wasn't the time or place for her to become involved.

She cut back through the campus. As she hurried along the path, she wondered if there would still be a crowd near Curry Hall, holding vigil for the missing girl. But everyone had dispersed. As she reached the quad, however, she found a cluster of students gathered around a tree. She realized that they were tacking up a white flyer of some kind. Scanning the quad, she saw that all the other trees were already plastered with them. She cut across to one of the maples to read the flyer.

The headline read "Missing" above a photo of Lily Mack. She was pretty, with blond hair falling far below her shoulders and a small cleft in her chin. With a start Phoebe realized that she recognized the girl. She wasn't in either of Phoebe's classes, but Phoebe had walked with her in the rain recently, and shared an umbrella.

And the girl had told her a secret.

# 2

Lowering her eyes, Phoebe tried to summon the few minutes she'd spent with the girl. It had been about two weeks ago, just before eight one morning. Phoebe had stopped by the cafeteria, something she rarely did in the morning—the sweet, cloying aroma of pancakes and French toast was too reminiscent of boarding school—but she'd run out of coffee at home and was desperate for caffeine.

After leaving the student union building, she saw that it had started to pour. Luckily she had an umbrella in her bag, and she stopped under the overhang to pop it open.

As she peered through the streams of rain, trying to estimate how much damage her Tod's loafers were going to endure, she noticed a girl standing a few feet away from her, dressed in jeans, a T-shirt, and a cotton sweater. Though she was strikingly pretty, Phoebe saw something tentative, sad even, in her eyes and wondered if she was a high school student touring the school, unsure of what to do. It seemed mean to ignore her.

"Do you need help?" Phoebe called out.

"No—thank you," the girl replied. "I was just wondering if I should wait out the rain. But I've got a class."

"I'm headed to Arthur," Phoebe said. "If you're going anywhere near there, you're welcome to share my umbrella."

"Oh, wow, thank you," the girl replied. "I'm headed to Arthur, too."

The girl ducked under the umbrella, and after Phoebe shouted, "One, two, three," they began a dash along walkways already flooded with puddles.

Before they'd run very far, the girl glanced over at Phoebe and called over the sound of the rain, "I really like your books."

So that's it, Phoebe thought: she was *waiting* for me. The phrase "No good deed goes unpunished" flashed in her mind.

"Thanks," Phoebe said. She hoped the blunt reply would discourage further conversation.

"Are you going to be teaching next term, too?" the girl asked.

"I'm not sure yet," Phoebe said. "That's still up in the air."

"I really wanted to take your writing class, but both sections were already closed by the time I heard you were subbing for Dr. Mason."

"Sorry. The department head decided to keep the classes small." Phoebe knew she should be nicer to the girl. "Are you thinking about writing professionally one day?" she added.

"Yes, I think so. Nonfiction like you. I like to explore things."

"Why don't you send me an e-mail," Phoebe said. "When I know if I'm staying or not, I'll let you know."

"Thanks. I'd really appreciate that."

Phoebe refocused on the walk and dodged a puddle. Despite the umbrella, she could feel that the back of her jacket was nearly soaked. At least Arthur Hall was now in sight. Students and faculty were scampering up the steps, eager to escape the downpour.

"Can I ask you one question?" the girl asked hurriedly.

Phoebe had no doubt about what was coming next. It was bound to be a variation on, "What's Angelina *really* like?"

"Sure," Phoebe replied without enthusiasm. All she wanted was to get settled in her classroom before twenty sopping wet students came tramping through the door.

"Is it really possible to start over? After you . . . you know . . . you've made a mess of things?"

Phoebe's body stiffened instinctively. She couldn't believe the girl was shooting this kind of question at her.

"You'll have to ask me in a year," Phoebe said bluntly. "I won't know until then, will I?"

They mounted the steps to Arthur, and Phoebe collapsed her umbrella, shaking the water out.

"I'm sorry, I didn't mean *you*," the girl said, flustered. Phoebe could see that her cheeks had quickly colored. "It's *me*. I—I've made kind of a mess of things."

"Oh, I see," Phoebe said, softening her voice. She felt a pinch of guilt for misunderstanding and being so curt.

"In your book *Second Acts*, you talk about people reinventing themselves," the girl said. "And I wondered, can they really do that?"

"I was writing specifically about celebrities, of course," Phoebe said. "And yes, some of them definitely do."

"I mean *anyone*. Regular people. After something bad has happened, after you've . . . you know . . . you've screwed up. Can you really escape?"

Phoebe took a small breath, gathering her thoughts. She didn't want to blow the girl off, but she also needed to get moving.

"Yes, I do think you can start over. But you have to do the work, as they say. That means figuring out what steps you must take to fix things. You've also got to be willing to look back at the mess and understand how it happened so you don't repeat the same mistakes."

The girl glanced away briefly, and when she looked back, Phoebe saw that her face was pinched.

"Thank you," the girl said. "I appreciate your advice."

"You're welcome," Phoebe said. She wondered if she should probe, but by now the stream of people headed into Arthur had been reduced to a trickle, a sign that classes were about to start. "Well, good luck."

The girl smiled wanly and started to move away. Then she stopped and turned back.

"Don't tell anyone what I said, okay?" she said quietly. "It's a secret."

"Of course not," Phoebe said. "And please send me that e-mail?"

The girl said she would and hurried into the building ahead of Phoebe.

Now Phoebe's stomach knotted as she passed tree after tree stapled with the flyer. Near the western edge of campus she saw that someone had scrawled something on one of the flyers. She approached to take a closer look. The letter *G*—or what looked like the letter *G*—had been written crudely in heavy black marker right across Lily's face. Phoebe pulled the flyer down and stuffed it in her purse.

When she arrived at her house, three blocks west of campus on Hunter Street, she made a cup of tea and replayed the brief conversation with Lily in her head once again, making sure she hadn't forgotten anything. What was the mess Lily had made? she wondered. Was it linked to her disappearance? Should Phoebe have done more to help the girl that day?

And why had someone scrawled across Lily's photo with a marker? Was there someone on campus who hated her?

Phoebe picked up her phone and called Glenda. A babysitter answered and said that Dr. Johns and her husband were attending a campus event. Phoebe left a message, asking that Glenda call her when she returned.

With mug in hand, she circled through the contiguous rooms of her tiny house—a rectangular living room that ran across the front of the house and, in the back, side by side, a kitchen and a small dining room, which Phoebe used for her office, turning the table into a makeshift desk. When she'd first looked for a place to stay in Lyle, she'd had something far more charming in mind—perhaps a house in the country—but this was one of the only decent rentals available, and in the end she'd been grateful for its location just a few blocks from campus. Being isolated in some rural area would have made her exile harder to adjust to.

At one point in her circling, Phoebe stopped in her office and surveyed the table. Toward the front was a stack of papers, articles, and blogs her students had written—that she was in the process of grading.

At the back of the table was a thick folder of magazine clippings and articles, all about celebrities, which she was periodically going through, hoping one of them would spark an idea for her next book. On top of the folder she had laid an antique porcelain pen. It had been a gift from her mother when she first became a writer, constantly writing poems as a teenager. Phoebe had always thought of it as a talisman, something that made the words flow—but it had proved absolutely futile lately.

At 11:30 she gave up waiting for Glenda. She dressed for bed and flicked off the lights in her bedroom, except for the night-light by the door. As she slid in between the soft cotton sheets she'd lugged with her from New York City, she could hear the muted chirping of crickets outside, the last of the year, and from far off, the mournful whistle of a train. Where was it headed? she wondered sadly. She felt so far from anything that had mattered to her, and at the same time she knew she couldn't go back to Manhattan yet. She needed to save her money. And she needed to figure out why things had gone so wrong for her.

For a dangerous moment she felt the tug of something from long ago, something dark and threatening. I'm just thinking too much about the missing girl, she told herself. She squeezed her eyes closed and forced herself to think of her classes on Monday.

At eight the next morning, just as Phoebe was making coffee, Glenda phoned.

"You up, Fee?" Glenda asked. There were voices and clanging kitchen sounds in the background.

"Yeah. I was just going to try you again."

"Sorry I didn't call last night. I was on the phone half the night—dealing with this whole situation. You heard about the missing girl?"

"Yes, that's why I called you. When I saw the flyers last night, I realized I'd had a conversation with her about two weeks ago."

"You're kidding. What did she say?"

"Nothing super revealing, but it might be relevant. She seemed to be looking for answers."

There was a rattling sound on the other end of the phone, as if someone had hurried by Glenda with a tray full of glasses.

"Look, I'm hosting a breakfast for a local group and they're just about to walk in the door. Can you come over in an hour? There's something I want to talk to you about anyway."

"Okay, will do."

For the next hour Phoebe thumbed through a stack of mail she'd been ignoring that week. At exactly nine, she walked the several blocks to the college president's residence, directly across the street from the campus. Though a bit run-down in places, it was still a grand, impressive house, apparently built for some captain of industry before the college was even founded. There wasn't a ton of rooms inside, but they were all spacious, decorated with a mix of antiques owned by the college and random pieces left behind by former presidents who had come and gone, a few with their tails between their legs.

For Glenda it was like living a fantasy. She had grown up in the projects in Brooklyn, and though she and her husband Mark had lived in a series of nice apartments and homes as she moved up through academia, this one topped them all. As Glenda had once told Phoebe, "It's even better than my black Barbie Dream House."

The housekeeper answered the door. Over her shoulder, Phoebe could see that there were a few stragglers from the breakfast still in the living room.

"Dr. Johns is expecting you," the woman said. "She asked that you wait in the conservatory for a few moments." She led Phoebe down there.

It was Phoebe's favorite room in the house. The windows were floor to ceiling, and the space was filled with lush ferns and miniature orange trees. She settled in one of the slightly worn black wicker armchairs. A coffee service had been set up on a table nearby, and Phoebe poured a cup for herself. Outside leaves from the maple and oak trees in the yard slipped from the branches and drifted silently to the ground.

Ten minutes later Glenda rushed in, dressed in a peach-colored wool pants suit that flattered her soft brown skin. Phoebe flashed a smile at her. They had met in boarding school, two scholarship students—both daughters of single mothers—thrust together as roommates. They had forged a friendship from day one. Though Phoebe had watched the gradual evolution of Glenda's kick-ass work skills and career, she still found herself in awe of the woman her friend had become.

"Sorry, Fee," Glenda said, flopping her five-eleven frame into another armchair. "It was like herding cats to get them out. You want anything to eat?"

"I'm fine with coffee, thanks. Any news about Lily?"

"Unfortunately, no—though we've pieced together some details about her whereabouts Thursday night. How much do you know about her disappearance?"

"Nothing, really."

Glenda let out a long sigh. "She was last seen on campus at about eight Thursday night," she said. "She told her roommate she was going to the library, and people recall seeing her there. But at some point she headed off campus. The cops discovered that she ended up at one of those bars I despise at the bottom of Bridge Street—Cat Tails. The bartender says she had two beers and paid the tab at around ten. Two people reported seeing her leave the bar and turn up Bridge Street—but she never made it back to the dorm."

"Why did the roommate wait so damn long to report it?"

"Lily has a friend named Blair Usher with an off-campus apartment over on Ash Street. When Lily left for the library, she told her roommate she might be staying there that night—she sometimes did that, apparently. The roommate was out of the dorm most of Friday, and when she returned to the room, there was no sign Lily had ever come back home. That's when the roommate started to get concerned. At dinner that night in the cafeteria, she went looking for Blair and found out that Lily hadn't stayed with her Thursday night after all."

"A girl last seen leaving a bar alone," Phoebe said soberly. "That's a story that doesn't usually end well."

"I know. And her cell phone has not been used since that night, so it's not looking great." Glenda let out a breath. "So, tell me about your conversation with her."

Phoebe related what Lily had said about making a mess of things and wanting to start over—or escape. When Phoebe finished, Glenda leaned back in her chair, folding her arms against her chest. Her eyes danced around as she mulled over what she'd heard.

"You think I'm a creep, don't you?" Phoebe asked after a moment.

"What do you mean?"

"For not trying to figure out what was eating away at her."

"Not at all," Glenda said. "And you know I'm always straight with you. The girl caught you off guard five minutes before class, and you did what you could at the time."

"I know. But I feel guilty now. And I just want to know she's okay."

"This information is helpful. I'll pass it along to the cops this morning."

Phoebe remembered another detail. "Val Porter told me Lily's boyfriend disappeared this spring. Do you think her disappearance could be connected to his?"

"His name was Trevor Harris, and yes, I wondered the same thing," Glenda said. "People weren't as worried, by the way, when he seemed to vanish. It was this past March. He'd apparently talked about just bagging it and heading out west. He wasn't much of a student, and he didn't get along super well with his family."

"Maybe Lily heard from him and went to meet up with him someplace."

"Possibly. Though she *is* close to her family, and they said she'd never just take off without telling them." Glenda shrugged. "Yet based on what she said to you, it sounds like she was toying with the idea of a fresh start someplace."

"Or a different kind of escape," Phoebe said. "Like taking her life."

"Also possible." Glenda looked stricken.

"What exactly are the cops doing?"

"They're interviewing everyone who knew her, as well as people who were downtown that night. And if she doesn't turn up in a few days, they may use cadaver dogs to see if they can pick up any scent along the river."

"Honestly, I'm surprised you haven't lost more students in the Winamac. It's right by those bars."

"There was one drowning about a year and a half ago—the spring before last. The guy had been doing a pub crawl that night, and they think he got disoriented, walked in the wrong direction, and accidentally fell in. Kind of hard to swim when you're drunk as a skunk and dressed in work boots and corduroy pants. But we're constantly warning kids about drinking and the river from the moment they arrive."

Glenda bit her lip and gazed out the window.

"There's something else on your mind, G," Phoebe said. "I can tell just by looking at you."

"Yeah," Glenda said quietly. "There *is* something else. That's the main reason I wanted you to come by. Last spring we learned that there might be a secret society on campus. A secret society of girls."

Phoebe could feel a breath catch in her chest.

"How big—and what's their agenda?" she asked after a couple of seconds.

"We have no idea on either count. In fact, we've got little proof they actually exist. In May a student of ours showed up at a local hospital having a panic attack. She was completely hysterical. After they calmed her down, she told one of the doctors that she had once been a member of a society of girls on campus, and that they were out to get her now."

"Does this so-called group have a name?" Phoebe asked.

"She called them the Sixes. Tom Stockton—the dean of students—went to see her, but she clammed up on him. She dropped out of school the next day."

Phoebe shifted in her chair uncomfortably. "Are you sure this girl wasn't just having some kind of psychotic break?"

"The doctor didn't think so. Plus, there's something else. Over the past year, maintenance has found the number six painted discreetly in various places—like on the foundation of Arthur Hall—but we never could figure out what it meant."

"Wait," Phoebe said. "Are you thinking Lily's disappearance is tied into the Sixes somehow?"

"I don't know. But Tom Stockton has reason to believe that Lily may be involved with the group."

Maybe that was the mess Lily had referred to, Phoebe thought. Had she been a member for a while but then decided she wanted out?

"What are you going to do about it?" Phoebe asked.

"I've got a plan, but I'm afraid you may not like it."

"What do you mean?"

"I want you to go on an information-gathering mission for me on campus," Glenda announced. "I want you to see if this society really exists and if so, what they're up to."

Phoebe couldn't hide her surprise. "*What?*"

"Hear me out. Even if there's no connection between the Sixes and Lily's disappearance, I need to shut them down. You know as well as I do how groups like this can get out of hand."

"But isn't that something the administration should be doing?" Phoebe said.

"Yes, that's our responsibility, and we've got procedures for these things. You start with the person being harassed and move outward from there. But Tom has been unable to turn up any real proof. If there's one thing I've learned about college kids, it's that they're very reluctant to throw any of their peers under the bus. In sensitive cases we sometimes use a person outside the administration."

"But why would girls talk to *me?* That's—"

"Oh, please, Fee. You're not only a bloodhound when it comes to digging up info, you're also brilliant at getting people to spill—whether it's about their secret lives or their sordid pasts or the affairs they've had with their half brothers."

"Still, I can't just start randomly pumping people, can I?" Phoebe said, running her hand through her hair. But she knew she couldn't say no. Besides the fact that she'd never be able to turn down Glenda—she owed her—Phoebe now felt an obligation to help the girl she'd had so little time for.

"I've thought of a way to handle that," Glenda said. "You can say that I've tapped you to assist with the internal investigation about Lily's disappearance. That gives you the perfect opportunity to ask questions and see where that leads you."

"Will I be stepping on anyone's toes—like Tom Stockton's?"

"I don't think so. Tom doesn't take it personally that we hit the wall with our own investigation about the Sixes. Kids just don't like talking to 'the man'—and in this case it's the administration. But you should arrange for Tom to brief you. He's expecting your call."

For a brief moment, Phoebe felt as if she was sinking in water or sand, but she forced herself to get a grip.

"Okay," Phoebe said, "I'm in. I'll need the roommate's name and info, and contact info for this Blair Usher, too."

There was no time to catch up on personal stuff today. Glenda said she needed to touch base with both the campus and local police before meeting with Lily's parents. They had arrived late last night by car, and she was seeing them in an hour.

As Glenda walked Phoebe to the front hall, they found Glenda's husband Mark buckling a bike helmet on their nine-year-old son, Brandon. Mark was striking looking, half white, half African American, with olive green eyes and skin so light that people often assumed he was white. Glenda had met him during her final year at boarding school and dated him on and off until they'd decided to marry ten years ago. He presently worked as a freelance management consultant, though Phoebe suspected he wasn't too busy in the general Lyle area.

"Hi, guys," Phoebe said. Brandon wrapped his arms around Phoebe in greeting. Mark offered only a nod and smile. She and Mark had never been close, but from the moment she'd arrived on campus, Phoebe had sensed a new coolness from him. She wasn't sure why. The obvious conclusion: he thought Glenda's professional rescue of Phoebe was potentially damaging to his wife's stature.

"Where's *your* helmet?" Glenda asked Mark.

"I'm not going with him today. He's done these streets alone before. It's good for him to get out there on his own."

"But it's Saturday morning. One of us should—"

"In a perfect world one of us would go, but we both have work to do this morning, don't we?" He had a sarcastic tone Phoebe had never heard him use with Glenda before.

"I'd better go," Phoebe said, feeling awkward. "I'll start today, Glenda—and I'll let you know tonight if I find anything."

Brandon tugged on the strap of his helmet as if it was choking him. Phoebe gave him another hug and said good-bye to Mark. Glenda walked Phoebe to the oversize front door and swung it open.

"It means a lot to me to have you do this," Glenda said quietly. "But if for any reason you'd rather not, just say so, okay?" She gave Phoebe a long look.

"No, I'm good," Phoebe said quickly, pulling her anorak closed.

As she hurried down the sidewalk from Glenda's house a few moments later, Phoebe could feel a mix of things churning inside her. There was concern—for Glenda and whatever headaches this situation might cause her, but mostly for Lily. Had the girl just taken off, trying, in her words, to escape a mess? Or had something terrible happened to her after she left the bar?

And there was also unease. The need to know had taken hold in her, as it so often did in her work, but this time, in investigating the Sixes, she would be traipsing over ground she'd sworn she'd never go near again.

She thrust her hands in her pockets, protecting them from the wind that had suddenly picked up. One hand brushed against a piece of paper, and Phoebe realized that it was the flyer about Lily that she had torn from the tree. She pulled it from her pocket and uncrumpled it.

Staring at it, she realized suddenly that it wasn't a *G* that had been scrawled on Lily's face. It was the number 6.

*I*t was in January that she first sensed she was in some kind of trouble.

The school was buried under two feet of snow, and everyone on campus seemed possessed by cabin fever, glum from endless term papers, soggy boots, and the biting cold. But none of that had bothered her. She loved the boarding school and everything about it, especially in comparison to her big, sprawling high school. For her there was nothing more pleasurable than sitting cocooned in a carrel in the library, reading and writing to the muffled sounds of girls outdoors calling out to each other as they hurried across campus in the snow.

The work was tough, but she didn't care. She'd gotten straight A's her first term, had four poems published in the literary magazine, and was up for a spot as an editor of the newspaper. Someone had whispered that she was a shoo-in. She'd written tons already for the paper, and her stuff barely needed editing.

But the spot went to another girl, one who had barely contributed to the paper. It had stung to hear the news.

She tried to pump herself up. There would be another opening at some point, she told herself, and she'd go for it. Until then she'd just contribute more ideas, write even more pieces.

Suddenly, however, her story ideas were routinely rejected, and she was given only one assignment in a whole month—a totally lame little story. It was as if she'd ended up on somebody's bad side.

The third-quarter literary magazine came out, and this time there was nothing of hers inside. What did I do wrong? she wondered. Her poems had seemed so good to her.

And then the study group thing happened. She'd been meeting once a week with three other girls from her American history class, preparing for the frequent and awful pop quizzes the teacher was famous for. One afternoon, a member of the group told her that she and the two others had decided to disband and study on their own. *But a week later, she stumbled on the three of them working in a lounge without her. It was as if they wanted her to see them. She hurried quickly by, as the blood rushed to her cheeks.*

*People have stopped liking me, she realized with a horrible sense of dread. And she didn't know why.*

**3**

Phoebe stuffed the flyer back in her pocket and hurried along the sidewalk, her mind racing. Was the scrawled 6 an indication that Lily had become a target of the Sixes? Phoebe wondered. She pictured the girl's sad blue eyes and felt a fresh swell of worry.

Phoebe had planned to bike along the river that morning, as she'd done most Saturdays and Sundays since she'd arrived in Lyle, but she scrapped those plans as she walked back home. There was no reason not to start her research immediately; in fact, the weekend would probably be the best time to pump students, when they weren't busy schlepping to classes. But first she had to connect with Tom Stockton, the school's dean of students. If she was going to hit the ground running, she needed background info and whatever leads he had about the Sixes.

Once home, she found Stockton's cell number in the faculty directory. His phone rang five times, and just when she was certain it was going to voice mail, he answered.

"Stockton," he announced, his tone firm.

"Hi, Tom, this is Phoebe Hall," she said. "I know I'm catching you at a crazy time, with this student missing, but I was hoping we could talk at some point today."

"Say again."

"Phoebe Hall. I'm teaching here this term, and I'm supposed to talk to you about the secret society—the Sixes. Glenda might have mentioned I'd be calling."

"Oh—right. Of course."

"Can you meet today—to fill me in?"

"I wish I could, but I'm up to my ears with this Lily Mack crisis. I'm on my way to a meeting about it right now."

"Could you grab a cup of coffee after that?"

He sighed. "I hate to commit to anything at the moment. We have no idea if this whole thing will turn really ugly."

The guy was starting to annoy her. Glenda had said he was on board, but it sure didn't sound that way.

"What if we at least set up a time, and then if you *can't* make it, we'll reschedule? I promised Glenda I'd work on this over the weekend. There's a chance the two things might even be connected."

"All right," he said after a second. Invoking Glenda's name had apparently done the trick, but he didn't sound pleased. "Why don't we meet at Café Lyle at noon."

Café Lyle was the coffee shop in the student union. If she was going to entice kids to open up to her, she could hardly be seen fraternizing with the enemy. "Do you mind if we meet at Berta's?" Phoebe said, referring to a little café on upper Bridge Street near Tony's. "I think it might be better to do this off campus."

After another audible sigh, Stockton agreed. As they ended their call, Phoebe considered her next move. Though she didn't want to do much until she had a full briefing from Stockton, there was no harm in talking to Lily's roommate right away. Glenda had already e-mailed her the name—Amanda Azodi—and her dorm.

She headed back out, this time to campus. It was just after eleven when she arrived at Curry Hall. Students, she'd discovered, tended to sleep till noon on Saturdays, but she suspected that Lily's roommate would probably be up already, given what was going on. Phoebe tried the main door of the dorm and realized that it was locked. She'd forgotten to ask Glenda for any kind of access card to swipe. She'd have to wait for someone to exit the building.

After ten minutes a sullen-looking girl emerged, dressed in jeans, a baggy sweatshirt, and Uggs. Her ponytail, Phoebe noticed, was tied with what appeared to be a pair of stretchy yellow panties. The girl allowed Phoebe to catch the door without even a glance in her direction.

Phoebe rode the elevator to the fourth floor and stepped into the hallway. Directly in front of her was a lounge and kitchenette, with a garbage can overflowing with trash and several pieces of sagging, modular furniture; one sofa had been turned upside down. Except for the low groan of the refrigerator, the floor was absolutely still. Phoebe glanced at the number on the first door to the left: 406. It looked as if 424 would be farther in that direction. She realized this was the first time she'd been in a college dorm in twenty years.

Walking down the silent hallway, she imagined the students who lay sprawled in their beds behind the doors, sleeping off hangovers or exhausted from all-nighters they'd pulled during the week. The cinderblock walls of the corridor were plastered with announcements, including flyers pleading, "Help Us Find Lily!!!" When Phoebe reached 424, she saw that there was a makeshift paper pocket taped to the door with dozens of the same flyer inside, obviously there for people to grab and distribute. She rapped lightly on the door several times. From inside she thought she heard someone stir. As she raised her hand to knock again, the door opened partway, and revealed a young woman's face.

Phoebe had only seen Lily's roommate from a distance the previous night, and up close the girl's looks surprised her. At Lyle the pretty girls traveled in packs, and she had expected that Lily would be rooming with someone equally attractive. But her roommate was almost homely, with a wide, flat face, deep-set brown eyes, and shoulder-length brown hair styled in a structured under-curl that seemed from another era.

"Amanda?" Phoebe asked as the girl stared at her in confusion.

"Yes?"

"My name's Phoebe Hall. I'm part of a team at the school looking into Lily's disappearance. May I come in?"

"What's the matter?" Amanda asked, alarmed. "Did they find her?"

"No—not yet. But I'd love to ask you a few questions."

"I already talked to the police, you know. I told them everything."

"Yes, I'm sure you were very helpful. But the college has to do its own investigation. We want to turn over every stone."

"Okay," the girl said after a moment's hesitation. "You wanna come in, then? Sorry . . . our room's kind of a mess."

That turned out to be the understatement of the century. Phoebe entered a space that looked like it had been in the path of a tornado. The two beds, with twisted sheets and comforters drooping over their sides, were on risers, allowing for the desks and dressers to fit underneath, and every inch of extra space below was filled with wadded clothes, splayed books and magazines, plastic dishes, soda cans, and flattened cookie boxes. All the surfaces in the room—desktops, dresser tops, and windowsills—were covered, too, with more books, boxes of tampons, and jumbo plastic bottles of shampoo and hand lotion. One side of the room seemed particularly messy. Phoebe realized that it must be Lily's side, which the police had probably searched.

"Do you wanna sit?" Amanda asked, gesturing to her desk chair.

"Great, thanks," Phoebe said, unbuttoning her coat. As Phoebe took the chair, Amanda plopped down cross-legged onto a spongy-looking throw rug in the middle of the floor and pulled her knees up under her faded Lyle College T-shirt. The air, Phoebe noticed, smelled vaguely of mildewed towels.

"I take it the police have searched through Lily's things?"

"Yeah. And they took some of her stuff last night—like her laptop and her notebooks. Her parents came by first thing this morning. They just kind of stood here for a few minutes and then they left. They're like, totally freaked out."

"I'm sure," Phoebe said. "It must be so awful for them. And awful for you, too, Amanda. I had a friend who disappeared years ago, and the waiting was unbearable."

It was a slight exaggeration. But there were several strategies Phoebe used again and again when interviewing people. The first: Find common ground with the person.

"I couldn't sleep last night," Amanda said, rocking back and forth on her butt. "I didn't want to say this to her parents, but it just seems something bad must have happened to her. I mean, why else would she be gone so long?"

"She's never gone off for a while and not told you?"

"No—though I've only known her for two months."

That news surprised Phoebe. Wouldn't an upper-classman like Lily pick a close friend to live with?

"How did you end up as roommates, then?" she asked.

"The girl I was supposed to room with flunked out. It was too late to find anyone else and way too late to ask for a single. Lily ended up stuck, too. She was gonna live off campus with her boyfriend, but then he took off. The college paired us, and the funny thing is, it's worked out okay. I know I'm never going to be one of her close friends or anything, but we get along good."

"Was she pretty upset about her boyfriend?"

"Yeah. But not like *suicidal* or anything. I think she was sad at first, but then she started to get mad. She said that's what happens when you date a guy like that."

Phoebe didn't say anything. Just waited. That was another technique: Leave a silence alone, no matter how awkward it felt. Invariably the other person filled it, often with something unexpected.

Amanda shrugged a shoulder. "He was kind of a bad boy, if you know what I mean," she said.

"Oh, one of those," Phoebe said, offering a knowing smile. "Can't be trusted or counted on for anything?"

"Exactly. Lily said she thought he'd cheated a few times. But then, what do you expect? That's what you have to pick from at Lyle—bad boys or losers."

"That's a shame. Why is that, do you think?"

"The admission standards for the guys are much lower here than for the girls."

"Really?" Phoebe said, caught again by surprise. "Why would that be? I'm new here, so I don't know a lot about how things work."

"What I hear is that tons more girls apply to colleges these days so most schools have way fewer guys to pick from."

"Got it," Phoebe said. "That doesn't sound like a great situation."

Amanda smiled ruefully. "It isn't. Maybe you can help me explain to my mother why I never have a boy-friend."

"Sometimes, though, as bad as a bad boy is, he can be hard to resist," Phoebe said, prodding. "Do you think there's any chance Lily heard from Trevor and went off to meet up with him?"

Amanda shook her head quickly, as if the cops had already asked that question. "I don't think so. If she'd heard from him, I think she would have mentioned it."

"Had she started seeing someone new?"

"Sort of. I mean, maybe."

"Maybe?"

"I heard her on the phone a few weeks ago. She was arranging to meet someone for a drink. I asked her, 'Hot date?' and she said it was just a guy she was start-ing to get to know."

"A guy here on campus?"

"I don't think so. I asked her if he was our year, and she just kind of smiled and said, 'Wouldn't I be a fool to date a little boy again?'"

"Someone from the town, you think?"

Amanda wrinkled her nose. "Lily's real smart, and she wouldn't date a townie. I just got the feeling it wasn't a student. Maybe Blair knows."

"That's the friend she sometimes stays with off campus?"

"Yeah, she lives over on Ash Street. Number 133."

"How often does Lily stay there?"

"In the beginning of the term, once or twice a week. She'd crash on their couch. But then I guess she got too busy. When she said she might stay there Thursday, it was the first time in weeks."

"Is there anyone else she's particularly friendly with?"

"People like her, but she's sort of kept to herself lately."

"Is she involved in any extracurricular activities?"

"She writes for the school paper and magazine. She really wants to be a writer. And she's on the volleyball team."

"And what about a sorority?" Phoebe asked. "Is she in anything like that?" She kept her eyes on Amanda as she asked this question, observing her body language.

"Oh, sororities aren't allowed here," Amanda said without a trace of guile. "Which is fine with me, because I wouldn't have been picked for one anyway."

"Is there anything else you can think of?" Phoebe asked. "Something you might have forgotten until now?"

Amanda shook her head, woefully.

"Well, I appreciate your talking to me," Phoebe said. "Let's hope Lily *did* just go off somewhere—to clear her head, maybe."

"Yeah," Amanda said hopefully.

At that, Phoebe said good-bye. As she pulled the door shut, she saw Amanda still sitting on the floor, looking morose.

From the dorm Phoebe had planned to go directly to Berta's to meet Stockton, but when she checked her phone outside, she found a message from him saying he had to cancel. "I need to spend most of today with Lily Mack's parents," he said. "Why don't we plan to meet at Berta's tomorrow—same time."

Damn, she thought. She wondered if his excuse was legit or if he'd pulled a power play because he didn't like her on his turf. Regardless, it left her in limbo until tomorrow. She thought about walking over to Ash Street and trying to talk to Blair now, but she knew it would be better to wait until she had a clear sense of what she was looking for. One truth she lived by as an experienced interviewer was that your first encounter with someone when their guard was down only happened once, and you had to do your best not to blow it.

She returned home, and for the next hour or so, she researched college secret societies on line. The most famous one by far was Skull and Bones at Yale, but there were plenty of others around the country. Some concentrated on playing pranks, while others had more aggressive goals, like taking control of student government and organizations. There were a few that actually did philanthropic work.

So what was the Sixes' agenda? Phoebe wondered. There were no sororities at Lyle, so maybe it functioned as one. But if it was just a social club, why terrorize a member?

When she'd finished her search, she turned to schoolwork, completing some of her critiques of the student papers that she'd promised to return this coming week. Most of the kids in her classes were average at best at writing, but a couple showed real promise, she'd discovered. There was a gutsiness to their writing that impressed her.

As she stuffed the finished papers into her tote bag, thinking about Monday morning, Duncan Shaw crossed her mind unexpectedly. She'd been so preoccupied with Lily's disappearance that she'd forgotten about the awkward encounter last night. She wondered if he was ticked at her. Picturing him, she realized how much more attractive she'd found him without the professorial beard and mustache. But it didn't matter anyway. The last thing she wanted to do was become entangled in a campus romance.

From there, her mind flew to Lily once again. Maybe the mess Lily had alluded to was actually related to a romantic entanglement and *not* the Sixes after all. Could she have taken off with the new guy she was apparently seeing? Or been harmed by him? Phoebe was still tossing these thoughts around as she slid into bed later that night.

She woke the next morning at around seven, and after a quick breakfast, loaded her bike in the trunk of her car. She drove through town toward a small park along the river, which spread out from either side of the old steel bridge at the base of Bridge Street. A bike path shot off from the north end of the park and ran for miles along the river, and though it wasn't scenic near the town, farther north Phoebe had discovered some beautiful secluded areas and several stunning vistas across the muddy brown Winamac. Her weekend bike rides had become one of the few pleasures she'd found in Lyle.

Phoebe stopped her car in the parking lot near the park and tugged her bike from the trunk. According to the weather report she'd checked earlier, it was going to be overcast most of the day, but right now there were only a few scattered clouds scuttling across a bright blue sky.

As she walked her bike toward the path, Phoebe glanced around the empty park with its weathered benches and granite war memorial. Across the street was a row of shabby buildings—an old barbershop, a hardware store, and the two grungy tavern-style bars that Glenda hated. One was Cat Tails, where Lily Mack had last been seen the night she vanished.

Phoebe mounted her bike and began to pedal. Even this early on a Sunday she usually passed other people— mostly gray-haired walkers and other bikers—but today she seemed to have the path to herself. Soon she'd gone a mile, and the malaise she'd been feeling began to dissipate. The air was crisp and cool, woodsy scented and almost intoxicating to breathe. And the trees here were brilliantly colored—no fiery reds like you saw on the sugar maples in her home state, Massachusetts, but bright yellows and oranges and burnt sienna. For the first time in ages she felt a surge of something like joy.

After she'd ridden for about forty minutes, she stopped for a drink of water. She was on one of the most isolated parts of the bike path now—dense thickets of trees lay between the path and the two-lane highway that ran parallel—and there wasn't a soul in sight. In fact, she had yet to pass a single person during her ride. She found the isolation suddenly disconcerting. I'll go just a little farther, she thought, and then turn back.

As soon as she climbed back on her bike, an older couple in tracksuits emerged on foot through a cut in the trees, walking a husky. Phoebe relaxed at the sight of them. A short time later she heard bikers coming up behind her, and soon three men whizzed by, suited in full spandex. Okay, no need to worry, Phoebe told herself. A few minutes later a man approached on a bike from the opposite direction. He was in his forties, probably, dressed casually in athletic shorts and a T-shirt. As he passed, she saw him furtively check her out. Give me a break, she thought.

Suddenly the air grew cooler, and Phoebe glanced up. The promised blanket of clouds had finally begun to unfold across the sky, instantly dulling the colors of the leaves around her. It seemed like a good time to turn back. Rather than stop her bike, Phoebe slowed down and made a U-turn in the path.

She'd gone only a short distance when she spotted another biker approaching her from the front. To her surprise, it was the same guy she'd passed five minutes ago. After he'd shot by, she turned; simultaneously he snapped his head back in her direction.

Maybe the guy was only retracing his route, like she was doing herself. Maybe he was trying to pick her up. Regardless, she felt uncomfortable. She began to pedal faster, anxious to reach town. She checked behind her again. There was no sign of the guy. She was relieved when she glimpsed the tip of a church spire through the trees, indicating that the town of Lyle lay just ahead. I'm probably just being silly, Phoebe thought, letting my city fears affect me here.

As she neared the park, she suddenly heard noises ahead—the murmur of voices and also the hum of running motors. She quickened her pace, curious. Emerging from the path into the park, she was stunned see a fire truck, an ambulance, and two police cars parked haphazardly along the street. Yellow police tape had been used to cordon off a large section of the park closest to the river, and about thirty people gathered alongside it.

She dismounted and raced ahead, her bike rattling. She could now see that there were several boats bobbing in the river, black Zodiacs filled with cops and men in wet suits. But the real action was on the bank of the river. One Zodiac had already pulled up there, and several cops hovered around it. Oh, God, Phoebe thought. They had found Lily Mack.

**4**

P lease don't let it be her, Phoebe pleaded to herself. Nearly shoving her bike along ahead of her, she followed the yellow tape until she found an empty spot where she could better see. As if on a count of three, several cops hoisted something out of the boat and onto a black tarp lying on the ground. It was a body, and the crowd gasped in unison. Phoebe could view only the lower half, dressed in sodden jeans.

One of the men stepped back from the body, and suddenly Phoebe could see the upper half. Her heart lurched. The face appeared bloated and partially covered with strands of matted long blond hair, but Phoebe knew that it had to be Lily. A photographer began to move around the body, snapping pictures.

Phoebe needed to call Glenda, but she could barely drag her eyes from the scene. She watched for another minute—until the police formed a human barrier around the body, blocking it from view. Leaning her bike against her hip, she quickly dug her phone from her jacket pocket.

"I just heard," Glenda said after Phoebe had blurted out the news. "I'm headed down there now. Is the body still in the river?"

"No, they've brought it to that little park by the bridge."

"Do you think it's definitely her?"

"It must be. I can't really see the face, but she's got long blond hair."

"I'll be there in five minutes."

Phoebe turned her attention back to the grim scene in the park. A woman with a black bag—most likely the coroner—approached the body and crouched down next to it. The crowd was growing, and people strained their necks for a better view. Phoebe felt gripped by an overwhelming sadness. The smart, pretty girl who wanted to be a writer and had waited in the rain to talk to her was dead, her lifeless, bloated body on display for a crowd of strangers. There would be no fresh start now.

While the coroner busied herself with the body, two EMTs rolled a trolley toward the body and stopped, waiting. Phoebe wondered where Lily's parents were. It would be horrible for them to come upon this scene.

Phoebe glanced back at the people who had gathered around her. Many of them seemed to live in the apartments above the shops and bars across the street or in some of the small old houses that climbed up from the river. There were also a few people in jogging clothes, who, like her, must have come off the river path. At the very fringe of the crowd were four guys in jeans and saggy sweatshirts who Phoebe thought must be Lyle College students. Two of them were talking animatedly on cell phones. It would be only minutes, Phoebe thought, before the entire campus was on fire with the news.

Inside the police tape, the officials mostly milled around, talking to each other or speaking into cell phones and walkie-talkies. The coroner touched her right hand to the ground for leverage and stood up. She nodded, just one flick of the head down and up to the EMTs, who zipped the dead girl into a black body bag and hoisted it onto the trolley. They rolled the trolley to a dark-colored van and lifted it inside. A minute later the van pulled away, with the coroner in the passenger seat, followed shortly afterward by the ambulance. The ambulance was leaving empty.

No sooner had the two vehicles driven away than two cars turned from Bridge Street onto River Street and parked, one behind the other, in front of the hardware store. One was an SUV with "Lyle College Campus Police" on the door. The other was a white Mini Cooper. Phoebe saw that Glenda was sitting hunched over in the passenger seat of the Mini Cooper, as if she'd been shoehorned into the space.

The campus cop in the SUV jumped out first. Phoebe wasn't sure of his name, but she recognized him. He was the head honcho, one of the two she'd seen in the thick of things outside Curry Hall the night before last. He was about forty, with thick silver hair, and he was oddly tanned for this time of year. She didn't know the older woman who emerged from the car with Glenda, but she assumed the woman was part of the college administration. The three of them hurried in unison toward the park. Phoebe waved toward Glenda. When her friend caught the gesture, she signaled with a raised finger that she would join Phoebe in a minute.

It turned out to be longer than that. After the campus cop exchanged a few words with one of the town cops inside the cordoned-off area, the yellow tape was lifted and the three delegates from the school were ushered inside. A man in a sports jacket immediately approached them, likely a detective. At several points the detective shook his head back and forth, as if the group from the college kept asking him questions he either couldn't or wouldn't answer.

Phoebe shifted from one foot to the other. She hated being on the other side of the tape, not knowing what was going on.

After about fifteen minutes Glenda and the older woman ducked back out under the yellow tape and, with Glenda in the lead, walked toward Phoebe. The crowd had continued to balloon, and now there were at least a hundred people rimming the park. Phoebe backed her bike up so that she and Glenda would intersect in a more private spot. As soon they reached each other, Phoebe saw that her friend's eyes were strained with worry.

"It's definitely her?" Phoebe asked, though she knew the answer.

"Yes. She's barely recognizable, but the clothes and jewelry match. Phoebe, do you know Madeline Bloom—our VP?"

"Sorry we have to meet under these circumstances," Madeline said, offering a very firm handshake. She was probably close to sixty, short and shaped like a fireplug. She looked like the kind of person who got the job done, no matter what it was.

"Did the cops use cadaver dogs?" Phoebe asked.

"No, a boater spotted the body a little north of here, bobbing in the water. This was the easiest place to bring it to shore."

She was floating along the river as I rode my bike, Phoebe thought sadly—maybe just a short distance from me through the trees.

"Do they have any idea what happened?" Phoebe asked. She kept her voice low, aware that they were the focus of attention now. Phoebe realized that even if some Lyle residents had never seen Glenda, they probably knew that a tall, attractive black woman ran the college, and this had to be her.

"They were pretty tight-lipped," Glenda said. "The only thing they volunteered was that there doesn't seem to be any obvious sign of foul play—though of course, nothing is certain until they do the autopsy."

Then what happened? Phoebe wondered. Could Lily have killed herself? That thought was as chilling as the notion that the girl had been murdered.

"I overheard one interesting tidbit when you were talking to the detectives," Madeline volunteered in a near whisper, and Glenda and Phoebe turned to her in unison. "A couple of the cops were talking about a sweater. I got the feeling Lily was wearing one earlier, but they haven't been able to find it."

"That could be a key detail," Phoebe said. She turned to Glenda. "And what about Lily's parents?"

"The police are going to break the news, but Tom is planning to head over to the hotel later," Glenda said.

"I need to get back to campus and deal with everything else." She glanced down at Phoebe's bike. "You biked down?"

"No, I came by car."

"Give me a lift back to campus then, will you? That way Madeline can hang here and see if she can pick up any new information." She turned to the VP. "Stay on top of Craig, okay?"

Madeline snickered. "Oh, that sounds like fun," she said.

"He'll want to box you out, but don't let him," Glenda said.

"I hear you," Madeline said, and held Glenda's eyes knowingly. "I'll call you with an update in a little while."

While Glenda slid into the passenger seat of the car, Phoebe loaded her bike into the trunk. Backing out of the parking lot a minute later, Phoebe saw people trailing Glenda with their eyes. Her friend kept her own eyes ahead, her expression neutral, until they were two blocks away. Then she covered her face with her hands.

"What a nightmare," Glenda said, her voice muffled.

"I know," Phoebe said. "I just keep wondering how in hell she ended up in that river."

"No matter what happened, it's bad for the school, of course," Glenda said, lowering her hands. "If she got drunk and fell in, that's bad. If someone killed her, that's bad. If she killed *herself*, that's bad. We're expecting a record number of applicants this year. Can you imagine what this could do to admissions?"

She looked over at Phoebe. "Sorry, I know I'm sounding selfish. I feel terrible about this poor girl. And I feel sick for her parents. But I have to think of the college, too."

"Of course," Phoebe said. "By the way, I talked to Lily's roommate yesterday. I'm pretty sure she doesn't know a thing about any secret society. But Tom Stockton and I are supposed to meet in a few hours, and once he's briefed me, I can really dig in."

Glenda shifted in her seat, and Phoebe could sense her friend studying her with her deep brown eyes.

"You're okay with this, right? I mean, looking into the Sixes."

"I told you, I don't want Stockton thinking I'm stepping on his toes, but I'll make it work."

"No, I mean are you okay digging into something like this, considering . . . considering your *own* experience?"

Phoebe cocked her head and smiled faintly. "Well, isn't that partly why you asked me to do it?" she said quietly.

"Yes," Glenda admitted. "I thought you would bring an understanding to the task at hand. But you must let me know if it hits too weird of a nerve with you."

"I'm okay. I made a vow a long time ago to never let what happened control my life. If anything, it only makes me more determined to help out here. I know just how evil girls can be."

"Do you think if the Sixes really do exist, they could be connected to Lily's death?"

"It's possible. A prank gone wrong. Or maybe she wanted out and they were tormenting and bullying her the way they'd done to that other girl. That could be the mess she was referring to. And she decided to 'escape' by drowning herself." She told Glenda about finding the flyer with the number 6 scrawled across Lily's face.

Glenda sighed loudly. "It would hardly be the first time a student killed themselves because of bullying." Her voice hardened. "If the Sixes really *are* tormenting students, we need to shut them down. We've got to use every possible resource the college has."

"What's the deal with the campus cop?" Phoebe said. "You seemed a little wary of him."

"Craig Ball. He's fairly new in the top job, and so far his performance has been good—he's been able to make a dent in the drug problem on campus. But he's a bit of a glory hog. Plus, he seems to like to hoard info. I'm not a hundred percent sure I can trust him."

"I'd have a hard time trusting anyone that orangey-looking," Phoebe said. "The guy looks like he's starting to *rust*."

Glenda scoffed. "I think he's a regular at the local tanning bed. And he seems to take every vacation in Miami Beach."

"Was he hired on your watch?"

"Yes, but it wasn't some conscious decision of mine. There was an older guy in charge when I started here— Hutch Hutchinson. Kind of crusty, but a real gem. Craig was his number two, hired a couple of years ago. We've got mandatory retirement here, but we'd found a way to ignore it with Hutch because he was so good at his job. Then word started getting around about it, and people were asking why I was playing favorites. The next thing I knew, Hutch was bowing out late last fall, and we had no legit reason not to give the top job to Craig. Later I came to realize Craig was the one who stirred the pot about Hutch and helped push him out."

"Too bad." Phoebe couldn't imagine the headaches Glenda had to deal with. "So what's next for you today?"

"Devising a press strategy. And trying to figure out how to inform the students. Feels weird to put news like this in an e-mail blast, but that's how it's generally done these days." They'd reached East Gate, and

Glenda pointed toward the curb. "Just let me off here, okay? I want to walk around campus and take the pulse."

"Call me if you hear anything," Phoebe said as Glenda stepped out of the car. "I'll do the same."

As soon as she was home, Phoebe phoned Stockton on her cell. She wondered if he'd try to blow her off again, using the latest news as an excuse.

"My, *you've* had a busy morning," he said as soon as she'd identified herself. "Glenda just filled me in."

"Yes, pretty harrowing," Phoebe admitted.

"You can tell me more when we meet today."

So he wasn't blowing her off after all.

"Noon still good?" she asked.

"Yes, see you then."

She stripped off her bike clothes and showered. As hot water streamed over her, the image of Lily's dead body fought its way into Phoebe's brain—the sodden jeans, the long, wet hair clinging to the bloated face. And then she could see Lily underwater, submerged, terrified. Don't go there, she told herself, fighting back tears. Stay focused.

Thirty minutes later, she was headed toward campus. Berta's was to the east of the college, but Phoebe first wanted to check the mood on campus, just as Glenda had. Passing through the western gate, she saw that the

Lily flyers were still up—though some had come partly unstapled and now flapped forlornly in the wind.

How many people know by now? Phoebe wondered. The campus seemed busier than she expected. Bunches of students, dressed in jeans, sweatshirts, and sneakers, stood gathered together at various spots, talking. Phoebe guessed, from the troubled expressions they wore, that the talk was of Lily.

It was a relief to enter Berta's. Something about the atmosphere there—the raffia-wrapped dried herb bouquets and the countless rooster tchotchkes—seemed to repel anyone under twenty-five, giving the town at least one student-free zone besides Tony's. The crowd was generally a mix of faculty and administration, as well as locals, who sat for hours drinking lattes and eating muffins the size of cantaloupes. She surveyed the half-filled room, first for Tom, and then, when she didn't see him, for a table with a little privacy. There was an empty one against the back wall, and Phoebe snaked her way toward it. Though not even crowded, the place seemed to be oddly energized. People surely had heard about the body pulled from the river and were buzzing about it.

Phoebe ordered coffee and waited. Finally, nearly twenty minutes late, Stockton arrived, ducking his six-something length under the upper doorframe as he entered. He was good-looking in an uptight, Waspy way, and probably in his late thirties. Catching Phoebe's hand wave, he wove through the tables to the back of the café.

"Sorry I'm late," he said, pulling a chair out. "It's been perfectly crazy."

"I can only imagine," Phoebe said.

"Nice to officially meet you, by the way," he said, reaching across the table to shake her hand. His grip was so hard it pinched her fingers. He shrugged off his navy barn jacket, letting it sag behind him. He was wearing pressed khaki pants with a crisp blue cotton shirt and a belt of buttery brown leather. His dark blond hair was short, worn in a classic side-part style, and his skin was smooth and clear, except for a tiny razor cut on his strong chin. He looked like the kind of guy who should be working at a distinguished college like Williams or Middlebury; she wondered how he'd ended up at Lyle.

"Same here," she said, forcing a smile. There was a snootiness to the guy that was already rubbing her the wrong way.

"How are you liking teaching?" he asked. "It's a whole different ball game for you, isn't it?"

"Completely different ball game," Phoebe said. "But I'm enjoying it."

*Enjoying* was a stretch, but Phoebe was hardly going to be candid with Stockton.

"And I hear you and Glenda go way back," Stockton said, his slate-colored eyes curious. "You went to boarding school together."

"Yes, that's right," she said, hurriedly. She was anxious to abandon that topic and get on to what mattered. Thankfully the waitress came by to take Stockton's order.

"So, tell me about this morning," he said, turning his attention back to Phoebe. "You just happened to be downtown in the park when they found the body?"

What the heck was he implying, she wondered. That she was some sort of ambulance chaser?

"Actually I was coming off the bike path after a ride," Phoebe said. "I saw the commotion in the park and headed over."

"Was there any bruising on the body? Any indication that she'd been attacked?"

"I never got that close."

"Did you have any sense of what might have happened?"

"No, just that she'd clearly been in the water for a while. Are there surveillance cameras downtown, do you know? I've been wondering if one of them picked up something the night Lily disappeared."

Stockton scoffed. "I'm afraid we local yokels in Lyle haven't quite caught up with New York and London in that regard," he said. Was that a dig? she wondered. Regardless, she wasn't going to snipe back and risk pissing him off.

"At least more eyewitnesses may come forward now that they've found her body," Phoebe said. "Glenda says Lily was last seen going up Bridge Street—after she'd left the Cat Tails bar. For some reason she turned around and ended up back down at the river."

"Don't you think it's obvious that someone intercepted her walk home?" Stockton said.

"And convinced her to go back down along the river?"

"*Convinced* isn't the word I had in mind," he said.

"What about the possibility of suicide?" Phoebe asked.

"Why start up the hill if you were planning to drown yourself?"

The waitress arrived with a mug of black coffee for Stockton and slid it in front of him.

"Do you mind if we switch gears for a minute?" Phoebe said. "As you know, Glenda wants me to look into this secret society—the Sixes."

"I'm more than willing to discuss it, though I must admit it's fairly low on my list right now."

"Why's that?"

"Because Lily Mack's death is one through ten on that list." His voice sounded impatient. "Don't get me wrong. We don't want any kind of secret society on our campus. But the death of a student takes precedence over everything."

"But don't you think there's a small chance that Lily's death might be related to the Sixes somehow?"

Stockton leaned back in his chair and pinched his lips together.

"As I said, I'm concerned about the Sixes," he said. "But even if they *do* exist—and that's still an if—I don't think they had anything to do with what happened to Lily."

"What *do* you think, then?" she asked, because it was clear to her now that he had a theory. She took a sip of her coffee.

Stockton narrowed his eyes and stared intensely at Phoebe.

"I think we may have a serial killer on our hands."

# 5

Phoebe gulped down her coffee in surprise.

"*What?*" she said.

Stockton quickly turned his head to the right and then to the left, making sure no one was eavesdropping.

"This has to be under the cone of silence, all right?" He waited for Phoebe's nod. "I think there may be a predator out there who gets his jollies from drugging college students and drowning them in the river."

"But who are the other victims besides Lily?" Phoebe asked, still taken aback. She wondered why Glenda hadn't mentioned anything about this.

"We had a student drown in the Winamac the April before last. A senior named Scott Macus."

"But Glenda told me he'd been out drinking and stumbled into the river."

"That's what everyone assumed. But after I heard about Lily this morning, I went back and looked at Scott's file. The blood alcohol report indicated he'd had about three beers. Hardly enough to make most guys disoriented. The last place he was seen was at Cat Tails—sound familiar? Then, according to his friends, he just disappeared. They said it was totally unlike him to go off without telling them."

"Were there any marks on his body?" Phoebe asked.

"Nothing to indicate a struggle. But if someone's been drugged, it wouldn't take much to force them into the river."

"Two deaths don't necessarily add up to a serial killer," Phoebe said.

"You're right," Stockton replied. "But those aren't the only deaths. Ever hear of Parker-Hyde College? It's about an hour and a half north of here on the river. A male student drowned there a year ago. And there have been a number of similar cases in the Midwest—all involving college students who mysteriously drowned after a night out but who didn't appear to be inebriated."

"How awful," Phoebe said. "Have any of the drowning victims other than Lily been female?"

"Not that I'm aware of. But I've just begun to look into this. I haven't even had a chance to mention this to Glenda."

Phoebe glanced away, thinking. Stockton's theory made her skin crawl. Could it really be true? It seemed far-fetched, and yet she'd read that serial killers did migrate from one area to another. God, she thought, if Glenda was concerned about the impact of a secret society on Lyle's admissions, Phoebe could only imagine what news of a serial killer would do.

"Do you mind if we get back to the Sixes for a minute?" Phoebe asked. "Lily's death might not be connected to them, but Glenda wants me to look into the group regardless. As you said, it's a problem in its own right."

Stockton pinched his lips together again and examined some imaginary thing floating on the top of his coffee.

"I hope you won't take offense," he said, lifting his head up. Then he shot her a patronizing smile. "But I've got to be perfectly blunt here. This kind of problem should be handled by someone from the administration, or at the very least by a regular faculty member. Not . . . an outsider."

Phoebe took a breath before answering. "But as we both know, sometimes an outsider has a better shot at obtaining information," she said.

"You're not telling me anything I don't know." Stockton sniffed. "But you've been at the college for less than two months."

It took everything Phoebe had to smile nicely at him. The guy was pompous and arrogant, but she needed his full cooperation.

"Why don't I start with my research and see how it goes," Phoebe said. "If it doesn't work, or if it creates problems, Glenda certainly isn't going to want me to continue."

He shrugged, forced to resign. "Okay. What do you need to know?"

"Glenda said you first heard about the Sixes when a student ended up in the ER last spring."

"Correct. It was early May. I received a call one night from the manager of the ER at Cranberry Medical Center—it's about ten miles north of here. A student named Alexis Grey had arrived there hyperventilating. She was alone, by the way, and it was unclear how she'd gotten to the hospital. After they examined her, it was obvious she was having a panic attack, which intensified when they suggested having someone from the college come and fetch her. She blurted out something about having been a part of this secret society called the Sixes, and that when she'd quit the group, they'd begun to torment her. But that was the most anyone was ever able to get out of her. I went to see her that night, but she refused to talk to me. Her parents arrived the next morning, and brought her home—she's from the Baltimore area—and she refused to return to Lyle. There were only a few weeks left of classes, but she chose to forfeit the entire term. I tried to get the parents to talk to me, but either Alexis had forbidden them to or they knew nothing."

"And other than that incident, the only hint of the group has been the number six showing up on campus?"

"Yes, painted in spots, carved in others. Sometimes six things collected in places. But in hindsight, I realized I'd also picked up an odd vibe here and there. For example, at the start of this term I put together a student committee with the so-called purpose of examining quality of life on campus, but really I was following up on what had happened to Alexis. I wanted to see if I could spot any fault lines. At one of our sessions I mentioned that I thought it was a good thing that Lyle didn't allow sororities. I saw a look flash between two of the girls—it was the kind of look that said, Well, we *do* have something like that. I tried to probe, but they went instantly incommunicado."

"Do you think that's what the Sixes basically is—a sorority? Or is it sinister in nature?"

"*Sinister* seems far too strong of a word," Stockton said. "If they're the ones marking things with a six, then it would seem they're just about making a little mischief. True, Alexis was pretty upset, but her meltdown might have been due to a combination of other factors."

Phoebe touched her finger to her lip. "Glenda said you had reason to believe Lily might be involved."

"Shortly after the term started—we're talking the first week of September—maintenance complained that someone had been dragging some of the Adirondack chairs from the quad out onto the plaza in front of the student union every night. Turns out it was always six chairs. So I asked Craig Ball to position a guy to watch one night. Lo and behold, at three in the morning, he discovers two girls dragging the chairs across the grass. Lily Mack and Blair Usher."

"Did you talk to them?"

"You bet. Separately. But they'd worked out their cover story by then. Claimed they'd been up studying and wanted to chill. Said they could see the stars better out on the plaza, away from the trees. And they denied doing it previously. Unfortunately the cop intervened before they'd dragged over more than two chairs, so there was no way to prove they were behind the other incidents."

"What do you know about Blair?"

"Senior. Excellent student. Varsity field hockey. Beautiful. What your Hollywood pals might call an It girl."

"I heard that Lily told her roommate she might stay with Blair Thursday night. Don't you think it could be more than a coincidence that Lily planned to see Blair on the night she disappeared? I'm not sure if Glenda told you, but I spoke to Lily two weeks ago. She said she'd made a mess of things, and she seemed anxious to break free. Maybe the mess Lily wanted to pull back from was the Sixes, and they didn't want to let her go."

"College students are always making messes. There's no reason to believe that the mess she referred to involved the Sixes or that her death has anything to do with what she talked to you about."

Before Phoebe could respond, Stockton cocked his wrist to check his watch. "I should go," he said. "I want to follow up on what happened with the parents at the morgue." He reached back and tugged his wallet from his pocket. More buttery brown leather.

"Please, let me pick this up," Phoebe said. "But before you go, can I get the names of the two girls who exchanged the look?"

Stockton's eyes widened, as if he finally understood that she was really going to look into this.

"Why don't I shoot you an e-mail as soon as I return to campus?" he said, then nodded good-bye and threaded his way through the tables and out the front door.

Rather than ask for the check, Phoebe ordered another coffee and mulled over what she'd just heard. God, she thought, secret societies and serial killers—Lyle is sounding more and more like the college from hell.

Regardless of how Lily had died, Phoebe's job was to investigate the Sixes. She decided she would swing by Blair's apartment as soon as she left Berta's, and later, once she had the info from Stockton, she would try to speak to at least one of the two girls from the committee.

Phoebe also wanted to make contact with Alexis somehow. Maybe the girl had calmed down enough over the past six months to be willing to spill some information. There was a decent chance Alexis had transferred to another college, but it might be in the mid-Atlantic region like Lyle, and therefore fairly easy to drive to.

Outside, a few minutes later, Phoebe pulled her jacket tighter. The sky was low and dark now, and the temperature seemed to have plummeted in the forty-five minutes she'd been inside. Later, when she was back at her house, she'd have to dig out her down coat from whatever box it was still stuffed in. Well, at least that will give me something to do, she thought ruefully. Since she'd moved to Lyle, she found Sunday evenings to be particularly lonely, exacerbated by a type of back-to-school blues that must have been stirred up by being on a campus again. As a counterattack, she'd begun a ritual of making pasta on Sunday nights and eating it with a good wine. Tonight, of course, would be even tougher to contend with. She'd have the memory of Lily Mack's body running roughshod over her brain.

Unbidden, Duncan came to mind as she walked, followed a second later by a crazy idea. What if she invited him for dinner tonight? Having company would help chase away the blues, and what's more, she'd be making amends for the awkward situation on Friday. They'd exchanged contact information when their committee work started. She dug out her phone, found his number, and without giving herself a chance to reconsider, called him.

"It's Phoebe," she said after he answered. "Don't hang up, okay?"

"You sound like you're in a wind tunnel."

"I am, sort of. I'm just walking up Bridge Street, and it's windy as hell. Look, I'm sorry again about Friday night."

"Don't worry," he said. "I've licked my wounds and recovered." His tone was good-natured.

"Have you heard the news about the missing girl—Lily Mack?"

"No, I've been holed up in the lab. Is she okay?"

"They found her body in the river this morning. I was downtown when they pulled her out."

There was silence on the other end, and she wondered if the news had upset him.

"That's tragic," he said after a moment. "Do they know what happened?"

"Not yet." She paused. "Um, look, I was wondering if by any chance you're free for dinner tonight. I was going to make pasta."

"You're not trying to put Tony out of business, are you?"

"That would be tough. I only know about ten recipes really well."

He chuckled. "Sure, dinner sounds good. The only hitch is that I've got to hang in the lab until about seven."

"Why don't you come at seven thirty, then?" She gave him the address.

"Red or white?" he asked.

"Red would be great."

As soon as she hung up, she wondered if she'd been stupid to make the call. Would Duncan misinterpret the gesture? All she knew for sure was that it would be a relief not to be alone tonight.

She had a rough idea where Ash Street was and found it easily on foot after asking someone for directions. The house at 133 was a two-story clapboard, barely ten feet away from its neighbors on each side, its hunter green paint peeling badly. A rusted aluminum beach chair, the kind you fold up and toss in the back of your car, sat forlornly on the sagging porch. Phoebe climbed the steps. The front door was already ajar, and she pushed it open all the way. She found herself in a foyer strewn with boxes, old boots, mail circulars, blow-in cards from magazines, a couple battered skateboards, and one half of a badly dented bike. A row of pegs had been nailed to the wall, and a small jean jacket, probably a woman's, as well as a pink slicker, hung limply from them. There was a door to the left, likely leading to the downstairs apartment; up a staircase she could see another door. She glanced at the two mailboxes, thinking they might provide a clue as to which apartment was Blair's. But they listed only names—three male names on one, and on the other, Blair Usher and Gwen Gallogly.

She was about to rap on the downstairs door when it opened and a shaggy-haired guy, probably a student, stepped outside, a backpack slung over his shoulder.

"Can I help you?" he asked, narrowing his eyes.

"Sorry to bother you," Phoebe said. "I was looking for Blair Usher."

"Upstairs," he said, lifting his chin.

"Thanks," Phoebe said. She turned and took a step toward the stairs.

"But I don't think they're there," he added. "I heard somebody go out earlier."

"Why don't I give it a try anyway," she said. That's another thing she'd learned over the years from her work: Believe only half of what people tell you.

After mounting the stairs, she rapped lightly on the door up there. It was heavily chipped, but there was a new-looking straw doormat on the floor in front of it, and tacked to the door was a Pennsylvania Dutch hex sign designed with two black-and-red birds and the word *Wilkum*. Both items were the kind of things a mother would send in a care package. Getting no response, Phoebe rapped again, harder this time. She waited. Nothing.

Just as she was about to leave, she heard soft footsteps making their way to the door. It swung open and revealed a tall, pretty redhead with pale skin. Her hair was pulled back in a high ponytail, and there were faint smudge marks beneath each eye, as if she'd slept in her eye makeup and hadn't washed her face yet today. She was wearing a neon green camisole and tight jeans tucked into knee-high gray suede boots. A frown began to form on her face as she took Phoebe in.

"Yes?" the girl said. She cocked her head as she spoke, and the ponytail followed.

Phoebe introduced herself and explained she was a teacher at Lyle. "Are you Blair?" she added.

"No," the girl said bluntly. "She's not here right now."

"Will she be back soon?"

"I'm not sure. What's this about?"

Obviously the phrase "teacher at Lyle" had failed to elicit even a soupçon of respect.

"I'm sure you've heard about Lily Mack," Phoebe said.

"Of course. Why—is there some other news?"

"No, but I've been asked to help in the internal investigation the college is doing. You must be Gwen, then."

"Yes—and we've already told the police everything we know."

"The school has to look into what happened as well. May I come in for a minute?"

"I guess," Gwen said, petulantly. "If you're saying it's absolutely necessary." Gwen opened the door fully, and Phoebe stepped into the apartment. To her surprise she saw that it was in total contrast to the junk-strewn foyer downstairs. Though the walls were cracked and blistered in spots, they'd been painted a pretty yellow in the hall and red in the living room beyond. There was an old gilt-framed mirror in the entranceway and a small table, both the type of used but respectable booty you lugged home from Goodwill. Everything was neat and tidy, almost disarmingly so. The only sign of student life were two field hockey sticks leaning against the hall wall, along with a padded knee brace. A ripe, sweet smell filled the air, as if a vanilla candle was burning somewhere.

"Sooo?" Gwen said.

"Do you mind if we sit down?" Phoebe said, pointing with her chin toward the living room.

"I have to meet someone in a minute," Gwen said.

"It won't take long, I promise," Phoebe said. Begrudgingly the girl led Phoebe into the living room. Though Gwen continued to stand, Phoebe perched on the edge of a faded floral sofa. Above the mantel of the walled-in fireplace hung another Pennsylvania Dutch hex symbol. When you were this age, weren't you supposed to have *Twilight* movie posters plastered on your walls? Phoebe wondered.

"I love how you've fixed up your apartment," Phoebe said, smiling. "This reminds me a little of my college apartment, but ours didn't look nearly as nice."

"Thanks," Gwen said, unmoved.

"I'm so sorry about Lily's death. Were you friends with her too?"

"I knew her. But she was really Blair's friend."

"I heard she was thinking of staying here the night she disappeared." She let the comment hang there.

"You'll have to ask Blair that," Gwen told her after a moment. "I really have no idea."

"So you hadn't heard that?"

Gwen rolled her dark green eyes back and sighed in exasperation.

"Yeah, I heard that—after the fact. To be perfectly honest, she hadn't really been staying here much anymore."

"Did Lily ever seem depressed or worried to you lately?"

Another sigh. "I just told you, I really never saw her."

Phoebe didn't even consider broaching the subject of the Sixes. Gwen would only tip Blair off, and Phoebe would lose her edge when she spoke to the girl directly.

"Understood," Phoebe said. She let her eyes roam absently, as if she was gathering her thoughts, when she was really checking out the space.

"Could you ask Blair to call me, then?" she said finally. She took out a pen from her bag and scribbled the information on a piece of paper.

"Sure," Gwen said, taking the paper limply, as if she planned to let it flutter to the floor the moment Phoebe departed.

As Phoebe started on her way back home, she found it hard to judge whether Gwen's attitude was just the general sullenness that Phoebe often witnessed in girls that age or something else—a defensiveness because she had something to hide.

The apartment had surprised Phoebe. Its tidiness, its pretty decor. And then there were the hex signs. Such an odd choice for college girls. One would have said a gift from Mom; two said something more intentional.

Phoebe herself had never liked hex signs. She'd first seen them on a trip to Pennsylvania Dutch country with Alec. The Amish farmers didn't display them, but other people in the area did, and they popped up everywhere—on barns, houses, calendars, and half the souvenirs at the various tchotchke shops. She had almost bought note cards designed with them, just for something to take back, but she realized that she found them creepy. Maybe it was because of the flat, two-dimensional design—or the fact that they were supposed to ward off evil, hinting at witchcraft.

Could that be what the Sixes were about? Phoebe wondered, stopping abruptly on the sidewalk. Didn't the word *hex* mean to put a spell on something? Maybe the girls in the Sixes pretended to be witches and threatened to cast evil spells on girls they didn't like or who broke their code. If so, that could explain Alexis Grey's hysteria. Nothing like finding out that a witch's curse has been placed on you to send you over the edge.

And then with a start Phoebe thought of something else. The word *hex* also meant "six."

# 6

Back home, Phoebe flipped open her laptop and did a Google search for hex signs. She discovered that they'd been introduced by German settlers in the 1600s, though there wasn't a consensus as to why. The most common theory, as Phoebe had suspected, was that they were used to ward off evil. The word *hex* was actually derived from the German word for witch. So wait, Phoebe thought, does it not have anything to do with the Greek word for *six*? It seemed it didn't, but as she read more, she learned that many early hex signs had six-pointed stars, and surprise, surprise, one theory held that the name *hex* had evolved from a mispronunciation of the German word *seches*—meaning "six."

So maybe the hex signs in Blair and Gwen's apartment had nothing to do with witchcraft, but were simply a way for the girls to sneakily announce that they were part of the Sixes. Funny, she thought, how secret organizations always had to make sure they had their damn symbol down, to give members a way to show that they belonged. Because what secret societies invariably wanted was to *not* be a total secret— they wanted people to whisper about them, to yearn to belong, and in some cases, to be very afraid of them. Phoebe had learned that all too well.

Next, she Googled information about drowned bodies. When a person drowned, she read, the body generally sank at first, but as it decomposed, the resulting gases forced it to the surface. The colder the water, the longer it took for those gases to form. At this time of year it might take well over a week for a body to rise to the surface, even if the weather was as warm as it had been. But a body didn't always sink to the bottom. Sometimes it got caught on tree roots or wrapped in nautical rope along a dock. Maybe that's what happened to Lily's body, Phoebe thought, which would explain why it had been found so quickly.

Then she checked out the story Stockton had mentioned about students dying in the Midwest. He hadn't exaggerated. In the past five or six years a dozen young men in just a few states had been found drowned after a night out. In all the cases, authorities had declared the deaths accidental, though some family members bought into the notion of a serial killer. Again, Phoebe felt her skin crawl. She instinctively glanced up to the window above the table. How horrible to even consider, she thought. But serial killers did move around. She'd read enough about Ted Bundy to know that he had begun his deadly spree in Oregon, moved on to Colorado, and killed his last victims in Florida. Stockton might be right.

Thinking of Stockton made her remember to check her e-mail. As promised, there was a message from him with the names of the two girls who'd exchanged the look during the committee meeting: Molly Wang and Jen Imbibio.

Bingo, Phoebe thought. Jen Imbibio was in one of the sections of her writing class. It would be easy to find an excuse to talk to the girl after class tomorrow.

She opened the file she kept on her students on her laptop and scrolled down to Jen Imbibio's name. Jen had earned B-, C, and C+ on her three assignments so far. Phoebe had yet to review and grade Jen's most recent assignment. She'd asked her students to write a reported article on any topic they wanted, and also a separate, first-person blog on the same subject, done in a much chattier, breezier style. Jen had chosen reality TV as her subject.

Phoebe reached across the table to a stack of papers, located Jen's two pieces, and read through them. Her research for the reported piece had been decent enough, but the writing was stilted. For the blog, Jen had gone off on a total tear about the girls who were on the shows, girls who flaunted their fake breasts and were famous for nothing. The writing here was sassy and provocative in parts, a refreshing surprise.

Phoebe glanced at her watch. It was close to four o'clock, and she'd done nothing yet for dinner with Duncan. She jumped up from her desk and hurried into the kitchen. She'd decided earlier that she'd make spaghetti carbonara, which she'd planned to prepare for herself that night anyway. There were arugula and lemons in the fridge, which meant she could put together a salad with lemon vinaigrette. What about dessert, though? she wondered. There was still time to make a mad dash to the supermarket before it closed. But that would be trying too hard, turning the evening into more than it should be. There was fruit in the fridge, she realized—grapes and tangerines—and she could get away with serving those.

The doorbell rang at a little past seven thirty, just as she had finished beating the Parmesan cheese into the eggs. She'd already fried the pancetta, and the house was redolent with the scent of meat and garlic. It smells like a damn souvlaki stand in here, she thought with annoyance, wiping her hands quickly on a dish towel.

She swung open the door. Even though she expected Duncan, seeing him on her doorstep startled her a little. She realized that she was still not used to him sans beard and mustache.

"Come in," she said, offering a smile.

"Sorry I'm a few minutes late. I spent the afternoon with thirty feisty little rats, and I decided I'd better shower again. . . . Wait, this is Herb Jack's place, isn't it? At first glance, I'd say you've improved on it by about 400 percent."

Phoebe laughed. "Thanks. Lucky for me he decided to put all his Civil War memorabilia in storage before he went on sabbatical."

"You *are* lucky. I can't really picture you surrounded by bayonets and muskets." Duncan handed her a bottle in a shiny silver sack. "You said pasta, so I brought a Brunello di Montepulciano."

"Terrific," she said, impressed by his choice.

She hung up his coat, opened the wine in the kitchen, and returned to the living room with a glass for each of them. Duncan accepted his and sank into the sofa, one leg crossed over the thigh of the other. Beneath his jeans he was wearing weathered black cowboy boots.

"That must have been tough this morning at the river," he said, as she took a seat in the old rocker across from him. "How are you doing?"

"It *was* tough," she admitted. "And it's hard to chase the image out of my mind."

Duncan rubbed his thumb back and forth along the curves of the wineglass. "Have you learned anything about how the girl died?" he asked, looking back at her. "You have the inside track, of course."

"I know as little as you do. But coincidentally, I had an interesting encounter with Lily two weeks ago." She described the rushed conversation in the rain, and then decided to share what she learned from Glenda and Stockton about the Sixes.

Duncan placed his wineglass on the coffee table and leaned back into the couch. He was wearing a beige henley shirt with his jeans, the top two buttons undone, and though not tight, it fit his body well enough for Phoebe to see what good shape he was in.

"What do you think?" she said.

"Hmm," he said. "On one hand, no, I've never heard about any secret society. But as soon as you said the words, it pricked a nerve with me. I've had the weirdest sensation from time to time—when I'm around some of the students."

It was the kind of creepy comment, Phoebe thought, that someone makes in a horror movie, when they begin to sense that their house is haunted by a girl who died a hundred years ago.

"What do you mean?" she asked quietly.

"Hard to describe—in fact you're the first person I've even mentioned this to because it's been so vague. Sometimes when I'm talking to kids—usually outside the classroom—I have a weird sense there's something they're just not saying. Have you ever suspected you're the only person in a group that doesn't *know* something? You'll see someone shoot another person an odd look. That kind of thing." Tom Stockton had seen a look exchanged, too, Phoebe recalled. "Are you thinking Lily was a member?"

"Yes, she may have been."

"If the right moment ever presents itself, I'll probe the students a little."

"That would be great—I'm trying to find out all I can. Speaking of the right moment, are you hungry?"

"Famished, actually," he said. "I never broke for lunch today."

She'd set up the drop-leaf table in the living room for dinner, and while Duncan refilled their wineglasses, she dumped the spaghetti in the pot of boiling water and then served the salads.

"So you know Herb, then?" she asked, after they'd begun to eat.

"Not super well," Duncan said. "But I've been to a couple of his Christmas parties here."

"Is there a lot of socializing among the faculty?

"About average, I'd say." He craned his head around. "Why am I remembering a dining room? I keep picturing a big table with a steaming crock-pot of Swedish meat balls."

Phoebe laughed, though she wondered why he'd been so quick to change the subject.

"It's through that door over there," she said, gesturing with her chin. "But I've set it up as my office. Herb used the second bedroom upstairs as his, but it's under the eaves and feels so claustrophobic to me."

"I can imagine a lot about Lyle makes you feel claustrophobic. Has it been hard leaving Manhattan behind?"

"Definitely a little strange. But I felt I had to get away. I was looking for a place to think, to regroup, that sort of thing." She smiled, feeling a little self-conscious. "And then Glenda made me an offer I couldn't refuse."

"Someone told me you two went to the same boarding school."

"More or less."

He cocked his head in a gesture that said, Please explain. He's a little like me, Phoebe thought. He likes to go below the surface.

"Glenda graduated from there," she said. "I ended up staying for just my sophomore year and then finished up back at my hometown high school." She paused for a moment. "Homesick."

He narrowed his brown eyes, studying her.

"You don't seem like the kind of girl that gets homesick."

"Well, I've had my wuss moments in life," Phoebe said. She looked away involuntarily and kicked herself for it.

"What's amazing," Duncan said, "is that you and Glenda stayed friends after knowing each other for just a year when you were, what, fifteen?"

"I know. But she'd helped me through a tough situation, and we forged a pretty strong bond. We did drift apart for a bit—this was before cell phones and e-mail. But right after college we both ended up in New York—I was in the magazine business, and she was getting her doctorate at Columbia—and we started spending time together again. It was fantastic to reconnect, and since then we've been very close."

"And are you glad you accepted her offer to come here?"

"By and large, yes. But like I said, I miss the city." She smiled. "You cannot get a red velvet cupcake in this town. But at the same time I've enjoyed the quiet, the lack of chaos. And teaching has given me something to focus on besides my recent fuckup."

"I bet the kids find you utterly fascinating."

"Oh, yeah, but not necessarily in a good way. There's that whole elephant-in-the-room thing to contend with—with both students *and* faculty."

He cocked his head. "Meaning?"

"The whole *scandale*," Phoebe said. "The plagiarism charges. I know people start buzzing about me the minute I walk into a room. I feel like Jordan Baker in *The Great Gatsby*. They're all wondering whether I really cheated in that golf tournament."

"*Did* you?" he asked, holding her eyes intensely. It was the first time she'd been asked so bluntly, and she found it strangely appealing.

"No," she said, shaking her head with a rueful smile. "A freelance researcher mislabeled some research notes. And yet . . ."

He didn't say a word, just looked at her. So he knows how to do the pregnant pause just like I do, she thought.

She shrugged. "I'm not blameless. I've always been such a stickler for detail, but in this case I hired a person without the right experience and didn't pay enough attention to the process."

"Maybe something about the process didn't interest you anymore."

"Maybe," she said.

God, she thought, how did I get into this? He was asking all the questions. Mercifully the timer she'd set for the pasta went off just then.

In the kitchen, she tested a strand of the linguine, drained the pot, and then stirred the creamy sauce into the noodles. Perhaps it was the glass and a half of wine she'd already drunk, but the carbonara smelled heavenly to her.

"Does Tony know you can do this?" Duncan asked after she served the pasta and he'd consumed two big forkfuls. "This is amazingly good."

"Thank you. I don't have much of a repertoire as a cook, but I'm generally pretty decent at pasta. My Italian grandmother loved to teach me in her kitchen."

"You're adopted, then. You can't be Italian with that fair skin and blue eyes."

"I'm just a quarter Italian, the rest is English and Irish." She needed to get the attention off herself. "Do you like to cook?"

"Some nights, though nothing fancy. A lot of nights I end up working late in the lab and I just grab takeout."

"Is it strange—working with rats?"

"Why, do you find them unnerving?"

Phoebe shuddered a little. "Yes," she said. "I—I can't stand it when I see them on the subway tracks in New York."

Duncan laughed that deep, melodic laugh of his. It was the kind of laugh that made you want to linger in a room with him.

"They have their charms, believe it or not. One of the things we've been studying is how cleverly they teach their pups. They make pretty good mothers, too—except, of course, when they eat their young for reasons we don't quite understand." He laughed again. "Sorry about that. Not the kind of comment I should be making over dinner."

Phoebe smiled. "No problem—it's very interesting stuff." But she was anxious to get off that topic, too.

Duncan set down his fork and leaned back in his chair.

"So how did you end up writing about actors?"

"I've always found them intriguing—though not so much because of the sexcapades and outrageous behavior. I had a second cousin who had a fair amount of success doing TV and off-Broadway theater, and I could always see that she was desperately trying to be something she wasn't. I kept wondering what demons she was running from. And as I began to do celebrity profiles, I saw that they *all* were trying to be something different than they were, that they all had these secrets. I love figuring out what makes them tick; there's an exhilarating rush when I find a clue that helps me piece everything together."

For the next few minutes they tossed around several different topics: why Duncan had chosen psychology as a field; Lyle's issues as a college; and how different Gen Y was from their own generation. I like this, Phoebe thought.

They finished their pasta, and Phoebe realized that the night was going faster than she wanted it to.

"Would you like an espresso?" she asked, rising from the table. "I lugged my machine out here from the city."

"That would be great," Duncan said. "Let me help you clear, though."

"No, no, there's really so little to do." She returned from the kitchen a few minutes later with the espresso, the fruit, and a plate of chocolate biscotti she'd discovered while searching quickly through the pantry.

Duncan peeled opened a tangerine, not saying anything but seeming content, comfortable with the silence.

"So how long have you been at the school?" Phoebe asked. "And is it a good fit for you?"

He was the one who looked away this time, as if gathering his thoughts, but she knew from experience that people broke eye contact when the other person's words had thrown them off.

"About two years," he said, looking back at her. "And it's been pretty good. It's just not the kind of place where I saw myself."

"I hear it's hard to get a job in academia these days."

"It wasn't that, actually." He sounded grave. "I take it the campus grapevine hasn't served up my personal story, then?"

She suddenly felt a prick of anxiety, though she wasn't sure why. "No," she said.

"My former wife's parents were from Lyle. She was diagnosed with terminal cancer two years ago, and she wanted to come back here to die. I'd been teaching at Northwestern—we were living in Chicago—and fortunately a job opened up at the college here not long after we moved back."

Phoebe realized she'd been holding her breath. She let it out slowly.

"And?" Phoebe asked haltingly.

"She died fifteen months ago. But ironically not from the cancer. She was in the final stages when she fell asleep reading in the bathtub and drowned."

# 7

Phoebe woke just after three with a jolt, her heartbeats tripping over each other. A sound, it seemed, had punctured her dream, but she could hear nothing now. She struggled up in bed, listening, straining to see with only the dim glow of the night-light.

Then she heard it again. Something was scampering over the roof. It's just a squirrel, she told herself, one of the groups she sometimes saw in the tiny backyard. Just don't let the damn things find their way into the attic, she prayed. She switched on her bedside lamp and let her eyes adjust. For some reason she felt unbearably thirsty. She threw off the covers and padded downstairs.

She flicked on the kitchen switch. Bright light burst into the room from the overhead fixture, like a flash going off. She poured a glass of water from the jug in the fridge and sat down at the small wooden table. Outside, the night pressed against the kitchen windows. She felt exposed suddenly, discomfited by all that darkness out there, so she took the water upstairs with her. As she settled herself in bed again, her back against the headboard, she replayed the evening in her mind.

The revelation Duncan had made toward the end of dinner had thrown her. She'd figured that he must have been married at some point and was now divorced, that he might even have older kids somewhere. The last thing she'd expected was a wife found dead in a bathtub.

"I'm so sorry," she'd said. "These past couple of years must have been very hard."

He pulled his mouth to one side. "Yes," he said. "And yet not exactly in the way you'd expect. Allison and I had agreed to get a divorce just days before she was diagnosed with cancer. The marriage had become a disaster. But I wanted to stay with her during the last year of her life. Plus, I was the one with the health insurance."

"That was good of you to do," Phoebe said.

"Part of me actually thought that things might get better between us given the new set of circumstances, but I'm afraid that never happened." He offered a small smile. "And as you can imagine, my experience as a widower has been pretty strange. People look at me with pity because they think I lost the woman I loved. That's not to say I didn't grieve, but my experience hasn't been what people assume."

"How much . . . sooner did she die than she would have from the cancer?"

The question was probably going farther than she should have, but Phoebe felt compelled to know. And he'd opened the door.

"A couple of months, maybe a bit longer," he said. "Ordinarily someone might wake if they were taking in water while sleeping, but because she was so ill, her systems weren't functioning right. I had warned her about falling asleep in the tub, but sometimes I wonder if she almost let it happen that night. I'd gone out to a school event—and remembered she'd seemed very down. When I came home two hours later, she was dead."

He set down his espresso cup and leaned back. "So is this what always happens with you? People confess things they generally never tell a soul?"

Later, at the door, as he was leaving, Duncan let his brown eyes roam over Phoebe's face, discombobulating her slightly; she wondered if he was going to kiss her.

"Thank you for dinner," he said instead. "You'll have to let me return the favor at some point."

Now in bed, Phoebe thought about what it would have been like if Duncan *had* kissed her. She imagined that soft, full mouth on hers, his hand on the back of her neck. This is crazy, she thought. During the past seven nightmarish months, her libido had left the building, and she couldn't believe it was finally showing its face here in little old Lyle, Pennsylvania. And yet she couldn't deny her attraction to Duncan. She'd liked his inquisitiveness, his easy laugh, the slight air of mystery. And she liked that face and body.

She tried to shake Duncan from her mind in time for her eight o'clock class the next day. It didn't help that her students seemed so glum. She was sure it had to do with Lily's death. Last week she had sent the twenty students jpegs of several articles from magazines like *Vanity Fair* and the *New Yorker*, and today they were to discuss what made each story compelling. But Phoebe ended up doing most of the talking.

She then had an hour before her eleven o'clock class, the one with Jen Imbibio, and she decided to use the time to stop by Blair's apartment again.

The house on Ash Street seemed even more dejected than the day before. The dark, junk-strewn foyer was absolutely silent, and this time no one answered the door to the upstairs apartment. It was going to take forever to connect with Blair if Phoebe resorted to just popping in now and then. She scrolled through her e-mail for the information Glenda had sent about the girl. A cell phone number had been included. Phoebe would have preferred her first conversation with Blair be face-to-face, but she needed to speed the process along. While walking back down Ash Street, she punched in Blair's number on her phone.

"Hi Blair, this is Phoebe Hall," she said, after being greeted by an automated message. "I stopped by yesterday to see you. Would you give me a call? I'd like to arrange a time to talk."

Her eleven o'clock class turned out to be like the first. Students were listless and morose. As Phoebe offered her own comments on the articles she'd sent the class, she studied Jen closely for the first time. She was tiny, barely five feet tall, with long, slightly curly brunette hair and blue eyes in a heart-shaped face. She looked like someone out of a fairy tale, Phoebe thought, the kind of girl you'd expect to find riding a deer in the Romanian forest. Yet she also had a very modern air of entitlement about her. Interestingly, Jen had less to say than anyone else today.

At the end of class, Phoebe announced that she'd be passing graded papers back on Wednesday. Students filed out of the room quietly, with no one stopping at Phoebe's desk to ask a question as they normally did. Before Jen could reach the door, Phoebe called out her name.

"Me?" the girl said, surprised.

"Yes. Do you have a minute?"

"Um, okay," she said, looking slightly put out.

"Why don't we go to my office? It'll be easier to talk there."

They made their way to the second floor of the building. One of the hall lights was out and the corridor was gloomy, like everything else that day. After slipping into her office, with Jen following without enthusiasm behind her, Phoebe switched on two lamps and scooped the papers off the guest chair facing her desk.

"Here, have a seat," she told Jen. Phoebe wondered if she should close the door but decided against it; Jen already looked ready to jump out of her skin.

"Okay," Jen said, sitting down with her backpack still on. "Just so you know, though, I'm supposed to meet someone in a few minutes."

"This will only take a sec," Phoebe said, smiling. "I wanted to talk about the assignment I'm handing back on Wednesday."

Jen twitched in her seat. Her expression morphed into mild alarm.

"There's nothing to be concerned about," Phoebe said quickly. "I just wanted to tell you that I liked your blog. It's really terrific."

"Oh, wow," the girl said, breaking into a smile. "I—wow."

"You're doing something much stronger in your blog than in your regular magazine pieces, and I think we should figure out how to bring that quality to your other stuff. I see your next magazine assignment is going to be on childhood obesity. But how about picking a topic that allows you to use the same sassy voice that you used in your blog writing?"

"But isn't the next assignment a *reporting* piece?" Jen asked.

"Yes. But you can still add attitude if the topic allows for it."

"Um, wow, okay," the girl said. "So it would probably have to be something I have a strong opinion about?"

"That's right. Take a day to rethink your topic. . . . Of course, I know this is a hard time to focus right now."

Jen knitted her tiny brows, not sure at first what Phoebe meant. Then she got it. "Right," she said quietly.

"Were you friends with Lily?" Phoebe asked.

The girl took a breath before answering.

"Sort of," she said. "I mean, we used to be friendly last year. Lately, though, we didn't see very much of each other."

"From what I know, they're still not sure what caused her death," Phoebe said. "Do you think she may have been depressed?"

"I wouldn't have any idea," Jen said. "Even if I'd seen her, she wouldn't have confided in me. We were never that close."

"I happened to speak to Lily myself—a week or so ago."

"Really?" the girl said.

"Yes, just briefly. I got the sense she was struggling with some things."

Jen said nothing this time. She just bit her lip, and shifted in the chair.

So, Phoebe thought, the easy-does-it strategy was going nowhere; time for a bolder approach.

"I feel so bad that I wasn't able to help Lily," Phoebe said. "I've thought a lot since then about what might have been troubling her. I wondered if she might have gotten caught up in something she regretted . . . like the Sixes."

Jen's whole body froze, except her blue eyes, which danced around anxiously. "I—um, I don't know what you mean," she said.

"The Sixes," Phoebe said, glancing surreptitiously toward the door to make sure no one was outside. "The secret society on campus."

"I don't know about any societies," Jen said hoarsely. "I'm really focused on my own stuff. Gymnastics. And dance."

"And you've never heard about a group that might be bullying or threatening other students?"

Jen shook her head back and forth slowly.

"No," she said. "I can't imagine the girls here doing something like that."

"Maybe it's just one of those urban legends then," Phoebe said, smiling, trying to break the tension. "When I was in college this crazy rumor went around, claiming that a psychic had predicted a guy was going to kill six coeds at a school that began with the letter *W.* Guess what school I went to? Wisconsin. As you can imagine, all the girls were hysterical."

There was no response. Phoebe could see that bold hadn't worked either, and if she kept at it, she was going to make the girl's tiny heart stop in her chest. She needed to drop the subject and establish some trust, which she could possibly tap into later.

"I should let you get to your appointment," Phoebe said. "But there's a book I'd love to loan you."

The girl's face relaxed just a hair. Just then, a noise from the hall caught Phoebe's attention. It sounded like the soft scuff of a shoe. Phoebe waited for the person to pass by the door, but no one did. She had the sense that someone was standing on the other side of the doorway, listening. But Jen, distracted, had clearly not heard anything.

Phoebe rose quickly but quietly from her desk and stepped over to the other side of the office. She leaned her head out into the hallway. There was no one there. When she pulled her head back in, Jen was standing up, waiting eagerly to be dismissed.

"Here it is," Phoebe said, tugging a book from the shelf. "It's a collection of articles by a terrific writer named Ron Rosenbaum, who first made his mark in the 1970s and '80s. There's a lot of attitude in his reporting pieces. I think you'll be inspired."

"Thanks," Jen said, smiling weakly.

After the girl had departed, Phoebe stepped into the hallway. She could hear Jen nearly tripping down the steps in her hurry to leave, but otherwise it was quiet. Phoebe walked down the hall to the department reception area. Four or five offices fanned off it, all belonging to senior members of the English faculty. The receptionist, Bev, was sitting at her desk, staring at her computer screen, while the department chair Dr. Carr stood nearby, thumbing through a stack of mail.

"Why hello, Phoebe," he said, looking up. He was about sixty, built like a bear, and surprisingly gracious to her, considering she'd been foisted on him by Glenda. She suspected he was slightly intrigued by her, as if he'd been asked to employ a parolee who'd served time for murdering her husband years ago. "What can we do for you?"

"I was just wondering if anyone was looking for me. I thought I heard someone come by my door."

"Not that I'm aware of," he said. "Bev, do you know?"

"I think most people are at lunch," the receptionist said.

"Okay, thanks," Phoebe said. She turned to leave.

"Oh wait," Bev said, finally taking her eyes from the computer screen. "Maybe Dr. Porter."

"Pardon?"

"Dr. Val Porter. I don't know if she was looking for you, but she was up here a few minutes ago. I saw her at the copy machine."

Phoebe headed back down the hall and on her way glanced into Val's office, which was on the other side of hers. But it was empty. She wondered if it *had* been Val outside her door. It wouldn't surprise her. She sensed that Val kept a close eye on her, curious as to what Phoebe was up to.

Back in her office, Phoebe unwrapped a sandwich she'd brought from home and considered the conversation she'd had with Jen. She'd scored nothing of real note, but there'd been that one interesting slip on the girl's part. She'd told Phoebe, "I can't imagine the girls here doing something like that," even though Phoebe had never said the Sixes was a secret society of *girls*. It was another clue that the group actually existed and that Jen might be a member.

For the next few hours Phoebe read through material in her office and mapped out plans for future classes. But she had trouble keeping her mind on her work. She kept coming back to Lily and the Sixes. So far she hadn't made a lick of progress.

It was almost six and already dusk when Phoebe decided to call it a day. Before long the clocks would have to be set back, and it would be even darker by now. Something to look forward to, Phoebe thought grimly.

As she crossed the wind-swept quad, she caught a glimpse of Jen Imbibio, walking with another student from her eleven o'clock class—Rachel, a tall, very athletic-looking blonde. Jen's face was pinched, and her tiny hands moved animatedly as she spoke. Phoebe wondered if Jen was filling Rachel in on the grilling she'd been subjected to earlier, which could mean

Rachel was a member of the Sixes, too. It's like that movie *Invasion of the Body Snatchers*, she thought. You know the bad people are in your midst, but you aren't certain who they are.

As she continued down the path, she spotted Craig Ball, head of campus police security, coming from the opposite direction. With his silver hair and tanned, crinkly skin, he looked like he should be flying planes for Delta, Phoebe thought. When he was closer, he nodded at Phoebe and ran his eyes over her face but said nothing. She was pretty sure he recognized her from the park yesterday morning. For all she knew, she thought sardonically, he had her on a list of security risks because of the plagiarism charges.

"Mr. Ball?" Phoebe called out just as he started to pass her. "We haven't met yet." She gave him her name and explained she was a friend of Glenda's.

"Right, good to put a face to the name," he said. "Can I be of some assistance?" His tone was brisk, suggesting that the offer was only perfunctory.

"I just wanted to introduce myself. Glenda asked me to talk to some of the female students here about the Sixes. I'd love to speak to you at some point and learn what you know."

"Tom Stockton's probably the better person to talk to right now. I get involved when there's vandalism, of course, but so far there's been only a minimal amount."

"All right, thanks. If you do think of anything, will you let me know?"

"Sure."

As she started to head on her way again, Ball reached out and touched her sleeve.

"By the way," he said. "Did that guy ever find you?"

"What guy?" she asked.

"Mid-thirties, maybe. Dark hair. Came by our office asking for you this morning. I looked up your office phone for him, but said I wasn't at liberty to give out anything else."

"No one's contacted me," she said. "Did he leave his name?"

"Nope. Just said he knew you from Manhattan."

Who in the world could it be? Phoebe wondered. She had a number of male friends in the city, but she'd been out of touch with most of them recently and could hardly imagine one of them just showing up on campus.

When Phoebe unlocked her front door ten minutes later, she was greeted by the scent of fresh laundry and Lemon Pledge. The cleaning lady, Margaret, had come and gone. For the first time since Phoebe had been living there, she felt a sense of comfort coming home.

She changed into jeans and headed for the kitchen. To her surprise she saw that Margaret, a grouchy, taciturn woman, had left a bowl of Granny Smith apples for her. A scribbled note lay near them on the table.

Maybe I've begun to charm the old bat, Phoebe thought.

She picked up the note. "Please call me," it read. "I need to talk to you."

Oh, I get it, Phoebe thought. She's damaged something, and the apples are her way of priming me for the conversation. Phoebe dug her phone from her purse to call.

"We need to discuss Thanksgiving," Margaret said abruptly once Phoebe had identified herself. "I'm gone that whole week—at my daughter's. If you're goin' away yourself, you may not need me. But I have a friend who can fill in if necessary."

Thanksgiving, Phoebe thought. She hadn't even noticed it looming on the horizon. After her mother died several years ago, she had stopped traveling to Massachusetts for the holiday weekend, and she and Alec had generally ended up going to his brother's apartment in the city for dinner. She couldn't imagine what she'd do this year.

"Actually, I haven't thought that far ahead," said Phoebe. "I'll have to let you know."

"As soon as possible then," Margaret said brusquely. "If you want my friend, I'll have to give her advance notice."

"Of course."

"Good night then."

"Good night. Oh, and thank you very much for the apples."

"Apples?"

Phoebe hesitated, confused.

"The bowl of apples on my table. You didn't leave them?"

"Nope, wasn't me."

Then who? Phoebe thought, hanging up. She had no friends in Lyle who would have just popped by. Besides, the house had been locked.

She glanced back at the apples, and unconsciously her brain began to count. There were six of them.

# 8

It's them, she thought, her heart starting to thump. The Sixes. They've been here, they left the apples.

She spun around, almost knocking over one of the kitchen chairs.

How had they gotten in? Her eye shot to the kitchen door with the window on the upper half. Each week she left the key for the cleaning lady under a flowerpot on the back stoop. Maybe they'd been watching the house and seen Margaret retrieve it.

Phoebe couldn't believe they'd had the nerve to sneak into her house.

She flipped on the stoop light, opened the back door, and stepped outside. Peering into the twilight, she wondered if someone might be out there, watching her. She quickly turned over the flowerpot and grabbed the key still beneath it. Phoebe stepped back inside and turned the lock on the door. She also slipped on the chain lock. Next she checked the front door. Still locked. She did a quick circle through the rooms, making sure nothing was disturbed, and then tentatively mounted the stairs. She doubted anyone would still be in the house, and yet her pulse quickened as she opened each of the two bedroom doors and scanned the rooms. Nothing unusual.

Back downstairs she studied the table in her office. There was no indication that anything on her desk had been touched. They've been in this room, though, she thought. She could *sense* it.

Returning to the kitchen, she stood by the table and stared at the apples. I'm being paranoid, she chided herself. She didn't even know if the Sixes actually existed, and besides, there could be another explanation. Maybe Duncan had left the apples as a thank-you gesture. He might have dropped by and, not finding her home, checked around for a key. But she couldn't imagine him entering uninvited.

Phoebe dumped the apples in the trash with a thud, picked up her cell phone again, and called Glenda. She was surprised when her friend actually picked up.

"Hey, I was just about to call you with an update," Glenda said. "Have you recovered from yesterday?"

"Partly. But something weird just happened. I think the Sixes may have paid me a visit at home."

"What do you mean?" Glenda asked urgently. Phoebe described finding the six apples in her kitchen.

"Damn, I can't believe this," Glenda said. "I'm coming over."

"Don't be silly, I'm sure you're swamped."

"Then why don't you come by my place for dinner? We've scheduled a memorial service for Lily tomorrow night and I need to review the plans, but I'll be home in two hours. Mark's at a meeting and Brandon's going to eat early, which means we can sit and talk."

Phoebe agreed to the offer. She was eager not only for the company but for the opportunity to hash things out with Glenda. Until it was time to leave, Phoebe tackled her e-mail, but she found it difficult to concentrate. She kept trying to imagine who had come into her house. One person? A group of them? *Was it the Sixes?* Don't let them get to you, she told herself. You're not fifteen years old. But when it was finally time to head to Glenda's, she left at least one light burning in each of the downstairs rooms.

Glenda swung open the front door of her house only seconds after Phoebe let go of the heavy old-fashioned knocker, and to her surprise, Phoebe found her friend standing in the foyer with a man she vaguely recognized. There was something military-looking about him—the ramrod-straight posture, the cropped hair—and right away Phoebe thought *cop*. His overly pink skin made his piercing blue eyes nearly pop out of his face.

"Phoebe Hall, this is Detective Michelson," Glenda said. "He's leading the investigation into Lily's death."

"Nice to meet you," Phoebe said, reaching out her hand. Michelson gripped it firmly, but his eyes barely took her in, as if he'd instantly assessed her as unimportant to his efforts.

"Thank you for stopping by," Glenda told him. "It's very important that the school and community work together on this."

After Glenda closed the door behind him, she kicked her teal-colored high heels onto the faded Oriental runner. She was wearing a wool dress and jacket—the same color as the shoes—that Phoebe guessed she'd been in for the entire day.

"Follow me," Glenda said. "A roast chicken awaits."

Glenda led Phoebe to the back of the house. The kitchen was a cavernous room with miles of countertop geared for entertaining, but there was also a small eating nook with a banquette in a corner. Phoebe shrugged off her coat and slid onto the banquette. The table was already set for two.

"So tell me what happened," Glenda said, pulling a bottle of white wine from the huge, hulking refrigerator.

"First give me an update on Lily," Phoebe said. "What did this detective have to say?"

"I don't have much to report," Glenda said. She uncorked the bottle, filled two wineglasses halfway to the top, and handed one to Phoebe. "According to Michelson, cause of death was definitely drowning. She had the equivalent of two alcoholic drinks in her system. That could have made her tipsy, but it's hard to imagine she was so out of it that after getting partly up Bridge Street, she spun around, headed north along the river, and fell in. The only other thing he coughed up was that there was no sign of sexual assault." She sighed. "Every time I ask him a question, he throws out the phrase 'confidential police matter.'"

"They must have *some* theory about what happened to her. Could you read between the lines at all?"

"No, but Tom followed up with some of the students the cops talked to, and it looks like the police suspect that a guy might be involved. They kept asking if Lily was seeing someone or if she ever picked up guys in town. It's possible she met a guy on her way home from Cat Tails or bumped into one she knew on the street. Then the two of them found a spot along the river for a grope session. When Lily decided not to go as far as the guy wanted, he flew into a rage, shoving her into the river. According to her parents, she was a good swimmer. But because it was dark and she'd had a couple of drinks, she may have been disoriented and panicked."

"If there was no sign of sexual assault, I wonder why they think a guy was involved."

"Madeline knows someone who knows someone in the coroner's office, and she heard they found a bruise on Lily's arm about the size of a thumbprint. As if she may have been forced into the water."

Phoebe felt her stomach clench at the news.

"Has Stockton had a chance to share his serial killer theory with you?" Phoebe asked.

"Yup," Glenda said. She set the chicken and salad on the table and slid onto the short end of the banquette. "And can you imagine what *that* rumor would do to enrollment? Of course, I can't stick my head in the sand—not with kids' lives at stake."

"I know as much about serial killers as I know about the Andromeda strain," Phoebe said, "but I do know they often move around so they don't leave a trail. This could be someone who was operating in another area and has moved into this region."

"Tom's going to check in with the administration at Parker-Hyde and see what he can find out. But enough about that. Tell me about the damn apples."

Phoebe relayed what had happened, as well as details of her conversation with Blair's roommate and Jen Imbibio.

"Of course, we still don't know for sure that the Sixes exist or if they left the apples," Phoebe said, "but it seems like a fairly big coincidence that the apples appear at the same time I start asking questions."

"You're bringing them out of hiding at least, which is good," Glenda said. "But I'm furious about what they did. You need to report this to Craig Ball, okay? And you need to get your lock changed."

"I doubt that whoever snuck in took the trouble to make a copy of my key," Phoebe said.

"But they *might* have."

It could be categorized as overreacting, Phoebe thought, but she realized she *would* feel more comfortable doing as Glenda suggested.

"Okay, okay, I'll get the lock changed. Did you tell the detective about the Sixes?"

"No—I didn't think there was a reason to at this point. Like I said, the cops seem to be looking for a guy right now."

"Let's see how my research goes. If the Sixes turn out to be a real group with a vendetta against Lily, you'll need to let the cops know."

Glenda set her fork down and looked into Phoebe's eyes.

"Fee, if for any reason you want to bail on the research, I'd totally understand. When I asked you to help, I never expected that someone would end up sneaking into your *house*."

"I won't lie," Phoebe said. "Those apples rattled me a little. But they're just apples. I'd be silly to let them get to me. Next on my list is visiting Alexis Grey to see if she might be willing to talk now. Can you dig up her contact information on file?"

"Of course," Glenda said. As Phoebe took a sip of wine, she could feel her friend studying her.

"What?" Phoebe asked.

"There's a question I never knew how to ask you at the time," she said. "Your experience back in school. How much did it—you know, really affect you? You sounded so strong in your letters, I never knew for sure."

Phoebe shrugged. She could feel her throat constricting a little.

"Oh, I don't know," she said, setting her wineglass down. "I suppose it's why I hung back my first years at Wisconsin—because I couldn't risk getting burned again. And I used to wonder what would have happened if I'd graduated with you and gotten a scholarship to some Ivy League college. How might my life be different? But something good came out of it. You and me. Maybe we wouldn't have become lifelong friends if I hadn't had that experience and counted on you for so much support."

Glenda smiled sadly and raised her glass. "As my mother likes to say, thank God for small favors."

When they finished eating, Phoebe started to pull on her jacket. In light of what had happened earlier, she was eager to arrive home on the early side.

"I've got an idea," Glenda said. "Stay here tonight. We've got this big-ass, fancy guest suite for so-called visiting dignitaries."

"You're not serious," Phoebe said, laughing.

"I'm dead serious. I lured you into this, and I don't want you staying at your house until you change that lock. The bathroom is stocked with everything you need—even a toothbrush."

Phoebe started to argue, but she could see Glenda wasn't going to take no for an answer.

After Glenda showed her to the ground-floor guest room, decorated in yellow chintz, and said goodnight, Phoebe realized she'd never mentioned her dinner with Duncan. Tonight hadn't been the right time anyway. She washed up in the adjoining bathroom and left the light on and the door just an inch ajar. As she tugged off her jeans a minute later, she heard a car pull into the driveway along the side of the house. Mark, she realized. Wearing just her T-shirt and panties, Phoebe climbed into the high antique bed.

She had just begun to drift off to sleep when she heard a man's muffled shout from the floor above her. Her eyes shot open, and her muscles tensed. It was over so quickly she wondered for a second if she'd imagined it. But she knew she hadn't. She waited, holding her breath, but nothing else came. For the second time in a week, she wondered if there was trouble in Glenda's marriage.

The next morning, on her way to Ball's office to report about the apples, she dropped by the café in the student union for coffee.

"We have to stop meeting at local eateries like this," a male voice said behind her.

She spun around to find Duncan standing in line. She was surprised by the small rush of pleasure she felt at seeing him.

"Oh, hi," she said, realizing that she must look grungy from not having showered. "How's it going?"

"Pretty good, thanks."

She waited while he ordered a coffee himself and walked out with him onto the quad. It was much cooler today than yesterday, and the wind was driving crinkly maple and oak leaves across the grass. Students were bundled up.

"I take it you didn't check the weather forecast last night," he said with a smile, nodding toward her lightweight coat. Duncan himself was wearing a suede jacket.

"Um, actually I bunked down at Glenda's last night." She relayed the story about the apples.

"That's pretty damn nervy," he said, his eyes narrowing. "Shouldn't you turn this investigation back over to the administration?"

"I think I'm okay for now." His concern was making her feel anxious. "So the memorial's tonight. Do you think there'll be a big turnout?"

"I would guess so. Are you going?" He seemed to study her closely. Her hair was whipping around her face, and she could feel that the tip of her nose was reddening from the cold.

"Yes. Definitely."

"By the way, thanks again for dinner Sunday night," he said. He held her eyes, as if he was about to say something else, and she thought, Okay, here it comes—a request to get together again—but suddenly he broke his gaze and glanced at a group of students rushing by. "Oops, I've got a student meeting now. Take care— and please be careful, okay?"

She watched as he dashed across campus, his strides long and easy. She felt a twinge of disappointment. She'd wanted that invitation, she realized.

Taking sips of her coffee as she walked, she made her way to the small building on the eastern edge of campus that housed security. Since a student had just died, she expected to step into a scene of jangling phones and tense activity, but the room was quiet and there were only two people there—a pretty young woman manning the front desk and an older man, probably early seventies, on the other side of it. He was wearing a parka plastered with strands of yellow dog fur. It was clear Phoebe had interrupted a conversation between the two, but the man stepped off to the side to let Phoebe speak, as if he had the time to wait. He was tall, with a large frame, but there was something hat-in-hand about his stance.

"Is Officer Ball available?" Phoebe asked the girl at the desk.

"I'm sorry, he's not," she said with a light southern accent. "But if you leave a message, I'll make sure he gets it."

Phoebe offered her name and number, which the girl typed into the desktop computer, her nails clacking against the keys. Phoebe started to leave but then turned back. "Oh, just one more thing," she said. "I need a locksmith. Can you make a recommendation?"

"Mmmm, lemme see," the girl said, sliding open the top drawer of her desk. "I've got some cards in here."

"You lock yourself out?" the old guy said. Gruff voice, but his nearly translucent blue eyes were kind.

"No, just want to change one of my locks," Phoebe said.

"There's a place called Reliable Locks over on Broad. Tell them Hutch sent you."

"Thanks a lot," Phoebe said. She realized that this must be Hutch Hutchinson, the security head that Ball had nudged out of his job.

As Phoebe pushed the door open to leave, she could sense the old guy sidling back up to the desk.

"Well, tell Craig I stopped by again," she heard him say. His comment was followed by the sound of his parka being zipped.

"I will, Hutch," the girl said almost tenderly. "I'm so sorry he hasn't had a chance to call you back. It's been just crazy around here, you know."

Outside on the path, Phoebe called directory assistance on her phone and learned the exact address of the locksmith. She could swing by there right now, she thought. She was putting her phone back into her purse when she nearly collided with Hutchinson. In the bright light of day she saw that his face was leathered with age, but thanks to his striking blue eyes and thick head of gray hair, he was still a handsome man.

"You're the former head of campus security, right?" Phoebe said. "I'm Phoebe Hall, an old friend of Glenda's. I'm teaching a couple of classes here this term."

"Pleasure to meet you," Hutch said and pumped her hand with a firm grip.

"Glenda tells me you did a great job here."

"Well, I sure enjoyed working with Dr. Johns," Hutch said. "She's one of the best things that ever happened to this college."

"Do you still keep in touch with many people on campus?" Phoebe said, thinking of the comment he'd made inside about stopping by again.

"Not so much. But with this girl drowning, I thought they could use an extra pair of hands in the investigation." He didn't add that Craig was obviously not responding to his overtures. She bet Craig would rather be caught drinking a cocktail with a pink umbrella in it than encourage any help from his former boss.

"What's your take on the situation?" Phoebe asked.

Hutchinson puffed up his chest, clearly pleased to be asked. "Hard to say when I don't know any details. Could be suicide, but when a young lady ends up dead, there's often a guy in play. Could be a bad catch she picked up in a bar—or a boyfriend she dumped. One of the most dangerous things for a girl this age is breaking up with a guy who doesn't want to be broken up with."

Interesting, Phoebe thought. "Someone in the administration has a theory there's a serial killer on the loose," she said, deciding it was okay to mention it to him.

Hutchinson harrumphed. "By definition, then, I'd say there'd have to be more than one dead body."

"There was another drowning, though, right? The spring before last?"

Hutchinson looked off and didn't say anything

"Scott Macus," he said after a few seconds. "A crying shame about that. But the cops ruled that an accident. Besides, there's a year and a half between the two deaths. Serial killers like a cooling-off period, but it's rarely *that* long."

He tilted his head and scratched his neck with a knotted finger.

"Unless," he added, "you count the kid who ended up in the river but survived."

Phoebe felt cold in her thin jacket. "When was that?" she asked.

"Last November, just before I retired. A kid came into the security office one night, sopping wet and shivering his butt off. A senior, I recall. Said he'd come to in the river and didn't know how he'd gotten there. Last thing he remembered was being at that damn bar, Cat Tails. He managed to kick off his shoes and swim to shore. I wasn't on duty that night, but I followed up with him the next day. He didn't have a scratch on him, so there was no indication of foul play. My determination was that he'd been inebriated and had fallen in accidentally."

My God, Phoebe thought. Cat Tails was the bar that both Lily and Scott Macus had last been seen in. *Could* there be a serial killer?

"Does Craig know about this?"

"It's in the database, but since he didn't handle the call, he might not know to look there."

"Should you tell him?"

He smiled. "Craig doesn't seem to care about what I have to say. Besides, in my opinion, if you put a college next to a river, kids are always gonna fall in. This serial killer angle seems pretty out of the box to me."

"I have another question for you," Phoebe said, knowing he wouldn't mind. "Glenda asked me to look into whether there may be a secret society of girls on campus, called the Sixes. Ever hear anything like that?"

Hutch cocked his head, clearly surprised.

She continued. "They apparently sometimes leave their mark—for instance, the number six painted on a wall, or six objects clustered together."

Hutch shook his head. "Nope, never got wind of anything like that. But I'll keep my ears open."

Phoebe dug out a business card from her purse and offered it to Hutch.

Hutch smiled as he accepted it and gave her a small salute with his large hand. Phoebe sensed he'd enjoyed the exchange.

As she watched him walk off, she heard someone approach her too closely from behind. She spun around. Standing smack in front of her was the man she considered the incarnation of the devil on earth.

# 9

"Well, hello, Phoebe," Pete Tobias said smarmily. She half expected him to drop to the ground and begin to slither around her ankles on his belly. "Fancy meeting you here."

The last line was a total lie. It was suddenly clear to Phoebe that he'd been the guy who had asked Craig Ball about her. Tobias worked for the *New York Post* and was one of the reporters who'd treated her most viciously in print following the plagiarism charges. His distaste for her had seeped through every word, and she'd wondered if she'd once done something indirectly to enrage him, leading to a grudge against her. He'd obviously figured out where she'd fled in exile and driven out here so he could file an update for readers who craved the rush of schadenfreude her saga could provide.

"Oh, really?" Phoebe said, trying not to reveal how much his sudden presence disturbed her. "That's funny, because weren't you asking for me on campus yesterday?"

Though there was still a smug tug to his mouth, his too-small eyes flickered. She'd caught him in a lie, and it had thrown him off his game a little. "What I meant was that I'm surprised to see you in front of campus security," he said. "Everything *okay*, I hope?"

"What exactly do you want from me?" she asked. She could hear an edge in her voice and she warned herself to take it down a notch.

Tobias's lips curled into a full smile. With a start she wondered if there was a dreadful new development in her situation—someone else claiming she'd stolen his words and threatening to sue her ass off.

"I hate to disappoint you, Phoebe, but I'm actually here covering the death of Lily Mack."

"Why would a death in Pennsylvania interest the *New York Post*?"

"There's a very good reason. Lily's a New York City girl—from Cobble Hill, Brooklyn. Then someone told me that you were working here. What a coincidence! I'd love to buy you a cup of coffee and hear what you've been up to."

Sure, Phoebe thought, but you'll have to drag me back to hell with you to do it. "I'm sorry, but this is a very busy time for me," she said. "Now, if you'll excuse me."

She strode briskly away, headed to Glenda's house to pick up her car. Because she knew Tobias was probably following her with his eyes, or might even be tailing her from a distance, she kept her posture confident. But once she was in the car, she let her shoulders sag in dismay. She couldn't believe that prick had surfaced in her life again.

Phoebe drove directly home without bothering to stop by the locksmith's. She felt discombobulated by her encounter with Tobias, and right now she craved the sanctuary of her house. As soon as she entered, she made a sweep through the rooms, checking for any sign of disturbance. But everything appeared to be fine.

She was desperate for a shower, but that was trumped by her need to know what Tobias was really up to. She clicked on the *New York Post* Web site and searched under his name. Bless his evil heart, Phoebe thought. He'd been telling the truth. There were several reports with his byline on the disappearance of Lily and the discovery of her body, including a few details from anonymous sources about the drowning and some breathless quotes from kids on campus.

And then, to her chagrin, she discovered a reference to herself at the end of Tobias's most recent story.

"Lyle happens to be the college where disgraced celebrity biographer Phoebe Hall now teaches," he'd written. Next, she thought, the jerk would be insinuating that she was linked to Lily's death somehow. She imagined the headline: "Plagiarist Eyed in Death of Pretty Coed."

Enough about him, Phoebe told herself. She needed a game plan for tackling the Sixes. If only I knew more about them, she thought. Was membership simply about feeling important and superior—and the thrill that came from excluding other girls? Or was there something far more sinister at work?

Somehow she had to find a way to make direct contact with Blair Usher. The girl wasn't returning her calls, and it was pointless to keep trudging over to the house on Ash Street, where Gwen and Blair could just ignore her knocks on the door. She decided to ask Glenda for both a photo of Blair and the girl's class schedule. Then Phoebe would basically stalk the girl until she caught up with her.

Also, as she'd told Glenda, she needed to talk to Alexis Grey. Phoebe had no classes on Thursday and she decided to drive to the Baltimore area then.

Only in learning more about the Sixes would she have a chance of understanding what Lily had been referring to. Was there something awful she'd discovered about the group only after she'd joined?

Of course, Phoebe realized, Lily's need for a fresh start might have nothing to do with the Sixes. Maybe the mess was a romantic one—she'd hooked up with the wrong guy, for instance, after her boyfriend Trevor disappeared. It might be the guy she'd hinted to her roommate Amanda about. And her death might be linked to the romance.

She felt unsettled suddenly, almost claustrophobic. I'm letting those stupid apples still get to me, she thought. She headed upstairs, hoping a shower would relax her.

Later Phoebe returned to her study and gladly diverted her attention to grading the last few reports for class the next day. At one point her eyes drifted over to the folder at the back of the table, the one stuffed with clippings that were supposed to inspire her next book idea. The sight of it triggered a brief wave of anxiety. I've *got* to come up with something, she told herself. But not today. There was just too much going on.

As the day continued, Phoebe still couldn't shake her unease. She decided she would go back to Berta's before the seven o'clock memorial service and treat herself to a light dinner there. Before leaving the house, she remembered to call the locksmith Hutch had recommended and arranged for her lock to be changed after her second class tomorrow.

She cut through campus on her way to Berta's. The sun was already low in the sky, mostly hidden by swaths of sooty gray clouds. Students hurried down pathways and across the grass, shouting to each other in order to be heard over the wind. Halfway across the quad, Phoebe decided on a detour. She headed over toward the plaza in front of the student union, where the memorial would be held. She was curious to see what the setup was.

When she arrived, she saw that a platform and podium were already in place, as well as a hundred or so folding chairs. Nearby, a few boys tossed a small football back and forth, though the wind played havoc with their fun. A huge gust suddenly tore through campus, making the podium rock back and forth. Phoebe caught sight of the pathway that ran from the plaza toward Arthur Hall, the one whose puddles she had leaped over with Lily that day.

"Professor Hall?"

Phoebe didn't use "Professor" as a title because she wasn't one, but occasionally students made the mistake. She turned around.

She'd never met the girl who was standing before her. Phoebe would have remembered. She had long brown hair, which was glossy and smooth, even in the wind. Her eyes were a striking khaki color, set slightly far apart, and they glistened now, as if she had just blinked back tears. There was a pretty flush to her cheeks, and her full lips were naturally outlined in a rosy shade just a bit darker than the rest. Not a classic beauty in any way, Phoebe thought, but the kind of face you couldn't take your eyes off.

"Yes?" Phoebe said.

"I'm Blair Usher," the girl replied.

Phoebe had to fight to hide her surprise. So no need to stalk her after all, she thought.

"Ah," Phoebe said. "Nice to meet you." She wondered if she was standing face to face with someone who'd snuck into her home.

"You keep leaving me messages," the girl said, almost petulantly. "Can I help you with something?"

"Yes, you can," Phoebe said. "I'm part of a team doing an internal investigation into Lily Mack's death, and I'd like to ask you a few questions. Actually, I was going to grab a bite before the memorial. Can I treat you to a burger or a salad?"

"I have plans right now," Blair said. "Sorry." She didn't sound very sorry.

"Which way are you headed?" Phoebe asked.

"Why?" Blair demanded. She seemed wary but at the same time utterly confident. Certain animals in the wild are like that, Phoebe thought. Big cats, for instance.

"Just wondering," Phoebe said.

"That way," Blair said, pointing east with her chin. "Off campus."

"Me too," Phoebe said. "I'll walk with you for a bit, then."

Blair hesitated for a moment, and Phoebe was sure the girl was about to say she'd misspoken, that she was really headed north or west or anyplace other than where Phoebe was going. But Blair finally shrugged a shoulder. "Whatever," she said.

As they started to walk, Phoebe studied Blair from the side. She had to be one of the most attractive girls on campus, and she dressed as if she knew it. She was wearing skintight jeans, knee-high black suede boots, and a black coat nipped in at the waist with a flared skirt. Wrapped twice around her neck was a pink cashmere scarf. An It girl, just as Stockton had said. To her right Phoebe saw some of the touch football players pause and look, staring right through Phoebe at Blair.

"I'm sure the police have already asked you," Phoebe said. "But do you have any thoughts on what might have happened to Lily?"

"None whatsoever," Blair said. "I hadn't spent any time with her lately."

"But there was a chance you were going to see her that night, right? Her roommate said Lily had told her she might stay at your place."

"No," Blair said firmly, "Lily was never going to *stay* at my place that night. At the very beginning of the term she used to stay over sometimes. She'd gotten totally screwed in her living situation when her boyfriend took off, so we'd let her crash on our couch. But that was weeks ago."

So either Lily had lied to her roommate or Blair was lying now, Phoebe thought.

"Why do you think she told her roommate that, then?" Phoebe asked.

Blair paused on the cement path and turned to face Phoebe. "Maybe," she said softly, in a fake conspiratorial tone, "she didn't want her roommate to know what she was really planning to do that night."

"When you *were* seeing more of Lily, was she ever blue or depressed?"

"If she was, she never let on to me. Of course, I'm sure she wasn't pleased when her boyfriend bolted. He left without even saying good-bye." There was a hint of glee in the last statement, as if she thought Lily had gotten what she deserved. Phoebe told herself not to react.

"Had you heard whether she was dating someone new lately?"

"*Dating* someone?"

Oh, that's right, Phoebe thought. No one in college *dated* anymore.

"I mean seeing someone. Or hooking up. Her roommate mentioned that she thought Lily had started to see a new guy. Any ideas who that could be?"

A look crossed Blair's face, and then it was gone almost instantly, like the ripple made by a breeze across a puddle of water. But Phoebe had caught it: a micro expression of disapproval, perhaps even anger. Have I pricked a nerve? Phoebe wondered.

"Nope," Blair said. "No clue."

They were getting close to the eastern gate, and Phoebe guessed she only had a minute or two more.

"So you and Lily had drifted apart," Phoebe said. "Did you two have some kind of falling out?"

"Why would you think that?" Blair asked.

"Because that's often the case when people stop being friends."

Blair stopped and turned to Phoebe, holding her eyes. "I guess as a famous biographer, you know all about what makes people tick," she said smugly.

Phoebe smiled at her. "Sometimes it's just common sense," she said.

"Well, to be perfectly honest, Lily turned out to be someone who wasn't trustworthy. I decided it was better to keep my distance."

"What did she do that upset you?"

"I probably shouldn't say. It wouldn't be nice—with her being dead and everything."

They had just passed through the east gate, and Blair stopped on the sidewalk. She would make certain, of course, that she went the opposite way that Phoebe did.

Phoebe decided to go for broke. "Lily didn't join the Sixes, did she?" she asked. "Is that what upset you?"

The girl clearly hadn't expected Phoebe to go there, and, caught off guard, she looked briefly away. Phoebe could tell Blair's mind was racing, trying to figure out how to play it. The girl looked back at Phoebe.

"The Sixes?" she asked slyly. "I'm not following." Her tone suggested she was up for a little game.

"It's a secret society of girls here," Phoebe said. "Though it's hardly much of a secret anymore. I would have thought you'd heard of them."

"Oh, that's right," Blair said, and briefly touched the tip of her tongue to her pillowy upper lip. "There *have* been a few rumors about them."

"And what exactly have you heard?" Phoebe asked.

"Nothing really very specific," Blair said, staring straight at Phoebe. "Just that they're very, *very* powerful."

Phoebe's heart skipped. The last comment hadn't just been part of the game. It had been a threat, of course. I'm being warned off, Phoebe thought anxiously, just like I was years ago.

"Is there anything else?" Blair asked. "I really have to go."

"No," Phoebe said. "Thank you for your time."

Phoebe turned toward Bridge Street, and behind her, she heard Blair walk briskly off in the opposite direction, her boots tapping hard against the sidewalk.

As soon as she was at Berta's, Phoebe ordered a glass of wine. She had envisioned a quiet hour by herself, a chance to unwind, but she felt totally on edge. Phoebe had no doubt now that the Sixes existed, and that Blair was in the thick of it. There was something truly unsettling about the girl.

By the time Phoebe finally headed back to campus, it was dark and she was later than she'd planned to be. Reaching the plaza, she saw that a huge crowd of students and faculty was already milling around. Many of the students held candles, cupping the wildly flickering flames with their hands. Phoebe's eyes scanned the crowd. Far off to the left, she spotted Pete Tobias talking to a bunch of students, obviously coaxing information from them like a con artist. She headed to the opposite side of the plaza, aiming to steer as clear of him as possible.

Toward the edge of the crowd, a long rectangular table had been set up to sell coffee, and Phoebe bought a cup. Just ahead of her she spotted Craig Ball weaving through the crowd. She realized he had never gotten back to her.

A few minutes later, Tom Stockton opened the service and introduced Glenda. Her remarks weren't long, but they were sincere and moving. "The way we can remember Lily," she told the crowd, "is to take pieces of her spirit into our own lives."

Phoebe noticed that Mark, Glenda's husband, was standing near the front of the crowd. But rather than listening intently, he was glancing down into something in his hand. Probably his BlackBerry, Phoebe realized. She felt that nervous twinge again, like she'd experienced when she heard the shout last night. She was going to have to talk to Glenda about what was going on with her friend's marriage.

Two students spoke next, girls who choked back tears as they described Lily and paid tribute to her. It seemed that each knew her not so much as a good friend, but as someone they had interacted with in the course of a school activity—one had been on the volleyball team with Lily, another was a coeditor of the school magazine. Did that mean Lily didn't have many close friends? Phoebe wondered. Because she'd joined the Sixes? Because there was a new guy in her life? Phoebe glanced around at the faces of kids in the crowd. The students seemed somber, definitely upset, and some of the girls had tears streaming down their faces. There was no sign, interestingly, of Blair or Gwen.

The ceremony closed with a blessing from the school chaplain and a haunting song from the choral society. The crowd began to disperse into the darkness, though some students hung back, hugging or talking listlessly to each other. Phoebe thought of making her way up to Glenda, but she saw that her friend was surrounded by members of the administration. Time to head home, then, Phoebe thought, and the idea made her slightly uneasy.

"Excuse me, Phoebe?" Phoebe turned to see that it was Jan Wait from the English department, the lenses of her big red glasses fogged from the cold. "Miles and I are having people over for a glass of wine—we're just parallel to Bridge Street on Morton. Twenty-six. Would you like to join us?"

Phoebe almost said no, and then caught herself. Jan had always been pleasant to her, and Phoebe appreciated the invitation. It would be a relief to have company tonight.

"That sounds lovely," Phoebe said.

Before leaving the plaza, Phoebe spent a few minutes studying the thinning crowd. Still no sign of Blair. Or Duncan either. But maybe he'll be at the Waits's,

Phoebe thought. Miles Wait was in the psych department, too.

Their place turned out to be one of the restored wooden houses from the 1700s that dotted the town, especially closer to the river. As Phoebe shrugged off her coat in the small entranceway, she peered through the door into the living room, checking out the scene. There were already about a dozen people inside, sipping wine and chattering. And Duncan *was* there, at the far end of the room. He stood by the bookcase with a white bust of Freud on the top shelf, talking to a woman. Phoebe could only see the edge of her through the crowd.

She stepped into the living room, welcomed warmly by the tall, affable Miles. She glanced back toward Duncan and decided to approach. Suddenly the crowd around him shifted slightly, and she saw that it was Val Porter who was standing next to him, talking animatedly. And then, to her surprise, Val reached up and ran her hand down Duncan's back.

It was the kind of possessive gesture that only a lover would make.

## 10

Busy boy, Phoebe thought irritatedly. When Duncan had first asked her out to dinner, she'd assumed he was unattached, but he was clearly spreading his charms around. At least this solved one problem for her, she decided. She hadn't wanted to get involved with anyone, and this guaranteed she wouldn't. She had no interest in being part of someone's campus harem.

She made her way to the bar, a drop-leaf table set up with a hodgepodge of wine bottles and half a quart of Skyy vodka. To the left of it was one of those big brick fireplaces that must have been used for cooking centuries back and now featured a gas fire. The flames danced, repeating the same frantic pattern again and again, and the gas made a popping noise like a flag being whipped by the wind. Phoebe poured herself a glass of cheap Shiraz. Just to her left was a cluster of three people—a man and two women—and she sensed, by the quick pause in their conversation, that they had noticed her and exchanged looks. Many of the faculty would know who she was, the famous plagiarist in their midst.

"Phoebe, have you met Bruce Trudeau?" It was Jan bearing gifts, a man with a potbelly so big it looked as if he was carrying a basketball beneath his shirt. "He's in Miles's department."

"No, I haven't. How do you do?" Phoebe shook Trudeau's hand and then turned back to Jan. "This was so nice of you to do tonight. And your home is charming."

"I thought everyone could use a drink," Jan said. "We're all churned up. Miles had Lily in a class last term, and she was in one of Bruce's this fall."

"Oh," Phoebe said, surprised. "I assumed she was an English major."

"Yes, but a psych minor," Bruce said. "And very smart."

"From what you know of her, do you think she might have committed suicide?" Phoebe asked.

"My gut says no," Trudeau said. "She was a little distracted these past weeks, but not morose in any way.

And yet it's so hard to tell with kids this age. They hide it very, very well."

"Were you aware if she was dating someone?"

"I wouldn't know," Bruce said. "Why so interested? Are you considering writing about this?"

"No, no," Phoebe said. "Celebrities are my beat. I'm just curious."

"What about all this serial killer talk?" Jan asked. "Do you buy any of that, Bruce?"

So, Phoebe thought, *that* theory was now off the leash. She bet it was moving like a brush fire on campus—and she wondered if Tom Stockton had lit the match.

"It seems awfully farfetched," Bruce said. "But I *do* know there's a reporter from the *New York Post* asking a lot of questions, and if he picks up on that theory, he'll go crazy with it. And the media will descend like vultures."

"Did you know there's actually a target age for serial killers?" Jan said. "I read that female victims are usually between sixteen and thirty-eight. When I learned that, I put it on my list of reasons to not hate being over forty."

"And please tell—what are some of the other reasons?" someone asked behind them. It was Duncan's voice.

"Actually, that's the only one I've found so far," Jan said. "Phoebe, do you know Duncan Shaw?"

"Um, yes, hello," Phoebe said.

"Can I get you a refill?" Duncan asked, nodding toward her wineglass. She glanced down and saw that the glass was almost empty.

"Sure," Phoebe said.

As Duncan maneuvered through several clusters of people toward the bar, Jan asked Bruce about a study he was doing on delayed gratification. Phoebe only half listened. Her eyes roamed the room, searching for where Val had gone off to. She didn't look like the type who let a man out of her sight.

"Here you go," Duncan said, returning a couple minutes later. Phoebe turned away from Jan and Bruce, who were now deep in conversation, and reached for the wine. As her hand encircled the glass, her fingers brushed against Duncan's, and she felt a momentary spark. He looked into her eyes, holding them.

"Were you at the service tonight?" she asked. "I didn't see you."

"Yes, though I was a little late," he said. "For some reason I thought it started at seven thirty. What did you think of it?"

"Well done. But so sad, of course. I hear Lily was a psych minor."

"Yes, apparently," he said, forced to move a little closer to Phoebe as more people entered the room. "Miles said he had her in a few classes, but I never did. Any news about the police investigation?"

"I'm not privy to much. I did hear that the cause of death was drowning."

She cringed as soon as the comment escaped her lips. She wondered if hearing the word *drowning* was troubling for Duncan.

"How's *your* situation, by the way?" Duncan asked. If the topic was tough for him, his tone gave no indication. "Any more problems?"

"I had a weird chat today with someone I suspect is in the Sixes," she said. She offered him a few highlights of her conversation with Blair. "She was very cagey. And I can absolutely imagine her sneaking into my house."

"It's ironic, isn't it?" he said. "You leave New York, only to have someone break into your house here."

"I know. The worst thing that ever happened to me in Manhattan was having my car keyed."

Just then, someone jostled her from behind, and she was shoved forward, her breasts pressing into Duncan's arm. She righted herself, trying to look nonchalant, but she felt her cheeks redden.

"You aren't going to throw in the towel and head back to New York, are you?" he asked.

"Why?" she asked. "Are you afraid of the blow to the English department?"

The expression in his eyes shifted, no longer solemn.

"Actually, I'm not thinking of the English department."

Oh, please, she thought. If he was seeing Val, why make flirty little comments to her?

Before she could think of a response, she felt a long, thin arm brush against her own. She knew who it was before she heard the deep voice.

"Hello, Phoebe," Val said. She was wearing flowy black pants and a black jersey top, cut low. Around her neck were half a dozen silver chains, each dangling a different object—an antique cross, a burnished silver vial, a shark tooth—into her cleavage. If I gave her five dollars, Phoebe thought, she would probably tell me my fortune.

Phoebe nodded in greeting.

"What a surprise," Val said. "I've never seen you at a faculty get-together before." Then she laid her long, slim fingers on Duncan's arm.

"I've got an eight o'clock, so we should go now," Val said, turning to Duncan. "Ready?"

"Um, yeah, I guess," he said. "Do you need a lift home, Phoebe?"

"No, thank you," she said. "I'm all set."

She said good night and set down her mostly full glass, thanked Jan for the invitation, and snaked through the crowd, hoping to beat Duncan and Val to the door.

She didn't mind the walk home. The crisp October air was energizing. She'd left lights on in the house, and when she reached it, she saw that it seemed cozy and inviting from the sidewalk.

Phoebe let herself in the front door, and after peering around to make sure nothing was disturbed, she tossed her coat on a chair in the living room. She peeled off her boots, plopped on the couch, and laid her feet on the wooden trunk that she used as a coffee table.

Let Val have Duncan, she thought, allowing her body to sink into the sofa. There was no denying she found Duncan attractive, but no romantic entanglement here meant no chance for regret. Plus, she had other things to concentrate on right now—like figuring out what the Sixes were up to and staying out of Tobias's way.

Outside a car approached, its engine a dull hum, and then seemed to slow as it reached her house. She felt her body tense, on alert, but the car kept going. Don't be paranoid, she chided herself.

But then there was another sound, this one much closer. She bolted upright and strained to hear. It was a scratching sound—almost like branches blown by the wind back and forth across a window. It's coming from the kitchen, she realized with a start, or immediately outside the back door. Was someone trying to get in?

From where she sat on the couch, she could see part of the kitchen, including the back door. Frozen in suspense, she stared at the handle of the door. It wasn't turning, and she couldn't see anyone in the glass above it. The scratching stopped, but five seconds later, as she finally took a breath, it started again. Maybe it's a mouse, she thought. She'd seen a package of traps on a shelf in the pantry off the kitchen, so it was clear Herb had once been plagued by them. She forced herself from the couch.

By the time she reached the kitchen door, the scratching sound had stopped again. Her eyes flew over the room, searching, but she had no clue what had made the noise. If there *was* a mouse, it might be inside the walls or in one of the cabinets.

And then the noise was back. It was more of a knocking now, and as she turned in its direction, she realized it was coming from the refrigerator—from the freezer part on top. Was something wrong with the motor? she wondered, now completely baffled.

She moved across the room and closed her hand around the freezer door. She yanked, pulling it open.

She saw that there was something dark and clumpy at the back, like a wet wig, and then suddenly something sprang at her, hitting her in the chest. She stepped back as the thing fell to the floor with a hard thud. Her eyes shot to the ground. It was a rat, a brown one with a hideously long, hard tail. She gasped, watching as it writhed by her feet. After only a second or two, it collapsed, dead or dying. Her eyes were drawn back into the dark mass at the back of the freezer. To her horror she saw that there were more rats, huddled together and motionless. She started to scream, but all that came out of her mouth was a ragged groan.

She stumbled from the kitchen, her pulse pounding in her ears. Moving frantically around the living room, she searched for her purse. Finally she found it on the table by the door and groped for her phone. She needed to call the police, to get them here *now*. But then she stopped. Her thinking seemed muddled and slow, like someone trying to run through water, but she knew that she should call Glenda first. Because she knew the Sixes had left the rats, just as they'd left the apples.

Glenda answered her cell phone on the second ring, her voice low, as if she was in the midst of something. In the background was the murmur of voices.

"Can you talk?" Phoebe pleaded.

"What if I call you back in fifteen minutes? I'm just finishing up something."

"Um—okay. No, it can't wait. Something awful's happened. You have to tell me what to do."

"What is it?" Glenda urged, her voice barely above a whisper. Phoebe could sense her friend moving, walking away from the people she was with. "Are you okay?"

"I think the Sixes broke into my house again. Someone put rats in my freezer!"

"Oh, my God. Where are you now?"

"At home."

"Are the rats running around?"

"No, they're all dead, I think. It's horrible. And I bet there's six of them." She had to fight to keep her voice from breaking out into a wail. "Should I call the police now? I didn't want to do anything without checking with you."

"Um, let me think for a sec. Maybe we should have Craig take a look first. I'll call him, and we'll head right over. Will you be okay till we get there?"

"Yes. But hurry, please.'

As she hung up, Phoebe could feel her pulse still racing—from both nerves and fury. This had to be payback for her conversation with Blair, she guessed. She'd provoked the girl by bringing up the Sixes, and

Blair had decided to exact revenge. But where had she and her cohorts found a bunch of rats? They certainly hadn't gone off to the city dump and rounded them up with a net.

And then she knew. They must be rats from one of the labs at school. The girls could have broken in and taken them. All that work just to send her a message. Phoebe squeezed her head in her hands. Everything was accelerating, just like years ago. They weren't going to let up.

What's taking them so freaking long? she wondered, when she saw that fifteen minutes had passed since she'd called Glenda. But a few moments later a campus police car pulled up outside. Ball was driving, with Glenda in the passenger seat. As soon as Phoebe let them into the house, she blurted out the basic details of what had happened.

Ball, zipped in his leather uniform jacket, scrunched up his mouth and strode into the kitchen, with Glenda and Phoebe trailing behind him. "Damn," he said as he took in the scene. Glenda gasped. To Phoebe's disgust, she saw that a small amount of blood had trickled from the mouth of the rat onto the floor.

"This is outrageous," Glenda said.

"How'd they'd get into the house—do you know?" Ball asked.

"The *rats?*" Phoebe asked.

"No," Ball said, barely tamping down his impatience. "The girls. Dr. Johns said you think the Sixes did this."

Phoebe glanced at Glenda and then back at Ball. "Yes, I'm sure it was them," Phoebe said. "I think they must have made a copy of my back-door key yesterday." She explained about the apples, and that the locksmith appointment wasn't until tomorrow.

"That's the kind of information I should have been alerted to earlier," Ball said, narrowing his eyes at her.

"I know. That's why I stopped by your office this morning and left a message for you."

From the way Ball's upper lip lifted, Phoebe could tell he hadn't appreciated her comment. She'd busted him in front of his boss.

"Let me take a look around," Ball said, still securely in alpha male mode.

"But shouldn't we call the police now?" Phoebe asked.

Ball and Glenda hurriedly exchanged a look.

"Let's hold off on that for a second, okay?" Ball said. "Let me first see what we've got here."

"There's something else you should be aware of," Phoebe told him. "I assume these must be rats from one of the labs on campus."

"Of course—which means there's been a break-in there," Glenda said.

Ball whipped out his cell phone and commanded someone named Jake to hightail it up to the science center to investigate—and another cop named Buddy to head over to Phoebe's, along with some large trash bags. When he hung up, he suggested that Glenda and Phoebe take a seat. He headed back to the kitchen.

"Fee, I'm so sorry I got you into this," Glenda said.

"Well, at least we can be pretty sure now that the Sixes *do* exist," Phoebe said. She brought Glenda up to speed on her conversation with Blair. "It also means they're fairly organized. It took at least two people to pull this off, I'd say."

"And they're even nastier than we imagined," Glenda said.

Off to her left, Phoebe could hear that Craig was now in her study. She hated the idea of him in there, possibly pawing her things. When he eventually emerged, he made a beeline for the front door, opening it with a handkerchief.

"Which door did you use when you came home tonight?" he asked Phoebe.

"The front."

"You need to use a key to lock it when you exit, right?"

"Yes. I'm sure I locked it when I left, and it was locked when I got back. I also made certain the back door was locked when I left."

Ball didn't say anything, just moved around the periphery of the room, checking the windows. When he was done, he stood silently for a moment, his mouth twisted as he deliberated. Without asking, he headed upstairs, and they could hear the clomp of his feet above them. Five minutes later he was back downstairs, shaking his head.

"All the windows are locked, too," Ball said. "And the back door. Which means they must have made a copy of your key. Because if they got in through an entry point that you'd accidentally left unlocked, they would have been forced to leave either a door or window unlocked when they took off."

"So *now* do we call the police?" Phoebe asked.

Again Ball shot a look at Glenda, one that seemed to speak whole sentences. Phoebe glanced at Glenda. Her face was tense with worry, but Phoebe wasn't sure what she'd just telegraphed to Craig.

"Ms. Hall, I know this may be awkward for you," Ball said, "but I'm going to ask you a favor as a member of the school community. I'd like us all to keep a lid on this for the time being."

"A *lid* on it?" Phoebe said. "Why?"

"I think it's best that we handle this ourselves for now. I'll investigate discreetly and try to determine who exactly broke in—and then we'll go to the police. That way we don't end up creating a big stink that the whole world knows about. And I mean that literally. We've got a damn New York City reporter on campus."

Phoebe snapped her head toward Glenda, convinced her friend would nix the suggestion. But Glenda's eyes were imploring.

"Please, Phoebe," she said. "So much is at stake."

"But—" Phoebe started to protest but caught herself. Ball was right—the whole thing could blow up in Glenda's face.

"All right," Phoebe said. She wasn't crazy about the idea of covering things up, but she could understand Glenda's point of view. Besides, if they alerted the cops to what had happened, Phoebe would be told to stop her own investigation.

And she had no intention of giving up. Because that was exactly what the Sixes expected her to do.

A girl who lived across the hall from her was the one who gave her the first clue to what was wrong. They were in the laundry room one night, folding clothes side by side as the wind howled outside, and the girl complained about a friend who'd been passed over for a role in the musical.

"It's Fortuna," the girl said. "They made sure the part went to who they wanted for it."

"What's Fortuna?" she had asked. The girl's comment had begun to trigger an unease in her, but she wasn't sure why.

"You don't know?" the girl had said, wide-eyed. "They—they control everything here."

Fortuna, she said, was made up of the rich, pretty girls. They guaranteed, the girl said, that their own members—or girls they approved of—won elections, starred in the plays, ran everything that mattered. The administration turned a blind eye because the parents of Fortuna members were the biggest donors to the school.

They were named, the girl said finally, for the goddess of fortune. Their symbol was fortune's wheel. She suddenly remembered that one of the girls in her former study group always wore a charm bracelet with a single silver wheel.

"I don't care," she had said to the girl. "I'll make my own fortune."

"Don't ever let them hear you say that," the girl had told her. "Because they'll make you pay for it."

## 11

Leaving a few lights burning in the living room, Phoebe mounted the stairs to the second floor.

It had taken Craig Ball and the younger cop Buddy, who looked to Phoebe like he still had his baby teeth, over an hour to clean up the horror-movie scene in her kitchen. While they worked, Glenda had tried to convince Phoebe to stay at her house, and though Phoebe had been briefly tempted, she'd said no. She couldn't just start bunking down at Glenda's every night.

She told herself it wouldn't be so bad. Craig had promised that Officer Hyde would drive by her house at least every half hour. And of course the chain locks would be on the doors. But as soon as everyone had departed, she'd felt her dread begin to swell like a dry sponge dropped into water.

After changing into flannel pajama bottoms and a T-shirt, Phoebe slid into her icy-cold bed. Thanks to sheer weariness, sleep overtook her within moments. Then, suddenly, she was shaken back into consciousness. She was hearing knocking sounds again, coming from downstairs. She quickly sat up in bed. Were there more rats, she wondered desperately, trapped somewhere else? But as the sound continued, she realized that someone was knocking on the front door.

After grabbing her cell phone from the bedside table, she shot out of bed and hurried down the stairs. Maybe it was Buddy, checking on her in person.

From the stairwell, she had a direct view of the window in the front door. As she approached she saw, to her utter surprise, that Duncan Shaw was standing on the other side.

She crossed the room quickly and opened the door.

"Miles called and told me the news," Duncan said as he stepped inside. "Are you okay?"

Phoebe sighed. "To be honest, I feel pretty rattled. God, that's a bad pun, isn't it?" She led him into the living room. "Were the rats yours?"

"Fortunately, no," Duncan said. "In fact, there are no rats missing at all from the science center. They were probably bought at a pet store or a student may have owned them." He took a seat on the couch. "So tell me what happened. I've only heard pieces of the story."

Phoebe gave him the highlights. As Duncan listened, he shook his head in disgust.

"But the cops cleaned everything up?" he asked.

"Craig said they did the best they could for now, and I haven't dared look. I just won't ever eat sorbet again."

"How did someone manage to get access?"

"I think by making a copy of my key the day they left the apples. Would you like a shot of brandy, by the way? I'm suddenly feeling in need of one."

"That would be great," Duncan said. "So you're pretty sure it was this group again—the Sixes?"

He shrugged off his jacket and let it fall on the couch. He was wearing the same clothes he'd had on earlier— jeans, button-down dress shirt—but they were slightly rumpled, as if he'd stripped them off, dropped them on the floor, and then retrieved them ten minutes ago. Phoebe wondered if Val was back at his place, keeping the bed warm.

"Yep, pretty sure," Phoebe said. She crossed the room to a small butler's table where she'd set up a few bottles of after-dinner liqueurs. "There were six rats, just as there were six apples. And remember that slightly hostile conversation I had with Blair Usher today? This feels like retaliation."

As Phoebe opened the brandy bottle, she remembered that she was in her damn pajamas. The bottoms were decent enough, but the top was just a tissuey T-shirt that you could practically see her breasts through.

"Miles said we're supposed to keep all of this quiet from the cops for now?" Duncan said.

"Yes. Craig Ball wants to dig up more evidence, and figure out for sure which girls were involved. I guess he's afraid that if the cops are called in now, it'll be a mess on campus. I'm going to have the locks changed tomorrow, so they won't be able to get in again, and once Ball knows who broke in, he'll hand them over to the police."

"Reasonable from a PR standpoint for the college, but not exactly comforting for you."

"I just keep reminding myself that they're a bunch of twenty-year-old girls, not master criminals." She wished she felt as confident as her words boasted.

With brandy glasses in hand, Phoebe crossed back across the room to Duncan. When she handed him his glass and sat down next to him, their fingers brushed and she felt the same charge she'd experienced earlier at the party. I want him, she thought. Where did this come from?

"Still, this is pretty serious stuff," Duncan said. He smiled for the first time that night. "I can't imagine what it was like for you when you found them—knowing how unfond you are of the little creatures."

"Well, I really appreciate you coming over and checking on me," Phoebe said. She looked at him coyly, unable to resist making the next comment. "I just hope it didn't throw a wrench in your plans tonight."

It took him a moment to realize what she'd meant, and he threw his head back and laughed.

"Oh—Val," he said. "It's funny—suddenly she's completely interested in me. Maybe as a feminist she was operating under the premise that it's wrong for a woman to make a play for a widower until his wife has been dead and buried for well over a year. No matter what I do, I can't seem to discourage her."

"So you aren't seeing her, then?" Phoebe asked. She'd meant it to come out lightly, but her tone had sounded urgent, betraying her eagerness to know.

"God, no," Duncan said. He studied Phoebe for a moment. "I can tell by your face that you don't totally believe me."

Phoebe shrugged. "As a writer, I've always given far more credence to what people do than what they say."

"Right—and of course I left the party with Val. Will you believe me when I say she begged for a ride, claiming her generator was on the blink?"

"Ahhh," Phoebe said. "Did she mean her car's generator or her own?"

Duncan laughed again.

"Well, if actions dazzle you more than words, let me make a stronger case for myself, then," he said.

He reached his right arm behind her, pulled her toward him, and kissed her. His lips were warm and soft, and as they pressed deeply into her mouth, she felt a rush of intense desire spread through her lower body.

All too quickly, he pulled away. She caught her breath. Don't stop, she wanted to say. Duncan stared into her eyes so intensely she had to fight the urge to look away.

"Did I convince you?" he said.

"Almost," she whispered.

He took her glass from her hand and set it down on the table. Cupping her face in his hand, he kissed her again, this time more urgently, and within seconds his tongue was in her mouth, exploring. She reached her arms around him and kissed him back, harder and deeper. Her body felt on fire now.

Without taking his mouth from hers, he began exploring her breasts with one hand, massaging them through the tissuey fabric and circling her nipples with his thumb. Involuntarily Phoebe let out a moan, and pressed her body into his.

"So what's the verdict?" he asked, pulling away again. "Do you believe me now that I don't give a rat's ass—if you'll excuse the expression—about Val?"

"Yes," Phoebe said softly. She realized that she was trembling a little—from desire, from everything the night had entailed. Duncan said nothing back, just held her eyes, and she knew then that the next move would have to be hers. The kiss had come because she'd challenged him with her comment about actions versus words, but he wasn't going to push it. He'd learned his lesson with his first dinner invitation.

"Would you like to stay?" she asked him. God, I'm really doing this, she thought. "I mean, I may not be at the top of my game, considering everything that's happened, but I'd give it my best shot."

"Something tells me that not the top of your game is very good," he said.

She led Duncan upstairs. She was glad she'd left just the one bedside lamp burning in her bedroom. Though she was in good enough shape, she felt self-conscious suddenly. The last time she'd made love to a *new* man, it had been Alec and she'd been thirty-seven, with firmer breasts and a flatter stomach. But as Duncan pulled her pajama top over her head, she just stopped thinking. He took her breasts in his hands, stroking and kneading them. He kissed her urgently at the same time. He stepped back just long enough to nearly tear his shirt off and toss it on the small armchair. His chest was smooth and well defined. She ran her hands over it, feeling the softness of his skin.

Pulling her closer again, he slipped his hand inside her pajama bottoms. His fingers began to explore, softly at first, teasing her, and then more firmly. And then suddenly his finger was inside her, making her gasp. Phoebe reached between his legs and stroked him.

"Why don't we get in bed," he said.

While she found a condom in the dresser, Duncan peeled off his blue jeans and boxer briefs. As she reached the bed, he stripped back the comforter in one move and lay her down. He tugged off her pajama bottoms and began to explore her with his mouth and his tongue. She pulled on his hair, urging him up and inside her. The strokes he used at first were long and torturously slow, and she writhed beneath him. Suddenly he quickened his pace, moving faster and faster, and it was only seconds before she climaxed. He slowed his speed so that she could concentrate on the waves, and then moved faster and faster until she felt him come inside her.

Afterward he held her, spooning. He stroked her hair with his hand. "Was the invitation for the entire night?" he murmured into her ear.

"Absolutely," she said.

A little while later she thought she sensed him drift off to sleep. She had thought the sex would enable her to fall back asleep easily, but she suddenly felt wired. The image of the dead rats came rushing back. After lying quietly for a while, unsuccessfully willing sleep to come, she slipped out of bed and padded down the hall to the bathroom. In the mirror she saw that her cheeks were still flushed red. She wet a washcloth with cold water and, sitting on the edge of the bathtub, held it to her face. Had she been crazy to go to bed with Duncan, to start up a fling with someone at the school? Maybe, she thought mockingly, I was suffering from posttraumatic rat syndrome and couldn't think straight tonight. But she knew that wasn't true. Her desire for him had been building since he'd sat across the table from her eating spaghetti carbonara. And what she knew for sure was that tonight had done nothing to quell that desire. She wanted him all over again.

She stood up, hung the washcloth on the towel rod, and massaged lotion into her face. It was now after midnight, and she had to force herself to sleep so she would seem reasonably sane in class tomorrow. She switched off the bathroom light and snuck quietly down the hallway. The darkness made her heart skip just a little. As she approached the bedroom, she stopped in her tracks. She could hear the murmur of Duncan's voice. He was talking to someone.

# 12

As Phoebe stepped into the room, she saw a pinpoint of light floating above the bed. It was from Duncan's cell phone, she realized; he was talking into it in a low voice, propped up on an elbow. He muttered a good-bye, and from the dim glow of the night light, Phoebe watched him toss the phone onto the chair where his clothes were lying and flop onto his back.

"Everything okay?" she asked, puzzled.

"I was just checking my voice mail to see if Miles had called with any news. He was going to search the lab again just to be sure."

"Oh, I thought I heard you talking," she said, puzzled.

"I left a message on his voice mail at work, telling him to call me if he found anything. How you doing? Still feeling a little rattled?"

"Not so much," she said, shrugging off her robe. She slipped back into bed. Duncan shifted position so his body was facing hers. "You have a nice way of calming a girl down."

"Oh, is that right?" Duncan said. She could sense his mouth form into a smile. He dragged his other hand down the length of her body. They made love again, this time even more intensely, and seconds after he pulled out of her, she fell into a deep sleep.

Her alarm went off at six. Phoebe stirred, then reached up and slapped the snooze button. Suddenly she remembered Duncan, and her eyes shot open. The opposite side of the bed was empty. Oh, please, she thought. Don't tell me he's just taken off.

Then she heard him on the stairs. He came into the room—pants on, shirt off—carrying two espressos.

"I hope you don't mind me co-opting your prized espresso machine," he said.

"Hardly," Phoebe said. "And I can't believe I'm being served in bed."

He lowered himself next to her, and after Phoebe propped herself up, he passed her one of the small cups. The smell of the coffee mixed with the musky smell of Duncan's body. Phoebe wondered if in the rude light of day she would begin to find him wanting in some way, but no, that didn't happen. She liked the way he looked and sounded and smelled.

"I also took the liberty of tidying up your freezer a bit," he said, smiling.

"Oh, wow, that's even better than coffee in bed," Phoebe said. "I don't think I even would have worked up the courage to open that door again."

"I'm a bit more comfortable with rat fur than you are, and I hacked out the remaining traces of it. Besides, I had to figure out some way to thank you for last night."

I can think of one, she thought. Come back to my bed again soon.

She pulled on her robe while Duncan dressed. As they left the room a few minutes later, Duncan nodded at the night-light by the door.

"You know what I love about that," Duncan said.

"Oh, God, I can't believe you noticed it," Phoebe said, rolling her eyes

"No, no, it's good. It gave me another glimpse of the soft, tender side of Phoebe Hall."

"Hey, I'm in a strange house," she said. She nudged him with her elbow. "I need to wake up at night and know where I am."

A few minutes later they descended the stairs, and when they reached the front door, Duncan pulled Phoebe toward him and kissed her softly on the lips.

"So are you going to let me cook for *you* one night?" he asked.

"I'd like that," she said.

"How about Friday night?" he asked. "Unless, of course, you have plans to eat alone at Tony's."

She smiled. "What do I have to do so you'll finally let me off the hook about that?"

He laughed.

"Trust me, I'll think of something between now and Friday."

As she heard Duncan's footsteps tripping down the steps of her porch, some of the discomfort from the previous night rushed back. She walked hesitantly into the kitchen. It looked exactly as it had when she'd left yesterday afternoon: the two glasses in the drainer, the faded yellow dish towel threaded through the drawer pull, the row of small gourds on the windowsill above the sink.

Get it over with, she told herself, and yanked open the door of the freezer. Duncan had been good to his word—there wasn't a trace of anything foul in there. It was also totally empty inside; he'd tossed out her two tubs of sorbet and she found that he'd put the ice cube trays in the dishwasher.

An hour later, showered and dressed, Phoebe double-checked all the windows and doors before leaving the house. She took her car to campus this time, and bought a cappuccino and bagel at Café

Lyle—since she hadn't had the stomach to fix any-thing in her kitchen. Just as she planted herself at a table, Glenda called.

"You okay, Fee?"

"Yeah. I keep waiting to develop symptoms of bubonic plague, but so far I'm not hacking up any blood."

"You didn't stay up all night in a panic, did you?"

"No, no, I managed to get some sleep," Phoebe said.

There was no way she could blurt out the de-tails about her night with Duncan, not smack in the middle of the campus café anyway, and yet holding back made her uneasy. She hadn't even told Glenda about her first dinner date with Duncan, and the longer she waited, the weirder it would seem—the two of them had always been open with each other about their personal lives. Phoebe sensed that she might be dragging her heels this time for a reason. Was it because she thought Glenda would disapprove of her becoming involved with another member of the faculty?

"I wish I could say it helped to know Buddy was patrolling the neighborhood," Phoebe added quickly. "But he seems like the kind of guy people still give wedgies to. Any news from your end?"

"So far Craig hasn't been able to flush out any of the Sixes, but he's on it big-time. And I have the information you needed—Alexis's admission file. I know you have a class at eight, but can you come over afterward and pick it up?"

Phoebe agreed, and after nearly wolfing down her breakfast, she hurried to Arthur Hall. She'd told her students to come prepared to comment on the writing styles in the pieces she'd passed out on Monday, and she planned to save time at the end of today's class to describe some of the principles she'd learned from editors she'd worked with over the years. But as the students began tossing out comments, she found herself only half concentrating; instead her mind ricocheted between the dead rats, Blair, Lily—and Duncan, too. At one point she realized that one of the few boys in the class was calling out a question. She was forced to ask him to repeat himself.

"Isn't it silly for us to be studying magazine articles when print is on its last legs? I mean, many of us may never write for magazines."

"I disagree," Phoebe said. "Yes, if you write professionally, a lot of your content will probably be for the Web—and that's why I have you doing blogs. But there's no reason to believe that magazines are going to be dead any time soon. There's still a big market for long-form articles. In fact, I think that eventually you'll find far more long-form articles on the Web."

This led to lots of back-and-forth between the kids, leaving little time for Phoebe to share the editor wisdom she'd planned to dispense, but that was okay, since she didn't feel focused enough to do it justice. At the end of class she gave an assignment for Monday—write a pitch for any magazine of your choice—and was out the door before any students could grab her for questions or offer additional commentary on the tottering future of print journalism.

The president's office was across campus in the administration building, an older structure with marble floors and wide corridors. As Phoebe hurried up the stairs to the second floor, she nearly collided with Glenda's husband, Mark. He looked dapper as usual in brown pants, a beige car coat, and a thin brown scarf around his neck.

"Oh, hi, Mark," Phoebe said, greeting him with a smile.

"Someone's in a hurry," he said in response. He forced a smile after his comment, but she'd detected something snide in his tone. She knew she wasn't imagining it. Since she'd been in Lyle, he definitely seemed to be snubbing her.

"I was just going to catch Glenda between my classes. She's up there, right?" Phoebe said.

"You mean, instead of putting out fires all over campus? Yes, the president is ensconced."

Now *that* was definitely dripping in sarcasm, Phoebe thought. But she couldn't tell if she or Glenda was the catalyst.

"Well, I'll see you later, then," she said, eager to extricate herself before the conversation deteriorated. "Have a good day."

"Ditto," he called as he descended the stairs. *Ditto,* she thought. What the hell was going on with him?

Phoebe waited for Glenda's assistant to announce her arrival before stepping into the office. She was struck, as she had been the first time she'd visited, by the duality of the room's personality. The throw pillows on the couch and citrusy scent from bowls of potpourri made the space inviting, but at the same time the formidable desk clearly conveyed that someone powerful held court here.

Before Phoebe could even say hello, Glenda tossed her head back from her seat behind the desk and laughed.

"You look like you're ready for the red carpet. Clearly you aren't going to let some rats cramp your style."

Phoebe had dressed in a tight pencil skirt, a crisp white blouse, and a leopard-print belt, but she knew Glenda was picking up on more than that. The night with Duncan had left her feeling rejuvenated.

"That's nice of you to say, considering that the last Botox shots I had in Manhattan wore off about three weeks ago," Phoebe said.

Glenda rose from her chair and came around the desk, then perched on the front edge of it.

"Maybe life in lovely Lyle, Pennsylvania, is agreeing with you—despite a few recent disturbances," Glenda said.

"Let's not jump to any conclusions just yet," Phoebe said, smiling, deciding this might be the time to spill the beans about Duncan. "Speaking of life in lovely Lyle, I bumped into Mark on the stairs here."

"He was dropping off my BlackBerry," Glenda said. "In my frantic state this morning, I'd left it at home." She glanced down at the desk and scooted some papers out of the way, as if not wanting to meet Phoebe's gaze.

"Okay, talk to me, G," Phoebe said. "Something's up between the two of you—I can tell."

Glenda shot a glance at the office door, making sure it was closed. "Then maybe you can explain it to me," she said, "because I haven't a clue what's going on. Things just seem off between us lately, and I'm not sure why."

"Off *how*?"

"He's grumpy toward me—a lot. You saw it that day with Brandon. And if he's not grumpy, he's just cool, standoffish."

"Could it be your job? Your career's never been a problem for him before, but then again it's never been this *big*."

"That's the first thing I wondered, even before I asked myself if he might be screwing someone else. But I've been president for nearly three years, so why would it become an issue now? Of course, there's a chance that living in Lyle is finally taking its toll."

"How's his business going?"

"Pretty good, I guess. I probably should ask more about it, but you know me—I'm not the super wifey type."

"*Could* he be screwing someone?"

"I haven't seen any obvious signs of it," Glenda said, folding her arms across her chest. "And I'm not going to stoop to going through his texts. At least for now. Besides, he still seems pretty interested in screwing *me*—though he's a little more detached these days."

"Maybe the grumpiness has something to do with me," Phoebe said.

"*You?*" Glenda asked, perplexed.

"Yeah. To be perfectly honest, he doesn't seem very happy to have me around."

"How do you mean?"

"I get the feeling he thinks it was a bad idea for you to invite me here. That it could cause you grief professionally. When did all this grumpiness start, anyway?"

"Uh—about two months ago, I'd say. Around the time the semester started."

"Around the time *I* arrived."

"But I just can't—"

There was a knock on the door, making them both jerk their heads in that direction. Glenda's assistant stuck her head in.

"People are starting to arrive for your next meeting, Dr. Johns," she announced.

"Tell them I'll be right there," Glenda said. Once the door was shut again, she turned back to Phoebe. "To be continued."

Glenda slid off the desk, circled back around it, and retrieved a manila folder resting on the far corner. She handed it to Phoebe.

"Here's a copy of everything from Alexis Grey's file," she said. "I shouldn't be sharing this with you, so don't let anyone see it."

"Got it."

"And Fee? Thanks again for last night. For understanding why we need to keep this under wraps."

"Are you worried about Ball, though? You told me the other day that you don't totally trust him."

"I still need to keep my eye on him, but last night I actually felt that we were on the same page."

As Phoebe walked across campus moments later, she realized that she still hadn't said a word to Glenda about Duncan. She'd have to do it the next time.

As soon as her eleven o'clock class was over, Phoebe rushed home to meet the locksmith. He turned out to be about twenty, tall, with lanky black hair and a sleeve of tattoos on his right arm. While he drilled the back door, Phoebe made a sweep through the house, checking that no one had snuck in this morning, but everything seemed in order.

After the locksmith left, Phoebe fixed a late lunch and lit a sandalwood-scented candle. Getting the back-door lock fixed had brought all the bad stuff about last night rushing back, making Phoebe feel jittery again, and she wanted something to help her relax. Just a couple of days ago she had begun to finally feel at home in Herb's tiny house, but now the walls seemed to be pressing on her.

With sandwich in hand, she settled in her office and opened the manila envelope Glenda had turned over to her. There were about ten pages all together—Alexis's application to Lyle, her transcript, and notes Tom Stockton had made about her night in the ER. She spread the contents out across her desk. What Phoebe needed was a "cover" that would allow her to elicit info from Alexis's family about her whereabouts at this time, and hopefully the contents would inspire one.

As she began to peruse the pages, Phoebe felt the funny tingle that so often came when she submerged herself in research. She was good at interviewing people, she knew—good at probing and listening and teasing out the truth from the ramblings and lies—but just as much, perhaps even more, she loved the research. She called it "Sherlocking." She would comb through old letters and papers, or endless pages of information on the Web, for the tiny nugget that would open a secret door for her.

Alexis had earned only average college board scores, but she'd paid her dues in high school, not only finishing with all A's and B's but also working her tail off in a string of extracurricular activities—basketball, tennis, student council, community service. Obviously Alexis's family had money, because rather than work, the girl had spent three different summers with a group called Hartney, which offered teen cultural trips abroad. She'd been to Australia, France, and Spain. An idea formed in Phoebe's mind.

Alexis's mother was listed on the information form as a homemaker. With any luck, she would be home now. Phoebe tried the number.

"Mrs. Grey?" Phoebe asked after a woman answered with a clipped hello.

"Yes?" the woman said.

"Good morning, I'm Phoebe Smart from Hartney Student Travel. We're doing a major survey of parents whose kids have taken part in our programs—in the hope of enhancing what we do. Do you have a moment to answer some questions?"

"You've caught me just as I'm getting ready to go out. Is the survey long?"

"No, no, just a few questions. And your feedback will help enormously."

"All right, then," the woman said. "If it's only a few."

"Am I right to assume Alexis was happy with our programs? She did three of them."

"Yes, she was quite pleased with them. Needless to say they're exorbitantly expensive, but we felt they were worth it."

"And what did she like best about them?"

"She loved the kids," the mother said. "And the itineraries were good. She always felt she was learning something."

"Did one program stand out for her more than the others? She was in Australia the longest, of course."

"She loved Australia, yes. But they were all good in their own way."

"And what is she up to now? Is she in college?"

There was a moment's pause before the mother answered.

"She'll be going to the University of Maryland in January."

"Oh, that's a great school," Phoebe said. "But she's not studying anyplace right now?"

"No—she's working at the moment. At the Gap in the Crossgates Mall here. You know, just taking some time off."

"Of course. A lot of the kids we've tracked down have taken a break here and—"

"I hate to cut you off, but my ride for tennis is here. I really need to go."

"Not a problem." Phoebe thought of quickly asking for Alexis's cell number but was afraid it would set off an alarm. She knew where Alexis worked, and that was a good start.

After hanging up, Phoebe checked Facebook for Alexis but, interestingly, there was no page for her. She then Googled the mall and looked up directions. The trip was going to take roughly three hours. She decided she would leave right after an early breakfast the next day.

Phoebe was making the trip in the hope that time would have helped quell the girl's fears and that she'd finally be open to talking, but Phoebe knew there was just as good a chance Alexis would still be reluctant to divulge anything. If only I knew more about the Sixes, Phoebe thought, it would give me an advantage in trying to pry information from Alexis.

She let her mind wander for a moment and then reached again for her phone. Several years ago, for a book she'd written on former child stars, she'd interviewed a psychologist named Candace Aikens whose specialty was adolescent girls and women in their twenties. Phoebe had been more than impressed by the woman's insight, and she wondered if Aikens might have some wisdom to share on this subject. She looked up the number in her log, punched it on her phone, then left a message on voice mail.

Just thirty minutes later, as Phoebe was scrolling through e-mail she'd been ignoring for days, Dr. Aikens called back.

"I'm teaching at a small college for a semester, and I was hoping to pick your brain about something that's happening here," Phoebe explained.

"Sure, I'll do my best. Tough group to understand, aren't they?"

"Yeah, bit of a challenge for me. They just seem so different from people I knew in *my* twenties. Here's the issue I'm dealing with: there appears to be a secret society of girls here. We haven't got a lot to go on yet, but we do know that they like to play nasty pranks and that one of their former members ended up in the ER with a panic attack, saying they were after her."

"Ahh, I'm seeing a lot of mean girl behavior like that these days."

"But even at the college level?"

"Absolutely. They band together almost like a pack of wolves. I call it girl power gone wild."

"Define wild, will you?" Phoebe said. "What kind of things do they do?"

"Bully. Intimidate. They can be very aggressive sexually—predatory, almost. For instance, keeping track of guys they've slept with and sharing the info. It's behavior you used to only see with guys."

"I know that young girls can be mean. But it just seems so surprising in girls *this* age."

"Not anymore, because our culture has come to allow it. Look at what you see on these reality television shows. It's okay to be a roaring bitch or flip over a table on someone. In fact, it's *prized*."

"That sounds pretty scary."

"I'm not saying all girls are like this. There are plenty of terrific, dynamic girls out there. There's just a certain pathology with the girls I'm talking about—the ones who organize these wolf packs. They may have been abused when they were young or scarred by a certain experience. Years ago girls had to internalize anything that happened to them like that, but now they're allowed to act out."

"So all the girls in these groups have had a troubling experience in their past?"

"I'm talking mainly about the ringleaders. Other girls get lured in simply because they're needy on some level, they want to belong. Or maybe they're just seduced by the charisma of the queen bee."

"The queen bee?" Phoebe felt a chill as she said the words.

"The one at the center who's running everything and pulling the strings. In a way all the members are queen bees, but she's—how should I put it?—queenier than the rest."

Phoebe thought about Blair. Beautiful. Utterly confident. And fearless.

"And that's enough to sway a nice girl into doing something nasty?"

"Some of them don't know what's really going on until they're fully entrenched. And then it can be hairy for them. I'd love to talk more later, Phoebe. But I've got a patient coming in a few minutes."

"No problem. This has been very insightful."

When she set the phone down, Phoebe noticed that it had grown dark out. She sprang up from her chair and hurried from one room to the next, flicking on lights. She was out of breath by the time she finished.

She sat back down on her desk and scribbled down notes from her conversation with Dr. Aikens, wondering how it all related to the Sixes. Was their hidden agenda all about bedding boys and adding notches to their belts? Based on her brief encounter with Lily, that seemed so hard to believe, but Phoebe knew she might have misjudged the girl. She also wondered if Blair was really the ringleader. Or was there someone else in control?

Much later, when she couldn't put off bed any longer, Phoebe took a book upstairs with her and tried to read, but she could barely concentrate. Each time the house creaked or groaned, her eyes shot up toward the open door of her bedroom. At one point she let her eyes drift over the rumpled sheets and thought of Duncan, of making love to him last night. Though sex with Alec had been decent, more than decent at times, in the last year of their relationship he'd come to rely on a paint-by-numbers approach in bed, and she had found herself yearning for something exciting and reckless. And that had defined sex with Duncan. It had been intense, freeing. She also couldn't deny how safe she'd felt, having him with her. Don't be a baby, she told herself. Your lock is changed. You are safe.

Her cell phone, which she'd parked on the bedside table, rang suddenly, making her jerk. With Duncan on her mind, she immediately thought it might be him, just calling to check in.

But when she answered, she heard a gravelly voice on the other end.

"I hope I didn't wake you," the man said.

"Who *is* this?" Phoebe asked.

"Hutch Hutchinson. We met yesterday."

"Oh, hello," Phoebe said, her voice softening. "No, you didn't wake me."

"I've been thinking about what we talked about," he said. "About that group of girls you mentioned. And I think I may have some information you'll find interesting."

# 13

Hutch Hutchinson lived on the outskirts of Lyle, and his driveway turned out to be about a quarter of a mile long. As Phoebe reached the end of it, she saw that the house was actually a log cabin tucked into a cluster of fir trees at the edge of a heavily wooded area. There was an old red Honda in front of the cabin, as well as a black pickup truck, its hood and windshield scattered with pine needles.

Phoebe had tried to wrestle the information out of him over the phone, but he was adamant about telling her in person. It seemed to Phoebe that he might be craving face-to-face time with another person. She asked if he'd mind meeting at eight thirty the next morning because she was heading out of town.

"Sure, why don't you come over to my place," he said. "Coffee's on me." It would delay her arrival in

Maryland, but she was anxious to hear whatever he had to share.

As Phoebe stepped from her car, her nostrils were filled with the fragrant scent of fir trees. This was the kind of setting she'd envisioned for herself in Lyle, but she now knew she probably would have felt skittish living so far from anyone else. She strode up and knocked on the wooden door of the cabin. No one answered. Could he still be sleeping? Phoebe wondered. Just then she heard a sound behind her, and she spun around. A golden retriever, its muzzle whitened with age, was lumbering toward her from the direction of a large work shed. A tiny Chihuahua suddenly shot right past the retriever and nearly bounded into Phoebe's arms.

"Okay, Ginger, give her a minute to get the lay of the land," a voice called. Hutch had now emerged from the shed himself. He wore baggy khaki pants, work boots, and a faded plaid shirt. "We don't even know if the lady likes dogs."

"I *do*," Phoebe said. The retriever licked her hands with abandon as Ginger pranced at her feet like a tiny reindeer. "Though the combo is a bit of a surprise."

Hutch laughed deeply, but Phoebe heard a doleful chord somewhere in there.

"Ginger was my wife Becky's dog," Hutch said, scooping Ginger up with one hand. "She passed two years ago, and Ginger just goes nuts if she sees a nice looking female."

"I'm sorry for your loss," Phoebe said.

"I appreciate that. I'm not a toy-dog kind of guy. The retriever, Sunny, is more my style. But needless to say, Ginger's got a special place in my heart. Come on in."

The inside of the house was cluttered but homey looking and layered with smells from all sorts of things—dog hair, pipe tobacco, fresh coffee, and the smoldering logs in the wood-burning stove. Over the hearth was an oversize framed photo of Hutch and his wife. Becky had been a plump, pretty woman whose face exuded kindness and a fierce devotion to her man.

"Sit wherever you'd like," Hutch said, gesturing broadly with his large hand, "and just help yourself to coffee." Phoebe took the couch, figuring Hutch would prefer the big leather recliner for himself. She could practically see the shape of his body in it. On the coffee table in front of her was a tray with a glass coffeepot, mugs, sugar, and milk. Phoebe poured a mug for herself.

"You make a mean cup of joe," Phoebe said after taking a swig.

"Unfortunately it's about my only selling point as a bachelor," Hutch said. "That and the fact that I still have all my hair."

"Well, those things are at the top of a lot of girls' lists."

"Good to know," Hutch said, smiling warmly. The skin crinkled around his eyes. "Now, I'm not going to take up a lot of your time because I know you wanna be on the road."

"That's okay. I've recently had a harrowing experience with the Sixes, so I'm anxious to hear what you have to say." She told him about the rats.

"God damn," Hutch said, shaking his head in disgust. "Excuse my language, but that just makes me mad. We never had anything as bad as that happen, but after you told me about the group, I thought back, and something hit me. There *was* an incident that might be significant."

Phoebe leaned forward expectantly.

"Tell me."

"Because you said the Sixes was a group of girls, I first tried to think about stuff involving the coeds," Hutch explained. "They usually don't create much drama here—oh, sometimes they get drunk and throw up all over, and once I thought I was going to need a hose to break up a catfight between a couple of them."

"Over a guy?" Phoebe asked.

Hutch smiled. "Yup. And I'm sure he probably wasn't worth it. But I couldn't recall anything directly involving a group of coeds. Girls just aren't into pranks the way boys are."

He took a swig of his own coffee and set the mug down on the thick wooden table.

"But then," he said, "something popped into my mind when I was out with the dogs last night after supper. Early last fall, before I was handed my walking papers, a bunch of fellows at Lyle ended up with a big black check mark painted on their dorm-room doors over the course of a few days. They were all quick to report it because if the school thinks you've damaged your room yourself, you have to pay for the repairs out of your own pocket. I sent one of my deputies out to investigate. The boys claimed to have no idea who was responsible.

"Now, as you've probably figured out," he continued, "kids don't like to tattle on each other. But I ended up talking to some of these guys myself, and I got the feeling they really *didn't* have a clue as to who was responsible. Last night I dug out my notes from that time. You see, I kept some records of my own over the years, in addition to what we had on file at h.q. And guess what?"

"What?" Phoebe asked. She sensed Hutch was stretching things out a bit, enjoying having her company and attention.

"Six doors had been painted in all."

Another "signing" of the group perhaps, Phoebe thought. But what did it mean? "Was there any connection between the guys?" she asked. "Were they on the same sports team, for instance?"

"No, there wasn't any obvious connection. Interestingly, though, the doors were in three different dorms, which seemed to suggest that it wasn't all random—that the boys were targeted somehow."

"That's creepy," Phoebe said. "Targeted for what, do you think?"

"Don't know," Hutch said, but Phoebe sensed he had something on his mind. He took another swig from his mug.

"Do people still use the word *dork*?" he asked.

Phoebe laughed a little. "I think so. Why?"

"Like I said, I spoke to all these guys myself. And I remember they all seemed kind of dorky or nerdy to me. The kind of guys who never went to the prom in high school and who are smart in things like statistics."

"Did you think someone was bullying them?"

"The thought crossed my mind at the time, so I asked around a bit. Didn't find anything."

"Interesting," Phoebe said. "Though I can't see how it fits in."

She glanced at her watch. It was after nine, and she needed to get her butt in motion. She wasn't sorry she'd taken a detour to Hutch's this morning—a connection with him could prove useful as she kept digging—but what he'd shared hadn't amounted to much, and she was anxious to find Alexis. As Hutch escorted Phoebe down the driveway, with the dogs bounding alongside them, they agreed to keep each other in the loop. Then he told her he had one more piece of information to share that morning.

"That fella I mentioned the other day," Hutch said. "The one who woke up in the river? I got his name for you. Wesley Hines. And I was right. He graduated last spring."

Phoebe thanked him again, and before firing up the engine, she took a minute to program her GPS for the Crossgates Mall.

The first leg of the trip, just fifteen minutes long, took her down a two-lane road until she picked up the interstate to Lancaster, Pennsylvania.

The landscape constantly shifted as Phoebe drove. In between massive housing developments, which looked like eruptions of giant mushrooms, she passed sprawling old farms with silos and red barns, many with fields of dried corn stalks. Eventually a sign announced that she was now in Amish country. And then she spotted a hex sign, huge and ominous-looking, on the side of a barn.

At ten she made two calls as she drove. The first was to the Gap at the mall, asking for Alexis. Phoebe wanted to double check that Alexis was on duty today.

"She just ran down to the stockroom," a young man replied. "Do you wanna hold?"

"No thanks—I'll call back," Phoebe told him.

The other was to Glenda's assistant. Phoebe explained that as part of the investigation she was doing for Dr. Johns, she needed contact information on a former graduate, Wesley Hines. The assistant promised to e-mail Phoebe with it after she called alumni relations.

In Lancaster Phoebe picked up I-83 and headed south. The traffic was heavier here, bumper-to-bumper in places. Signs for Baltimore appeared. It all seemed so busy and oddly strange to her after the two months she'd spent sequestered in Lyle. She felt like a character in a movie who has been kidnapped and hidden someplace seemingly remote, only to discover when she escapes that the real world has been thundering by just outside the door the entire time.

Yet as surreal as the trip seemed at moments, she also felt energized. She had a mission, something she hadn't had since before the plagiarism charges brought a halt to her world. Though she had no reason to be particularly optimistic about today, she told herself she *would* return with something vital after meeting with Alexis. She had to.

From time to time her mind found its way to Duncan. Last night in bed, she'd kept thinking about the sex with him, but she knew that more than lust was involved in her preoccupation. She liked the *man*. Maybe that was why she'd turned him down for dinner in the first place. Because she'd been fighting an attraction to him without even realizing it.

But where could this possibly lead? she asked herself. She'd be heading back to New York as early as January—and May at the latest. The last thing she needed was to become emotionally entangled with someone in Lyle. Besides, for all she knew, that was what he was avoiding as well—especially considering what he'd been through in the past two years.

Despite heavy traffic in spots, Phoebe made decent time, and at just after noon she pulled into the massive parking lot of the Crossgates Mall. It had been years since she had been to a suburban shopping mall, and she felt slightly overwhelmed when she stepped inside. There was a cacophony of sound—Muzak, reverberating voices, gushing water from the fountains—and visual noise too: endless signs, banners, and flags. Phoebe used the map to locate the Gap on the main floor, and after sliding on a pair of black sunglasses, she slipped into the store.

There were only a few customers inside, flipping through stacks of jeans and shirts. Phoebe moved toward a table piled with cotton turtlenecks and feigned fascination. After a moment she glanced up and let her eyes sweep around the store. At the moment there appeared to be only two salespeople on the floor—an African American woman in her forties and a white guy just out of his teens. No sign of a woman of about twenty. Maybe Alexis was in the stockroom again.

Phoebe moved a few feet to a table piled with sweaters. Minutes passed, and still no sign of Alexis. Just as she was starting to worry that she'd blown it somehow, Phoebe noticed a doorway that led to the Gap kids' section. She sauntered toward it, and when she peered into the room, she saw a pretty brunette wearing a headset, folding tiny little sweaters. That's got to be her, Phoebe thought.

She hung by the doorway of the kids' room rather than going inside and drawing attention to herself. A short time later, the black woman drifted into the section and began talking to the brunette. Phoebe strained to hear, hoping the women might call each other by name, but it didn't happen. By this point, though, it was clear there weren't any other salespeople, and Phoebe was certain the brunette was Alexis.

Phoebe made her way back outside, settled on a bench directly across from the Gap entrance, and called the store again.

"I'm planning to stop by the kids' department, but I wanted to make sure that Alexis will be there today," she said to the employee who answered. "She was so helpful to me the last time."

"Yes, she's here," the girl said.

"Great. I hope she'll be there during lunch."

"Yes, she doesn't take her break till two."

Phoebe made a quick dash to the ladies' room and then, after picking up a newspaper and coffee, began her wait.

At about one forty-five, earlier than predicted, she saw Alexis walk briskly out of the store. Phoebe jumped up and followed her until, a few minutes later, she entered the food court. After buying a soda and slice of pizza, the girl took a seat at a white metal table for two. Phoebe grabbed a breath, then made her way in that direction.

"Alexis?" Phoebe asked when she reached the table. She noticed that the girl had pulled off all the cheese from her pizza, and it now lay in doughy clumps on the waxed paper. Alexis glanced up casually, perhaps expecting to see a coworker or a friend. When she spotted Phoebe standing there, she wrinkled her brow.

"Yes?" she said.

"My name is Phoebe Hall. May I sit down?" Phoebe didn't wait for a reply. She slid into the empty chair across from the girl. Though Alexis was pretty, up close Phoebe saw that there were angry red patches of rosacea on her cheeks and forehead, the kind of flare-up that was often stress-related.

"What—who are you?" Alexis demanded. She seemed flustered, but Phoebe also sensed anger beginning to boil beneath the surface.

"I'm a new instructor at Lyle College. And I was hoping to talk to you for a few minutes."

Alexis's face reddened even more, as if someone had suddenly held a blowtorch to it. She placed both palms against the table and shoved her chair back, making a metallic grating sound so loud and obnoxious that other customers snapped their heads to see what was happening.

"I already told people there last spring," Alexis sputtered. "I have *nothing* to say." She screwed the cap back on her Diet Pepsi, preparing to bolt.

"I know you went through a lot, Alexis," Phoebe said. "And I know it must be hard to talk about certain things. But if girls are being bullied or intimidated on campus, we need to stop that immediately."

Alexis stared at her soda bottle and shook her head quickly back and forth. She said nothing.

"Have you heard the news about Lily Mack's death?" Phoebe asked.

This time the girl's brown eyes flickered in response. "What about it?" she said. The lack of surprise indicated she'd already been informed somehow.

"We have reason to believe Lily was part of the Sixes. And we need to find out if they're connected to her death in some way."

Alexis had flinched when Phoebe said the name of the group, and now she was stuffing the remains of her pizza slice into the paper bag next to her.

"Will you tell me what they did to you, Alexis?" Phoebe said.

"Don't ever contact me again, okay?" Alexis said, jumping up. "My uncle's a lawyer. He can get a restraining order against you? Do you hear me?"

Phoebe didn't like hearing the L-word. She had tussled with lawyers during the writing of each book, and she'd learned not to let them intimidate her, but this situation involved Glenda and the college, and she couldn't risk causing trouble for either.

Phoebe rose from the table, but before turning to go, she tried to read Alexis's eyes. The girl seemed belligerent now, more than a little freaked, and Phoebe half wondered if she would let out a scream in the middle of the food court. That would be fun.

"I'm sorry to have bothered you, Alexis," Phoebe said calmly. "I'm sure this last year has been a terribly upsetting time for you."

"You have no clue," the girl said.

"Maybe I do," Phoebe said. "The Sixes have been after *me* lately. They broke into my home and did something terrible." She reached into her purse, dug out a business card, and dropped it on the table. "If you change your mind, please give me a call. I want to prevent the Sixes from ever hurting anyone else."

Alexis's expression had gone completely blank, as if she'd dove deep inside herself, though the patches of red on her skin seemed to be practically throbbing. Phoebe moved away slowly, hoping the girl might change her mind and call out, but she didn't. After Phoebe had walked to the end of the food court, she glanced back discreetly. Alexis was hurrying away from the table, back in the direction of the Gap. The pizza bag and soda bottle were still on the table, and so, too, Phoebe assumed, was her business card.

Phoebe kicked herself all the way to the parking lot. She had blown it, totally blown it. And yet she couldn't imagine what tactic *would* have worked with the jumpy girl.

She was all the way to the car when her phone rang. She glanced at the screen, wondering if it was Glenda with news, or maybe even Duncan. The screen read, "Caller Unknown."

"Yes?" she said, picking up.

No one spoke, though she could hear shallow breaths on the other end.

"Yes?" Phoebe asked again, her pulse kicking up a little.

"No one must ever know I talked to you, okay?" a strangled voice said suddenly. Alexis. So she had picked up the card after all.

"They won't," Phoebe said. "Trust me."

"I mean it. If they find out, they'll try to ruin me again. At my next school."

"Why are they doing this to you, Alexis?" Phoebe asked. "Because you wanted out?"

"Yes," she said, nearly in a moan. "And I said I would tell."

"Tell about the group? What they're up to?"

"Yes, I said I would tell the school. About them. About what they did. About the freaking *circles*."

# 14

Somehow she had to entice Alexis to meet her. It would be easier to elicit information face-to-face, and the girl would probably be less likely to bolt again if they made a personal connection.

"Can we spend a few minutes together, Alexis?" Phoebe asked gently. She felt as if she was tiptoeing toward a tiny bird, praying it wouldn't fly off. "I think you'll feel more comfortable talking face-to-face."

The girl sighed, obviously undecided. Phoebe stayed silent, fearful of tipping things the wrong way.

"Are you still here—inside the mall?" Alexis asked finally.

"I'm just outside, in the parking lot," Phoebe said.

Another sigh, this one practically a groan.

"I'll meet you, but not in *here*," Alexis said begrudgingly. "There's this big dumpster—right behind Friendly's. I'll meet you there. And I only have ten minutes. That's all."

Phoebe had no clue where the Friendly's was, and she didn't want to waste precious time running inside to check the map again. She squinted at the back of the huge mall in the bright autumn sunlight. There were hulking dumpsters in both directions—every store had one. She won't wait if I'm late, Phoebe thought anxiously. As she hurried back toward the mall, she asked a woman struggling with two toddlers and sagging plastic bags for directions to Friendly's. "Up there," the woman said, flinging her head to the right. Phoebe broke into a jog and zigzagged through endless rows of parked cars, making her way around the perimeter of the mall. Finally she spotted the back of Friendly's. Alexis was already there, standing by a green dumpster with her arms wrapped tightly around her and shifting her weight back and forth from one foot to the other.

"Thank you for doing this, Alexis," Phoebe said when she reached the girl, nearly out of breath. She thought briefly of touching Alexis's arm, just to show support, but quickly scratched the idea. Alexis looked like the slightest touch would make her head blow off.

"Are you sure they'll never find out?" Alexis said. She shot a frantic look to the left and then to the right, scanning the parking lot as if the Sixes might be lurking behind one of the SUVs.

"They won't," Phoebe said. "The only person who knows I'm here is the president of the school. And she's going to be very grateful for your help."

"It's what you said—about not letting them hurt anyone else. I—I just don't want that to happen."

"I know. So help me understand. What are the Sixes all about?"

Alexis snorted in disgust. "They're *supposed* to be about female power. About being fierce and fearless and ruling the world—and getting what you want out of life. It's always the same type of girl who gets tapped. Pretty and smart. And a jock. Always a jock."

"How big is the group—and what do they *do*, exactly?"

"There're about forty members," Alexis said. "They're supposed to help each other out—have each other's backs. You exchange stuff about classes, about guys. And then when you leave school, they help you out, too."

"What do you mean?"

"I'm not sure. They set you up somehow. With contacts, stuff like that, I guess."

"Is Blair Usher the leader?"

Alexis flinched at the sound of the name.

"I think so. I mean, she was the one who always ran the meetings. But sometimes—I don't know . . . It felt like she was checking in with another person."

"You said something about circles. You mean, you'd put six chairs or something in a circle?"

"*What?*" Alexis said, her confusion tinged with irritation. She was getting riled up just talking about the Sixes, and her patience seemed as fragile as an eggshell. "No, not actual circles. Circles of *membership*. To get to the inner circle, you have to work your way through these six freaking circles."

"Is that where the name of the group comes from?"

"Yes—and the fact that there were six girls who started it."

"Are the circles like tests, then?" Phoebe said.

"Yes," Alexis said. She began to twist and writhe her neck, as if she were struggling to free it from her body. "The first circle is 'Proclaim.' You have to leave the number six someplace—like on a building—to declare your allegiance. That one's easy, like a sorority prank."

"And then?" Phoebe asked.

"The next is 'Reveal.' You have to tell something totally private about yourself—a secret that you've never shared with anyone." Alexis held Phoebe's eyes for a moment, looking stricken. "Something not good."

"So it's a way for you to show your loyalty. Does each circle become harder?"

"Yes," she said, spitting out the word. "And—and when I found out about the third one, I didn't want to do it. But you don't have a choice. They make you think there's no going back."

"So what was it, the third circle?"

" 'Dominate.' You fuck somebody up who is a jerk— another student. Somebody who hogs all the talking time in class or is a total showoff or is just a slut. You're supposed to send a nasty e-mail blast about them or delete their term paper from their laptop or steal their cell phone. Blair kept saying they *deserve* it."

"The school didn't realize this sort of thing was going on?"

"I don't know. Some stuff, like the term papers, probably just looks like mistakes. I swear I didn't want to do it. But when you start to protest, they make these little threats. Kind of funny at first with a wink, wink, but then you remember—" Her voice had become almost hoarse. "*They know your deepest secret now.*"

"So they forced you to do the next one, too—the fourth circle?"

"I—I almost did," she said. Her lower lip began to tremble. "But then I changed my mind. I couldn't. You have to sleep with a guy. Some total loser, and then completely dump him and do an unsigned post about him. It's called the 'Bewitch' circle. It's supposed to teach you how to use power and put guys in their place. But the kid they picked for me, he—I heard he had tried to kill himself in high school, and I just couldn't do it. What if that had made him try *again*?"

Alexis started to cry a little, tears slowly streaming down her rough, reddened cheeks.

Was that what the painted doors had been about? Phoebe wondered. She was remembering what Hutch said about the dorky boys.

"Did they paint a check mark on these boys' doors, do you know?"

Alexis widened her eyes, clearly surprised that Phoebe knew about this.

"Yes," she said. "Though I don't think those guys ever realized *why* the check was there. They just ended up humiliated and ashamed later and didn't understand it was part of some master *plot*."

"So this is when you broke away for good."

"Blair said I *couldn't* leave, that I'd be sorry if I did. But I told her I didn't care, that if she did anything, I'd let the administration know about the Sixes. And then she said that there'd be payback, that I'd regret it for the rest of my life."

Alexis began to sob, her chest heaving. Phoebe found herself swept back, as if caught in a flash flood, to her awful year in boarding school. At night she had sobbed into her pillow, hoping Glenda wouldn't hear. Now she bit down hard on her lower lip, forcing herself back to the present.

"And *was* there payback, Alexis?" she asked softly.

"Yes," Alexis said. "You know what those bitches did? The summer before junior year I'd made this— this stupid sex tape with a boy I'd met. That was the secret I shared. They made me show it to them. And once I left the Sixes for good, Blair sent it to this new boy, Chris, I was dating at Lyle. I loved him, and the minute he saw it, he broke up with me. And then they said that if I talked to anyone in the administration, they would send it to my parents and the whole school. If the Sixes find out I'm going to the University of Maryland, they'll send it to everyone *there*."

"All to keep you from telling?"

"Not just that—for *revenge*," Alexis exclaimed. "In a way Blair *wants* girls to betray her. That way she can have a vendetta against them. One of her greatest pleasures is getting back at someone."

"Did she—"

"Look, I have to go back inside," Alexis said. "I don't know how I'm even going to work now. I'm all freaked out." Using her fingers, she tried to wipe away the mascara smudge marks that her tears had caused.

"But wait," Phoebe said, nearly pleading. There was still so much she needed to know. She fished in her purse for a clean tissue and handed it to Alexis. "What about the last two circles? Do you know what they are?"

"No. And I don't want to know either." She hitched the drooping strap of her handbag higher on her shoulder. She was getting ready to fly.

"Just one more question," Phoebe pleaded. "What about Lily—was she in the Sixes?"

"Yes. She joined in the spring. I tried to say something to her because I'd started to see what monsters they were. But her boyfriend had just dumped her, and she seemed so bummed. She was looking for something, something to belong to."

"Do you think she could have tried to leave this fall?"

"I don't know," Alexis said numbly.

"Can you tell me the names of some of the members? That would help a lot."

Alexis shook her head back and forth vehemently.

"No, I can't. They'll know it came from me. And they'll punish me again."

"Please—"

"I said *no*. I just can't."

Before Phoebe could say another word, Alexis had turned and begun to race along the outside of the mall, headed toward an entrance.

Watching her go, Phoebe finally exhaled. She felt drained from the conversation. She was so distracted it took her a while to find her car, but finally she spotted it. She unlocked the door and nearly threw herself inside. As she leaned against the seat, she realized that despite how the cool temperature was, her back felt damp with sweat.

It was past lunchtime, but Phoebe had no desire to eat. Once she had maneuvered her way back onto I-83, she dug her phone from her purse and called Glenda. According to her assistant, Glenda was in a meeting and couldn't be disturbed. Phoebe asked her to deliver the message that she had information worth sharing and could be reached on her cell phone.

Phoebe drove as if on autopilot, her mind running back and forth over what she'd learned from Alexis. After the rats in her freezer, she'd had no doubt that the Sixes existed and that they were nasty as hell, and her conversation with Alexis had backed that up. But she needed to find out what the last two circles involved before deciding if they could actually be behind Lily's death. That would tell her just how far the girls were willing to go to get their way—or to enact the kind of vendettas that Blair seemed to relish.

Thirty minutes later, after pulling off the highway to fill her gas tank, Phoebe checked her e-mail. Glenda had written, saying that she was anxious to hear Phoebe's news, but she was jam-packed for the rest of the day and evening. Therefore she'd arranged for Stockton to meet Phoebe in his office at 6:30 and receive the update.

Damn, Phoebe thought. It made sense for Glenda to delegate the meeting to Stockton—that way he could jump-start any investigation that needed to be done—but she'd promised Alexis that only she and Glenda would know about their meeting. Besides, Phoebe just didn't *like* Stockton, and she hated having to turn over what she'd learned to him.

Phoebe scanned down her other unopened e-mails. With a start she saw that there was one from her agent, Miranda, with "Priority" in the subject line. Ever since last spring anything urgent-looking from her agent had flooded her with dread. As it turned out, Miranda had seen Tobias's mention of her in the *Post* and wanted to be sure Phoebe was aware of it. "You need to get out of this guy's line of sight," she wrote. "He's a real bastard."

Duh, Phoebe thought. She briefly considered calling Miranda and filling her in, but she knew her agent would ask if Phoebe had an idea for her next book yet. And that was one discussion she wanted to avoid.

She kept scrolling and found that there was also the promised e-mail from Glenda's assistant about Wesley Hines. Though the college had no cell phone number or e-mail address for Wesley, it did have a current home address, and to Phoebe's surprise, it was in Doring. That was a town just a few miles from Lyle. As she stared at the address, she wondered if Hines had grown up in Doring, gone to Lyle because it was close, and resettled temporarily with his parents as tons of kids seemed to be doing these days.

I need to talk to him, she thought. *As soon as possible.* Hutch had assumed Hines had fallen into the Winamac drunk, but that might not be the case. If there was a serial killer in the area, as Stockton believed, Hines might have been a victim—one who miraculously survived. She wondered suddenly if the Sixes could have been involved in the incident. Was Hines the kind of dorky boy they targeted?

She glanced at her watch. She'd been making decent time on the road, and that meant she'd definitely be back in Lyle before six—which left just enough time for her to swing by Hines's home before her meeting with Stockton. If Hines had a nine-to-five job, she might catch him as he was arriving home from work. She punched his address into the GPS and fired up the car.

The rest of the drive was uneventful, and she pulled into Doring a few minutes earlier than expected. She'd assumed that Wesley Hines was still bunking down at his parents' place, so she was surprised when the GPS led her to a subdivision of attached gray town houses—row after endless row of them, and with new ones under construction at the end. These were the kind of units you lived in when you downsized after retirement or landed yourself a decent job after college. Hines was likely living here alone.

As she drove down the road that wound through the town-house "village," scanning the numbers on each house, Phoebe realized that Hines's place—2118—was going to be near the end of the row, and she grabbed an available parking place there.

Hines's house was indeed the very last in the row. It abutted a cluster of oak trees, which surprisingly the bulldozers had left standing. As Phoebe headed down the sidewalk in that direction, she discovered that she wasn't in luck. The windows of 2118 were dark, suggesting that no one was home. But then she spotted a young guy emerging from around the far side, probably coming from a parking lot behind the house. He crossed the yard and walked up the three steps of the porch, where he opened the mailbox and dipped his hand inside.

That's him, Phoebe thought, and then immediately she found herself thinking, No, it couldn't be. The silhouette seemed too grown-up-looking to be just out of school—he was wearing a three-quarter-length dark green coat, pressed khaki pants, and loafers. But as she cut across the lawn to reach the house, she got a closer look and realized that he couldn't be any older than twenty-three. He was a bit heavyset, clean-cut looking, with blond hair that spiked up a little in front.

Before Phoebe could call out to him, he caught her movements from the corner of his eye, and his head swiveled in her direction.

"Can I help you?" he asked, studying her. She suddenly realized that she had seen him someplace before. But where? she wondered. He didn't go to Lyle anymore.

"Are you Wesley Hines?" Phoebe asked.

"Might be," he replied coolly. "Depends on who's asking." Clearly the town-house village wasn't one of those charming little neighborhoods where people just popped over to say hello to new neighbors.

"Sorry to bother you," Phoebe said. "I teach at Lyle College. I'm on a committee looking into a few campus issues. I was hoping to talk to you for a few minutes. "

"I doubt I'd have much to tell you," he said, now friendly, the edge gone from his voice. "I only spent two years there—I transferred from a community college. And I wasn't all that involved when I was there."

"I know what you mean," Phoebe said. "I wasn't in the thick of things at college myself. But I'm interested in something that *did* directly involve you—that night you found yourself in the Winamac River."

For a few seconds Wesley just stared at her. She sensed the wheels in his brain spinning rapidly.

"Why curious after all this time?" he asked finally.

"Because, as you may have heard, a girl was found dead in the river this past weekend. Her name was Lily Mack. And I'm wondering if there might be a connection somehow. That someone could be targeting students."

Again the stare. Then Wesley exhaled loudly.

"Wow," he said. "I've waited a whole year for someone to take me seriously about that night. I guess better late than never."

*Yes*, Phoebe thought with excitement. Here we go.

"Would you have a few minutes to talk now?" she asked. "I really want to hear your version of the events."

"Uh, sure," Wesley said. "Why don't you come in? Though you'll have to excuse the mess. I didn't have a chance to tidy up before I left this morning."

As he dug through his coat pocket for his keys, Phoebe crossed the rest of the lawn and climbed up the stoop steps. Wesley unlocked the door, and Phoebe followed him into the house. For one brief moment, as they were both standing side by side in the darkened space, Phoebe wondered nervously if it was wise to walk into a strange man's house this way, but as soon as Wesley flicked on the light, she relaxed.

The comment about tidying up seemed absurd in light of how the town house looked. The L-shaped living room was incredibly neat, except for the Eagles mug on the coffee table. The place was pleasantly fixed up, too, with a leather sofa and matching chair.

"What a nice spot you've got," Phoebe said. "I take it you found gainful employment, unlike other recent college grads."

"I'm pretty lucky," Wesley said, slipping off his coat and dropping it over a wooden coat peg behind the door. He was thinner than she'd realized outside—his coat had added bulk, and his head, which was disproportionately large for his body, had helped foster the illusion. He was wearing a gray crewneck sweater that matched his eyes, and underneath, a crisp white button-down shirt. Not exactly a dork, but neither what any girl would describe as a hottie. "My dad owns a feed company in the area, and I'm managing it right now. Don't get me wrong, though. I work my butt off."

"Feed company?" she asked.

"We make feed for livestock—cattle, pigs, chickens. Of course, with all the farms around here dying off, it isn't exactly a booming business, but I've added a lawn care department, which is going gangbusters. In fact, I'm going to be doing business with the college. I just signed a deal with them."

Suddenly she realized where she'd seen him. He had been one of the two guys standing next to her in the crowd in front of Lily's dorm that night.

"That's terrific. Though it sounds like you had a tough time convincing people from the school to take you seriously last year." She wanted to maneuver back to why she was here.

"Yup," Wesley said, easing past the coffee table to sit on the couch. He let his legs fall apart and rested a hand on each knee. "I suppose I can't totally blame them, though. They figured I'd been drunk, your typical college boy, but it was still—if you'll excuse the expression—frustrating as hell."

"Would you mind if I took notes?" Phoebe asked, slipping a pen and pad from her purse.

Wesley flipped over his palm in a gesture that said she could do as she pleased. "I'm just glad someone's finally listening," he said.

"So tell me what happened that night," Phoebe said, her pen poised above an empty page. "You just came to and realized you'd ended up in the river somehow?"

"Not *somehow*," Wesley said, narrowing his eyes. "Someone dumped me in there."

# 15

Wait a minute, Phoebe thought, Hutch hadn't mentioned that part. Were there details about the incident that Hutch wasn't privy to?

"Did you *see* the person?" Phoebe asked.

Wesley shook his head defensively, as if he'd detected a trace of doubt in her voice.

"No, I didn't see anyone, and I don't remember anything about going in. But I would never, *ever* have ended up in that river on my own. I had one beer that night. I'm not a drinker."

*Not a drinker.* Those were the same words that the friends of Scott Macus, the student who had drowned over a year ago, had apparently said about him.

"Start from the beginning, will you?" Phoebe said. "You were at Cat Tails, right?"

Wesley pursed his thin lips together and then blew out a sigh.

"Yup. It was around this time a year ago—November 16. When I got back from the library that night, a couple of guys on my floor said they were going out, so I decided to tag along. We ended up walking into the place around ten."

"Is it mostly kids from Lyle who hang out there?"

"On weekends, yes, but not so much on weeknights. The place was pretty full that night, but I'd say over half the crowd was townies."

"Okay, so what did you do when you got there?"

"We bought a round of beers at the bar and just stood there for a little while, shooting the breeze," he said. "There were a couple of local women at the bar— at least ten years older than we were—and they started chatting us up. I had zero interest, but my buddies seemed pretty into them. After I'd played wingman for a while, I wandered over to the other side of the bar and ended up throwing darts with a couple of guys I recognized from school but didn't know by name.

"After a few games I looked over and saw that my buddies were still talking to those cougars. I could have just taken off, but I didn't feel like walking back to campus—one of the guys had driven. I bought another beer but only had a couple of sips."

"You're sure about that?"

"It's the God's honest truth. I needed to get up pretty early the next day to finish a paper, so I wasn't taking any chances. Once I'd bought the second beer, I wandered over to this old jukebox against the wall and pumped a few quarters in it. Played a few Stones songs. Then all of a sudden this guy I didn't know came over to the jukebox and asked me if the machine gave change. I said I didn't think so. I remember he just stood there, and then he said, 'Well, at least someone had the good taste to play the Stones.' And that's the last thing I remember. Until I came to in the river."

"That must have been terrifying."

He stared off for a minute, massaging his forehead with one hand.

"I thought I was in a dream, some kind of nightmare," he said, looking back at Phoebe. "I'm a good swimmer, but I felt so weighed down in my clothes, I could barely keep my head up. Thank God I had loafers on. I kicked them off and swam to the shore. I was about half a mile farther south from Cat Tails. There's a fair amount of trees around there, so somebody could have pushed me in without anyone noticing."

"What time was this?"

"My phone was dead, but I had a waterproof watch on. It was half past one when I made it to shore. I'd lost, like, two hours. Cat Tails was closed by then, and there was no one around. I tried to flag down a couple of cars, but the drivers wouldn't stop. I looked like the swamp monster, so why would they? I walked back to campus and went right to the security office. There was some young kid on duty, and you could tell he thought I'd probably been pounding back Buds all night. The next day the head guy—that geezer who'd been there for years—stopped by my dorm and talked to me, but he obviously thought I'd been hammered, too."

"What do you think really happened?"

Wesley made a sharp *tiih* sound as he exhaled air. "Someone must have drugged me," he said. "Not with a drug that knocked me out, but one of those date-rape drugs where you still seem to be functioning but you don't actually know what the hell is going on, and you don't remember a thing afterward. Whoever it was talked me into going outside and away from the bar and then pushed me into the river."

"Did you ever set your drink down and take your eye off it?"

"Yeah, a few times, like when I was playing darts. In hindsight it seems stupid, but what guy expects his beer to be drugged? The mug was basically right in front of me, but I kept turning around to shoot. I also put it down again when I was picking songs at the jukebox."

"What happened to your friends?"

"That's exactly what *I* wanted to know," Hines said. "The next day they told me that they looked for me just before the place closed at midnight and didn't see me. They decided that I must have hooked up with some girl and bolted."

Interesting, Phoebe thought. Again, that's what Scott Macus's friends had assumed about him.

"So it sounds like you were someplace outside of the bar from before midnight until one or so, but you have no idea where. Go back to the guy by the jukebox. Did you mention him to me because you thought he might be significant?"

Wesley touched his upper lip with the side of his forefinger and looked away momentarily.

"Yeah, I keep thinking about him," he said. "I mean, the way he approached me seemed a little weird, even at the time. He was older—late thirties or early forties, and better dressed than a townie."

"Is it possible you were assaulted that night?"

"You mean, like *raped*?" he said. There was a flash of disgust in his eyes. "No way. I would have, you know, figured that out. The person got his jollies just from pushing me into the river and hoping I never came up.

You know, a kid from Lyle drowned in the river last year around this time, and nobody had any idea how or why, but I'm thinking he was drugged, too. And maybe the same thing happened to Lily Mack."

"I just realized that I actually saw you outside her dorm the first night she was missing."

He narrowed his eyes at Phoebe.

"Oh, yeah, you look kind of familiar. I'd been on campus that night, meeting with the head of maintenance about our lawn-care deal. And then I heard people buzzing about something happening to this girl Lily. I knew her. I mean, I didn't *know* her know her, but she was in a class of mine. And right away an alarm went off in my head—because of what happened to *me*."

Phoebe glanced down at her notes, scanning them. Her mind was racing. Wesley's story added credence to the theory Tom Stockton had raised: that there was a serial killer drugging college students in river towns and tossing them to their deaths in the muddy Winamac.

"Wesley," she said evenly. "This is important information, and you need to go to the police with it as soon as possible."

He shifted in his seat, not happy with the thought.

"I just don't want to end up feeling like a jerk again," he said.

"I don't think that will happen this time," Phoebe said. He shrugged. "I have one more question, if you don't mind." She needed to get back to what her true focus was.

"Sure," he said. "Shoot. But then I need to move. I have to call a supplier before dinner."

"Do you recall if there were any girls from Lyle College in the bar that night?"

It seemed to be the last question Wesley was expecting, and his gray eyes widened in surprise.

"Yeah, there were a few around, I guess. Why?"

"Have you ever heard of a secret society of girls at Lyle? One called the Sixes?"

Hines looked closely at Phoebe again, thinking something but not saying it. Finally he shook his head.

"Nope. Doesn't ring a bell. What are you getting at, anyway?"

"They're apparently pretty wicked. Up to a lot of bad stuff."

Wesley wrinkled his face, perplexed.

"You mean they're like a cult?" he said. "Or like witches or something?"

"It's more that they like to bully people—both male and female students," Phoebe said. "And they play nasty tricks on them. I've wondered if they might be connected to the drownings in some way. One of the members is named Blair Usher. Another, I believe, is Gwen Gallogly."

Wesley shrugged. "Never heard of either one."

"Did anyone ever paint a check mark on your dorm room door?"

"No—that sounds like frat boy behavior and Lyle doesn't have frats."

"Well, I'd better let you make that phone call," Phoebe said. "If anything else occurs to you, will you get in touch?" She drew a business card from her wallet and passed it to him. Wesley glanced at the card, then flicked it a couple of times with his thumb. Sensing he was growing restless, Phoebe dropped her pad into her purse and rose from the couch.

"Sure," Wesley said. "And thanks for listening. You're the first person who's seemed to care."

As Wesley walked her to the door she glanced around the apartment.

"You didn't decorate this place all by yourself, did you?"

"You mean, did I use a professional?"

"Or I thought maybe your mom helped you. Or your girlfriend."

He smiled ruefully. "My mom died quite a few years ago. And I don't have a girlfriend at the moment." His smile turned cheerier. "But hey, when I find somebody, maybe she'll appreciate the fact that I'm not a slob."

"Absolutely," said Phoebe. She shook his hand and thanked him once again.

Driving out of the town-house development a few minutes later, Phoebe weighed how she felt about Wesley's story. She could see how the campus police might have viewed him skeptically when he'd arrived sopping wet at two in the morning, but she had to admit, he sounded credible enough now. Plus there didn't seem to be any reason to keep flogging his story after all this time if it wasn't true.

Did she believe he'd been the intended victim of some kind of roving serial killer? Stockton would surely think so—and she would have to share this story with him tonight—but Phoebe still found it tough to embrace the whole idea. At this point, there was no evidence that Scott Macus had been murdered, and the verdict was still out on Lily.

And as harrowing as the experience had been for Wesley, it still could have been just an accident. Phoebe remembered once reading that the most common date-rape drug was alcohol. In certain instances a woman woke up with a strange man, couldn't remember how she'd ended up there, and assumed she'd been drugged, but the amnesia was in fact the result of her suffering an alcoholic blackout. Wesley said he hadn't drunk much that night, but he could have had more than he remembered, or maybe his tolerance was extremely low.

And what about the Sixes, she wondered. There didn't seem to be anything linking Wesley's experience to the group. They might be mean as hell, they might want to show loser boys who was boss, they might have even played a role in Lily's death somehow, but there was no apparent reason to believe they were luring male students to the river late at night. And yet she couldn't let go of the idea they might be involved.

Phoebe had planned to stop by her house before meeting with Stockton—to turn on lights and to make sure everything was okay—but her impromptu meeting with Wesley put her behind schedule. She drove directly to the campus, found a parking spot, and bounded up to the second floor of the administration building. Stockton's office was just down the hall from Glenda's. His assistant had apparently left for the day—it was dark in the anteroom, the assistant's desk deserted. But the door to Stockton's inner office was cracked enough to reveal a strip of light. Phoebe tapped on the door. From inside she heard Stockton's muffled voice call for her to enter.

Unlike most of the others on campus, this office had a clubby, old-boy-network feel—wall-to-wall bookshelves, an Oriental rug, and black-shaded lamps casting soft puddles of light around the room. Phoebe suspected that Stockton must have coughed up a bit of his own dough to help create the ambience, since the school hardly had a decorating budget.

Stockton didn't look up right away. Instead, with horn-rimmed reading glasses perched midway down his nose, he continued to peer at the sheaf of paper in his hands. Reminding me of who's in the power position, aren't you? Phoebe thought. A few seconds later Stockton lowered the sheets and glanced up.

"Thanks for dropping by," Stockton said, as if it had been he who had summoned her. "Why don't we sit over there? It'll be more comfortable."

He motioned to a seating area with a matching leather sofa and chair. As Stockton made his way around the desk, Phoebe took a seat on the sofa. There was a coffee table in front of her, displaying a carved wooden box and leather coasters. The only thing missing, Phoebe thought, was a stack of *Horse and Hound* magazines.

"So you've had a bit of a road trip today," Stockton said, lowering his large frame into the chair. A dash of sarcasm had laced his words, and though Phoebe wasn't sure what she'd done to tick him off, she had a feeling she would find out soon enough.

"Yes, but it was worth it in the end," Phoebe said.

"The famous author's powers of persuasion at work?"

"I wouldn't attribute anything to my so-called persuading skills," Phoebe said. "I think in light of Lily's death, Alexis realized it was essential to speak up now."

"I would have appreciated a heads-up about your trip." Stockton sniffed. "As the dean of students, anything involving student life here is under my domain."

So that's it, Phoebe thought. I've stepped on his big fat toes. She felt a sudden urge to let a little air out of that ego of his, but quickly submerged the instinct. If she were going to continue with her investigation, she would need his cooperation.

"I'm sorry, Tom," Phoebe said. "I'd run it by Glenda, and I thought you were in the loop. She probably assumed I'd informed you."

"So tell me what you learned from Alexis," he said, moving on now that she'd been duly reprimanded.

She described what the girl had shared—including all the gory details about the circles of membership.

"Jesus," Stockton said when she'd finished. "Not exactly the campfire girls, are they?"

"No, they're certainly not. Does this circle stuff ring any bells with you? The deleted term papers, for instance?"

"Actually, yes," he said, stroking his chin between his thumb and forefinger. "We're used to those 'dog-ate-my-homework' kind of excuses here, but there were a couple of incidents recently that concerned me. Within one week, two different students reported having a term paper they were working on deleted from their laptops while they were in the library. They'd been sitting in the same section of the library, and had gotten up briefly. In one case to go to the ladies' room, and in the other to locate a book. From what I could determine, they didn't know each other."

"What about anonymous postings about sexual encounters?"

"*That* I'm not aware of specifically. We know that cyber bullying goes on with kids, but it's an elusive thing because they don't like to come forward. I hope Alexis named names."

"No, she refused."

"Well, that's the only way we can speed up shutting these girls down. I had Blair Usher in for another talk this morning, but she just plays totally dumb. Claims she's heard of the group, but has no idea if anyone she knows is in it. Why would Alexis insist on protecting them at this point?"

"She's fearful of further recriminations."

"You mean, reaching-beyond-the-grave kind of thing? I'd say that's overreacting a bit, wouldn't you?"

"No, these girls seem pretty fierce. Has Glenda had a chance to tell you about what the Sixes did to me—the rats?"

He wrinkled his nose, as if a putrid smell had just blasted into the room.

"Yes, a grisly business. I wish I could devote more of my attention to it, but I've got the Lily Mack situation to deal with. And that comes first."

Phoebe realized she needed to bring Stockton up to speed on her conversation with Wesley. But as she started to speak, someone knocked on the door. Stockton called for the person to enter, and to Phoebe's surprise, Val Porter stepped inside.

"Oh good, Val, you're here," Stockton said.

What was *this* all about? Phoebe wondered. Val smiled at Stockton but only ran her eyes quickly over Phoebe's face, as if she were a stranger on a train platform.

"I've asked Val to join our discussion," Stockton told Phoebe. "Needless to say Val has a wonderful understanding of female adolescent behavior, and I thought it would be helpful to obtain her input on the Sixes."

Phoebe could barely hide her annoyance. Just because the woman taught courses like Introduction to

Feminist Theory and Geographies of Gender hardly
made her an expert on secret girl societies.

Val took a seat at the other end of the sofa, but close
enough for Phoebe to pick up the scent of patchouli.
Val's hair was pinned on her head tonight, and silvery
tendrils hung loosely around her face in that boho style
she favored. Phoebe wondered what Val's reaction
would be if she learned Phoebe had been to bed with
Duncan.

"So how can I help?" Val said, addressing the question mainly to Stockton. She grasped a silver tendril between the index and middle fingers on her right hand
and slowly slid it through her fingers.

"I'll let Phoebe fill you in," Stockton said. "She's
had an interesting trip to the Baltimore area."

"*Baltimore?*" Val said. "What has that got to do
with anything?"

Phoebe practically glared at Stockton.

"Unfortunately," Phoebe said, "it's not appropri-
ate for me to share details about my visit down there
with anyone else, since I promised confidentiality." She
turned to Val. "What I *can* share is that the Sixes is capable of being extremely cruel and nasty. A psychologist I talked to said that it's girl power run amuck, and
it isn't uncommon at this stage of their lives. Does that
jibe with what you've seen in your gender classes?"

"Until Tom mentioned it to me, I'd never heard of this little group, so I really don't have much to contribute." Val's self-satisfied tone, however, suggested that they were about to hear an opinion regardless. "That said, I *could* see female students here banding together to encourage a sense of empowerment."

"Are you saying the girls here need a boost?" Phoebe asked.

"Good God, no," Val said. "The women at Lyle—like the women at most colleges today—are smart, proactive, and ambitious. They arrive here thinking that they'll meet men of their equal, men superior to the slacker boys they attended high school with, but that's not the case. They soon discover that it was much tougher for them to be admitted to the school than their male counterparts—we have fewer male applicants these days, so we lower the standards for them. The boys aren't up to par socially or intellectually, and that can wear on the women very quickly. Banding together would at least be a way for them to experience solidarity and sense of purpose."

"You're not suggesting it's a good thing, are you?"

"No, Phoebe," Val said. "I don't believe that's what I said at all."

"Are there any girls in particular who you think might—"

The door to Stockton's office suddenly flew open, and all three of them turned in unison. Glenda stood in the doorway, her face etched with concern.

"What's happened?" Tom asked.

"Trevor Harris—the student Lily Mack was dating?" Glenda said. "They found a body in the river late this afternoon, and the cops are pretty sure it's him."

# 16

"What?" Tom said, shooting up from the chair. "How did you hear this?"

"Craig and I were called down to the police station just a little while ago. Michelson told us."

"And does it mean Trevor was actually living in the area this whole time?" Stockton asked.

Glenda shook her head quickly back and forth.

"The body's badly decomposed, so he probably died last spring. I assume, since it's too soon for DNA results, that they found some type of ID on him. He never took off for parts unknown, as everyone suspected."

Phoebe felt numb. It was another endorsement of Tom's serial killer theory. There was even a pattern emerging, she realized. Scott had died a year ago this past spring. The following fall Wesley Hines had found himself in the river. Trevor had obviously died this spring, and now Lily this fall. It felt to Phoebe like one of those ridiculous but terrifying slasher movies she'd seen trailers for—where bodies of teen victims pile up at regular intervals.

Phoebe started to blurt out what she'd learned from Wesley, but then caught herself. She didn't want to share the info in front of Val.

"But I don't get it," Stockton said. He'd started to pace, arms across his chest. "Bodies eventually pop up from a river. What took this one so long?"

"Michelson said that the body was snagged in some tree roots close to the shore. It's similar to what happened to Lily."

"Who spotted it?" Stockton said.

"Michelson was being cagey, but it sounded like the police actually came across the body. You know that antique place, the Big Red Barn on Route 1? If you cross the road to the bike path, there's a picnic area right in front of the river. The body was found nearby in some fairly dense vegetation. The police were apparently searching the area for some reason."

"Perhaps they're still trying to figure out where Lily went into the water," Phoebe said.

"But why—" Val started to say, but Stockton interrupted her.

"You know what this means, don't you?" he said. "There *is* some maniac out there preying on our students. We've got a total nightmare on our hands."

Here we go, Phoebe thought.

"But how big a nightmare it becomes depends on our actions," Glenda said. "We have to keep cool and use our heads. We can't have a single regret later about how we handled this."

"So what's the plan?" Stockton asked. "Have you talked to the parents?"

"I've left a message for them, but I'd like you to follow up," Glenda said. "I've got the PR team coming to my house in a few minutes to devise a strategy on that end."

"I should join you," Stockton said.

"No, Tom, I need you here," Glenda said. "Our first priority is the students. I want you to draft an e-mail alerting them to the news. Tell them I've already arranged for the campus police to beef up security, but they also need to watch out for each other. And draft an e-mail to the parents, too. Full disclosure. I also want you to brainstorm with Craig about any additional safety recommendations we should be making. We don't want to set off a panic, but we may want to tell kids to travel in pairs." She paused. "And finally, I want to know if we have any rights in controlling student behavior *off* campus."

"What do you mean?" Stockton asked, wrinkling his brow.

"That bar Cat Tails keeps turning up in every story," Glenda said. "Can we restrict students from going to the river bars? I know that's extreme, but if we're going to prevent another death, we may need to practice tough love."

Glenda checked her watch and then turned to Phoebe. "Have you got your car? I walked today, and I'd love a lift home."

"Of course," Phoebe said, relieved at the request. She was anxious to talk to Glenda alone.

"What can *I* do, President Johns?" Val asked. "I want to be of assistance."

"I appreciate the offer, Val," Glenda said, "and I'll let you know if something comes to mind. Right now all I ask is that everyone be discreet."

Phoebe followed Glenda from the room. The building was eerily quiet now. Though the hall lights were on, most of the staff had left for the day, so offices were dark. They passed no one in the building, but outside, as they hurried to the parking lot, groups of students dashed by them, chatting and laughing. They won't be laughing so hard tomorrow, Phoebe thought, once they've learned the news about Trevor.

As Phoebe pulled the car out of the parking lot a few minutes later, Glenda threw her head back on the seat of the car.

"Three deaths in two years," Glenda said. "I can't believe it."

"Actually, *four* incidents," Phoebe said. She relayed what she'd learned from Wesley.

Glenda shook her head and blew out a breath. "Well, at least the police seem to be giving it their full attention now. It was like an overturned beehive down there tonight."

"I just wonder if they're equipped to handle something this big," Phoebe said.

"I could ask myself the same question," Glenda said. "You know, I've worked at four different colleges and been trained to deal with just about everything—budget cuts, student protests, faculty caught sleeping with students. But no one ever took me aside and said, 'Here's what you need to do if a Ted Bundy type shows up on your campus.'"

"What if there really *is* a serial killer," Phoebe asked quietly, "but not some Ted Bundy type? What if it's someone we know?"

"What do you mean?" Glenda said. Even with her eyes on the road, Phoebe could sense her friend's shock at the comment.

"What if the Sixes did it?" Phoebe quickly spelled out what she'd learned from Alexis about the circles and how Blair loved to exact revenge.

"My God, this is worse than I thought. We've got to nail these girls. But you don't really believe they're cold-blooded killers, do you, Fee? I can entertain the idea that they might have accidentally killed Lily as part of some prank gone wrong, but *three* murders? It seems unfathomable."

"It's just something worth mulling over." Phoebe knew she needed to learn what the fifth and sixth circles entailed. "We should finally mention the Sixes to the cops now, don't you think?"

"Let's continue to let Craig investigate the Sixes for a bit longer. I don't want to open a Pandora's box unnecessarily."

Phoebe felt a pang of doubt but kept her mouth shut. She had to take Glenda's lead on this one.

"Why didn't you want Tom to come to your house, by the way?" Phoebe asked.

Out of the corner of her eye Phoebe saw Glenda cock her head, deliberating.

"I *do* need him on campus right now, taking care of business there, but I've also picked up a weird vibe from him lately, like he's saying one thing and thinking another. Or maybe this whole mess has made me paranoid."

"There's a vibe *I* pick up from him," Phoebe said. "That he seems to really *like* the serial killer theory. As if he's dying for it to be true."

"And why would that be, do you think?"

"Well, would he be a candidate for your job if this whole thing exploded in your face?"

Glenda nodded slowly. "So you mean he's pushing it in order to throw the campus into even bigger turmoil?" she asked. "And give the board a reason to boot me out?"

"Maybe," Phoebe said. "He just seems awfully slick to me, and worth keeping an eye on." Glenda was silent.

"So you think there'll be a full-scale panic tomorrow?" Phoebe asked.

"Not so much from the kids," Glenda said. "But the parents are going to go nuts. Trust me—some will be showing up with U-Hauls to whisk their kids away."

When they reached Glenda's house, Phoebe put the car in park and leaned over to hug her friend.

"Hang in there, okay?" Phoebe said. "There's nothing you can't handle."

Alone in the car, Phoebe headed home. As she drove down the dark, empty streets of Lyle, she could feel her unease rising. About Trevor Harris being found, about everything. Plus, she hadn't had time to go home earlier to turn the lights on, and she couldn't bear the idea of walking into a pitch-black house.

As she pulled into the driveway, her eyes raced quickly over the front of the house. The glowing porch light, controlled by a sensor, seemed to accentuate how absolutely dark the inside of the house was. Phoebe stepped out of the car, locked it, and scanned all around her. There wasn't a soul anywhere.

Phoebe unlocked the front door, pushed it open a few inches, and listened. The only sound was the low purr of the furnace. Patting her fingers along the living room wall, she located the switch for the overhead light, which she rarely used. When she flicked it on, the room exploded with light. At first glance, everything looked exactly as she'd left it.

After locking the door behind her, Phoebe made her way to the kitchen and quickly flipped on the light. Her eyes roamed the room—the back door, the windows, the fridge. Everything seemed okay.

As she shrugged off her coat, Phoebe felt her stomach growl from hunger. She hadn't eaten a thing since the morning. She dumped a can of New England clam chowder into a pan. While the soup heated, she dug her phone from her purse to check e-mails. There was one from Duncan, sent a short while ago.

"Looking forward to tomorrow night," he'd written.

"Me, too," she typed back, smiling. "What time? And where?"

She almost jumped when another e-mail appeared from Duncan almost instantly. So he was online right now.

"Why don't you come by my office in the science building at six," he replied. "I'll show you around the lab and then we can head to my place."

"Great," she wrote, though the idea of seeing the lab made her squirm. "Btw, have you heard the news about Trevor Harris?"

She watched the screen, waiting, but nothing else appeared. Their brief exchange had lifted her mood, but now she felt her unease return, weighing down on her.

She took her soup to her office and typed up notes from her conversations that day with both Alexis and Wesley. When she was done, she printed out a set for Glenda and one for Hutch as well, which she would drop off tomorrow. It would be good to get his input, though she wondered if he'd feel he'd been wrong not to take Wesley seriously.

Next she went online and searched date-rape drugs like GHB and roofies. She quickly learned that victims often appeared normal after they'd been slipped the drugs, and people around them might have no idea they were under the influence. And just as Wesley had told her, they might later experience total amnesia about what had transpired.

When she'd finished reading, she closed her eyes and massaged the area between her eyes. Her brain hurt, and so did her body, from so many hours in the car. She shut off her laptop and, leaving several lights downstairs blazing, mounted the stairs to her bedroom.

As her head sank into the pillow a few minutes later, she picked up a faint musky scent, and she realized it was Duncan's cologne, still lingering in the fabric from the other night. Until she'd received his e-mails, she had kept thoughts of him mostly at bay since the morning, but now, as sleep began to overwhelm her, she allowed a few to roam her brain. I can't help it, she realized. I'm dying to see the man again tomorrow. Sure, it's just a fling, she told herself, but that didn't mean she couldn't relish it. In fact, maybe that's why the sex had been so intense and exhilarating the other night—because they both knew it was destined to end before long.

She woke with a start after three, cold all over. Searching the bed with her hand, she found that the duvet had slipped off onto the floor. She slid out of bed and began to drag the duvet back onto the mattress. As she stood barefoot on the cold floor, adjusting the duvet, she froze. There was a noise, like a machine running. Her heart seemed to ram into her rib cage.

Phoebe flicked on the bedside light and listened. There was definitely a noise, the low, steady hum of a motor of some kind. She grabbed her phone and forced herself to tiptoe into the hallway. Whatever the noise was, it was coming from downstairs. With her heart still pounding hard, she made her way to the top of the stairs. It's the dishwasher, she realized after a moment. She could now hear the rush and swirl of water.

But she hadn't run the machine after dinner, and even if she had, it wouldn't still be running *now*. The dishwasher in her city apartment had a delay feature so it could run hours later. Did this one have the same feature, and had she set it accidentally? She didn't think so; it was an old model.

Damn, I've got to go down there, she told herself. She flicked on the stairwell light and edged down the stairs. As soon as she reached the third step from the bottom, her eyes flew to the front door, to the chain lock. From the light she left on, she could see the lock was still in place.

She'd left the kitchen light burning, too, and as soon as she approached the room, she could see that the chain was still in place on the back door, too.

She relaxed a little. This has got to be a mechanical fluke, she told herself. She entered the kitchen and ran her eyes rapidly over all the fixtures. Nothing was amiss. The only sound in the room was the swish and swirl of water.

Phoebe approached, set her phone on the counter, and rested her hand on top of the dishwasher door. Open it, she told herself. You have to open it.

*If she'd been smart, she would have just backed off, concentrated on her work and on things that couldn't be taken away. But she hated the fact that she'd been shut out of doing any writing and editing. So she bided her time for a bit, mulling over her options, and then went to an English teacher who seemed to like her. She had an idea, she said, for a quarterly poetry magazine with a twist. There'd be no selection or rejection process. Everyone would have the chance to have one poem published in it. "That's a lovely idea," the teacher had said.*

*There was hardly anything special about it, and some of the poems that were submitted were like the stuff you found in greeting cards. But it was a success in terms of volume and participation. The first issue debuted at thirty-one pages long.*

Four days later the note arrived in her mailbox. *"You think you're hot shit, don't you? But you're not. You'll see."*

Below the words, the writer had drawn a tiny wheel.

# 17

Phoebe took a breath and slid over the rusted lever on the dishwasher door. The rushing-water sound ceased instantly, and the house was now utterly quiet. She paused for a moment, steeling herself. Then she slowly opened the door. A spray of water splashed onto her, and she glanced down instinctively. But it wasn't just water. The wet mark the water had left on her white pajama bottoms was tinged pink.

She gasped. The water was mixed with what looked like blood.

Letting the door flop back into place, she stumbled backward. It was them again, she realized—the Sixes. They'd gotten inside again somehow—*while she was sleeping.*

She grabbed her phone from the counter. She'd programmed in Craig Ball's number the other night, and she hit it now. Her fingers, she saw, were trembling. As the phone rang, she rushed into the living room, checking all around her. Since both chain locks were still on, they must have gone out a window, she thought. But how had they gotten *in*? She felt as if she was in one of those nightmares in which the walls and the doors of your house dissolve, and you feel completely exposed and vulnerable.

"Ball," a voice said. It was low but not groggy, as if he'd already been awake.

"It's Phoebe Hall," she blurted out. "They've broken into the house again. Please, you've got to help me."

"You're talking about the girls—the Sixes?"

"Yes—and I think there's blood. In my kitchen. I don't know who it belongs to."

As she talked, she positioned herself by the front door, ready to bolt if she had to.

"Okay, I'm ten minutes away, tops."

"Should I call the police, too?"

"Uh, just wait till I arrive, okay?"

As soon as the call ended, she froze and listened again. Could they still be in the house? she wondered frantically, but she heard nothing now, only the low groan of the furnace. She leaned back against a small cabinet to the right of the front door. They'd raised the stakes, she realized. As bad as the rats had been, breaking into her house while she was *there*, was a whole new level of audaciousness.

Though the wait seemed interminable, Ball was good to his word. The car pulled up exactly ten minutes later. This time, however, he wasn't wearing his campus police jacket. He was dressed in jeans and a black leather coat.

"You okay?" he asked as Phoebe let him in the front door. She knew that she must look panic-stricken.

"I've been better," she said. "I woke to the sound of my dishwasher running, and I think there's blood inside it. I'm wondering if they put a rat in there."

"Christ," he said, grimacing. "Let me see."

She trailed behind him as he went into the kitchen. He scanned the room, and then, using a handkerchief that he'd drawn from his pocket, he slowly opened the dishwasher door.

For a few seconds he just peered, squinting, into the machine. Phoebe stood behind him, and from her vantage point she saw that the dishwasher looked empty, except for the pool of bloody-looking water at the bottom. She fought an urge to retch.

"*Is* it blood?" she asked.

"I think so," he said. "There's that telltale smell. But at least I don't see anything dead in there."

Slowly, he pulled out the top rack. It was empty. He squatted close to the ground. As he pulled out the lower rack, Phoebe spotted something in the utensil holder. It was a cluster of spoons, wrapped in soggy cardboard that had been secured by a rubber band and was now tinted pink.

Using his handkerchief again, Ball lifted the little package from the dishwasher.

"If there were any prints, they sure aren't there now," he said. After yanking a paper towel from the dispenser, he laid it on the counter and set the spoons on top.

It took Phoebe only a split second to see that there were six spoons altogether.

"I don't believe this," she said, throwing her hands up. "What are they trying to do to me?" She didn't want to freak out in front of Ball, but inside she was roiling.

"They're getting bolder each time," Ball said in disgust. "What I want to know is how they got in."

"Exactly—and I have no damn clue. I checked the doors and windows before bed, and the chain locks were still on both doors when I came downstairs."

"Well, this ain't some locked-room murder mystery, so there's gotta be an answer," Ball said. "They may have pried a window open. Why don't you take a seat in the other room while I look around. Try to relax."

Oh, yeah, *right*, Phoebe thought, but she went into the living room and plopped onto the sofa. Leaning into the cushions, she could feel that she was sweating through her pajama top. Calm *down*, she told herself. You need to have all your wits about you.

As Ball began to make his way through her rooms, she tried to imagine the ugly little scene that had unfolded in her kitchen earlier. The girls—because surely there was more than one—had clearly counted on the fact that the sound of the dishwasher would wake her. That way she would see the blood when she opened it.

But was there a particular reason for *this* visit? she wondered. The apples had materialized after she'd dropped by Blair and Gwen's apartment. The rats had shown up after she'd talked to Blair. Maybe they'd somehow found out about her trip to see Alexis. Or Blair blamed *her* for being called in to see Stockton.

Ball had gone up to the second floor, and now she heard him descending the stairs, the steps creaking and groaning from his weight. He paused at the foot of the stairs. There was a consternated expression on his face, indicating he'd yet to solve the puzzle.

After a few seconds he crossed the room and stopped again, just in front of Phoebe. He cocked his head, still thinking, and then blasted back into the kitchen.

"Okay, I've got it," he called out a minute later, his voice muffled.

Phoebe nearly leaped from the couch and hurried into the kitchen. But Ball wasn't there.

"In here," he called. He was in the small pantry off the kitchen. Though Phoebe kept some kitchen supplies there, the space was mostly being used to store boxes of Herb's belongings that he'd packed up before his leave. As Phoebe stepped inside, she saw that Ball had shoved a stack of boxes out from the wall. Behind them was a window—small, but still big enough for a body to crawl through.

"It's unlocked," Ball declared. "And look—there are a bunch of scuff marks on the sill."

"It's been hidden from view since I moved in here," Phoebe said, chagrined. She could have kicked herself. "If the driveway were on this side of the house, I would have at least noticed it from the outside."

"You know what my guess is?" Ball said as he turned the lock into place. "They unlocked it after they snuck in with the apples—so they'd have a way back in if they wanted. Or maybe they never even came in through the door that first time. You might have changed that lock for nothing."

Jeez, Phoebe thought, that's the least of my concerns.

"So *now* do we call the cops?" she asked. "I mean, how can we not?"

"Tell you what. Let me do it. I can take the heat and explain that I'd asked you to let me handle things initially."

"Okay, I'd appreciate that."

"But I don't know how soon they'll investigate this. Right now they're focused on the two drownings. The good news is that we've figured out how those girls have been sneaking in, and you should be okay going forward. But if I were you, I'd investigate having better-quality locks put on the windows."

After he left, promising to have security continue to patrol the block, Phoebe sat back on the couch, collecting her thoughts. There was no point in trying to get back to sleep, even though it was barely four o'clock.

She hated how rattled she felt. She had sworn she wouldn't let the Sixes get to her, but they finally had. It wasn't that they'd simply scared the bejesus out of her; now they were fucking with her mind. And there might be more visits in the offing. At least tonight she would be with Duncan, staying at his house.

A few minutes later, she finally forced herself into the kitchen to make tea. The cluster of spoons sat on the counter, mocking her. She tore off a paper towel and, holding it in her hand, pushed the little package toward the back of the counter.

Once the first light had appeared outside, she went back upstairs, showered, and dressed. When she returned to the first floor, she still felt jittery. But she couldn't just crawl up in a fetal ball, she told herself. She had prep work to do for her Monday-morning classes, and she hoped to get some of it out of the way today. But first, out of sheer curiosity, she wanted to check out the spot where Trevor Harris's body had been found. After throwing on her coat, she grabbed the set of her notes that she'd planned to give Hutch. If she had time, she would drop them off at his place.

She headed north for just over a mile along the river on Route 1, the road that ran parallel to the bike path she used, until she reached the Big Red Barn. Since the body apparently had been found across the road by the river, this would be the best place to park, she realized. Phoebe had shopped at the store once, just after she'd skulked into Lyle, hoping to find a few items that would help make Herb's house seem more like her own. But to her chagrin the store seemed to sell mostly baskets, old metal spoons, and painted milk cans. It was too early for the place to be open, but there were half a dozen cars in the parking lot, some official vehicles, others probably belonging to people who'd come to rubberneck.

She parked at the far end of the parking lot and climbed from the car. Though the sky was clear, the air felt close to freezing, and she was glad she'd dressed in plenty of layers.

As she hurried to the road on foot, she noticed that there were two large carved pumpkins and about a dozen dried corn stalks leaning on either side of the wide barn door. Halloween is coming, Phoebe realized, and then after a brief mental calculation, she realized that the festivities were Sunday night. Perfect, she thought. It would feed nicely into any terror the students were experiencing now.

Though it was early in the morning, cars zoomed down the road in both directions, and it took a minute for Phoebe to find an opening in the traffic. Once across the road, she hurried through a cut in the tree border and emerged onto the bike path. On the other side of the path, in front of the muddy river, was an area that had been partially cleared of trees and set with five gray wooden picnic tables.

A movement caught Phoebe's eye, and she glanced in that direction. Farther down to the right, about two dozen people, a few with bikes, stood on the path, staring into the wooded area in front of the river. Phoebe followed their eyes. Yellow police tape had been looped through the trees closest to the path. Deeper into the woods she could see four or five men and women in uniform moving, sometimes lurching, through the trees and underbrush along the riverbank. That was clearly where Trevor's body had been found. It was horrible to think of him lying along the water's edge for months as his friends and family—and of course Lily—frantically wondered where he was.

Phoebe glanced back at the crowd and let her eyes roam over the faces. There seemed to be a mix of townspeople and students, in addition to the cyclists, who must have just stumbled onto the scene. And then suddenly she spotted Hutch at the far end of the crowd, dressed in baggy pants and a heavy black-and-red lumberjack-style jacket. Considering how much he clearly missed the action, it wasn't a surprise to see him here.

"Hey, Hutch, hello," Phoebe said after wandering over to him. His expression had been solemn, but as soon as he turned and recognized Phoebe, his face relaxed into a smile.

"Professor Hall, good morning."

"Phoebe, please."

"Okay, Phoebe it is. So you came to check out the scene. Grim business, isn't it?"

"Yes—things seem to be going from bad to worse," Phoebe said. She gazed back through the woods at the cops stepping clunkily through the brush. "How did the cops discover him, do you know?"

"I talked to an old buddy of mine on the force, and he told me that they were hunting for a sweater the girl had worn, hoping to find where she went in. They found the sweater here, then the boy."

Phoebe gasped. "So they died at the same spot. The cops must be thinking serial killer," Phoebe said.

"Not necessarily. Since these two were boyfriend and girlfriend, they might have gotten into something over their heads—something that caught up with them at different times."

"You mean something like drugs?" Phoebe said. She'd never considered anything like that.

"Could be," said Hutch. "We've got a problem around here with that stuff. Marijuana, OxyContin going for eighty dollars a pill, and even heroin."

"But just to play devil's advocate, what if the deaths are part of a larger pattern?" Phoebe asked. "You mentioned the other day that a year and half was too long of a cooling-off period for a serial killer, but now we're looking at four incidents spaced no more than six months apart."

"If you count Wesley Hines."

"Right. By the way, after you gave me Wesley's name, I found out he lives near here, and I paid him a visit. He's still saying someone drugged him and tossed him into the river that night. I suppose he could be a pathological liar, but he seemed genuinely upset to me."

Hutch shook his head slowly, as if both doubtful and yet deliberating what she'd said.

"I took notes during my conversation with him yesterday and made a copy for you," Phoebe added. "I was going to drop them off at your place later." She fished the notes out of her bag and offered them to him.

"I'll take a look," he said, accepting the pages and tucking them into the breast pocket of his jacket. "You know, I'm going to feel like hell if I completely misjudged the situation with that boy back then. It happened just around the time I was being forced out. Maybe I was too distracted to see the situation clearly."

Phoebe felt a rush of sadness, thinking of Hutch at that moment in his life. With his wife dead, work was all he had. And how honorable of him to acknowledge now that he might have been wrong. She couldn't imagine Craig Ball admitting to as much as misdialing a phone number.

"One thing I know from writing biographies is that things often only make sense in context," Phoebe said. "I included other notes in there, too. Yesterday I talked to a girl who'd been victimized by the Sixes, and she told me they've done their share of tormenting students here. I keep wondering if *they* might be behind the drownings—either directly or indirectly."

Hutch whistled through his teeth. "I haven't stopped thinking about what they did with the rats. You get kids in a group, and things can definitely escalate."

She then told him about the little horror show at her house last night.

"I don't think I like the way this has been handled," he said, looking sincerely worried. "I'm concerned about your safety."

"I'm calling the locksmith for extra security as soon as they open," she promised. "And I'm staying with a friend tonight."

There was some movement down by the woods, and instinctively Phoebe and Hutch turned their heads in unison. Phoebe's heart sank a little at what she saw. Pete Tobias was now standing toward the front of the crowd, talking to two guys who looked like Lyle students. There was something downright feral about him—he always had his nose in the air, hyper alert—and she knew he'd soon turn and scan the crowd with those beady black eyes. If he noticed her here, he'd try to make something of it.

"I'd better get up to campus, Hutch," Phoebe said. "Call me after you read the notes, okay? I'd love your take on them."

"I will," he said. "And Phoebe . . . please be careful?"

After saying good-bye, Phoebe turned quickly and hurried away, hoping Tobias hadn't spotted her.

She drove to campus next and went directly to the library. She spent the next few hours prepping for class on Monday. As soon as she thought they'd be open, she called the locksmith and arranged for someone to come by her house that day and install better window locks.

As she headed home later to meet the locksmith, she was struck by how electrically charged the campus seemed. People—faculty as well as students—were clustered in knots, talking, their faces pinched in concern. It was clear the news about Trevor had spread all over by now, and people were not only sharing whatever they'd heard but also probably speculating wildly. Passing a cluster of four girls, Phoebe heard one of them suggest that Trevor and Lily had made some kind of suicide pact, but that Lily had taken longer to fulfill her end of the bargain.

Right outside the western gate to the campus, things seemed just as crazy. There were five or six Winnebagos belonging to various news outlets, all with satellite dishes on top. Phoebe imagined that there were more like those positioned at the other gates.

The locksmith was pulling up in his van just as she arrived home. It was the same guy as before. When he was done, he walked her from window to window, showing off the special locks he'd installed.

"It's tight as a drum in here now," he said, flicking his lank hair out of his face. After he left, she told herself that unless the Sixes arrived with glass cutters, she was truly safe. And yet her body felt weighed down with worry.

At five o'clock she freshened up, applied makeup, and changed into jeans, a black cashmere sweater with a V neckline, and her tight suede boots. The anxiety she'd felt all day seemed to seep away, replaced by a growing sense of anticipation. She was looking forward to the evening, more than she would have ever expected. Knowing she'd be spending the night at Duncan's, she stuck her toothbrush and clean underwear in her bag.

She walked to campus this time, assuming they'd take Duncan's car to his place. After heading through the western gate, she followed the path toward the quad. Some of the excitement she'd noticed all around her this morning appeared to have simmered down. As she passed Curry Hall, the dorm where Lily had lived, she paused momentarily. I have to know what happened to you, Lily, Phoebe thought. She couldn't abandon her the way she herself had been abandoned so many years before.

Rounding the dorm, Phoebe spotted Craig Ball at the edge of a small parking lot that abutted the building. He was talking intensely to a male student dressed in a green Philadelphia Eagles sweatshirt. Was he interviewing a friend of Trevor's? Phoebe wondered. She would have liked to ask Ball if he'd talked to the cops yet about her situation, but it clearly wasn't the right moment.

She crossed the quad and swung left onto a path that would take her to the north side of campus. Soon the Grove, the wooded area at the northern end of campus, appeared on her left. Bright orange and yellow leaves still covered the lower branches of the trees, and there was a thick, lush blanket of them on the ground as well. On any other day it might have looked like a storybook forest, but to Phoebe it held no charm today.

Before long she could see the top of the science building peering above a cluster of tall maples. It was just around the next bend. She picked up her speed a little, anxious to arrive. As she walked, the ground lights along the path popped on, momentarily diverting her attention. When she looked up again, she saw two female students emerge from the other side of the bend, one in a black coat, and the other, a redhead, in a fake fur vest over a sweatshirt. It took Phoebe a few seconds to realize that it was Blair and Gwen. Her stomach flipped over as soon as she'd processed the thought.

"Hello, Ms. Hall," Blair said as she drew closer. She found Phoebe's eyes in the dusk and boldly held them. Gwen, however, lowered her eyes to the ground.

"Hello, Blair," Phoebe said, staring straight at the girl. Her unease was quickly morphing to anger.

"It's getting dark so early these days, isn't it?" Blair said slyly, slowing down as she passed. A tiny smile formed on her face, making the edges of her full lips curl upward.

You little bitch, Phoebe thought. I won't let you intimidate me.

"We all need to be careful, then, don't we?" Phoebe said. "Bad things can happen in the dark."

The nasty little smile evaporated as Blair passed. She didn't like two playing at her game.

Was I being warned of another visit? Phoebe wondered, hurrying up the path. Or was Blair simply trying to remind me who was boss? Phoebe turned to look behind her, but the girls were now out of sight.

It wasn't until she was inside the science building that Phoebe finally let out a breath. Duncan's office turned out to be on the second floor, in a warren of a half-dozen or so offices that branched out from a single reception area. The receptionist had gone for the day, but after making a guess, Phoebe hung to the right, and two doors down she found Duncan reading what looked like a term paper, his cowboy boot-clad feet propped on the desk.

"Hey there," he said, looking up at the sound of her footsteps. He swung his feet off the paper-strewn desk and pushed his reading glasses onto the top of his head. He'd paired his jeans with a plain white button-down shirt, open at the neck and rolled at the sleeves, the color setting off his dark brown eyes. Phoebe felt desire surge through her. How the hell did this happen? she wondered. A week ago I was completely irritated when he asked me for dinner, and now I'm nearly weak-kneed at the sight of the man.

"So this is the nerve center of the psych department at Lyle College," she said, smiling.

Duncan tossed down the paper and rose from the desk. "If you took a look at these papers I'm grading, you'd hardly call it a nerve center. Of course, it takes lots of nerve to turn in crap like this."

"Are the students just not trying? Or do you think what's happening on campus is affecting their work?"

"Possibly the latter. Though with some of the guys, I worry it's just plain over their heads. Here, let me clear a seat for you."

There it was again—the problem with boys. Duncan came around the desk, scooped up the papers piled on a leather-covered wingback chair, and plopped them on the floor. Then he turned back to Phoebe.

"My, don't you look lovely today?" he said. He stepped closer and kissed her softly on the mouth.

"Thank you," she said. She leaned back, looking into his eyes. "Though I'm a bit wigged out at the moment." She briefly described what happened with the dishwasher and then bumping into the girls on the path.

"Gosh, Phoebe, why didn't you call me?" he said. "I would have come right over."

"You were already forced to come to my rescue once this week. How many times can I drag you out of bed?"

"Well, is Ball taking this seriously enough?"

"Yes, I think so. And he's involving the police now."

"Would you prefer to bag the tour and just head to dinner then?"

"Oh, no, a tour would be fine."

"Great. Wait here for just a sec, though, would you? Bruce wanted to ask me something up on four."

As soon as Duncan departed, Phoebe let her eyes roam the room, trying to see what the space would divulge about him. There were stacks of term papers on the desk and on the counter behind it, shelves full of books, and Post-it notes stuck to the computer screen, typical items in any professor's office. The only personal objects were a mug that read "Musikfest, Bethlehem, Pennsylvania," a wall diploma for a doctorate from the University of Michigan, and two small photos on the desk. In one Duncan stood with several students, holding an award; the other featured him and Miles, in hip waders, standing in a stream. Not much to go on. She took a seat and tried to relax.

For a while her thoughts wandered, and then finally she brought them back—to the room, to the night ahead. She glanced down at her watch. To her surprise Phoebe realized that Duncan had been gone fifteen minutes already. She rose from the chair and sauntered down the short hall to the reception area and then out into the main corridor. It was empty and silent, not surprising for this hour on a Friday night. Suddenly there was the sound of footsteps echoing in a nearby stairwell. She waited, thinking it was Duncan, but he failed to appear. She felt a sliver of annoyance at his having left her for so long.

She started to turn, to go back to Duncan's office. Then suddenly the hall lights went off in unison. Phoebe was standing in total darkness.

# 18

Phoebe froze, her mind momentarily blank in surprise. Had the janitor turned the lights off? she wondered, soon grasping that every light along the corridor was out. She spun around in the dark toward the doorway of the pysch department. Duncan's desk lamp had been on, but now there was absolutely no light seeping into the reception area. There'd been a power failure, she realized. She felt a sudden surge of panic. Take a deep breath, she commanded herself. Just get control.

She swung back around toward the hall again. As her eyes adjusted, she saw that the emergency exit signs above the doors to the stairwells were still lit. They cast an eerie, ghostlike ball of light at each end of the corridor. Where in hell was it that Duncan had said he was going? she wondered. The fourth floor. But why in the world wasn't he hurrying back now? She quickly began to make her way to the stairwell at the end of the corridor, where she figured she was bound to meet him coming down. She wondered if the power was out over the entire campus.

It turned out the stairwell had emergency bulbs, but they cast only the dimmest light. There was no one on the stairs, and no sound of anyone descending.

"Duncan?" Phoebe called up the stairs anxiously. "Are you there?"

From far off she thought she heard the sound of a door slam, but then nothing else.

She felt annoyed, pissed really, that Duncan had not only left her for so long but wasn't bothering to rush back. She had no intention of standing around in the dark. I'll just go outside, she decided, and wait for him in front of the building. But first she needed to grab her purse from his office. She'd left it on the floor by the chair. In fact, maybe the smartest thing to do, she realized, was to call him on her cell. Hopefully, he had his own phone in his jeans pocket.

She reentered the corridor. It was utterly silent there, and her heart rate quickly accelerated even more. Relax, she willed herself again. It's only a stupid power failure. She made her way back toward the psych department.

Peering into the reception area, she saw that it was even darker there than in the corridor because the windows faced the Grove. Phoebe took several tentative steps into the room and turned right, in the direction of Duncan's office. She edged along with a hand out in front of her, feeling for the open door to the hallway. She found it the hard way, as the left side of her head smacked into the doorframe. Phoebe groaned in pain.

Taking a breath, she corrected her position and entered the hall. Her eyes started to adjust, and she could see a little in the darkness. With both hands now in front of her, she groped her way down the hall to the entrance to Duncan's office. She stood for a second in the doorway, gaining her bearings. Finally her eyes found the dark shape of the chair, and she moved clumsily in that direction. It was only when she touched the chair and felt the fabric that she realized she wasn't in Duncan's office after all. His chair had been made of leather.

Cursing in frustration, Phoebe retreated to the hall and made her way jerkily to the next office down. This one was definitely Duncan's. Even in the dark, she could see the dull gleam of the yellow Post-its on the computer screen. She moved toward the chair, and felt around by the base until she made contact with her purse.

As she stooped to pick it up, Phoebe heard a sound out in the hall. She rose and spun around in that direction.

"Duncan?" she called out. Thank God, she thought.

But no one spoke back. Phoebe crept out into the hall and listened. From outside the building, probably from the path that ran in front of it, she heard the muffled sound of a guy yelling boisterously to a friend—"Max, hey," and then, "Wait up, okay?" Inside, though, there was only silence. But then, from somewhere very close to her, Phoebe thought she heard a person sigh—a low, rough sigh like the kind a dog makes in its sleep. Her legs went limp with fear.

"Who's there?" she said. The words caught in her throat. She turned and looked behind her, where there were several offices beyond Duncan's, and then back into Duncan's office. She had no idea where the sigh had come from. Darkness seemed to be throwing sounds, like a ventriloquist. Then she heard the same thing again. It was close, but she couldn't tell if it was behind or in front of her.

Frantically, Phoebe lurched toward the reception area. Once she stepped into the main corridor and had the emergency exit signs for guidance, she flew toward the stairwell doors and then down the steps to the ground floor. After flinging open the door and bursting outside, she nearly collided with a man in the dark. It was Bruce Trudeau. The moment she recognized him, all the lights inside the building popped on.

"What's going on?" Bruce demanded as they both looked up at the building. He was out of breath, as if he'd been running.

"I don't know," Phoebe said, breathless herself. "Someone . . . where's Duncan?"

"Duncan?" Bruce asked. "I have no idea. I was on the lower campus and saw the lights go out up here. Figured I'd better investigate."

"You weren't *with* Duncan?" she asked. It was starting to feel as if she were in the tail end of a dream, when everything becomes even more absurd and horses sit down at the dinner table.

"No, why?"

She could see the curiosity in his eyes. The last thing she wanted right now was for the whole world to know she and Duncan were together.

"Um, he was going to show me the rats," Phoebe said. "He thought I'd be interested. He had to go to another floor first—I thought to meet with you—and while I was waiting in his office, all the lights in the building went out."

"How odd," Bruce said. "Let me see what's going on. Do you want to wait here or come back inside?"

"I'll wait here," she said, forcing a smile.

As the front door of the building closed behind Bruce, Phoebe grabbed a deep breath. If Duncan hadn't gone to meet Bruce, where in God's name was he? She started to dig around her purse for her phone.

But as if in answer to her question, the front door of the building swung open, and Duncan came bounding out.

"*There* you are," he declared and gave her arm a squeeze when he reached her. "Bruce said you were out here."

"Me?" she said. "What happened to *you*?" There was an edge to her voice, but she couldn't help it.

"I'm sorry about that," Duncan said. "The conversation took longer than I planned, and then just when I started to leave, the lights went out and Miles had an angina attack."

"But you said you were meeting Bruce."

"Did I say Bruce?" he asked, furrowing his brow. "Sorry, just a slip of the tongue."

"Is he all right now?" Phoebe asked.

"Yes, he took a nitroglycerin tablet, but I wanted to wait and make sure it worked. Plus I think the lights going off is what triggered the attack to begin with. I would have called you, but I hadn't brought my cell phone with me."

"Um, don't worry about it," she said.

"You okay?" he asked, guessing there was something going on.

She started to tell him about the sounds by his office, but changed her mind. Maybe it was the radiator she'd heard, or else her imagination had gotten the better of her, heightened because of the darkness, and she didn't want Duncan to think she was becoming a paranoid basket case.

"Yeah—the power failure just threw me."

"Let's skip the tour after all and head over to my place."

Phoebe smiled, relieved. "Good. Right now I feel in need of a couch and a glass of wine. My shoulders are up around my ears."

"How about a couch, a glass of wine, and a neck massage?"

"Even better."

"Just let me grab my bag from my office. I promise not to go MIA again."

As Duncan darted inside, Phoebe perched on the balustrade outside the building. Down the hill the rest of the campus twinkled enchantingly in the night, belying all the turmoil going on at the college—and the fact that Phoebe felt so discombobulated. I heard something, I *know* I did, she thought.

"I'm surprised you're letting me drive," Duncan said a few minutes later as he backed his car out of the science-building parking lot. "I was almost positive you'd insist on following me in your car."

"What do you mean?" Phoebe asked, puzzled.

"I know you like to be in control," he said. He glanced quickly over to her, smiling. "That's not a bad thing. Just making an observation."

"You're saying I would have felt more in control if I'd driven my own car to your house?" Phoebe asked.

"It's more about *later*. Now you've got to rely on me to take you home."

Phoebe laughed. "Oh, I see," she said. "Well, as long as you're not planning to drive me home at eleven o'clock tonight, I'm okay."

She surprised herself at how forthcoming she'd just been with him.

"You better be careful," Duncan said. "I might hold you captive for the entire weekend."

The last line caught Phoebe off guard. She'd thrown the toiletries and underwear into her purse certain that she'd be spending the night, but she hadn't thought beyond that. The idea of staying the *weekend* was tantalizing and yet also mildly discomfiting. She didn't want things getting ahead of her.

"Well, let's see how good a cook you are," she said, smiling, keeping it light.

They had circled around to the front of the science building on their way out of campus. To Phoebe's surprise, she saw Glenda's husband hurrying down the front steps.

"What's Mark Johns doing up here?" she asked.

"Hmm, not sure," Duncan said, glancing over. "I'd heard at one point he was thinking of teaching a class in organizational psychology as an adjunct."

Don't let him see me, Phoebe prayed, discreetly sinking down in her seat. *She* had to be the one to tell Glenda about her little fling.

A minute later they passed through the northern gate of the college. "Where *do* you live, by the way?" Phoebe asked.

"In Winamac Acres," Duncan said. "It's ten minutes from here."

She was vaguely familiar with the area—a fairly upscale subdivision that unfolded from the town.

"It's not ideal, but I was in a hurry to find something new after Allison died," he added. That's good, Phoebe thought. I won't be forced to use the bathroom where his wife died.

The outside of the house was attractive but standard—a shingle-covered ranch with a poplar tree on each side of the entrance. The inside, though, was totally unexpected. The walls between the kitchen, dining room, and living room had been knocked down to create a loftlike great room with a big gray stone fireplace. It had been decorated in a contemporary style but with comfy pieces—including a long L-shaped couch slipcovered in white canvas. The place was totally inviting.

"Did *you* knock the walls down?" she said as Duncan took her coat and hung it in the closet. "It's a terrific space."

"Yes, it was a bit of an extravagance, seeing that I don't plan to be in Lyle indefinitely, but after everything that had happened, I needed a place that I felt really at home in."

She followed Duncan into the kitchen area and slid onto one of the stools along the island while he uncorked a bottle of Bordeaux. He poured them each a glass. Then, after lighting the gas fire in the fireplace, he pulled out a large red pot from the fridge.

"Hmm, what do you have there?" Phoebe asked.

"Hunter's chicken," he said smiling. "With a name like that, I figured I could prepare dinner for you with my masculinity totally intact." He set the pot on the burner of the stovetop and lit the flame. "Let's give it about ten minutes to reheat, and then we'll eat."

He washed off his hands, wiped them on his jeans, and plopped on a stool perpendicular to hers on the island. After taking a drink of wine, he set the glass down and looked into her eyes. "Okay, Ms. Hall, tell me the whole story about last night—from start to finish."

She went over what had happened with the dishwasher, filling in the gaps she'd left before. She also told him about her talks with Hutch, Alexis, and Wesley. Despite the relaxing effects of the wine, she found herself getting churned up as she rehashed certain details.

When she'd finished, Duncan didn't say anything for a bit, just twirled the wineglass between his fingers.

"So tell me your opinion," Phoebe urged. "Do you think there *could* be some kind of serial killer on the loose here?"

He shrugged. "It's just so hard to know without being privy to any real evidence—what the cops have found. But there's one thing I *do* know."

Phoebe looked at him expectantly and was surprised when his expression became stern.

"Yes?" she asked.

"Maybe it's none of my business here, but it seems you've gone beyond the call of duty for Glenda—and it's time to let the authorities take over."

"You're right, of course," Phoebe said. "Everything's escalating. Besides, I feel I've done all I can do." Which wasn't true, she knew. She hadn't found out yet what the other circles were. And she hadn't learned who had killed Lily. But she could see it would be pointless to try to make any kind of case with Duncan.

"Is that a promise to cease and desist?" Duncan asked, smiling.

"Promise," Phoebe said, without meaning it.

"Great. And you know what your reward shall be? *Hunter's chicken.*"

For the next few minutes, she let Duncan do his thing while she sat curled up on the couch. She tried to keep the drownings and the Sixes at bay, forcing herself to concentrate solely on the flames dancing in the fireplace, the taste of the wine, and the reassuring sound of Duncan moving around in the kitchen. Once she jumped up and, smiling, used her phone to snap a picture of him cooking.

The stew was just the kind of comfort food she needed, and she devoured it. Over dinner she asked about Duncan's background, something she hadn't had time to probe much about yet. He was from the suburbs of Chicago, he said. He'd done his under-graduate work at UCLA but had missed the Midwest and gone to Michigan for his PhD—as she'd seen from the diploma—before finally teaching at Northwestern.

"Is that where you met your wife?" Phoebe asked. "At Northwestern?" She found the subject of his marriage slightly unsettling but also utterly compelling, and she'd been fighting off her curiosity since their first dinner.

"I met her when I first started teaching, but not at the school." He cleared the plates then, and she wondered if this was terrain he wanted to avoid.

"What about you?" he said, returning with salad and a plate of cheeses. "I realize I've assumed you're from the East Coast, but I never asked."

"A small, uncharming town in Massachusetts. Since my mother died a few years ago, I've been back just once—for a cousin's wedding."

"Not your favorite place in the world?"

"No. I have some happy memories—my mom tried hard to make things special for me, even though my father took off when I was two, never to surface again. But I hated the town. I wanted to be out in the world, forging a new life."

"Then why leave boarding school and go back there?" he asked quietly.

Phoebe smiled ruefully to herself. She felt like a witness on the stand in a courtroom drama who has just answered the wrong way, accidentally opening the door to a line of questioning that her lawyer has warned her to avoid at all costs. She met Duncan's eyes briefly and looked away, picking a piece of bread from the basket.

"So you didn't buy my answer the other night about being homesick?" she said.

"I sensed there was something you weren't telling me," he said. "If you feel comfortable talking about it, I'd love to hear."

"You'll actually find it fairly ironic," she said, meeting his eyes again. She hesitated. "I was bullied by a bunch of girls. They were part of a secret society, not unlike the Sixes."

Be careful, she warned herself. You don't really want to go here. Glenda knew all about it, of course. But very few others. Even Alec had been offered only cursory details in their four years together.

"Okay," Duncan said. "That explains why you're passionate about trying to root out the Sixes. So tell me about these bullies."

She touched the tips of her fingers to her forehead and lightly brushed her hair away. God, she thought, why did I start this?

"There's not all that much to tell. They sent mean notes, that sort of thing. Glenda was like a rock for me then, and I think that's why our bond has been so strong all these years."

Phoebe realized she'd been talking without drawing a breath. She breathed now, trying not to look as if she was gulping for air, and then took a long sip of wine.

"It's hard to picture Phoebe Hall fleeing town just because of some mean notes."

"Well, things got worse. They boxed me out of things I wanted to belong to. It was pointless to stay at the school if I couldn't participate. And it's no fun being shunned by other girls."

"It must have been a very difficult time."

"I don't think anyone escapes adolescence scot-free. Look, let's change the subject, okay? I hate dwelling on something from so long ago. It's not worth the time."

"Sure," he said. "I remember promising a neck massage earlier, and now seems like the perfect time."

"Yes, I'd like that," Phoebe said, glad to be delivered from the topic. She stood up from the table and began to clear the salad plates.

Duncan rose too and followed her into the kitchen. As she was setting the dishes on the counter, he slipped behind her and placed his hands on her waist. It was the first time he'd touched her intimately since the kiss in his office, and desire spread through her like a brush fire. "Or we could just go to bed," he said. "I can do some things there that are even better than a massage."

"Option B," she said, smiling.

They made love—first slowly and sensuously and then afterward in a fierce, raw way that almost shocked her. She felt herself letting go and briefly shucking off all the craziness happening around her.

In the morning Duncan was up ahead of her again. She could hear dishes clacking lightly together in the other room and classical music playing softly. When she padded into the great room, she found that he'd set out fruit and a basket of muffins.

"Okay, you didn't bake *those*, did you?" she asked.

"Berta's," he said. "I made a guess you're a blueberry girl."

"You guessed right," she said.

Their conversation over breakfast was easy and relaxed, no naked-light-of-day awkwardness. After breakfast they cleared the table together, their movements in sync, she noticed.

"This is the last weekend for good foliage," Duncan said. "If you're up for it, we could hang around here for a bit and then drive along some great back roads. Afterward we could eat lunch at an inn I know where they have really great mussels."

So he *was* kidnapping her for the weekend.

"That sounds perfect," Phoebe said.

The sky was crystal clear that morning, and as promised Duncan took them along charming back-country roads, past farms with big silos and old red barns. They drove around for about two hours, stopping at several roadside antique stores just to poke around, and then finally reached the inn. It was a little shabby, but bustling with people. Phoebe made a stop in the ladies' room first. When she caught up with Duncan again, she saw that he'd scored a table in the bar area next to a roaring fire. They both ordered mussels and shared a bottle of ice-cold pinot grigio. Duncan seemed less talkative during the meal than he had been in the car, but she figured he was simply chatted out for now. Just after they'd finished eating and ordered espressos, a young guy with a Lehigh University baseball cap strolled into the bar. Lehigh, she knew, was in Bethlehem.

"Tell me what you think of college men today," she said, setting down her espresso cup. "Especially the ones at Lyle. I keep hearing that they're not on par with the women."

"I have a few amazing guys in my classes this term, but it's true that many guys seem clueless these days. As a society, we've done a good job of empowering girls—deservedly so, of course—but some boys have gotten lost in the shuffle. The female students at Lyle often seem very frustrated with them."

"That reminds me of something that I turned up about Lily, something I don't want to lose sight of."

"What's that?" he asked.

"Right before she died, she had apparently started seeing someone new who wasn't a student. It sounded as if she was frustrated by the guys here, too."

"You've really been quite the sleuth," Duncan said. "Who told you that?"

"Her roommate. And serial killer theory aside, it's possible that this guy is tied to her death somehow. I wish I could find out who he is. As Hutch pointed out to me, women are vulnerable when they dump guys who don't want to be dumped."

Just then Phoebe's cell phone rang. When she glanced down, she saw that Hutch was calling.

"Speak of the devil," she told Duncan. "Excuse me for a sec."

"Thanks for those notes you took," Hutch announced after she'd said hello. "They turned out to be very insightful."

"What do you mean?" Phoebe asked. She felt a prick of excitement. "Did you find something in them?"

"In a sense, yes. Mindy, that girl you talked to at campus security, was nice enough to make me a copy of some of my old notes that I didn't keep here, and when I compared them to yours, a lightbulb went off. Can you drop by and see me again?"

Natch. It was just like Hutch to insist on a one-on-one.

"I'm in a restaurant right now, but why don't I give you a call in a bit. I can arrange to meet you." Even if she was going to spend the weekend with Duncan, she could still pick up her car and swing by Hutch's at some point.

"He found something in the notes I took," she explained to Duncan after she ended the call, "but he'll only tell me in person."

"I thought you were going to back off from this whole business." Duncan looked displeased.

"I'm just going to follow up on this one matter. Sounds like it may be important."

"Are you all set, then?" Duncan said. "We should probably hit the road."

"Okay," Phoebe said, surprised by his sudden urgency. She had imagined them lingering by the fire over another espresso.

Duncan swiveled his head, hunting the room with his eyes for the waitress. As soon as she brought the bill a moment later, he handed her his credit card without bothering to even check the math. Phoebe offered to contribute, but he shook his head.

"Did you leave anything at my house you need to go back for?" he asked.

"No—I don't think so," Phoebe said. What's going on? she wondered.

"Then I'll take you back to your place," he said. "I'm sure you've got as much work as I do today."

"Yes, tons," she said, trying not to seem disconcerted.

"Do you feel safe enough with the new window locks?" he asked. "I hate the idea of you home and afraid."

"I've got to face the music at some point," she said. "There's no point in prolonging it."

That was the truth. But still she felt her stomach doing a weird flip about this turn of events. So much for being Duncan's captive for the weekend.

# 19

Duncan was polite as they left the inn, helping her on with her jacket, opening the door for her. Maybe, Phoebe thought, I simply misinterpreted the hold-you-captive comment he made last night—he might have been playful and hadn't intended the remark to be taken literally. And he *had* extended their original date by almost an entire day.

But during their drive back to Lyle, he seemed distracted, even slightly aloof, and her gut told her something was definitely up. She realized he might be annoyed that she'd promised to go see Hutch after assuring Duncan she'd cease playing private eye. And yet she remembered she'd actually noticed a slight change in him when she'd first returned from the ladies' room. He'd seemed more pensive.

Perhaps what she'd witnessed had just been a gradual mood swing—intensified by the wine at lunch and spending hours in the company of the same person. She remembered how right from the start she had wondered if Duncan was prone to moodiness and retreating into himself.

As they drove, Phoebe watched the landscape roll by and commented from time to time on how lovely it was. Duncan acknowledged her comments pleasantly but added nothing more.

"Is everything okay?" Phoebe asked finally. Men hated that line, she knew, and it rarely produced an honest answer, but she felt she had to give it a shot. "You seem kind of quiet all of a sudden."

"Oh, sorry," he said. "I got a call when you were in the ladies' room about a few things I need to take care of today. I apologize for seeming distracted."

"Not a problem," she said. "Just wondering."

Once they reached the outskirts of Lyle, Duncan seemed to relax more into his seat, and she sensed his remoteness dissipating. As he pulled up to her house, he glanced over and smiled.

"This isn't going to cause your neighbors' tongues to start wagging, is it? It's not quite the walk of shame at this hour, but if any of your neighbors have hawk eyes, they'll realize you're basically wearing the same clothes you had on yesterday."

"Well, they didn't notice anyone climbing in my window or hauling rats through the back door, so apparently their observation skills aren't all that good," Phoebe said.

He put the car in park. "Why don't I come in for a minute and make sure everything's okay."

Part of her was tempted to say yes, but she shook her head instead. She didn't want to prolong the awkward vibe that had taken hold since lunch.

"Thanks, but I should be fine now," she said. "The locksmith declared the house tight as a drum."

A large vehicle came rumbling down the street at that moment, and they both looked up in unison. It turned out to be from a Philadelphia television station, and it was obviously headed toward campus.

"I wonder if there's some new development," Duncan said, narrowing his eyes.

"Or they've just come back from a late lunch at Taco Bell," Phoebe said. "Speaking of lunch, thanks for a lovely day."

He reached his hand behind her neck, pulled her close, and kissed her on the mouth.

"I had a great time this weekend," he said. "Call me if there's any problem—no matter what time it is, all right? I'll just be grading papers tonight," he said. It was as if his detachment during the drive home had been a figment of her imagination.

As she unlocked the front door of the house, she could hear the motor of the car humming behind her, and she realized Duncan was waiting until she checked inside. She scanned the living room and then turned and waved out the doorway. Duncan waved back and drove off down the street.

Once inside, she went window by window, checking that the locks were all on. It was clear nothing had been tampered with. But as she walked through the kitchen to check the back door, the thought of the bloody pool at the bottom of the dishwasher made her gag. Craig had promised to talk to the police about the incident on Thursday night, and she thought someone from the precinct would have been in touch with her by now.

As soon as she finished her inspection, Phoebe called Hutch. She wanted to arrange to stop by his cabin and find out what lightbulb had gone off for him. But he didn't pick up.

"Hey, Hutch, it's Phoebe," she said to his answering machine. "I'm home now and I can stop by any time." She imagined him out in the truck with his dogs, maybe picking up firewood or some grub for dinner tonight, probably listening to someone like Patsy Cline.

Next she phoned Glenda. She'd been surprised not to hear from her either. Just when she thought the call would go to voice mail, Glenda picked up.

"Sorry to be out of touch," Glenda said. "I barely had time to *shower* today with everything that's going on."

"What's the latest?"

"The campus is like a zoo. The kids are freaked, and so are their parents and the board of trustees. And we're not just a regional story anymore—apparently a crew from *Dateline* is barreling in our direction as we speak. The fact that Halloween's on Sunday isn't helping. There's a rumor running rampant that the next victim will be found this weekend."

"Do you think Tom is fueling any of this?"

"To some degree, yes. I keep reiterating to him how crucial it is not to fan the flames, and he gives me that haughty look as if he's shocked I'd suggest he *would*. But more than once I've spotted him huddled with someone on campus, and I don't like it. Plus, he sent an e-mail update to parents that he didn't clear with me first, and I thought the tone was all wrong. Yes, you've got to shoot straight, but you shouldn't create mass hysteria."

"How about you? How are you coping?"

"I've never felt so agitated in my career. I don't think I'm giving that away in public, but inside I'm like that expression the kids here use—'a hot mess.' And poor Brandon. I haven't been able to give him an ounce of time lately."

"What about Mark? How is this affecting things?"

"I once thought I had a good marriage, but instead of having my back, Mark seems even *more* distant these days. I've asked him to help with Brandon, to spend more time with him, and all he says is that he's too busy with work. But enough about me. How are you?"

From the casual tone of the question, Phoebe realized that her friend wasn't in the loop about the latest incident.

"Well, there's been a little development on my end, which Ball was supposed to tell you about." She relayed the dishwasher story to Glenda.

"Oh, my God," Glenda said. "Why the hell didn't he inform me? And you had to stay there alone last night?"

"It's not a problem," Phoebe answered vaguely. "I've beefed up my locks." As she spoke, she felt the guilt surge back. She still hadn't told Glenda about Duncan, and the longer she waited, the more awkward it would be. She started to say something, but Glenda cut in.

"Fee, look, I appreciate all you've done," Glenda said. "But this is now totally out of hand. I want you to stop your investigation. I can't put you in danger."

"Oh, come on," Phoebe said. "They've played a few dreadful pranks, but there's no sign I'm in any real danger."

"But you said yourself that we don't really know what these girls might be capable of."

"Are you thinking that as part of the fifth or sixth circle of membership, the Sixes will now demand the head of a tarnished celebrity biographer?" Phoebe tried to joke.

"I'm not kidding. I want you to stop. Why don't you stay here tonight, and we'll talk about it."

"I'll be okay, really."

"At least come over for lunch tomorrow. I need to discuss this with you in person."

Though Phoebe had no intention of letting Glenda force her off the hunt, she knew it would be good to hash out everything that had transpired in person. And she could finally tell her about Duncan. She agreed to stop by just after noon.

As the day quickly turned to twilight, she could feel dread begin to nudge her again. All of the ease and contentment she'd felt at Duncan's last night was gone. Her perturbed mood, she realized, stemmed not only from having to face a night alone in her house, but also from the abrupt end to her afternoon with Duncan. Now that she had a few hours' distance on the experience, she was sure that the shape-shifting his mood had undergone was due to something other than a phone call about work.

Keeping her gaze off the dishwasher, Phoebe made a cup of tea. She'd just sat down when her cell phone rang. Hutch, she thought. But she didn't recognize the number on the screen.

"Professor Hall?" the voice asked. It sounded like a student. Don't tell me someone's pleading for a grade change during the weekend, she thought.

"Yes?"

"It's Wesley Hines. You gave me your number, and said I could call you."

"Oh, of course," she said. Something was up. "How can I help?"

Wesley blew a gust of breath loudly into the receiver. "Wow, it's been a weird two days since I saw you last," he confessed.

"How so?" she asked. He'd been to the police, she suspected.

"Well, I did what you told me to do. I went to see the cops and told them my story."

"That's good. How did they react when you told them?"

"They took it seriously, real seriously. Let me tell you, it's been a relief to have people finally pay attention— and you were the first one, so I appreciate that."

"I'm sure it was frustrating when you talked to the campus cops last year, but I hope you can see it from their perspective. They had no reason to suspect it was anything more than an accident."

"Yeah, well, I take it you heard about the drowned guy they found?"

"Yes, Trevor Harris. Did you know him?"

"Nope—though I knew the name. I guess Lily Mack must have mentioned him at some point, and then people were buzzing about him last spring, when they thought he just took off."

"Are you thinking that the same thing happened to him that happened to you—but he didn't make it out alive?"

"I'm no expert, but hey, I've watched enough crime shows to know that you're supposed to put two and two together, and this sure looks like two and two together. It gives me the creeps when I think how close I came to dying myself."

"Well, I'm just so happy you're okay. And I appreciate your calling me to let me know you saw the cops."

"Actually, that's not the only reason I'm calling. You told me to get in touch if I thought of anything else—and I did. It may not mean much, but I don't know, I guess I thought I should share it."

Instinctively Phoebe sat up straighter, her curiosity fully engaged. She was sure the police wouldn't want her getting involved in the investigation, but she wasn't about to let that discourage her.

"Go ahead," she said. "I'm anxious to hear."

"Oh shoot, two people just walked into the store. Is there a chance we could meet after we close today? Then there won't be any interruptions."

"Today's complicated, unfortunately," Phoebe said. She was eager to hear what he had to say, but she needed to leave the evening open for Hutch. "How about tomorrow morning—at around ten?"

"Yeah, we're closed on Sundays, so that should be fine. There's a diner on Route 412 called Sammy's. Ever hear of it?"

"No, but I'll look it up. I'll see you there at ten then."

As soon as she hung up, Phoebe began to pace the living room. Hutch had something interesting to share, and now so did Wesley. Maybe, just maybe, the truth would begin to emerge this weekend.

She stopped pacing and massaged her temples. She could feel a headache coming on, partly from hunger, but there was no way she was going to cook anything in her kitchen. It had been a week since she'd been to Tony's, and she realized that the quiet back room and a glass of Montepulciano might help her take the edge off. Before she locked up, leaving several lights on, she tried Hutch again. No answer. She left another message saying that she was anxious to talk to him.

She drove to Tony's this time, and parked the car along Bridge Street. Stepping inside the restaurant, she wondered if she might see Duncan there, lingering again over a bowl of pasta. But the only people at the bar were two middle-aged guys watching a hockey game with the sound barely audible. Tony wasn't even there tonight. The hostess led her to a table in the back room, past about a dozen diners. Phoebe started to order her usual chicken with rosemary, but then realized that she suddenly had little appetite. She asked instead for a Caprese salad and a glass of wine.

She could feel a funk begin to descend, blending weirdly with her anxiety, as if she'd taken two medications that shouldn't be mixed. She closed her eyes and thought of Lily once again. She pictured the pretty girl she'd met that day, her blond hair wet with rain. You wanted out of the Sixes, didn't you? she thought. So what did Blair do to you when she found out?

Later, when the waitress cleared away her unfinished salad, Phoebe started to order an espresso and then changed her mind. She suddenly felt as eager to hightail it out of Tony's as she'd been to get down here. She paid the bill and stepped outside the restaurant. The air was crisp and clear, and Phoebe could hear the thump of rock music farther down Bridge Street. Cat Tails, she realized. And then an idea grabbed her. It's time I finally check out this place, she thought.

She left her car where she'd parked it and descended the hill, forced to bend her knees because of the steep incline. The music grew louder with each step she took, and was soon mixed with shouts and laughter. She'd planned to slip into the side entrance of Cat Tails, but there was a snarl of obnoxious-looking guys by the door there, so she continued down the street, turned right, and used the main door of the building. I'm going to feel like a fool in here, she thought as she entered, especially if I run into any students I know. But her curiosity was on fire now, and there was no turning back.

Surprisingly, the place was only half full. She surveyed the crowd. It was a mix of townies, a pack of older women flashing their cleavage, and kids who were clearly Lyle College students. One, whose sex was unclear, was wearing a rubber werewolf mask. Another, a girl, had on an absurdly tall witch's cap. Phoebe remembered it was Halloween weekend.

The place itself was an utter dive. The only decor to speak of were lights boasting different beer brands and a huge, weathered print of a catfish over the jukebox—the one where Wesley had played the Stones songs. Phoebe crossed the sticky floor and ordered a glass of red wine at the bar, suffering a smirk from the bartender. Then she turned and almost gasped. Tom Stockton was standing two feet away at the bar, his face turned mostly away from her.

Her gut instinct was to move, not to let him catch her, though she wasn't sure why. It didn't matter. Stockton seemed to sense her presence, turned and spotted her. He was clearly as surprised as she was.

"Well, well," he said. "Of all the gin joints in the world."

"Hello, Tom," Phoebe said. "I could say the same to you. You're the last person I expected to see here."

"Hardly surprising, really," Stockton said over the music. He was wearing a cropped brown jacket; underneath was a dark blue button-down shirt, the color of which perfectly matched his eyes. No doubt intentional, Phoebe thought. "This bar just might be the epicenter of our problems, and it seemed critical to check it out—especially tonight."

He backed a few feet down the pockmarked wooden bar, making a place for her to stand next to him. He slid his drink with him—scotch on the rocks, it looked like. Not having a choice, Phoebe slipped into the spot next to him. "Living on a Prayer" had been pounding on the jukebox, but once it stopped, nothing else came on. It was like being in a room where someone uninvited has suddenly sashayed in, leaving the other guests speechless.

"I know what you mean," Phoebe said. "The name Cat Tails kept turning up when I spoke to people, too."

"In some ways, it's just like every other college-town bar I've been in. But frankly, I don't like the vibe here."

"I hear a rumor's going around that something will happen this Halloween weekend. Do you think there's any basis for that?"

"No idea. What I do know, however, is that the students are hysterical. As an administration, we *really* need to get a handle on this thing."

Was that a dig at Glenda? she wondered.

"I'm sure Glenda will bring things under control," she said. "And I'm sure you're an enormous help to her right now."

Phoebe had allowed her tone to be the teeniest bit sarcastic, which she knew she shouldn't have, but he didn't seem to notice anyway.

The music started again, making it tough to talk. Phoebe followed the sound and let her eyes rest on the jukebox. Wesley had been approached by a slick-looking guy in his late thirties or early forties, but there was no one in here like that tonight—unless, Phoebe thought to her amusement, I count Tom. She noticed that the jukebox was right near the side door that opened onto Bridge Street. If someone had indeed drugged Wesley, it might have been easy to urge him out through that door without anyone really noticing.

"Well, that's it for me tonight," Phoebe said, setting her wineglass down, still half full.

"Why not stay a little longer, and we can grab a bite of dinner afterward? My treat."

"Thanks," she said, taken aback, "but I just ate at Tony's." Based on Stockton's previous attitude toward her, his invitation surprised her. He probably wanted to pump her for info.

She said good night and climbed the hill to her car, nudged along by the river wind at her back. As soon as she was at the wheel, she knew what she was going to do. She was going to drive by Duncan's. It seemed so high school, but if he was really home grading those papers he'd mentioned, she would at least know that he'd been honest with her.

But the house was dark, except for a light over the front door, and there was no car in the driveway.

Annoyed at how upset she felt, she tried to shake thoughts of Duncan as she pulled into her driveway. As she walked across the short expanse of lawn, she stopped in her tracks. The outside glass door was partially open. Someone had stuffed something white between that and the front door.

# 20

Phoebe looked quickly left and right and then swung around to face the street behind her. There was absolutely no one in sight. With her heart starting to gallop, she turned back toward the house and stared at the package protruding from the space between the two doors. What have those little brats left me now? she wondered.

She continued to the porch and mounted the front steps. As she inched toward the door, she saw that the pale thing was a manila envelope. Her name was on it, written in thick masculine scrawl with a black marker. Probably not the Sixes, then, she thought. After glancing once more behind her, she stooped down and plucked the package from between the doors. As soon as she had it in her hands, she could tell there was a sheaf of papers inside.

She quickly unlocked the front door and hurried inside. After checking doors and windows, she brought the package to the small table in her living room and tore open the envelope. There were actually two separate batches of papers inside, each set held together with a paper clip. Attached to the first was a note, signed "Hutch."

"Prof Hall, sorry I missed you," it read. "I was out with the dogs. Let's talk as soon as possible on Sunday. I'll be home most of the day. In the meantime, take a look and tell me what you see."

The papers felt charged in her hands. Is this where the truth lies? she thought. Am I about to finally figure something out? She plopped down at the table and tugged the note away from the two sets of papers.

The first batch were the notes about Wesley she'd given to Hutch when she'd seen him down by the river. As she thumbed through the pages, she saw that he'd underscored a bunch of lines pertaining to Wesley's time in Cat Tails—Wesley chatting briefly at the bar with the so-called cougars, the trip to the men's room after shooting darts, how he'd played a few songs on the jukebox, and the comments from the man asking if the machine gave change and then complimenting Wesley on playing the Stones song. The only other part that was underlined related to Wesley kicking off his loafers and swimming to shore. There wasn't a single comment in the margins explaining why these details mattered.

Phoebe tossed those pages down and stared at the second batch. It took only a second to realize that these were the photocopies Mindy had given Hutch of the notes he'd made while interviewing Wesley a year ago. They were all in his big scrawl, and portions had been freshly underscored with pencil here, too. As Phoebe scanned the pages, she saw that Hutch had drawn attention to the same details he'd marked in *her* notes— the cougars, the jukebox, the man asking for change, etc. These were clearly the parts that had made the lightbulb go off in his head.

Next Phoebe spread out both sets of notes, positioning the pages that corresponded to each other side by side. She began to study them, sweeping her eyes back and forth.

Based on her earlier conversation with Hutch, it seemed as if he had figured out a clue about what had happened to Wesley that night. The clue was certainly within one or some of the underlined portions. And it probably registered with Hutch when he had both sets of notes in front of him. But what the hell is it? Phoebe wondered.

She peered more closely at the pages. For the first time she noticed that the detail about the stranger at the jukebox had been underlined, on both sets of notes, more heavily than any other part. Obviously Hutch had found that piece significant. Did he think the man had drugged Wesley?

But then why also underline the part about the cougars? Perhaps Hutch thought that the stranger by the jukebox had worked in tandem with one of the cougars. Maybe the women had slipped the drug in Wesley's drink, and then a short time later, when Wesley's thinking had become fuzzy, the stranger had lured him outside.

Phoebe glanced at her watch. She would have liked to call Hutch right then, but it was after ten, and she knew there was a good chance he'd gone to bed. It would have to wait until morning, as he'd suggested. She made a copy of Hutch's notes on her printer, tucking one set into her purse to study more later and the other into a book for safekeeping, along with the notes she'd taken.

Before going up to bed, she stole into the kitchen and eyed the spoons the Sixes had left her. The card wrapped around them was totally dry now, and Phoebe wondered suddenly if it might contain some sort of message. Using a paper towel as a buffer, she tugged off the rubber band. Then she wiggled the cardboard from around the spoons.

As disgusting as it was to hold the piece of cardboard, she brought it into her office to study under the desk lamp. Slowly she pried it open. There were patches of faded color on the inside, but no message. She left the cardboard there on the table she used as her desk.

She climbed up the stairs to bed. But though she felt frayed from exhaustion, she soon saw that sleep wasn't going to happen. Handling the spoons had spooked her all over again. She just lay there, listening, trying to guess whether the creaks and groans she heard were cause for alarm or just the old house settling. Finally she dragged her pillow and duvet downstairs and plopped down on the couch with them. At least there, she thought, she'd be more apt to hear anyone prowling outside the house. The last time she squinted at her watch, it was just after three. Finally she drifted off.

She was awake by 5:45, feeling hungover with fatigue. She forced herself to wait until eight to call Hutch. When she reached him, however, his chipper voice suggested that he'd been up for hours.

"I'm afraid I'm not much of a detective," she told him.

"And why is that, lovely lady?"

"Because I studied your notes last night and again this morning, and I didn't find a single clue hidden in there."

Hutch chuckled. "I should have been clearer. What I discovered is not hidden at all. It's right in front of your eyes."

Phoebe conjured up the pages in her mind, trying to figure out what he meant.

"You've got me," she said after a moment.

"Well, then, I guess I'll have to give you a little lesson in detective work. Hold on a second. Ginger, get out of there. That's not for you." He returned his attention to Phoebe. "You up for that?"

"Absolutely. How soon can instruction begin?"

"I need to run up and see my nephew Dan in Allentown for a few hours. Ever since Becky died they've been good about having me over for Sunday lunch—or 'brunch,' as they call it. Why don't we plan on getting together at my place around three this afternoon? But let me call first to let you know I'm home."

"That sounds good," Phoebe said. "Two twenty-one B Baker Street, right?"

Confused, Hutch started to ask what she meant and then got the joke. He chuckled again in his deep, husky voice.

"Exactly."

She had a little time to kill before meeting Wesley, and she used it to review some of the notes she'd made for her classes on Monday. But she was anxious and ended up leaving earlier than she needed to. The day was raw and overcast, with a sky that looked like it had been smeared with soot. She found the diner that Wesley mentioned easily enough, its parking lot already jammed with cars. After locking up, she crossed the lot behind three beefy men dressed head-to-toe in camo, obviously planning to carbo-load for hunting down deer. In unison they flicked their cigarette butts to the ground before swinging open the door to the diner.

Inside, the place was overripe with the smell of eggs, bacon, French toast, and pancakes. Rather than increase her appetite, the aroma made her queasy. After she'd been shown to a booth, Phoebe ordered coffee and waited.

Wesley arrived fifteen minutes later, exactly on time. Despite the fact that it was Sunday, a day off for him, he looked as buttoned up as he had when she'd ambushed him after work: pressed khaki pants, an open-neck dress shirt in pale yellow, and a short, baseball-style wool jacket. His skin seemed freshly scrubbed, and his hair was spiked at the front of his massive scalp. Movie stars, she'd discovered over the years, often had heads slightly too big for their bodies, which worked brilliantly for them in films. But unfortunately she didn't see this as a plus for poor Wesley.

"Thanks for meeting with me, Professor Hall," he said, sliding in across the booth seat from her. He unzipped his jacket and folded it next to him.

"Please, call me Phoebe," she said, smiling. "You're not in school anymore, and I'm not even a real professor."

He cocked his head and smiled back. "Got it," he said.

"What would you like for breakfast?" Phoebe said. She wanted to quickly take care of ordering so they could get down to business. "I'm probably just going to stick with coffee myself."

"Actually, coffee's good for me, too," he said. "My dad's getting ready to head to Florida, and I promised I'd go over a few things with him at the mill later this morning."

"I thought it was a feed business," Phoebe said.

"Yeah, but we operate out of an old gristmill. It's a neat place, and my dad bought it cheap about thirty years ago when he outgrew his old building. They actually used to make feed there, too."

"Is there still water pumping through it?" Phoebe asked.

"Nah. We keep the sluice gate closed. But you can see the old water paddle and the gears and the millstones. Sometimes people come in just to take a look."

Phoebe signaled for the waitress to bring another coffee.

"You said on the phone that you had something else to share," she said.

"Yeah, it's a detail I never thought to mention to anyone," he said, "but something you said made me realize it might be important."

"It's about the night in Cat Tails?"

"Yeah. I think I mentioned to you that there were a few girls from Lyle College that night. At one point I could tell they were staring at me. And then it looked like they were saying something to each other about me—something kind of catty. I know it sounds stupid, but I felt so flustered I didn't even hit the board one time."

Jeez, Phoebe thought, why didn't he say anything about this earlier?

"Was there a reason you didn't mention this to the campus police?" she asked, her voice neutral.

"Maybe I *should* have," Wesley said. "But it didn't seem to matter at the time. They were the kind of girls who always looked down their noses at me, and they never came that close to me in the bar—at least that I noticed. When I talked to the campus cops back then, I was concentrating on people who were right near me—like that man by the jukebox.

"I wouldn't have even remembered it," he added, shrugging his shoulders, "if you hadn't mentioned that freaky girl group."

"Did you know any of the girls by name?" Phoebe asked.

"No, not at the time," he said.

"What do you mean?"

"Well, that's the most important thing I wanted to tell you. Like I said, I didn't know the girls personally, but I'd seen one of them around. She was really pretty—in a different kind of way—and super stuck up. After you and I talked, I looked for her in my old student handbook, and guess what? It was the name you mentioned to me. Blair Usher."

Phoebe's brain was already on alert as soon as he'd said "pretty—in a different kind of way." She couldn't believe what she was hearing.

"And *none* of these girls ever came close to you that night?"

"Like I said, I didn't notice. But they might have without me being aware. It got pretty crowded in there after a while."

Phoebe let out a breath slowly. Could *Blair* have spiked Wesley's drink that night? she thought. But why? Because he'd been targeted as a loser guy? She wondered if there was any way to find out if

Blair had been in Cat Tails the night Scott Macus had died.

She sipped her coffee. She could feel an odd disquietude taking hold, but it didn't seem to be about the Sixes this time. Something was bugging her, but she couldn't tell what it was.

"This is all very good to know, Wesley," Phoebe said, setting down her cup. "Did you tell this to the police when you talked to them this week?"

"No, I didn't. I wanted to speak to you first."

"Well, this is something you need to share with them, okay?"

"Do you think I'm in danger? Do you think those girls did it?"

"I don't know, but as I said, it's key to talk to the police. Will you do me a favor and not tell them we spoke? They generally don't like civilians intruding on their turf."

Wesley nodded soberly.

Phoebe picked up the saltshaker at the end of the table and ran her thumb over it, thinking. Something was gnawing at her.

"Is there anything else, Wesley?" she asked. "Anything else you remember from that night?"

He shook his head. "No, that's it. I'm surprised I even remembered about that girl. Like I said, if I hadn't talked to you, I probably never would have."

Phoebe thought of the material Hutch had left for her. She knew she shouldn't mention it to Wesley—at least until Hutch gave her the okay—but there was no harm in an indirect approach.

"One last question," Phoebe said. "Do you think there could have been anything significant about that stranger asking you for change?" That was the part Hutch had underlined most heavily.

"Well, if he's the guy who dumped me in the river, he would have needed to get close enough to me to slip something in my beer."

"But why that line?"

"I'm not following," he said.

"Why ask about change?"

"I guess he had to start someplace."

Phoebe wasn't getting anywhere. She signaled for the check and, after paying, walked with Wesley out to the parking lot. They promised to keep each other posted.

She wasn't due at Glenda's for an hour. On her way there, Phoebe stopped to buy a few supplies and groceries at the massive Walmart outside of Lyle—though the idea of cooking anything in her kitchen made her stomach turn. As she passed the boxes of pasta in the store, she thought of how exactly a week ago she'd served Duncan the spaghetti carbonara. Why hasn't he checked up on me today? she wondered suddenly. It seemed like the right thing to do, considering what had happened to her. Maybe what was really going on in the car was a realization on his part that he wasn't as attracted to her as he'd first assumed. Well, she thought ruefully, that solves the Where-is-this-thing-headed? problem.

She shoved her cart through the store, only half paying attention. As she reached the checkout, she spotted a depleted display of candy for trick-or-treaters and grabbed two bags of miniature chocolate bars.

She arrived at Glenda's at exactly noon. Though she knew she was going to have to do some fancy footwork to convince Glenda to let her stick with her research, she was determined to make it happen. The housekeeper answered the door, unsmiling, and led Phoebe into the wood-paneled study off the far end of the living room. Glenda was standing there, but to Phoebe's surprise, the expression on her face registered consternation, not welcome.

"Why are you looking at me that way?" Phoebe asked. The words were barely out of her mouth when she sensed the presence of someone else, and she snapped her head to the right. Tom Stockton and Craig Ball were standing over by the weathered antique desk, both looking stern. Clearly, there'd been some new development, and it was not a good one. Phoebe looked back toward Glenda for an explanation.

"Phoebe, we need to talk to you," Glenda said solemnly. "Something's happened."

Phoebe didn't like the tone of Glenda's voice any more than she liked the expression on her face.

"What's going on?" she asked bluntly.

"A student has accused you of plagiarism."

"That's—that's impossible," Phoebe exclaimed, and even as she spoke, she realized they were the same words she'd used last spring about her book. Her legs suddenly felt like liquid, as if they were about to dissolve. "I mean, I haven't even published anything since I've been here, for God's sake."

"Take a look at this," Glenda said, gesturing toward the desk.

A laptop had been set up there, and Stockton and Ball had clearly been studying something on it. Phoebe crossed the room, forcing herself to breathe slowly. I've got to stay calm, she told herself. It's all some dreadful mistake, and I can't lose control now.

"This is what the student brought to our attention," Glenda said, pointing to the screen. "It's on the blog you do for writers."

Phoebe leaned forward and stared at the page that was up on the screen. It was titled "On Words and Writing," fairly crudely designed, and there was a photo of Phoebe in the upper right-hand corner. She could tell from the dress she was wearing that the picture had been taken at a movie premiere in New York about a year ago. There was a short bio, which oddly stated that she had once edited a poetry journal. The most recent blog entry was titled, "Is Shorter Better?" It took only a moment of scanning the article for Phoebe to realize that though her byline was on the piece, it was actually an essay that one of the male students in her class had handed in as an assignment several weeks ago.

Phoebe reached a hand toward the keyboard, and as she did, Ball jerked forward slightly, as if his first instinct had been to stop her.

"Do you mind?" she said. "I'd like to see what else is here."

Ball nodded curtly, and Phoebe studied the site. There were just two other entries, and both were pieces she'd written as a guest blogger for Huffington Post within the last two years—one on memoirists making things up, and the other on unnamed sources.

Phoebe turned back to Glenda, who looked ashen. "So the guy from my class came across this," Phoebe said, "and reported it to you?"

"To me, actually," Stockton interjected. Phoebe thought she could detect a little excitement in his eyes, like a hound that's just picked up the scent of a fox.

"I hope you don't honestly believe that *I* put this site together?"

"But who else could have done it?" Ball said.

"*Anyone* could have," Phoebe said. She could feel her anger begin to boil, and she warned herself again to simmer down. "All anyone would have to do is go to a site like blogger.com and set up a blog in my name. They could drag a picture of me onto it from another site. And they could add on material I'd written for other sites. The two other pieces here are things I *did* write. As for the essay here that my student wrote, I shared it with everyone in class."

"Are you saying it's a hoax, then?" Stockton said. "That someone created this to make you look bad?"

"Of course it's a hoax," Phoebe said. "Can't you see how crude and amateurish this site is? Trust me, if I was putting together my own blog site, I'd do a hell of a better job than this."

"See what I said, Tom?" Glenda interjected. She turned to Phoebe. "I never thought you had done this."

"Then why call in the cavalry?" Phoebe asked sarcastically. Glenda flinched, and Phoebe turned back to Stockton and Ball.

"If you track the e-mail that set up this site, you'll see it has no relation to me. I'll bet it leads right back to the Sixes."

Then Phoebe stormed out of the room without looking back. As she hurried toward the front door, she nearly collided with Mark, coming out of the conservatory. He gave her a withering glance.

"You're more than welcome to bring yourself down, Phoebe," he said scathingly. "But please don't do the same to Glenda."

Shocked, she just stared back at him. So she'd been dead right about the source of his recent coolness. She started to speak, but bit her tongue. It would only make things worse.

She barely remembered the drive home. She was livid. Evidently the Sixes had created the blog, and Glenda, despite her comment to the contrary, had clearly indulged Stockton and Ball in their investigation. Was that the price that she was always going to have to pay because of the plagiarism charges? Would people always doubt her integrity?

And then there had been the odd reference to the poetry magazine. That was something she'd done in boarding school. Had the Sixes dug up info about her past?

As she entered the house, her heart sank even more. If the Sixes had gone to the trouble of creating the fake blog, they surely would want the word to leak out. Phoebe hurried to her office, shrugged off her coat, and brought up the *New York Post* Web site on her laptop. And there, to her utter dismay, was a short item by Pete Tobias, "Is Phoebe Hall Up to Her Old Tricks?" He stated that a student had accused her of posting his blog as her own and that the school was investigating.

Completely ruffled now, Phoebe called her agent and left a message asking her to call ASAP. I have to fix this fast, she told herself, before it explodes. She also sent an email to the student who'd written the essay, explaining the situation. By the time three o'clock rolled around, she realized that she'd been so distressed she'd forgotten about Hutch. But he hadn't called, so he probably wasn't back yet.

When her phone finally rang at four, it was her agent, Miranda. "What's going on?" Miranda asked bluntly. Phoebe gave her the broad outlines of the situation.

"Why would students do such a thing to you?" Miranda asked.

"I'm caught up in a bit of a mess, which I'll explain later, but you've got to trust me—I've done nothing wrong in this whole thing." Phoebe knew she sounded defensive—guilty even.

"I think we need to marshal the PR team again," Miranda announced. "Let me try to reach them, though it's going to be tough on a Sunday."

By five Phoebe still hadn't heard from Hutch. She called his number, thinking he might have forgotten that he'd promised to call first, but she reached his answering machine.

The doorbell rang shortly after, throwing her off guard. As she pulled the front window curtain aside, she saw four young trick-or-treaters standing outside. "Just a minute," she called. She opened a bag of the miniature candy bars, dumped them into a wicker basket, and headed outside. After the kids trooped away, she left the basket on the porch and turned off the lights in the living room.

By eight thirty she still hadn't heard from Hutch. She felt a small wave of worry, but let it pass. Maybe, she thought, he's been out in his work shed all afternoon and hasn't heard the phone. He might have been thinking she would just come over. She decided to do just that. Not only was she anxious to see him, but also it would be a relief to be out of the house.

She threw on her coat and tore out to the car. As she drove to Hutch's house, she passed bunch after bunch of trick-or-treaters. She felt entirely detached from the world around her, as if she was living in an alternate reality.

As soon as she turned from the road into Hutch's driveway, she smiled in relief. Even through the dense trees, she could see that there were lights on in the cabin, and as she drove closer she spotted both of Hutch's vehicles. He was definitely home.

As Phoebe slammed her car door shut, Ginger shot out from the dark of the yard, making Phoebe jump.

"Hey, little girl. What are you doing out all by yourself?"

Ginger whimpered and leaped into Phoebe's arms. Her body was wet, as if she'd been prancing around in a puddle of water.

"Oh, I hope you haven't been a bad girl," Phoebe said. "Does your daddy know you're out?"

With Ginger still in her arms, Phoebe mounted the porch steps. The dog was wetter than Phoebe had first realized, and she set her down.

Before knocking, Phoebe brushed at the large wet mark now on her coat. It felt sticky, and she pulled her hand away to look. In the porch light, she saw that her palm was smeared with blood.

**21**

P hoebe scooped Ginger up again and scanned the little dog's body for a wound. But she knew she wouldn't find anything; she knew, with a rising sense of dread, that something was horribly wrong. Where was the old retriever? she wondered. Where was Hutch?

She clasped Ginger to her body again and stepped closer to the house. She saw through the outer screen door that the inner wooden door was slightly ajar, opening onto the darkened hallway inside. Phoebe rapped on the frame of the screened door and called through the opening.

"Hutch? *Hutch*, are you there?"

There was no reply, though from somewhere far off in the house—the kitchen, she guessed—came the faint murmur of radio voices.

"Hutch, are you okay?"

Behind her the wind snaked through the trees, making the branches moan. Phoebe spun around. The lamps behind the curtains in the living room were casting a jagged circle of light into the yard through the windows, but beyond that it was totally dark, and she could see nothing but the faint outline of trees. She was anxious to get inside.

"Hutch," she called again, turning back to the door. "It's me, Phoebe." Ginger whimpered softly.

Phoebe breathed deeply and opened the screen door. The spring made a creaking sound as the door opened wide. She pushed open the inner door next and stepped into the entranceway. In the air was the familiar blend of wood smoke and pipe tobacco—and something else. Ginger twisted in Phoebe's arms, fighting to get down, but Phoebe gripped her tightly.

"Hold on, Ginger, it's okay," Phoebe said.

But a second later, Phoebe could see that it wasn't. Stepping from the hall into the living room, she discovered Hutch lying facedown on the floor, just in front of the couch. A pool of bright red blood bordered the right side of his head. And then she saw that blood was everywhere. It was spattered on the couch cushions and on the walls, even on the television screen. Phoebe groaned in despair.

Clutching Ginger, she staggered toward Hutch and knelt beside him. She knew she shouldn't touch anything, but she had to see if he was alive. She set the dog down and groped around his neck for a pulse. She felt nothing, but wasn't sure if she was doing it right. Grasping his shoulders, she heaved the old man onto his side.

She could tell instantly that he was dead. His eyes were blank, his mouth slack. His right temple had been battered and was now a caved-in, bloody mess. Pieces of what seemed to be tree bark protruded from the wound. At the top of his head was another wound, caked with blood.

"No, no," Phoebe wailed, and choked back tears. Ginger scooted from behind her and tried to lick Hutch's face. Phoebe grabbed the dog in her arms and struggled back up to a standing position. She had to call the police—but first she needed to get the hell out of there. She would call 911 once she was in her car and safely out onto the road.

She turned from Hutch's body and started to cross the floor, careful where she stepped. She noticed for the first time that flames were dancing in the wood-burning stove, and it was piled with logs, as if Hutch had filled it only a short time ago. Instantly her brain processed the fact: *This just happened.* Her legs felt rubbery. Get out, get out, she told herself.

And then, directly above her, a floorboard groaned.

She froze in terror. Ginger began to squirm in her arms again, this time more forcibly, and then let out a sharp, tiny bark. Someone was up there, Phoebe realized, directly above her. Was it the retriever? she wondered. But it had sounded too heavy for a dog. No, she told herself, her mind strangely clear and precise. It's the killer.

She didn't dare go back through the front hallway— the stairs leading to the upper floor were there. Instead she lurched through the living room into the kitchen. The radio was playing music now, a peppy song that seemed absurd to her in light of everything. Phoebe flung open the kitchen back door and clattered down the steps.

It was pitch-dark out back, except for a faint glow from the kitchen light and some illumination from a sliver of moon. With Ginger still in her arms, she tore across the yard and into the first few feet of the woods that rimmed the back of the house. If only she could reach her car, she thought frantically, but by the time she made her way around to the front of the cabin, the killer might be down the stairs and outside the house. She had no choice but the woods, where at least she had the cover of darkness.

She plunged deeper into the trees. What little light the moon cast was obscured now by the dense branches.

She could see almost nothing, just the bare outlines of things directly in front of her. She was wearing boots, at least, which made it easier to scramble over tree roots and logs, but the ground was also covered with mounds of dead leaves, and they made a whooshing noise with each movement of her legs. She was afraid the killer would hear her, know where she'd gone. When she was about twenty yards into the woods, she stopped to catch her breath. And to listen.

There wasn't a sound now. The wind had stopped momentarily, Ginger was quiet, too—as if she knew she mustn't make a peep—though Phoebe could feel the rapid beating of the little dog's heart. Phoebe raised the dog slightly, so she could reach into her shoulder bag with her left hand and dig for her phone. Just as she'd managed to unsnap the purse, she heard a noise from back where the cabin was. It was the whooshing sound of someone else moving through the dead leaves.

God, no, please, Phoebe pleaded to herself. She began to move again, but slower this time, trying not to make noise. Branches snagged at her jeans and the sleeves of her coat, and one whipped across her face, stinging her. Still moving, she stuck her hand in her bag and rummaged desperately for her phone. Finally she felt its smooth surface and grabbed it. She quickly pounded in 9-1-1.

"Help me," she told the operator in a whisper. "I'm in the woods, and someone is after me."

"Can you speak up, ma'am, I can't hear you."

"I'm in the woods," she hissed. "Behind Seven—um, Seven-ninety Horton Road. There's been a murder, and the killer is after me."

"Can you describe your location?"

"No—it's just in the woods. Behind the house. Please, I can't talk anymore. He'll hear me. Just send someone."

"I'm dispatching the police, ma'am. Please, leave your phone on."

"Okay," Phoebe said breathlessly.

She began to move again and realized that her feet were soaking wet. Glancing down, she saw that she was in mud, moving along the edge of a small stream. Behind her to the right, she could still hear the whooshing sound. Go faster, she screamed to herself. Faster.

The woods were deeper now, even thicker with trees. She could see only a foot ahead of her, and she was constantly forced to look down, to watch the ground for logs and underbrush. With a jerk, a branch suddenly snared the sleeve of her jacket and wouldn't let go. Her fingers raced in a frenzy over the fabric as she tried to free herself. Finally she just yanked her body away. The sound of the fabric tearing seemed to carry through the woods. But beyond it she heard something else. Somewhere, off to the left, was the distant sound of cars passing by. The road, she thought. If she could reach it, she could flag down a car for help.

The whooshing sound behind her had stopped. Had the killer given up chasing her? She turned around, to be sure. At first all she saw were endless black trees, but then, as her eyes adjusted, she spotted a figure. The person, with a head as smooth as a bulb, stood on a rise not far behind her, illuminated slightly by the moon. Then the person began to move.

"He's right behind me," she nearly moaned into the phone. And then she screamed into the night, "I've called the police. They're coming." Ginger let out a low growl that made her whole little body hum.

Phoebe picked up her pace, forced every few seconds to catch herself from stumbling. Just get to the road, she told herself. The car sounds had receded. She stopped for a split second, just trying to listen. Close by, came the deep, shuddering sound of a truck moving. There, she told herself, and hurled herself forward.

Suddenly she seemed to be in midair, her feet no longer in touch with the ground. Two seconds later she landed hard, and she was rolling, rolling, rolling, over rocks and stumps and logs. She tried to hold on to Ginger, but seconds later she felt the dog being yanked from her. There was a crunching sound next, and pain shot through her arm and her head. Then it seemed as if she was under water, swimming slowly toward a place far away.

There was nothing next, just darkness and silence. And then a light was forcing her eyes open, making her head ache even more. It was from the beam of a flashlight, she realized. Someone was crouching just to her right. Her heart lurched. Was it the killer? But as she tried to lift herself, she saw that the person with the light was in uniform. A policeman. She let her head flop back onto the ground. She realized that she'd passed out, clearly for more than a minute or two.

"Don't worry, you're safe," he told her. He said something else, but she couldn't hear the words, and she closed her eyes. She just wanted to sleep, even though she was wet and cold.

"Miss . . . *miss.*" It was the cop again, his voice stirring her.

"Yes?" she muttered, after struggling to open her eyes. She saw that there were now two cops, one just behind the other. Her head was pounding, and one of her arms ached badly, but she could barely tell which one. She began to shiver.

"An ambulance is on its way," the cop said. "Try not to move, all right?"

Had she been trying to move? she wondered. She didn't remember.

"Okay," she said.

"Can you tell me your name?"

She had to think for a moment. "Phoebe," she said finally. "Phoebe Hall . . . Where am I?"

Even as she spoke the words, she saw from the flashlight beams that she was at the bottom of a small hill. She could see the outlines of two other people with lights walking up on the ridge.

"You're in a ravine," the cop said. "You must have tripped when you were running."

"The dog?" Phoebe blurted out. "She—"

"Don't worry," the cop said softly. "We've got her. She led us to you, in fact."

Then Phoebe remembered Hutch and started to tear up.

"Can you tell us what happened?" the cop asked.

"Hutch. I came to see him. He was dead. And the killer—he was still in the house—upstairs. I . . ."

She wanted to say more, but she couldn't. Everything felt so heavy—her legs and her arms, even her eyelids.

"Can I just sleep?" Phoebe whispered hoarsely. "For a little while?"

"You might have a concussion, so you need to stay awake," he said. "At least until the ambulance comes. Can you do that for me?"

"Uh, I don't know." She felt so weary.

"Is that your dog?" he said. "She's awfully cute."

The cop talked to her then about little things. She could hear his voice droning in her ears, and sometimes she answered. Then there were more people moving around, lifting her. There was so much noise now, and she wanted to tell them, Shush, be quiet, I can't sleep, but no words came out.

She was in an ambulance after that, but she couldn't remember being lifted inside. There was something around her head—one of those protective braces, she thought. The siren made her head ache all over again.

Finally she was in the ER. Doctors and nurses stood over her, tugging off her clothes, prodding her.

"I'm Dr. Morton," a woman said. She was tall and seemed to tower over the table Phoebe was lying on. "Can you tell me where it hurts?"

"My head," Phoebe said. "And my arm. The um— left one."

"We're going to fix you all up, okay?" the doctor said. Her green eyes were warm and caring. "You may have had a concussion, and your left elbow is broken. We'll need to do some tests to see if there are any internal injuries."

"Thank you," Phoebe muttered.

"Is there someone you need us to call?" another woman asked. A nurse, Phoebe thought.

"No, that's okay," Phoebe said. She didn't want Glenda around, but she knew she would have to alert her eventually.

"There are two detectives who want to talk to you, but I suggested they come back tomorrow. We need to make sure you're okay," the doctor said.

Phoebe was in the ER for what seemed like hours. They X-rayed her elbow, and then secured it, and right after that she was wheeled off to another location for a CAT scan of her head. As an orderly rolled her gurney back to the ER later, she wondered what would happen after all the tests were done.

"How will I get home tonight?" she muttered to the orderly.

He chuckled. "Oh, don't worry about going home. We're checking you into our fine hotel for the night. Rest assured, it's four stars."

Eventually she was brought to another floor and hoisted onto a bed for the night. She drifted off again, though she was aware of people coming in and out of the room, checking on her.

At some point her eyes popped open, and she felt suddenly wide awake. It was dark outside, but there were low lights on in the room, and she could see that she was in a private room with just one bed. The door was open, and from the hall she could hear the low murmur of voices and the occasional sound of something being wheeled. She was on painkillers, she knew, but she sensed they'd begun to wear off—there was a dull ache in her head, her elbow, and, she realized for the first time, also in the left cheek of her butt.

As the minutes passed, her mind began to clear. She forced herself to go over everything, picking up a thread and following it backward. She had injured herself falling down a ravine in the dark. Someone had been chasing her. Hutch's killer. Her face tightened in anguish as she thought of the kind man she had known so briefly. He had been brutally murdered, beaten to death. There was a chance, of course, that it was a burglary gone bad, but her gut told her it was about the investigation—the one she had lured Hutch into. She felt sick with guilt. Who was the person who had stood on the ridge? She had seen only the outline, but she remembered that the person's head had seemed smooth as a skull.

Phoebe thought of Ginger then. Where *was* she? With relief she remembered what the cop with the flashlight had said. *She led us to you.* The police must have her. But what about the retriever—where had he gone? Hutch had said he had a nephew, and somehow

Phoebe needed to contact him—to tell him about Hutch and to ask him to track down the dogs.

Odds and ends began to fight their way to the surface of her mind. *Her purse and her phone.* Surely the police had found them, or at the very least they would still be in the woods. *Her car.* It was still at Hutch's. It was almost Monday, she realized, and she would have to miss class. She had to let the school know.

She shifted position, turning a bit onto her right side. She became aware that the pain was getting stronger now. She found the call button, and a nurse came in, giving her more medication. As she drifted off to sleep again a few minutes later, a gray light was seeping in around the edges of the window blinds. At least the night is over, she consoled herself.

The police wasted no time getting there in the morning. Phoebe had woken around seven, when a nurse came in to check on her. He'd helped her out of bed, and in the bathroom she was surprised to see that her tumble had remaining her with a black eye and a crosshatching of scratch marks on her face. The nurse had pointed out that her purse was safely tucked away in a cabinet by the bed. With the little battery power she had remaining in her phone, she left a message for the department chairman, Dr. Parr, explaining she had been injured and would not able to teach today.

Breakfast arrived next—damp toast and limp-looking scrambled eggs.

As she was poking at the food, she heard a light knock on the open door to her room. It was the pink-faced Detective Michelson, who walked in without waiting for her to reply. A slim Asian man accompanied him.

"Feeling any better?" Michelson asked her.

"Yes, much," Phoebe said. As she scooted up to a seated position in the bed, she nearly yelped from how much her butt hurt.

"This is Detective Huang," Michelson said, nodding toward his colleague. "As you can imagine, we're both anxious to talk to you."

"Of course," Phoebe said. She hadn't been forthcoming with the police previously, but she was now going to do everything she could to help. "Did you catch the killer yet?"

"Unfortunately, no, the person is still at large."

Michelson took the chair closest to the bed, splaying open his legs; Huang dragged an extra chair across the room for himself.

"Why don't you take us through everything—from the beginning," Michelson said. Huang drew a notepad from his coat pocket and flipped the cover over. Both men reeked of fresh aftershave, and the smell, mixing with the gamy hospital odors, nearly made Phoebe retch.

"First, there's one thing I need to tell you about Hutch," Phoebe said. "He has a nephew in Allentown. Can someone contact him?"

"Yes, we've already been in touch with him," Michelson said.

"And what about the dogs? Are they both okay?"

"The nephew has the little one. She's fine."

"But what about the retriever? I never saw her last night."

Huang shot a glance at Michelson that wasn't returned.

"Unfortunately," Michelson said, "she was hit and killed by a car last night. She must have wandered out onto the road after Mr. Hutchinson was murdered."

Phoebe lowered her head as she felt tears well in her eyes.

"Miss Hall," Michelson urged. "We need to hear your story. It's essential for our investigation."

She obliged, taking them through every detail she could think of, knowing it all could be important. At the end she thought to add that the only vehicles she'd seen in the driveway were the Honda and the pickup truck, which she assumed were both Hutch's since they'd been there on her previous visit. For the first time she wondered how the murderer had arrived at the cabin.

"And you can't make a guess whether the person who chased you was a man or a woman?" Michelson asked.

Phoebe shook her head. "Last night I thought it must be a man because the head seemed so smooth—as if he was bald. But since then I've realized it could have been a cap or the hood of a sweatshirt."

"Any revealing characteristics?"

Phoebe shook her head. "Not really. I'm not sure of the height because I couldn't see where the ground began. My sense, though, is that the person wasn't *short*. Or particularly large."

Michelson glanced down at his notebook, thumbed back a few pages, and then looked back up.

"And what were *you* wearing last night?"

"*Wearing?*" Phoebe asked, puzzled.

"Yes," Michelson answered bluntly, not bothering to elaborate.

"Jeans, a sweater . . . um, a wool peacoat. They're probably in there." Phoebe pointed her chin toward a closet. Huang jumped up, crossed the room, and opened the closet door. Everything was there and folded, except for her coat, which drooped forlornly from a hanger. She saw that the left sleeve had been sliced open by someone who'd treated her last night, but she had no memory of it.

"That's it—no hat, gloves, scarf?" Michelson asked.

"Some gloves," Phoebe said. What was this about, she wondered. "I assume they're still in the coat pocket."

"All right, let's switch gears now," Michelson said as Huang returned to his seat. "What prompted you to visit Mr. Hutchinson last night?"

His tone had suddenly shifted from courteous enough to plain blunt. Phoebe could feel her head start to throb again.

"I'm glad you got to that, because it may be relevant," Phoebe said, though she knew Michelson would be ticked once she came clean. "As Wesley Hines may have told you, I spoke to him last week. I then shared what I'd learned with Mr. Hutchinson. He asked me to come over to discuss it."

Michelson looked incredulous at this news. "It's hard to imagine how a faculty member came to be pals with the former campus police chief," he said, frowning.

"On behalf of Dr. Johns, I've been checking out some of the problems created by the River Street bars—and I ended up speaking to Mr. Hutchinson for background. He had interviewed Wesley last fall after the river incident, and we talked about whether it might be connected to the drownings. Hutch—er, Mr. Hutchinson, thought he'd found something important."

"Are you saying Mr. Hutchinson was *investigating*?" Michelson said. His face seemed to get even pinker. She realized that his blue, blue eyes and hot pink skin were a color combo that definitely appeared in nature—pink-tinged clouds on the horizon at sunset, for instance— and yet it just didn't work well on a human face.

"Not investigating per se," Phoebe said. "Hutch was worried that he might have been wrong to dismiss Wesley's story last year, and so he'd reviewed his old notes. Can you pass me my handbag?"

Huang retrieved it from the cabinet. With her right hand, Phoebe dug out Hutch's notes and handed them to Michelson, glad she'd made a copy since she was sure she wasn't getting these back. She didn't have a copy of her *own* notes to give him but she saw no reason to bring it up. The exact same things had been underscored by Hutch in both sets of notes.

"He told me a lightbulb went off for him when he saw the notes again," Phoebe said as Michelson scanned the pages intently. "He didn't want to discuss it until we were face-to-face."

"As far as you know, did he share these notes with anyone else?"

"He didn't say. But of course, now I'm wondering if he *had*."

"I'll keep these, then," Michelson said, folding the notes and tucking them into the inner pocket of his jacket. "And I'm going to tell you just this once, do you hear me, Ms. Hall? Let the police handle this business."

"Yes, of course," Phoebe said, trying to look contrite. "I never meant to interfere. I thought I was just helping the college."

"There's one other matter we need to discuss—these incidents at your home. As you can imagine, I wasn't happy to learn that the first ones hadn't been reported to the police."

Phoebe started to offer an explanation but bit her tongue. The less said the better, she knew. Besides, she wasn't sure exactly how Ball had worded his excuse.

"Well, I'm glad you can investigate *now*," she said. "I hope you can find someone to look at my kitchen. There's still blood in my dishwasher, and the spoons are on the counter."

They made arrangements, and Phoebe handed over her front door key, which Michelson promised to return as soon as possible. He also said he would have the police deliver her car to her house.

Michelson rose from his chair then; Huang followed suit just a second behind him, as if, like the perfect sidekick, he'd picked up an infinitesimal cue. As Michelson buttoned his coat, he trained his eyes directly on her.

"You live alone, correct, Ms. Hall?" he asked.

His tone was ominous, almost disapproving.

"I do," she said. "Why?"

"You need to be very careful going forward. Do you understand?"

"Are you saying you think the Sixes might try to pay me another visit?"

"I have no idea. But there's a chance that the person who murdered Mr. Hutchinson will."

# 22

"I don't understand," Phoebe said, flustered. "What threat do I pose to the person now? They managed to hightail it away from the scene of the crime."

"If Mr. Hutchinson discovered something incriminating in the notes and alerted the person, it may be the reason he was killed. And the person, having seen you at the cabin, may suspect you'd been talking to Mr. Hutchinson about what he'd found and are still putting two and two together."

Phoebe swallowed hard. "Tell me. Were Lily and Trevor murdered?" she asked. "If you think Hutch's death is connected to the drownings, then you must suspect those drownings weren't accidental."

"Ms. Hall, it seems you like playing Nancy Drew. You need to stop."

His comment was almost as good as a yes.

"I'm not playing detective now," Phoebe said. "I'm simply trying to assess what kind of risk I'm facing."

"I think you need to take this seriously—that's all I'll say. If possible, stay with a friend for a few days just to play it safe."

Fat chance, she thought. She basically knew only two people well in Lyle, and she wasn't on wonderful terms with either of them at the moment.

"Good day, then," Michelson said. "And just so you know, we're not sharing your involvement last night with the press. It's a detail we want to keep under wraps for now, partly for your own protection. And of course, we expect you to remain mum about what you know of the crime."

With that, the two cops departed. Phoebe drank the last of the tepid tea. She could feel fear creeping up the sides of the bed around her. I can't just lie here and come undone as I did at fifteen, she told herself. She had to try to figure out the revelation Hutch had experienced. As soon as she was home, she would scour the notes again. But first she had to spring herself from the hospital.

She reached for the call button, but before she pressed it, a man with a stethoscope draped around his neck entered the room and introduced himself as Dr.

Awad, part of the same "team," he said, as the doctor who'd treated her last night.

"You feeling a bit better today?" he asked. He was good-looking, Phoebe thought, and no more than thirty-five.

"Yes, much better," Phoebe said. "I'd like to be able to go home today."

"Well, let's see how you're doing first," he said. "You did have a mild concussion, and we like to keep an eye on those. How's the pain on a scale of one to ten?"

"No more than a one or a two," she told him, which wasn't exactly the case. But she thought she could manage if they sent her home with painkillers.

After scanning her chart, he listened to her heart, asking her to take quiet breaths. Next he drew a penlight from his pocket and examined her eyes with it. Then he explored her skull with his hands—searching for swelling, she assumed. When he was finished, he stepped back and studied her.

"Your elbow has just a hairline fracture, but you need to keep your arm in a sling for six weeks. As for your head, your tests were all good, and you seem fine now. Why don't we let you enjoy our fabulous lunch here, and then send you home in the afternoon. It will give us a bit longer to monitor you."

As soon as the doctor left, Phoebe felt suddenly ambushed again by fatigue, and within moments she was asleep. She had a dream, an endless, irritating one in which she was overheated and sweaty, stuck in a room where people were making too much noise. "Please transfer me," she told someone who refused to listen to her. She woke to her good arm being lightly touched. Forcing open her eyes, she found Glenda hovering over her.

Phoebe grinned before memory caught up with her. She was still pissed at how Glenda had handled the fake blog incident; her friend had sandbagged her.

"Hey," Phoebe said neutrally.

"Fee, tell me you're okay," Glenda said.

"Yeah," she said, struggling. She pulled out one of the pillows from behind her and tucked it under her injured arm for support. "Unless you count the fact that I look like I fell face-first into a briar patch."

"I feel totally to blame—I dragged you into this awful mess."

"Neither of us could have predicted anything like this. When did you hear the news?"

"I heard about Hutch last night. At first I assumed he'd been killed during a break-in. This morning Craig told me that he'd heard from his contacts in the police department that someone else had been injured at the scene—a woman. But I had no clue it was you. I knew you'd talked to Hutch that one time, but I would never have guessed that you were out there on a Sunday night.

And then, late this morning, Dr. Parr's office called to make sure I knew you were in the hospital, and suddenly I put it together."

"Sorry not to call you myself. My phone ran out of battery."

"I figured you didn't call because you were still livid with me."

"Well, that too."

Glenda slipped out of her dark red coat and folded it across the arm of the chair near the bed. She was wearing a long-sleeved black dress with a flattering high waist. On her neck was a pearl choker. Glenda's motto had always been: If you *look* cool in a crisis, people's first impression will be that you are. And yet Glenda's face told another story. It was drawn, and she had deep circles under her eyes.

"Fee," Glenda said, settling into the chair. "I *never* for a second thought you'd concocted that blog site or lifted that kid's essay. You've got to believe me."

"Then why not discuss it with me alone and hear my take? Why subject me to an inquisition in front of Stockton and Ball?"

"It was all coincidental. Tom had a number of urgent things to discuss with me, so I asked him over before our lunch. While we were talking, Ball burst into the house with the laptop. He'd told us about the blog seconds before you arrived. I should have demanded they leave and talked to you myself. I wasn't in any way accusing you, though. I was just shocked by it, and concerned."

Glenda was right, Phoebe thought—she *should* have asked the men to beat it before discussing the matter with Phoebe. But it wasn't such a big infraction that Phoebe couldn't let Glenda off the hook now.

"Have the tech people made any progress tracing it?" Phoebe said, her voice softening.

"Yes and no. They traced it to a fake e-mail account, but it's a dead end from there."

"Well, the *New York Post* has already posted an item. I need the school to release a statement saying I'm completely in the clear."

"It's already in the works. Now tell me about last night."

Phoebe shared the story, as well as the conversations with Hutch that had led up to it. When she'd finished, Glenda slumped back in her chair and let out a ragged sigh. Phoebe could see her friend felt truly anguished by what she'd heard.

"I just have such an ache in my heart about Hutch," Glenda said. "He was a good, good man—and it's horrible that he died in such a brutal way."

"This must be making things even worse on campus," Phoebe said.

"You bet. Everything up to now seems like one big May Day festival. Two girls have actually withdrawn—forced to, I'm sure, by Mommy and Daddy."

Glenda pinched her lips together. "I've got to ask you," she said. "Do you think the Sixes killed Hutch?"

It was a question Phoebe had asked herself more than once as she lay in her hospital bed—both in her drugged stupor and later with a clearer head.

"My answer's probably going to surprise you," she said. "Because for days I've been trying to figure out if they were behind the drownings. And yet my gut tells me they didn't do this."

"Are you thinking it seems off-brand for them?" Glenda asked. "That they may run around in their Frye boots pushing students into rivers, but they wouldn't beat an old man to death?"

"I'm not saying they *didn't* do it. Wesley remembers Blair being at Cat Tails the night he went into the river, and it could be she drugged him as part of this pattern of targeting so-called loser guys. There's a chance that as Hutch looked back into the river incidents, he saw something that clearly implicated the Sixes and he called Blair, tipping her off. She then showed up at his house—alone or with other members—and killed him.

"But there's a flaw to that theory," Phoebe continued. "I keep coming back to the fact that Hutch told me that a big clue lay in the notes about Wesley. And there was nothing in those notes about either Blair or, for that matter, *any* girls from Lyle College."

"If the Sixes didn't kill Hutch, who did? Are we back to the serial killer theory then?"

"Possibly," Phoebe said somberly. "But with a twist."

"Explain," Glenda said.

"Stockton talked about drownings in the Midwest and north of here and how those deaths might be related to the ones in Lyle—that they could be all the work of a killer who moved around the country. But I'm thinking the killer may be someone local. In the notes, Hutch heavily underlined a part about this guy who tried to chat Wesley up at the jukebox. That could have sounded familiar to Hutch for some reason. He mentioned to me that he had pals on the police force here. Maybe in the last year he'd heard tales of a local predator that operates this way but hadn't connected it back to Wesley until he reread the notes."

"You're scaring me big-time," said Glenda.

"I know, it's a sickening thought, but if Hutch figured it out, I might be able to too."

"*You?* Phoebe, you cannot take this on, especially after what happened. Do you hear me?"

Phoebe reassured Glenda that she wouldn't do anything that put herself in more danger. Before Glenda left, Phoebe asked that she track down the number for Hutch's nephew in Allentown.

The next few hours were interminable. A patrol cop stopped by to return Phoebe's house key, but that was her only visitor. After lunch an elderly woman rolled in a cart, offering the local newspaper, which Phoebe snatched eagerly to see the murder coverage. There was a small box on the front page about it, likely squeezed in at the last minute because the paper wouldn't have had time for a longer report. As guaranteed by Michelson, there wasn't a word about her.

Using her right hand only, she thumbed through the rest of the paper, just to give herself something to do. There were endless pictures of trick-or-treaters—kids dressed as Wolverine and Bat Girl and Harry Potter, and babies posing as strawberries, pea pods, and bumblebees. Someone *had* been killed on Halloween after all, Phoebe thought ruefully. Against her will, her mind found its way back to the sight of Hutch lying dead on the floor. If the killer hadn't come by car, how had he or she gotten there? she wondered. Hutch's cabin was too far out of the way for someone to have walked the entire distance. The killer must have parked somewhere and then reached the cabin by foot through the woods. Phoebe decided that as soon as she could, she would drive along the road and see if she could locate the spot—it might offer insight into who the person was. Something seemed to swim in front of her brain about this, but as she reached out for it, it slipped away.

Finally she was cleared to go home, and she alerted Glenda, who had offered to come back to pick her up. A nurse helped her dress, stretching the sweater carefully over her elbow, replacing the sling, and then draping her ruined peacoat over her shoulders. She was given an envelope of Tylenol with codeine and instructions on caring for her injured arm. The idea of going home filled her with dread. She thought of Duncan. She wondered if he had heard she was in the hospital.

It was cold and bleak outside, the sky once again covered with sooty smudge marks. But Glenda was back in kick-ass mode, a woman on a mission.

"By the way," Glenda said, as she navigated their way out of the parking lot. "Stockton was asking about you earlier today. He heard from Cameron Parr that you'd had an accident, and he was trying to suss out the facts. I told him you'd been injured but that I didn't know any details yet."

"Is he using Hutch's death to keep fueling the flames of panic?"

"Don't know. But Madeline told me that at one of their strategy meetings, he made a comment about how the college should have put more pressure on the police when Trevor Harris disappeared. By the college, he means *me*. It's pretty clear he's finding little ways to undermine me."

"You know, I'd almost forgotten," Phoebe said. "Saturday night I stopped in at Cat Tails to see it for myself, and I found Stockton there. Claimed he was scoping the place out because it was tied to all the drownings."

"Or he was looking for a student to hook up with."

"What do you mean?" Phoebe asked.

"When I first started at Lyle, I tried but couldn't get a bead on him—like why he'd leave a really prominent institution to come here. About six months ago, an old pal of mine started working at the college Stockton left, and so in light of his behavior lately, I called her the other day to see if she could learn anything on the down-low. I heard back yesterday. Apparently Stockton was rumored to have had flings with female students. It's not illegal for a professor to have an affair with a student, but it can be dicey, and most colleges frown on it, particularly if it's a pattern. And a dean of students is technically in charge of all the students, so it's even more complicated. Apparently he tried it one too many times at the last place, and they eased him out."

"Any hint he's done it here?" said.

"None. He's either wised up or has learned to be more discreet. But regardless, it backs up my instinct that he's not to be totally trusted." She paused as she switched car lanes. "By the way, you're bunking down at the presidential palace tonight. We can swing by your place first to get a change of clothes and whatever else you need."

Part of Phoebe longed to be tucked away safely in that yellow guest room tonight, but she knew she had to take a pass.

"I really appreciate it, G, but like I said before, I'd only be putting off the inevitable."

"I'm not taking no for an answer."

"There's another reason why it's probably best that I don't." She told Glenda about Mark's comments to her in the hall.

"He's got a lot of nerve," Glenda snapped. Phoebe had never seen her speak of her husband with such bite.

"What's happening on that front?" Phoebe asked.

"It's just more of that secretive thing, and it's started to work my last nerve. This past weekend I found a receipt for a restaurant that he hadn't mentioned eating at. He claims he was with a client, but he seemed flustered when I asked him about it."

"Are you thinking he's having an affair?"

"I came right out and asked him, and he told me I was being paranoid. It's funny. He's the one guilty of weird behavior, but I'm the one who's being made to look crazy."

Though she'd never been tight with Mark, Phoebe hated the idea of Glenda's marriage possibly unraveling. Especially now, in the middle of all this other mess.

"What about trying some marriage counseling?"

"Yeah, I've thought about that. But I can't do it right this moment. I need to focus on keeping the damn college together."

Driving down Hunter Street, Phoebe saw long strands of toilet paper dripping eerily from the tree branches. They were from last night, she realized, the handiwork of some devilish trick-or-treaters, and yet to her they seemed like a warning. *Go away. This is not a place for you anymore.* I don't *want* to stay on this street tonight, she thought, but where the hell can I go?

As they pulled up in front of her house, Phoebe spotted her car in the driveway and she grabbed the keys from inside, where the police had left them for her, before entering the house with Glenda. The cops had definitely checked out the scene inside—there were sooty marks on the kitchen counter where they'd taken fingerprints, and the spoons were gone. Slowly Phoebe eased open the dishwasher door and saw to her relief that they'd run the wash cycle. As Glenda waited, she did a search of the other rooms, and then the two hugged good-bye.

Once Glenda had left, Phoebe charged her phone and called the number for Hutch's nephew, which Glenda had provided. Reaching only voice mail, she left a message offering her condolences and saying she wanted very much to talk to him.

Next she listened to a string of voice-mail messages on her own phone. Craig Ball had made contact, asking that she debrief him about Hutch's murder. Though Michelson had said they were keeping her involvement under wraps, Ball had managed to find out about it—probably from contacts he had in the police department.

There was also a follow-up call from her agent, as well as the Lyle College tech guy, wanting to discuss the fake blog. Dr. Parr had tried Phoebe twice to see how she was doing, as had two other people in the English department, including Jan. And to her surprise, two of her students had called just to tell her they were thinking of her. She was surprised at how good the calls from them made her feel.

Not a peep, though, from Duncan. Surely by *now* he would have heard she'd been injured, and his failure to contact her stung. It also told her everything she needed to know. He'd been attracted to her initially, she was sure of it, and yet something had happened to dampen his ardor—perhaps he disliked her playing detective as much as Michelson did. She doubted she'd ever find out the real answer.

She was anxious to go through Hutch's notes again, but she had also begun to feel slightly lightheaded, probably from having eaten so little. She rooted around the fridge for dinner, trying to find something that wouldn't involve chopping, and finally plucked out two eggs to scramble. She could tell that having one arm in a sling was going to be a bitch to deal with.

It was nearly dark out, and she felt her unease starting to grow. The house seemed oppressively silent. I need music, she thought. She popped in a Neko Case CD and turned the volume up high.

The eggs turned out not to be as easy to prepare as she'd counted on, but she managed to beat them and pour them into a frying pan. While they cooked, she tried to focus on the music, but she could feel panic circling her. What if the killer was staking out her house right now? Tomorrow, she would investigate getting a security system installed. She didn't care what the hell it cost.

She flipped off the gas, and at the same time a song ended. There was utter silence. And then a sound. A footstep. Her whole body froze. Someone was walking in her living room.

*S*he was never sure how they'd snuck into her room. Glenda had gone home that weekend, and she was on her own, but she was sure she had locked the door. Somehow they had gotten their hands on the master key. She wondered later if the RA had let them in.

At first she thought there was someone crumpled on the floor in a heap, and she had frozen, startled, and fumbled for the light. Her clothes had all been shredded into pieces. But it took her a moment to realize that they'd been arranged in a pattern—the shape of a wheel. Fortune's wheel.

# 23

She spun around, instinctively grabbing the handle of the frying pan—to hurl or to swing it. To her utter shock, she saw Duncan standing in the doorway of the kitchen.

"What are you doing here?" she blurted out. Whatever relief she felt at the sight of him was overridden by her distress. How had he gotten *in*?

"Uh, sorry," he stammered. "I just needed to find out how you were. The mailbox on your phone was full, and then when I showed up at the hospital, they said you'd already been released."

"But how did you get in the house? The door was locked."

"It wasn't, actually. I knocked a few times, but I guess you couldn't hear me over the music. I tried the door, and it was open."

Phoebe brought her right hand to her forehead and massaged it, thinking.

"Sorry I sounded so frantic," she said after a moment. "Glenda brought me home, and in my foggy state, I must have forgotten to lock it again after she left."

"Well, I didn't mean to scare you out of your wits. I'm just glad to set eyes on you." He smiled mischievously. "I'm also thrilled to know you're a Neko Case fan."

She let out a long sigh and smiled back. So he'd obviously been concerned about her.

"Want some scrambled eggs?" she asked. "For some reason I've decided to prepare the same thing they served at the hospital."

"I've already eaten, but why don't you sit down and let me do it?"

"I'd like that. Have a glass of wine at least. On the counter."

He slipped out of his coat and hung it on a peg by the back door. As he slid the eggs onto a plate, Phoebe settled at the table. She watched him butter the toast. She could feel her earlier panic subsiding. After Duncan finished serving her, he poured a glass of wine for himself and sat across from her.

"I've been really worried about you," he said. "I heard about Hutch, and the fact that you found him."

She wondered how he could have heard, since the cops told her they were keeping things under wraps.

Before she could ask him, Duncan reached out and stroked her forehead.

"I'm just glad you're okay," he said. "Or maybe I shouldn't assume that. *Are* you?"

"A mild concussion, a small fracture on my elbow."

"Tell me what happened."

As she went through the saga again, Duncan asked only a few questions, and mostly let her talk, but his eyes betrayed how disturbed he was by her story.

"You must have been terrified," he said when she'd finished.

"Completely," she said. She'd lost her appetite as she spoke, and now her eggs lay cold and bloblike on her plate. "It was like one of those recurring nightmares where you just can't seem to move fast enough."

"And you never got a good look at who was chasing you?"

"No. But I started thinking that if I stop trying to force my mind to work, something is eventually going to come to me."

"What do you mean?" he asked. His soft brown eyes were quizzical.

"Have you ever had the sense that something is scratching at your brain? That there's a thought trying to reach you, but when you try to grab it, it retreats like a mouse. So you just need to be patient and wait. Sorry, there must still be a trace of painkiller in my system. I sound kind of loopy."

He cocked his head. "No, I hear you. What you're saying is that there's something in your subconscious trying to break free. Do you think it's about the killer?"

"Maybe," Phoebe said. "It could be something I saw last night that I didn't fully acknowledge, or maybe something I picked up from reading Hutch's notes." But even as she spoke, she realized that the sensation had first started with something Wesley had said at the diner. Maybe, she realized, the smell of the eggs tonight had retriggered that disquietude.

"Why don't I take a look at the notes at some point," Duncan said. "Maybe a fresh pair of eyes will help."

"Sure, good idea," she said.

"And if something *does* come to you over the next day or so, don't keep it to yourself. This is a dangerous situation. You understand that, right?"

"I know," she said. She felt her panic rear its ugly head again. "I appreciate your coming over tonight. I thought—I guess I had this feeling I might not hear from you again. Something seemed off between us Saturday afternoon."

Duncan leaned back in his chair, crossing one leg over the other and resting his wine glass against his chest.

"That was completely my fault," he said. "And I'm sorry about that. It didn't reflect how I feel about you."

Phoebe waited, not saying anything. It seemed best to let it all just unfold.

Duncan brushed twice at an unseen object on his thigh. She realized how seldom she'd seen him make a nervous or awkward gesture. Finally he looked back up at her.

"Something a little weird happened on Saturday," he said. "At the inn."

So she'd been right about the timing then, she thought. "Between us?" she asked.

"No, no," he said. "It happened when you went to the ladies' room. A couple that Allison and I used to spend time with came into the restaurant. I was never crazy about them, but the woman was a friend of Allison's from high school and the two of them became tight again when we moved back East. I waved to them from the table—I was about to get up to go over and say hi—and they just completely ignored me. Made eye contact and looked away very intentionally."

"Was it because they'd seen you with me, do you think?"

"No, you were in the restroom when they walked in. I'm pretty sure Allison badmouthed me to this woman right before she died. Allison grew very bitter as her illness advanced, and though I couldn't blame her, it was tough to live with. Her take was that our marriage was on the rocks because of me—that I had just announced one day I was bailing. And that I was sticking around through her illness just to make myself look good."

"I'm sure when I came down and joined you at the table, it only made things worse."

"Probably. Right after you showed up, they paid for their half-finished drinks and left. I'm sorry I let it get to me. The whole situation with Allison sometimes comes back to haunt me."

"I can understand. I've been dragging around plenty of baggage myself this fall."

"Speaking of baggage," Duncan said. "I want you to come stay with me tonight. I don't like the idea of you being here on your own."

"That would be great, actually," Phoebe said. And she knew she was feeling more than just relief over not having to stay in her house alone, checking and rechecking every entry point. Things seemed back to normal with Duncan, and that, she realized, was something she hadn't thought would happen. "Let me just round up my toothbrush and a change of clothes."

"Why don't you plan to stay for at least a couple of nights? I think it would be smart to hang out with me till the cops have caught this maniac, or at least have more information." Phoebe agreed.

In her office, she grabbed her laptop and with her good hand stuffed a tote bag with files she would need for class as well as her notes from Wesley and the copy she'd made of Hutch's. Her eyes roamed toward the back of the table where the file of inspirational clippings for her next book sat forlornly. She started to reach for it but then stopped herself. Who the hell am I kidding? she thought.

Next Phoebe hurried upstairs, took an overnight bag down from the top shelf of the closet, and tossed a few days' worth of clothes in it.

She followed Duncan to his house in her car so that she'd have it. Duncan kept his speed at around thirty, making it easy to follow him. When she arrived at his house, she felt suddenly exhausted and dressed for bed immediately. With her arm starting to ache, she popped one of the painkillers she'd been given. As she crawled into bed, Duncan slipped into the room and sat down next to her.

"I'm going to read in the next room for a while, but just give me a shout if you need anything," he said.

She slept deeply that night, stirring just once. When she woke in the morning, her brain felt sodden, as if it had been packed with wet towels. She was afraid she'd missed Duncan, that he must have already headed to class, but just as she inched her way into a sitting position, he popped into the room, carrying a mug with steam coming off the top.

"I heard you stirring, so I thought you might be ready for coffee."

"Oh, that's great. I still feel a little drugged out. Back to straight over-the-counter meds today." She took a sip. "You don't have a class this morning?"

"Not till ten, but I'm going to head out in a second to check on things at the lab. There's stuff in the fridge for lunch. Can you think of anything else you may need?"

"No, I'll be fine. I'll drop by campus at some point but probably hole up here for the day and rest."

"Sounds like a good plan." He lowered himself onto the edge of the bed, and with a firm stroke of his hand, brushed Phoebe's hair from her forehead. Then he leaned down and kissed her softly on the lips.

"By the way, don't even *think* about making dinner," Duncan said. "I already have a plan for that."

Two minutes later she heard his car pull out of the driveway. Somehow Duncan's presence had helped keep her grief at bay, but as soon as she was alone again, it was back. She had known Hutch only briefly, but she had liked him, had even imagined herself staying in touch with him through the school year, sharing the occasional cup of coffee. There was no escaping the fact that she could be partly to blame for his death. If she hadn't solicited his help, he may not have been murdered.

Her mind kept whipping back to the sight of Hutch dead, his face horribly battered. It was terrible to imagine his last moments and the pain he must have felt from those blows. Phoebe focused for the first time since that night of the rough, gray wood slivers protruding from Hutch's face. Had the killer used a piece of firewood as a weapon? she wondered suddenly. If that was the case, it seemed to suggest that the murderer hadn't arrived at Hutch's cabin with the express purpose of killing him.

So what did that mean? She'd surmised before that Hutch must have tipped off the killer—in person or by phone. But maybe Hutch hadn't said anything too specific; perhaps he had just *hinted* at his suspicions. So the person—or persons—had tracked down Hutch's address and dropped in on him, probably catching Hutch totally off guard. In the conversation that ensued, Hutch might have elaborated on what he knew, trying to flush the person out. And he could have overestimated his ability to control the situation.

The fact that the killer had parked his car elsewhere reflected a need for secrecy, so even if murder hadn't been premeditated, the person wanted to be sure his— or her—car wasn't spotted at the cabin by anyone.

After summoning her strength, Phoebe finally propelled herself out of bed. As she drank another cup of coffee, her phone rang from inside her purse.

"Where the heck are you?" Glenda demanded before Phoebe could even get a hello out. Glenda sounded more worried than miffed.

"You went by my house?"

"I'm out front now. I pounded on the door, but there's no answer."

I'm busted, Phoebe thought. Now I have to spill about Duncan, and she's going to be mad that I've kept this from her.

"I'm not there. I'm—I'm at someone else's house. A guy's."

Glenda snickered good-naturedly.

"Did you pick up some cute doc at the hospital?" she asked. "I have to say that those tread marks on your face haven't managed to make a dent in your looks."

"No, not a doctor. It's someone from Lyle. He came by last night and suggested I stay with him for a few days."

"You're dating a *townie*?"

"No, I mean Lyle College. We've only had a few dates, and I've been meaning to fill you in, but there's always been something more pressing to deal with these days. You aren't pissed, are you?"

"Of course not—unless it's my husband, of course. You gonna tell me who?"

"Duncan Shaw. I met him on a committee. He's in the psych—"

"Yeah, of course I'm familiar with him."

There'd been something abrupt in Glenda's tone that perturbed Phoebe. She wasn't sure if it reflected Glenda's views of Duncan or the fact that she'd been left in the dark.

"You don't sound that tickled," Phoebe said.

Glenda waited a half beat before answering.

"No, I hear great things about him as a teacher. The kids love him. I—I just don't know him socially. But I'm glad you've got someone now. This is a time when you could really use a safe haven—and a warm body, too."

"I'll fill you in more when I see you."

"Okay. How are you feeling, anyway?"

"Achy, but on the mend."

After she'd signed off the call, Phoebe sat quietly for a moment and replayed the conversation with Glenda. There'd definitely been a weird undercurrent, but she didn't know what it sprang from. She'd have to wait until she was face-to-face with Glenda and force it out of her.

Phoebe slid off the kitchen stool, retrieved her laptop, and checked the local paper on line for their latest coverage of the crime. This time it was a big story, prominent on the home page—though once again it contained no mention of her. For a brief moment it felt as if she had simply read about the crime and then envisioned the whole awful thing in her mind. But she *had* been there, and the terror she'd felt seemed to be hovering just over her shoulder.

Well, don't just sit there, she told herself. She found Hutch's notes in her purse and laid them out on the kitchen island. For the next thirty minutes she went over them again meticulously, even saying out loud the parts Hutch had underlined—in case the *sound* of the words triggered a revelation. But she got nothing. Frustrated, she dug out her own notes and went over the parts Hutch had underlined there. But they were virtually identical to what he'd marked in his. Still no insight.

I need a shower, she thought suddenly, something to help defog this damn brain of mine. It had been two full days since she'd had one. It proved to be slightly tricky showering with her injured elbow in a bathroom she was barely familiar with.

As the hot water streamed over her, soothing her aching muscles, Phoebe let her mind find its way back to the Sixes. Though she'd been fixated on Hutch's murder since Sunday night, she knew she also had to stay focused on exposing the group, since there was still a chance that they were tied to Lily's death—and even to Hutch's. I need to find out who else is a member, she told herself—and what the fifth and sixth circles are.

Maybe it's time for another chat with Jen Imbibio, she thought. Though Phoebe had been undecided about whether Jen might be a member, she sensed the girl *knew* something.

With just a towel wrapped around her, Phoebe typed an e-mail message to Jen on her laptop. She told her that there was a small matter she needed to chat with her about and asked that she get in touch by phone.

As she tramped back to the bedroom to dress, Phoebe could feel her energy starting to wane a little. She couldn't let that happen. There was plenty she needed to do today, including making a trip to campus. She planned to give Ball a debriefing, per his request, and also because she was eager to learn if he knew anything about Hutch's murder.

She dug out a fresh pair of jeans and a top from her overnight bag and struggled into them. She'd just run a brush through her wet hair when a sharp buzzer sound tore through the house, startling her. It wasn't until it had rung a second time that Phoebe realized it was the doorbell. Who could it possibly be? she wondered. An alarm bell went off in her head. Had the killer tracked her to Duncan's? Well, he sure as hell wouldn't be ringing the doorbell, she chided herself.

She slipped into the great room and made her way to the front door. It was solid wood, but there was a tall, narrow window on each side of it. She was going to have to look outside and see who was there. But before she could move toward the window, the person on the other side of the door took a step to the right on the stoop, and leaned forward, peering in through the glass.

Phoebe caught her breath. Val Porter was standing there, staring right at her.

## 24

Phoebe's first urge was to duck and scuttle back into the bedroom, but it was clear Val had seen her, and so she had no choice but to go to the door. What the hell was Val doing here, anyway? Phoebe wondered. Was this part of her plan to win Duncan over—just popping by in the morning to say hello?

Phoebe crossed the room and swung the door open.

"Good morning, Val," she said. "If you're looking for Duncan, I'm afraid he's already headed over to campus."

Val ran her eyes over Phoebe—her bruised face, her bare feet, and back up to her wet hair. Then Val smiled slyly, as if the two of them were in on the most wicked little secret.

"I was just dropping off something for him. Do you mind if I come in for a second?"

She's got to be kidding, Phoebe thought. She wants to *prolong* this awkward little moment?

"Sure," Phoebe said, not knowing how she could refuse.

"Looks like you've had an accident of some kind," Val said, as Phoebe closed the door behind her. Val was wearing a long plum-colored coat today, with brown stiletto boots, and her hair was pinned up on the top of her head again, showcasing those silvery tendrils around her face. "What in the world happened?"

"I took a bad fall off my bike," Phoebe replied. She'd already worked out this explanation as she lay in her hospital bed.

"Oh, dear. I'm so sorry. I bet it hurts."

"A bit, yes."

"But it appears that Duncan's taking good care of you. I didn't realize you two were seeing each other."

"I guess even at a school as small as Lyle, news doesn't *always* travel fast. How can I help you, Val? You said you wanted to drop something off?"

"Oh, right, I'm sorry," she said, with a trace of condescension. She dug into the brown leather tote bag she was carrying, withdrew a book from the bag, and then hesitated.

"Actually," she said, "I should really give this to him in person. Why don't I just catch up with him another time."

"Sure," Phoebe said.

Val smiled slyly again and tucked the book back in her tote. She gazed around the room appreciatively.

"He's created a wonderful space, hasn't he?" she said to Phoebe with a familiarity that suggested she'd been there before.

"Yes, very nice," Phoebe said. A code blue alert went off in her mind.

Val looked back at Phoebe and gripped her eyes with her own. "It's tragic about his wife, isn't it?" she said. "But at least she left him the money to do all the things he really wanted to, like this house."

Against her will, Phoebe could feel her face begin to form an expression—of perplexity, of surprise—but she fought it and tried to simply stare back at Val.

"Is there anything else I can help you with, Val?" she asked. "I need to get ready to go over to campus myself."

"No, no, I'm going now," Val said, heading back to the door. "Feel better."

After closing the door behind Val, Phoebe collapsed on the sofa and swung her legs onto the coffee table. She leaned her head back and closed her eyes. Her head was starting to ache again, not the agonizing hurt she'd experienced in the hours after the fall, but an odd sensation of someone gripping her head in their hands and squeezing.

She blamed Val for the headache. The zinger she'd delivered—the comment about Duncan and the money—had managed to get under Phoebe's skin. Had Duncan really inherited a bundle from his wife? she wondered. Had that had something to do with his decision to stay with her through her illness? He seemed like a good guy to Phoebe, not someone capable of using his wife. Val had probably deliberately misstated the situation because she'd been so pissed to find Phoebe at Duncan's. It was crazy to dwell on it, Phoebe realized. She needed to get moving.

When she reached the campus security building a half hour later, she found that the mood there seemed more energized than it had on her last visit. Phones were ringing, and two officers were huddled in the reception area, discussing their patrol plans for the day.

There was only one other visitor in the office, a girl reporting to Mindy that her meal card had been stolen. When the student finished and turned away from the desk, Phoebe stepped up and saw that Mindy's eyes were still puffy from an apparent crying jag. Phoebe gave her name and said that Ball had asked her to stop by.

"He's in with a student right now," Mindy said, "but I'll let him know you're here."

"I'm very sorry for your loss, by the way," Phoebe said after Mindy had buzzed Ball. "I'd come to know Hutch a little, and I'm sure you cared about him a great deal."

"He was like a granddaddy to me," the girl said, dabbing at her eyes with a wadded tissue. "I just feel so awful about what happened."

Behind Mindy a door creaked, starting to open. Mindy dropped the balled-up tissue in her lap, slid her chair up to the desk as tight as possible, and began to thumb through a stack of papers. A second later Ball stepped into the open area behind Mindy, followed by a male student whose boyish face suggested he was probably a freshman. Ball nodded toward Phoebe in recognition, and she saw his eyes circle over her bruised face. Then he turned to the boy.

"Think about what I said, Kevin, and get back to me," Ball told him bluntly. The kid nodded his head gloomily, and skulked off toward the door. As he passed by Phoebe, she saw that his green sweatshirt read Philadelphia Eagles, and she realized he was the same kid she'd spotted Ball talking to the evening she'd walked up to the science center.

"Thank you for stopping by, Ms. Hall," Ball said, commanding her attention. "Why don't you come in now?"

She snaked around Mindy's desk and followed Ball into his office. The space was as nondescript as the rest of the small security building—metal desk, file cabinets, industrial-looking lamps—except for the fame wall. There were at least a dozen photos of Ball with various dignitaries who'd obviously visited the campus—the governor, a few mid-level rock singers, and a book author Phoebe figured Ball had never actually heard of. He gestured for Phoebe to take a seat in the chair opposite his desk and slid into his own chair, which appeared to have been jacked up to give him extra height.

"Campus troublemaker?" Phoebe asked as she sat down.

"Excuse me?" Ball said, frowning.

"That kid who just left. Is he a campus trouble-maker?"

"Why would you ask that?" Ball said.

"I saw you talking to him the other day."

"Just some information gathering on my part," Ball said, folding his arms on the desk.

"Related to the drownings?" Phoebe said.

"No, Miss Hall, it was not," Ball said, brusquely ending that line of discussion. "Speaking of Mr. Hutchinson, why don't you tell me what happened. It will be just between us, of course. I know the cops are keeping your involvement hush-hush for now."

She gave Ball a bare-bones version of the events, mindful of the fact that the police didn't want her sharing key details, but also aware that Ball was in the loop to some extent because of his contacts. When she was done, she leaned forward in her chair. She could tell he was about to fire questions at her, but she wanted to jump in.

"I'd love your thoughts on the crime," Phoebe said, trying to sound just the right amount of ingratiating. "Do you think it was a burglary that went wrong—or something else?"

Ball twitched in his chair. Phoebe sensed that he was both annoyed at being cut off and flattered to be asked for his opinion.

"You can't expect me to hypothesize without seeing any of the evidence," he said. "And Michelson, unlike his predecessor, isn't one to share. But what I hear from some of my buddies on the force is that there was no sign of a burglary. There's a chance, of course, that you interrupted it when you arrived, but if that was the case, how were they going to cart anything out of there? They couldn't very well lug it through the woods to their car."

"So they parked along the road somewhere," Phoebe said, keeping her voice neutral. "That's what I'd figured."

Ball hesitated before answering. "Possibly," he said, though the slight shift in his eyes told her that he knew something in this regard, may have even checked out the site himself. It was clear Ball liked snagging info, but not sharing it.

"If it wasn't a burglary, then what's your best guess—without seeing any evidence?" Phoebe asked.

"You'd probably make a better guess than me," he said, "since you were at the scene. Did it look like he'd been taken by surprise?"

"I'm sorry, I'm not supposed to discuss details of the actual crime scene," Phoebe said.

Ball laughed, with a hint of a snicker to it. "We're all working toward the same goal here."

"I know. But as you indicated, Michelson is a real stickler about not sharing."

"Fair enough," he said, though his tone suggested he thought otherwise. He picked up a pencil and began to tap it against the fleshy palm of his tanned hand. "I've a question for *you* now. How'd you and Mr. Hutchinson get to be so buddy-buddy?"

"We were hardly that," Phoebe said. "I'd talked to him a couple of times because of the research I was doing into the Sixes."

"And what was that trip to his house Sunday night about? Just another chitchat session?"

"Yes, we were going to touch base. Mr. Hutchinson told me he had some information he wanted to share. It might have been important, but unfortunately I never had the chance to hear it."

Ball raised his eyebrows—they were same silver gray color as his hair—and pulled his mouth into a kind of trout pout.

"He give you any hints?"

"No, nothing, I'm afraid." Phoebe was suddenly anxious to leave. "Is there anything else? I should be on my way."

"That's it," he said. "This must all be very trying for you. Do you need a lift home, or do you have your vehicle?"

"I've got my car, thanks," Phoebe said, rising.

"Speaking of which, Officer Hyde told me he didn't see your car in the driveway when he drove by your home last night. I was concerned, needless to say, but assumed you might be staying with Dr. Johns."

"Um, actually, I'm staying with a friend for the next few days."

"Could you let me know when you return, please? I don't want to deploy a man to check an empty house each night when our resources are already stretched."

"Of course," she said. She assumed he'd enjoyed the opportunity to slap her wrist.

Her next stop was going to be her office, but as she headed toward the quad, she passed a couple faculty members and was struck by their double takes when they saw her face. She realized she'd be best off waiting until tomorrow to show up at Arthur Hall. Her bruises would be fading then, and she'd reduce the chances of people buzzing about her.

She turned and headed back to the eastern parking lot, feeling suddenly weary and achy again. This part of the campus, away from the quad and the plaza, tended to be quiet, and it was no different today, even with all the turbulence going on elsewhere. She had the path to herself, except for the dried leaves that chased each other ahead of her. It's so deserted here, she realized, and instinctively she spun around, checking behind her. What if the killer knew who she was and was tracking her movements? By the time she reached her car, her stomach was twisted in a knot.

The entire way back to Duncan's, she kept her eye on the rearview mirror, and she locked the door carefully once she reentered the house. She staggered into the bedroom. Not only was she fatigued, but her headache had intensified, and there was now a piercing pain in her elbow. Maybe she'd overdone it, she thought. Though her stomach was grumbling from hunger, she popped half a pain pill and fell onto the bed, letting sleep overtake her.

She stirred once during her nap, aware that dusk was descending and that she should turn on some lights, but she felt too leaden to move. She was asleep again almost instantly.

She woke the next time with a start, her heart racing and her body sticky with sweat. The room was dark. She'd had a nightmare, she realized, and the terror still had hold of her. In the dream she'd been back at Hutch's house. She'd just walked in the front door and discovered Hutch on the living room floor, but this time he was alive, moaning. It was an odd kind of moaning, almost like the mooing of a cow. And then there was someone else in the room, off to the left and wearing a black cloak with a hood covering his face. She'd gasped, and slowly the person had lifted the hood to reveal his face. It was Dr. Parr, the English department chair.

Where in the world is Duncan? Phoebe wondered, using her good elbow to prop her body up. She glanced at the digital clock: 5:20. She fumbled for the bedside lamp and turned it on, creating a pool of light along the side of the bed.

She struggled out of bed and into the bathroom. It had been ages since she'd napped during the day, and she felt jet-lagged, slightly disoriented. After dabbing a cold, wet washcloth on her face and pulling her hair into a ponytail, she wandered out to the great room. In the dark, the unfamiliar shapes of the room seemed ominous, almost threatening. She had no clue where the lights were, and she fumbled around the room for a minute, trying to locate the switch on the wall. Finally she found it by the door. The moment she touched the button, the room was flooded with light from the dozen or so small fixtures in the ceiling.

After pouring a glass of sparkling water, she found her phone and checked for messages. Duncan had called once to see how she was doing—she had stupidly forgotten to bring her phone into the bedroom with her. He'd also sent an e-mail about an hour ago. "I hope you're napping. I'm running later than planned but will be home by 7. DO NOTHING ABOUT DINNER." She smiled. His message assuaged some of the weirdness she was feeling.

Two hours later, when she heard Duncan's key turn in the lock, Phoebe was ensconced on the couch with her laptop, reading the news online.

"Hey there," he said when he spotted her, "how's the patient?"

"On the mend," she said, smiling.

"Sorry about being so late," he said. "I had an unexpected issue with a student."

She crossed the room to meet him. His hair looked a little wilder than usual, obviously ruffled by the wind. He was carrying a bag of groceries, and he set it down in order to shrug off his coat. When she reached him, he took her into his arms and kissed her.

"You look a little better," he said. "Your black eye is more yellow now than purple. That's a good sign."

"And a more flattering color for me, I think," she said.

"I want to hear all about your day," he said. "But first let me make a dent with dinner. I've got two great steaks I'm going to grill."

She returned to the sofa and to her laptop. As she read, she could hear Duncan moving between the kitchen area and the deck off the back of the house. After so many nights alone in her little house on Hunter Street, it felt both good and odd not to be all by herself.

"So Glenda called this morning," Phoebe said when they sat down at the table. "I hope you don't mind, but we're busted. She'd gone by my house, and I didn't feel comfortable lying to her."

Duncan smiled. "I don't mind. I mean, there's no policy against it. And people are going to start seeing us in public. Hell, we may become a fixture at Tony's."

So he *was* thinking of them as a couple, she realized.

"Well, there's one person who may *not* like seeing us in public. Val Porter dropped by to see you after you left today. I wouldn't have answered the door, but she saw me through the window."

Duncan smirked. "That's a woman who doesn't like to take no for an answer. Was she surprised to find you here?"

"Yes—and she even made a snide remark." Phoebe decided she was too curious not to bring it up.

"About?"

"About how nice it was that your wife left you plenty of money so you could buy this house."

He shook his head in disgust. "Val kind of redefines the word *feminist*, doesn't she?" he said. "Though she wasn't lying. I did end up with a nice nest egg."

"That doesn't seem like anyone's business but yours," Phoebe replied. She said it nonchalantly, but she knew she wanted him to elaborate.

"True, but I'm happy to explain it so you know the facts. Allison had a small trust fund from a grandparent. Nothing major, but decent enough. To my surprise she left it to me."

"How does Val even know about the money?"

"There was probably talk behind my back after Allison died. I've taken some trips; I've gutted this house." He smiled tightly. "But enough about Val. Any more news about Hutch?"

"Not that I've heard."

"We should take a look at the notes. You brought them, right?"

"Yes, we can look at them after dinner. I did have one interesting insight, though not related to the notes."

Duncan smiled. "I thought you promised not to keep this stuff to yourself."

"It just occurred to me a little while ago. I had a terrible nightmare when I was taking a nap. In the dream I was at Hutch's house, and this time the murderer was right there in the room with me. And it was Dr. Parr."

"Wait," Duncan said. He pulled his head back in surprise and then smiled. "Are you saying *Parr* is the murderer?"

"No, no, of course not," Phoebe said. "But I think what my subconscious was saying was that it's someone Hutch was *familiar* with. If I buy into the idea that he was killed by someone who he contacted after reading the notes, that would explain how he could find the person so quickly. He *knew* him. I'd already considered that the killer was a local person, but it could even be someone on campus."

"That's alarming," Duncan said. "Any thoughts who it might be?"

"I know so few people here yet, besides the students in my classes, of course. Does anyone jump to mind for you—anyone who's ever struck you as, I don't know, strange?"

"Off the top of my head, no, but as we know from history, killers so often wear the mask of sanity. They can seem perfectly ordinary by day. They sometimes even have wives and kids."

"Maybe something will occur to you when you see the notes."

Duncan insisted on doing the dishes, and Phoebe repositioned herself on the couch as he worked. A phone rang, and she realized after a second that it was hers. She upended her purse and grabbed it, seeing from the caller ID that it was Glenda.

"Hi there," Phoebe said.

"Are you sitting down?" Glenda asked.

"Yes, why?" Phoebe's whole body tensed, and in the kitchen area Duncan stopped in mid-action, sensing something from her tone.

"I've got news."

"What is it?" Phoebe demanded.

"The police have made two arrests in Hutch's death. Blair Usher and Gwen Gallogly."

## 25

"Fee?" Glenda asked.

"Yes, sorry—I'm just in a state of shock," Phoebe said. So it *had* been them, she thought. Her breath felt stuck in her chest. "How—how do they know?"

"Typically, Michelson is giving nothing up."

As she'd been speaking to Glenda, Phoebe had watched Duncan drop his dish towel and move toward the living area. He was standing directly in front of her now. He flipped his hands over, palm sides up, and let his mouth fall open. His whole body was asking, What the hell is going on?

Phoebe raised a finger, asking him to give her another minute. She was anxious to share the news with him, but she wanted to make sure she'd heard everything.

"Are they implicating them in Lily's death, too? And Trevor's?"

"I don't know if they've managed to do that, but I assume they're trying. The only motive I can think of for them killing Hutch is that he linked them to the drownings."

"How will you handle this?"

"I've scheduled a meeting with my staff in five minutes to figure out what kind of damage control we need to do. Word is out about the Sixes. We'll probably use the old there's-always-a-few-bad-apples-in-the-bunch approach. But listen, Fee, thank you for all your help on this. If you hadn't started this ball rolling—"

"—then Hutch would not be dead."

"You can't think like that," Glenda said. "We had no idea they were that dangerous. There's the doorbell. Everyone's coming to the house for the meeting, so I better scoot. Let's catch up tomorrow, okay?"

"Okay." Phoebe disconnected her phone and looked up at Duncan. "You're not going to believe this," she said. She relayed the news.

"Wow," he said, plopping down onto the couch beside her. "And so it must have been one of them following you through the woods."

"I guess so," Phoebe said. She hadn't been certain if her pursuer had been male or female, but she was having a hard time connecting either Blair or Gwen to the form that had stalked her. She wondered what evidence the police had found linking the girls to the crime.

Duncan raked his hand through his hair. "It's going to seem like a bomb went off on campus tomorrow. Too bad *U.S. News and World Report* doesn't measure notoriety for their college rankings. I bet we'd finally break the top one hundred."

"Yeah, I just hope the board doesn't hold it all against Glenda."

"And how are *you* feeling?"

Phoebe let out a long sigh. "Relieved, I suppose. Maybe I can stop looking over my shoulder now. It's just . . ." Her voice trailed off.

"What?" Duncan asked, his dark eyes quizzical.

Phoebe reached behind her head and shook her hair out from its ponytail.

"I guess I was wrong," she said.

"What do you mean?"

"I didn't really think that it *was* the Sixes."

"But you thought it was a *possibility*."

"Yes, but . . ." She struggled off the couch and paced before the stone fireplace. "I keep asking myself what Hutch saw in the notes that pointed in their direction. Of course, his contacting them may have had nothing at all to do with what was in the notes. Maybe he got a hold of them for another reason—he'd heard about them from me and might have begun to investigate them separately. And once he made contact with them, they went on the defensive."

"Could be," Duncan said. "Here, why don't you let me see those notes?"

After retrieving them from her purse, she brought them to Duncan, explaining the difference between the two sets. He tugged a pair of reading glasses from his shirt pocket and began to peruse the pages. While he read, Phoebe watched the flames do their repetitive dance in the fireplace. Her good arm touched Duncan's, and she could feel the warmth of his body through his shirt. It had been ages, she realized, since she'd hung out with a man on a couch after dinner. In the last years with Alec, their lives had been so busy in the evenings. After dinner there was more work, phone calls, answering e-mails, or often packing for a trip.

Duncan scrunched his mouth. "You're right about there not being a single reference to any college girls in here."

"Maybe Hutch found out about Blair being in the bar some other way," Phoebe said. She rested her head briefly against the back of the sofa. She was tired and knew she wouldn't figure this out tonight. "I probably should hit the hay so I'm fit for class tomorrow." She turned to smile at Duncan. "But what do I do about my face? I was hoping the bruises would be mostly gone, but they're turning out to be stubborn little bastards."

"Hey, you're the campus hero and those are your battle scars."

"But as far as I know, I'm still not suppose to disclose that I was at the murder scene. By the way, I never asked how *you* found out I was there."

Duncan ran a finger back and forth along his lower lip and looked off, thinking.

"It was Miles who told me you were in the hospital," he said. "I think he said he heard it from Cameron Parr."

"No, I mean about me being at Hutch's."

He paused. "Well, I hope this doesn't land him in hot water," Duncan said, tucking his glasses back into his pocket. "But Mark Johns told me." He eased up into a standing position and tossed the notes on the table.

"Mark?" Phoebe said, totally surprised by the revelation. "Why would he volunteer that to you? Glenda didn't know about you and me until today."

"It just came out during a brief discussion we had," Duncan said. "I think I mentioned to you that he might be teaching a course with us, and I bumped into him in the building on Monday. Miles had just told me you were in the hospital, and I'd also just heard about

Hutch's murder—though I didn't know the two were related. I brought up the murder to Mark, thinking he might know something via Glenda. And that's when he said that you'd been injured at the scene."

"That was before I'd told Glenda the cops were keeping it under wraps, so she wouldn't have told him yet not to say anything," Phoebe said, following the sequence but annoyed nonetheless. "And yet he should have known to be discreet."

"Please don't let Mark know I said anything," Duncan said. "I don't want him ticked at me. Ready for bed?"

"Hmm, yes. Though I might grab some fresh air out on the deck for a few minutes. I've spent most of the day indoors, and I could use it."

As Duncan headed for the bedroom, Phoebe slid open the back door. There was a real chill to the air, but it was just what she needed. The house had grown warm, because of the fire, and she'd been having a hard time focusing.

She crossed the deck to the railing at the far end. A light at the back of the house was on, and she could see that Duncan's yard was a decent size, nicely landscaped. In the far back were several rows of fir trees, blocking a view of his neighbors. She glanced up. A zillion stars were scattered across the sky, and she could see the filmy swaths of the Milky Way. Orion towered above the trees.

If Blair and Gwen really *had* killed Hutch—and she assumed the police had enough evidence to arrest them—that meant Hutch must have become suspicious of them and telegraphed that to them. They killed him to protect themselves. I was lucky, Phoebe thought, that they only used their scare tactics on me.

So that meant Hutch had stumbled onto something linking them to the drownings or to Wesley's fall in the river, or both. Something that wasn't in the notes. But *what*? she wondered, yet again.

Suddenly a thought jumped in front of her, like a night bird lighting on the railing of the deck. Maybe Hutch had contacted Wesley himself. He might have wanted clarification of a few points in the notes, and Wesley could have told him about Blair being in the bar. She would call Wesley first thing tomorrow and find out.

Of course that didn't explain all the underlines, she realized, but Hutch may have come to see that the clue he'd spotted in the notes didn't amount to anything in the end.

Phoebe turned to go inside and then stopped. Duncan had shut off most of the great room lights, but there was still a light burning in the kitchen. He must have left it on so she could find her way. She realized that now that Hutch's killer had been arrested, there'd be no reason for her to have to hole up at Duncan's. Well, she thought, it would be tough to function indefinitely in a space that was not her own.

When she entered the bedroom a minute later, Duncan was standing by the bed in his gray boxer briefs, setting the alarm clock. Despite her fatigue and achiness, she felt a surge of desire shoot through her. She slipped into the bathroom, quickly washed her face, and changed into her pajama pants and camisole. He was in bed when she returned, propped up against the headboard and staring at a corner of the room, as if deep in thought.

"I didn't even ask about *your* day," Phoebe said. She crawled in beside him, mindful of her elbow.

"Mine paled compared to yours," he said, directing his gaze at her now. "It was all pretty routine."

"What about your student?"

"Student?"

"The one with the unexpected issue."

"Oh, yeah. Smart kid, but the statistics part is totally over his head. He's tried tutoring, and it's just not working. He's probably going to have to switch majors. You ready for lights out?"

"Yup."

He switched off the swing lamp by his side of the bed. Phoebe lay on her right side, facing him, and in the dark she felt him shift his body closer to her. Duncan found her face with his hand, cradled it, and kissed her softly.

"Good night," he said. "I'm sure you'll feel even better tomorrow."

She felt a twinge of disappointment. Should she just boldly announce her intentions? she wondered. But Duncan was already on his back again, pulling the covers up. Of course he's not going to assume I want sex tonight, she told herself.

She thought she would fall asleep instantly, but when she closed her eyes, an image she had fought off all night made its way into her mind—Blair battering Hutch with a piece of firewood. Tonight should have brought a sense of closure, or at the very least the beginning of closure, but she felt troubled and discontent. And the nap had been too long. As she drifted off nearly an hour later, she realized she'd never heard from Jen Imbibio. She would grab her after class tomorrow. Blair and Gwen might be arrested, but the school still needed to shut down the Sixes.

In the morning she and Duncan took turns showering and drank their coffee quickly at the kitchen counter.

"Look, I know I offered my place while the killer was still at large," Duncan said, "but why don't you stay a few more nights? You're still in recovery mode."

"What if I take a rain check till later in the week," Phoebe said. "I need to organize things at home."

She left a few minutes ahead of him. It was colder out today than yesterday, and as she struggled to put on her gloves, one dropped to the ground. Stooping to pick it up, she felt a thought wiggling into her brain. At the hospital, Michelson had asked what she'd been wearing on Sunday night, and when she'd shown him her coat, he'd said, "Is that all?" The question had perplexed her. For the first time she wondered if the police had found an item of women's clothing at the murder scene, something they needed to eliminate as Phoebe's before linking it to the killer. So maybe that was one of the clues that had led them to Blair and Gwen.

Before heading to campus, Phoebe stopped briefly at her place. She unpacked her duffel bag, threw a load of clothes in the wash, and dropped some of the files she'd taken to Duncan's back on her desk. Before leaving, she scooped up a few pinecones from the edge of her backyard and arranged them in a bowl on the coffee table. She wanted to feel safe again in her little house, but she wondered if she was being naive. According to Alexis, there were at least forty members of the Sixes. If someone else was really pulling the strings, they might still be a powerful force, even with a piece cut off.

She drove to campus. The scene, when she arrived, was just as Duncan had predicted—as if a bomb had gone off. People were gathered everywhere in clusters—talking, gesticulating, shaking their heads in dismay. A strong wind added to the disarray and tore across the quad, grabbing papers and candy wrappers and tossing them aside in a snit.

It didn't take long to see that Blair and Gwen's arrest had had a big impact inside the classroom as well. Nearly every student in her first class appeared hyped up, as if they'd dropped a couple of Adderall at breakfast. Though Phoebe had applied makeup over her bruises and scratches, they were still partially visible, but the students seemed too wired to notice. She decided to confront the situation head on.

"You must all be feeling pretty churned up," she said once all the students were settled in their seats.

No one spoke for a moment, just looked at her in that slack-jawed style they so often resorted to in class, but finally a girl named Jackie lifted her shoulders in bewilderment and called out, "It just feels like, you know, everything's out of control. All the kids are going ape shit. There's press everyplace. And our parents want us to transfer."

"Yeah," a boy named Andy said. "I mean, I've heard of Skull and Bones. But who's ever heard of a secret society on campus that actually *murders* people they don't like? That's freaking crazy."

"Okay, I've got an idea," Phoebe said, coming out from around the table she generally sat at. "We're journalists, right? Let's *cover* this. I want everyone to form a big circle with their chairs. We're going to pretend we're a media company, and we're going to decide how to handle this on a variety of platforms. Some of you will report on it—talking to the police, and the administration. Some of you will write essay-style blogs. A good topic might be how you feel about the intrusion of the press in *your* life, or about the strain of trying to keep your parents from freaking out. You game?"

The students nodded their heads enthusiastically, and for the next hour they talked about the various angles of the crisis on campus and how they might cover it. Then they divvied up the assignments. It was part newsroom, part therapy session. The kids seemed enthralled. How ironic, she thought, that not one of the students suspected how deeply she was entrenched in the story.

As soon as class was over, she flew up to her office, closed the door, and called Wesley. He would be at work right now, but hopefully he would answer his cell phone. She reached only voice mail and left a message. Less than five minutes later, he called her back.

"I'm glad you phoned," he said. "I've been going to call you ever since Monday, but I was feeling so weird about everything."

"What do you mean?" she asked.

"That guy Hutchinson who died. I feel really strange about it."

"Why?" she urged.

"He was the head security guy who interviewed me after I woke up in the river. You know, the one who just seemed to dismiss my whole story."

"I know, I know," she said impatiently. "But why do you feel so weird?"

"Well, he called me last Sunday, after I saw you. He said he'd been reviewing some notes about the case. I was about to blow him off, but he admitted that he might have misjudged the situation last year.

"I went over the details from that night with him," he continued. "But this time . . . well . . ."

"What is it, Wesley?" Phoebe said. Christ, just spit it out, she wanted to scream.

"I told him about that girl Blair being there. That I hadn't mentioned it the first time because I didn't think it was important. And then he goes and gets killed, and those girls get arrested. I feel really guilty."

So Phoebe had been right. Hutch *had* contacted Wesley. After learning about Blair, he'd obviously pursued the lead on his own.

"You still there?" Wesley asked.

"Yes, I'm here. And no, you shouldn't feel guilty. How would you have known what they were capable of?"

"I know what you're going to say next. You're going to tell me to call the cops again. I already did. I called them right away once I heard about Hutchinson's death."

"Good," Phoebe said. "Did Hutch ask you any specific questions about that night at Cat Tails?"

"Hutch? Oh, did you know him yourself?"

"Yes, a little bit."

"I don't recall him asking any specific questions. He just wanted me to go over that night again. You know, describe everything I could remember."

"Did he give you any hint about what was on his mind—I mean, about any theories he might have had?"

"No, he didn't let on about anything to me. He just said once more that he was sorry he hadn't taken my situation more seriously last year—and that was it. Excuse me a sec, will you?" He turned from the phone. "If you're looking for the fifty-pound bags, they're against the wall."

"One more thing, Wesley," Phoebe said when she had his attention again. "Hutch reviewed the notes he and I both took about you being in the river, and he said he found something important in them—though he never had the opportunity to share it with me. By any chance, did he mention those notes to you?"

"Um, no. He just seemed interested in that girl, Blair."

"Okay," Phoebe said, frustrated. "If something occurs to you, just leave me a message."

After signing off, she tossed the phone down and rested her chin in her hand, thinking. Something still gnawed at her, something she couldn't see.

Her phone rang, and she swung her eyes toward it on the desk. The screen displayed a number she didn't recognize.

"Hello, Phoebe," a man's voice said as soon as she picked up.

Her body tightened in surprise as she realized the caller's identity.

Alec.

# 26

"Hello, Alec," Phoebe said trying to keep her voice casual. "What's up?"

"What's *up?*" he asked, as if her question had baffled him. But why wouldn't she ask that? The last time she'd actually spoken to the man was back in April, when he'd been sweet enough to update her on his new relationship status. After that there had been a few final details for the two of them to sort out about bills and joint possessions, mostly handled via e-mail. Oh, I've got it, she thought: he needs information of some kind—the name of the hotel they'd loved in Aix-en-Provence, or whether his winter coat might still be stuffed in the back of her hall closet.

"Well, I doubt you're calling to see what costume I wore for Halloween," Phoebe said. "What can I do for you?"

"To be perfectly honest, I was simply calling to ask how you were."

Oh, please, Phoebe said to herself. He can't think I'd buy that.

"My phone doesn't recognize the number on the screen," she said. "Did you change jobs?"

"I did, actually. I'm with a new firm—Searles, Minka and Holt. Still in midtown, though."

That was interesting, she thought. Had it become uncomfortable or too intense for him to work in the same firm as his new squeeze?

"I know you liked your firm," Phoebe said. "Was this just too good of an offer to turn down?"

"More or less. But I didn't call to talk about my new job. Like I said, I was wondering how you were doing."

"Um, good, I guess. I'm enjoying teaching. And it's been great to be around Glenda."

A few seconds of silence followed. Phoebe found herself growing annoyed. Obviously Alec had an agenda, and she wished he'd just get it over with.

"That's it?" Alec said finally. There was a tightness to his voice that Phoebe recognized. She'd ticked him off with the brevity of her response.

"I'm not really sure what you're looking for, Alec," Phoebe said. "It's been months since we've talked. Do you want to know how my love life is? Or if there's career life after plagiarism? If you can be more specific, I can probably do a better job of answering you."

Don't go all bitchy on him, she told herself. It's not worth the psychic energy, and besides, you'll regret it later.

She heard him take a breath. "There's no reason to be sarcastic, Phoebe," he said. "I read the *New York Post* stories. They said there might be some sort of a serial killer out there, and your name was mentioned in the same story. It also said someone on campus had accused you of plagiarism. I just wanted to be sure everything was okay."

She still sensed an agenda hiding cagily somewhere, but she knew the best strategy would be to respond politely—and then hustle him off the phone.

"It's nice of you to inquire, Alec. The plagiarism charges, by the way, were false. The *Post* will be running a retraction this week."

"And you're okay?"

She glanced down at her left arm, her fingers curling slightly out of the end of the sling.

"Yes, I'm fine," she said. "Thank you for asking. And how have *you* been? Happy with the job switch?"

"Yes, quite happy. Coincidentally, I have a client in Allentown, which isn't all that far from you, I believe. I need to see him next week, and I was thinking that if I met with him in the morning, I could drive down afterward and take you to lunch."

She nearly laughed in surprise. She'd not seen this coming at all. Not only didn't she have a shred of interest in his offer, but she thought he had a lot of nerve to ask.

"I don't think so, Alec. But thank you for thinking of me."

"Do you mind my asking why not?"

"Hmm, let me see how to put it. You announced out of the blue you were done with the relationship and moved out. You didn't even bother to get in touch when the tabloids were beating me to a bloody pulp. And then suddenly you want us to have a friendly lunch together."

She'd really lost it that time, but she didn't care.

"Out of the blue?"

"Pardon me?"

"You said I announced out of the blue that I was done with our relationship. Maybe if you'd been paying attention during the previous year, you would have realized things weren't right for us."

"Oh, were you sending smoke signals along the horizon, and I failed to notice them?"

"You just don't get it, do you, Phoebe?" Alec snapped.

"Obviously not. Why don't you tell me what I can't seem to get?"

"You never see when something's wrong because you're always too preoccupied with your research. You lose sight of everyone, including yourself. It's like you don't really want to connect—or ever get your feet wet emotionally."

She didn't think Alec could affect her anymore, but she felt the sting of his words.

"Which implies that on the other hand, you were there for me," she said. "But at a time when I needed you most, even just in friendship, you didn't bother to pick up the phone. I have to go now. Good-bye."

As she disconnected, she felt like hurling her phone across the office. She couldn't believe how much she'd let him get to her.

Her next class was in just a few minutes, and she needed to cool down and to splash some water on her face, which she could sense was beet-red. After gathering her things, she hurried to the ladies' room at the end of the hall.

As soon as she entered the small vestibule, she heard a noise coming from one of the stalls. She realized after a moment that someone was vomiting. The toilet flushed then, and a second later she heard the person emerge and turn on the water at one of the sinks. Phoebe stepped inside, expecting to find a student there, a girl with a painful secret perhaps.

But it was Val who was standing at the basin, dabbing at her mouth with a tissue. She made eye contact with Phoebe in the mirror for a brief second, then lowered her eyes and dropped the tissue into her purse. Was Val ill? Phoebe wondered.

"Hello, Val," Phoebe said. "Is everything all right?"

"What do you mean?" Val asked curtly. She was fishing in her purse for something, and seconds later pulled out a lipstick.

"I just thought that—well, maybe you weren't feeling well."

"I feel fine," Val said. She turned around finally, and Phoebe saw that she indeed had been sick. Her skin was white and waxlike, and her eyes were bloodshot, exactly the way they might appear if she'd just been busy hurling her breakfast into a toilet bowl.

"But thanks for asking," Val said, turning back to the mirror. She uncapped the lipstick and swiped a plum color on her lips. "How are *you* doing, by the way? Still recovering from that nasty spill?"

"Much better, thank you."

Val tossed the tube of lipstick back in her purse. "Well, have a good day," she said.

"You, too," Phoebe said as Val brushed by her. Val was dressed down a bit today, Phoebe noticed— black pants and a tight black jersey turtleneck. Simple dangling silver earrings. Clearly she wasn't feeling at the top of her game.

Though she had ten minutes before her next class started, Phoebe parked herself in the corridor outside the classroom. She was hoping Jen would come early and she could ambush her, arranging a moment to talk again. But by the time the class officially started, Jen had yet to arrive. Ten minutes into the class, Phoebe realized she definitely wasn't coming. But her friend Rachel was there, keeping her eyes glued to her laptop.

Phoebe used the same tack she had in the earlier class—a newsroom-style discussion about the campus situation and how it should be covered, followed by assignments for everyone. This group of students seemed equally engaged by the process. It's taken a series of tragedies for me to figure out how to connect with them, she thought, but at least I've done it.

"All right, lunch beckons," she said when class was over. "Writers need to eat, too."

Phoebe packed up her things quickly and put her coat on. Was Jen purposely avoiding her? she wondered. Or was she off in a panic someplace because of Blair and Gwen's arrest?

Phoebe hurried to her car. She'd been anxious to find the spot along the road where Hutch's killer had parked, and this was finally a good opportunity. Alec's words were still weighing on her, railroading her attention, but she needed to stay focused. Something was continuing to gnaw at her about Hutch's death, and she needed to figure out what it was. Seeing the spot where the killer parked might provide a clue, she thought, or spark an idea.

She knew it would be tough for her to drive by Hutch's place, but as she neared his driveway, the force of her reaction took her by surprise. A sob caught in her throat, and she choked back tears.

It didn't take long to find the spot she was looking for—or where the police suspected the car had been parked. That was because of yellow police tape. The cordoned-off area was a deep dirt shoulder of the road about half a mile past Hutch's driveway. Phoebe parked just beyond it, under two evergreen trees, and climbed out of her car. Michelson had better not drive by in the next five minutes, she told herself, or he might drop her in a vat of boiling oil.

After reaching the spot, she sidled up to the tape and searched with her eyes. There was room inside the tape for a car to park and be safely off the road, and though the car wouldn't have been hidden from sight, anyone driving by at night would have only seen the dark hulk of its shape.

She lowered her eyes to the ground. There were no tire tracks, but the ground had been disturbed— almost as if someone had swept the dirt. At first glance it seemed that after returning to their car, the girls had driven it up the road a bit, returned on foot to the shoulder, and quickly swept the ground here. Pretty clever. But was that really something Blair and Gwen would have been smart enough to do?

Phoebe raised her eyes and let them roam the woods beyond the shoulder. She realized she must be standing fairly close to where she had fallen and passed out. She shuddered, remembering her desperate scramble in the dark.

She returned to her car and slipped into the passenger seat, trying not to jar her elbow. There was one more stop she wanted to make.

She headed back into town, rounded the college, and then drove north to the antique store, the Big Red Barn. There were just a few customers this afternoon. As she climbed from her car, Phoebe noticed that most of the Halloween decorations had been taken down, but some tired corn stalks were still leaning against the building.

Traffic whizzed by on the highway, and after waiting for an opening, Phoebe hurried across to the river side of the road and turned right, in the direction of the spot she'd stood in last week. It was deserted today, except for a red cardinal bobbing along a tree branch that had been stripped of its leaves. This, she realized, was the last place she'd seen Hutch alive.

She had planned to fight her way through the trees and underbrush to secure a closer look at the spot where Trevor Harris's body had been found, but as she approached the woody area directly in front of the river, she saw that there was still yellow police tape looped through the trees. At the rate things were going, Phoebe thought, the cops were about to go through the county's entire supply of it.

She returned to the area across from the Big Red Barn and perched on one of the gray weathered picnic tables. There was police tape here, too, blocking off an area farther ahead along the riverbank. The muddy Winamac chugged along quietly, clearly oblivious to all the misery it had caused.

Phoebe glanced around at the other tables and the two blackened stand-up grills. She wondered how long it had been since one of the grills had been fired up. And yet it was clear from the scuffed ground that the area was used frequently by picnickers and nature lovers. And someone else—there was a very good chance, she realized, that this was where Trevor had gone into the river. The access to the water was so much better here than by the wooded area. His body would have drifted away briefly and then been snatched by the tree roots farther down.

And Lily, too, Phoebe realized. Her body might have been snagged close to where Trevor's body lay, reuniting the two briefly in death before it was dislodged several days later and made its way downstream.

If you were going to toss someone into the river, this would be a perfect place to do it, Phoebe thought. It was totally isolated. No one would hear any screams or the sounds of a struggle. Rows of trees lined the road, so that the bike path and the picnic area were blocked from the view of passing motorists. If Lily and Trevor had been murdered, it meant a car had been involved, just as with Hutch—and that the killer was pretty familiar with the area. And yet, she realized, *Wesley* hadn't been taken to this particular spot.

Once again, she wondered if the deaths were really the work of the Sixes. She couldn't imagine what the motive would have been, or how it linked back to the last two circles of membership.

A light drizzle had begun, and Phoebe scooted off the picnic table. It would be even trickier to drive in this weather, and she wanted to head home now. Once she was in the car, she e-mailed Glenda, asking her to find out what dorm Jen was in. She would just head over there and nab the girl coming or going. As Phoebe started to drop her phone into her purse, it rang in her hands.

"Ms. Hall?" the person asked when she answered. It was a male voice she didn't recognize.

"Yes."

"Dan Hutchinson here. Ed Hutchinson's nephew."

"Oh Dan, thanks for calling back," she said. "I'm so sorry for your loss."

"I appreciate your call. My uncle even mentioned you to us. He was hurrying back on Sunday to chat with you."

"I know. I just feel horrible about what happened. Will there be a service of some kind?"

"Yeah, definitely. It's been delayed because the coroner held on to the body for a while. I'll e-mail you the details when I have them."

"Thank you," she said and gave him the address. "By the way, is Ginger okay? Do you have her?"

"Yup, we've got her—though she seems awfully freaked out. Wish we could keep her, but my wife is allergic. We're asking around to see if any friends can take her while we look for a permanent home."

"Well, wait," Phoebe said, almost without thinking. "Why don't *I* babysit Ginger until you find a home for her. I can even ask around campus."

The last thing she needed was a dog, but she wanted to do it for Hutch.

"Gosh, that would be a lifesaver," Dan said. "I'm going into Lyle to sign some paperwork tomorrow. I could even drop her off for you."

They agreed on noon, and she gave him her address.

It was after two when she let herself into the house, and just like yesterday, she felt a mid-afternoon fatigue beginning to ambush her. But she couldn't take a nap, she told herself, she had too much to do. She made a double espresso and carried it with her into the study.

She opened her laptop and checked a few Web sites to see if any break in the case was being reported. She found nothing. Then she made notes about where she should take her class next. She had plenty of time before next Monday, but she'd loved the way things had gone today, and she wanted to be sure to build on that. Maybe she'd keep up the newsroom approach.

Finally she turned her attention to the files she had dumped on her desk after returning from Duncan's. As she sorted out several folders, her eyes drifted toward the back of the table. They found the piece of cardboard, the one that had been around the six spoons, and she realized that in her muddled state the other day, she'd neglected to mention it to the police. She'd have to give Michelson a call.

Grimacing, she picked up the cardboard, smoothed it out, and stared at it. When she'd studied it previously, she'd assumed it had come from some type of packaging, probably from the spoons themselves. But now she wasn't so sure. She peered more closely at it. At each of the upper corners there was a bit of faded yellow with short strokes of black over it. From the size and the thickness, she realized that it might be an oversize playing card. And then suddenly she knew. It was a tarot card. She took a deep breath. So maybe there had been a message intended for her after all.

There was probably enough color left, she decided, to figure out which tarot card it was. She opened her laptop again and Googled "tarot cards," then began running her eyes over the images.

It didn't take long to find the correct card. There was a man with yellow wings on the upper left-hand side and a giant bird on the right—the black strokes were the ridges of the feathers—and between and just below them was a sphinx. Her eyes dropped to the words at the bottom of the card on the screen: "Wheel of Fortune."

She lurched back in the chair, making it scrape along the floor. No, no, no, she thought. It's not possible. It was the same as the tiny silver wheel on the bracelets years ago.

She looked down and stared at the card again on the table. At the very bottom of the card, she now saw the faded lower edge of the W.

Blood had surged to her head, and she could hardly think straight. It must be a coincidence, she thought, trying to fight off panic, just the Sixes sending a message of some kind. She searched quickly for the meaning of the card: "A turning point, a change in fortune and destiny. Sometimes good, but also sometimes bad, a prophesy of luck deserting you."

But what if it *wasn't* a coincidence? What if the Sixes *knew* about her past? But how could they have? It had all been kept under wraps. She remembered the reference in the fake blog site to the poetry journal. It seemed that someone was funneling secrets about her past to them. Would they use the information against her somehow—even with Blair and Gwen under arrest?

She grabbed her phone and called Glenda's cell. When Glenda didn't answer, Phoebe tried her office line and barely gave the receptionist a chance to speak before she asked for Glenda. The woman reported that Dr. Johns was off campus at the moment.

Next, Phoebe tried Duncan. Maybe she would stay there tonight after all. She had to stay calm, she realized, or this could push her to some edge she couldn't see.

"Hey, it's me," she said into Duncan's voice mail. "I've got a problem. Can you call me as soon as you can?"

A buzzer rang, making her jump. It was the doorbell, she realized. She rose from the chair and hurried to the living room. Peering out the window, she spotted a child standing on the porch, dressed in a yellow rain slicker with the hood up. Why would a kid be coming to her house? she wondered as she opened the door.

"May I help you?" she asked.

The child reached up and tugged off the water-streaked hood of the slicker. To her shock, Phoebe saw that it was actually Jen Imbibio. She felt an alarm go off inside her head. Was this some kind of setup? But the girl appeared genuinely distressed.

"I have to talk to you," Jen said.

Phoebe ushered her inside and locked the door behind her.

"Okay, shoot," Phoebe said quickly. She was still reeling from the tarot card, and she had to force herself to focus.

"I'm one of the Sixes," Jen said.

"I see," Phoebe said, not knowing what else to say. It was just as she'd suspected.

"I need your help. Blair and Gwen—they didn't kill that old man. I know that for sure."

# 27

"Are you alone?" Phoebe asked.

The girl's face wrinkled in confusion. "Of course," she said. "Who would be with me?"

Phoebe motioned her into the living room and gestured toward an armchair. Jen took the seat, perching on the edge of the cushion. She looked vulnerable, but also a tiny bit impudent, like someone called into the principal's office who didn't feel deserving of punishment.

"So why do you think that—that they're innocent?" Phoebe said.

"First of all, I just know that they would never do anything like *that*," Jen said. "They're just not the type. I saw Gwen in the café on Monday, and she seemed perfectly normal."

"People who brutally kill people are often socio-paths," Phoebe said bluntly. "They can look and sound like the rest of us, but they do awful things without feeling a trace of remorse."

"Sociopaths?" Jen exclaimed. "Is that what you think they are?"

"You seem surprised I'd assume that, Jen. But aren't the Sixes by their very nature about hurting other people? You pull pranks, you steal, you humiliate vulnerable boys, you come after the people who want out—like Alexis Grey."

"No, we're *not* about hurting people. We're about female strength and helping each other gain every ad-vantage we can. Sometimes we put certain people in their place, but only because they're trying to *block* us—you know, hogging all the professor's time, stuff like that. And besides, you can't totally trust Alexis Grey. Blair said Alexis blamed us for posting that sex tape when a boy had actually done it."

"How long have you been a member?"

"I was just tapped at the beginning of the term. I'm only a junior member."

"And Blair was definitely in charge before she was arrested?"

"Yes, I guess." Jen gnawed on her bottom lip.

"What do you mean you guess?"

"There's this sort of council of seniors who run things, and Blair was the leader of that. But sometimes it seemed she consulted with other people. I don't know who."

Phoebe recalled that Alexis had also sensed that there was someone in the wings.

"You said first of all. What's the other reason you think they didn't murder Hutch?" Phoebe asked.

"The police found Blair's scarf at the murder scene, but I know for a fact it had been stolen," Jen said. "Someone is setting her up. People are jealous of Blair, and they want to bring her down."

So the cops *had* discovered clothing at the scene.

"Wait, start from the beginning," Phoebe said. "How do you know they found something?"

"I heard from this other girl who talked to Blair's mother that the cops showed Blair this pink scarf and asked if it was hers, and told her they found it at the scene. I'm sure Blair tried to tell them that the scarf had been stolen, and they probably thought she was just making that up to protect herself. But I know it's the truth. Because I was walking with her the other day, and she told me someone had taken it."

"But don't you see that she realized she'd dropped the scarf when she was at Hutch's house, and tried to cover her ass by telling you that she'd lost it."

Jen shook her head. "But she told me Sunday at *lunch.* That was way before the old guy was murdered. She'd just come from her house. I know she leaves some stuff downstairs in the entranceway, which isn't locked. Some girls had been hanging out at the apartment downstairs, visiting the guys who live there, and Blair thought one of them had stolen it just to be mean."

Now *that's* the pot calling the kettle black, Phoebe thought snidely, but she knew that the scenario was possible. In her mind she saw the coats drooping from the row of pegs in the dingy entranceway of the Ash Street house. Was Blair really being framed? she wondered. But how would the killer know that she would be a viable suspect?

"By the way, does either Blair or Gwen own a car?" Phoebe asked.

"No—why?"

"Would they have had access to a car?"

Jen bit her lip again and shrugged her shoulders. "Yeah, I guess they could have borrowed one."

"You need to tell the police about your conversation with Blair," Phoebe said. "I can give you the name of the detective you should talk to."

"I can't," Jen nearly wailed. "Don't you *see?* They'll know that I'm part of the Sixes then. And they'll suspect me, too."

So *that* was the real point of the visit, Phoebe realized. It wasn't at all about protecting Blair and Gwen—it was about protecting Jen's own hide.

"But the road may eventually lead to you anyway—everyone in the Sixes could come under suspicion. You should call your parents immediately and get legal advice about how to handle this."

Jen's eyes welled with tears. "My parents won't understand," she said. There was a trace of petulance in her tone. "Can't you try to help me first?"

"But help you *how*?" Phoebe didn't have an ounce of pity for the girl.

"I don't know. Can't you figure out who is setting them up?"

"I'm not a detective, Jen. That's what the police do."

"But you write those books. You find all sorts of things out."

Phoebe rose from the armchair and pulled a tissue from her purse for Jen. She needed a second to think. She had to work this situation to her own advantage—try to use Jen's inside knowledge about the Sixes.

"Okay, Jen, let me see what I can do," Phoebe said. "But first I'm going to need additional information."

Jen shifted on the couch, expectant.

"Let's start with me." Phoebe said. "You know, of course, that the Sixes have been after me, right?"

Jen looked away, unable to make eye contact. "I know they were upset with you," she muttered. "Blair said you were trying to expose us—and then ruin us."

"Were you one of the girls that broke into my house?"

"*What?*" Jen said. "I never heard they did that. Are you sure it was them?"

"Forget that for a minute," Phoebe said bluntly. "What does the word *Fortuna* mean to you?"

The girl looked genuinely puzzled. "Um, nothing. I've never heard of it. Is it a place?"

"I want you to ask the other girls in the Sixes about that name, okay? You won't want them to catch on that you talked to me, so tell them you overheard me on the phone after class, and that I was talking about the Sixes and Fortuna. See if it means something to any of them."

"Okay."

"Now tell me about the circles."

Jen's eyes widened in surprise. "But how—why do you need to know about them?"

"Just trust me. If I'm going to help you, you're going to have to provide me with information. I know about the first four. What are the fifth and sixth circles?"

"I really can't talk about them. We're never supposed to reveal anything about the circles."

"Jen, people are *dead*," Phoebe said. "It's time to talk."

The girl looked away and bit her lip again. At this rate, Phoebe thought, it was going to be a bloody pulp by the end of their conversation. Finally Jen looked back at Phoebe.

"You're only supposed to know about the circles you've done and the one directly above them," she said. "I've only done the first two. But someone told me about the fourth and fifth in secret."

Phoebe already knew about the fourth. "What's the fifth one?" she asked.

"'Seduce and Exploit.'"

"You're supposed to entice someone to have sex with you?"

"Kind of."

"*Kind of?*" Phoebe could feel her patience starting to fray.

"Well, yes, sex if you want. But you can find some other way to win their favor."

"And what's the exploit part?"

Jen looked away yet again, and this time when she turned her head back, she never looked directly into Phoebe's eyes.

"You entice them to do something for you or give you something you need."

"So you have sex with a boy and then have him write a term paper for you—something like that?"

"No, not a boy. You have to seduce someone in power. So what they have to share is really worthwhile."

Wow, Phoebe thought, it was just as the psychologist had told her—girl power totally run amuck.

"Like a professor, then?" Phoebe asked. "Or someone in the administration?"

"Yes," Jen said, nearly in a whisper.

"And you don't know the sixth circle?"

"No—just the name. It's called 'Secure.'"

"As in 'to secure'?"

"Yes. I think it might have something to do with forging your future somehow. That's all I know."

Her comment was vaguely similar to what Alexis Grey had said about the Sixes taking care of you after college. Phoebe was baffled. It was hard to imagine such a malicious group of girls morphing into a spunky career-networking operation.

At that Jen let her shoulders sag, like a kid who was growing bored and irritated. "I should probably go now." She rose from the couch and stuffed her hands in the pockets of her slicker. "They might wonder where I am. So you're going to help, right?"

"The Sixes are still in operation—even with Blair in jail?"

"It's sort of a mess, but they're trying to keep it going," she said.

"Who's in charge now? Another senior?"

"Yes, but I can't tell you who," Jen said. "She's a friend of mine. We—"

She broke off, looking like she'd given too much away. Phoebe bet it might be Rachel, the girl she saw Jen yammering to that day after class. Rachel was a senior.

"Okay, Jen, I'll see what I can find out. But you have to do the same for me. About Fortuna. I expect to hear from you." She paused. "I also need you to find out what the sixth circle entails."

"But they'll never tell me that," Jen said. "Besides, I don't see how knowing any of that would help."

"Let me worry about that. Just find it out."

Jen started to move toward the door

"There's one more thing I need to know before you go," Phoebe said. "Was Lily Mack trying to extricate herself from the Sixes?"

Jen sighed, thrusting her hands deeper into her pockets.

"Yes, she wanted out. And I heard Blair was furious about it. She felt really betrayed."

"How long had Lily been a member?"

"Just since last spring. After her boyfriend left."

"And why did she want to quit this fall? Because she started to find out what the Sixes were up to?"

Jen finally met Phoebe's eyes and held them.

"No, it wasn't really that. She was going through the fifth circle this fall, and the man she was supposed to, you know, seduce . . . she fell in love with him. And she didn't want to use him in any way. That's why she wanted out."

Phoebe found herself swallowing hard. She didn't like where this was going.

"So who was it?"

"I don't know. I swear. The only thing I know is that she was on a committee with him. Blair said that was how Lily first got to know him."

The school, Phoebe knew, seemed to form a committee every time you turned around. That's how she had met Duncan, after all—on a committee made up just of faculty. There were others for students only, and some that included a combination of faculty, students, and administration. Jen had been on the committee Stockton had organized about student life—that's where he'd seen her exchange a look with the other girl, Molly Wang, when he raised the topic of sororities. It should be easy enough, for Phoebe, to figure out which one Lily had participated in this fall.

As soon as Jen left, scurrying down the porch steps, Phoebe began to pace. She felt totally wired from the tarot card and now from Jen's visit. Her gut told her Jen didn't have a clue about Fortuna. Other members— Blair and the senior council—certainly might. But how could they have ever found out? Glenda was the only one here who knew about Fortuna. Could her friend have told someone?

Phoebe stopped abruptly. She debated whether she should even bother calling Michelson to tell him about the tarot card. Would he even care? The fact that the Sixes might know horrible details from her past and choose to torment her about them would have no relevance to the deaths they were investigating, even if Blair and Gwen were guilty.

She thought back on what Jen had shared about the scarf. If the story was true, it meant that someone was trying hard to implicate Blair—and perhaps by association, the other Sixes. That clearly suggested that the killer was someone at Lyle College, someone who knew the Sixes made a perfect target.

And that took her right back to where she'd started on Monday. If the Sixes hadn't killed Hutch, then the murderer could very well be a psychopath, someone who received his kicks purely from killing. But there was now something new to factor in, something she should have followed up on before: the new man who'd been in Lily's life this fall. In her mind she heard the line Lily had supposedly said to Amanda: *Wouldn't I be a fool to date a little boy again?*

Phoebe glanced at her watch. It was almost four and she hadn't heard from Glenda yet. She tried Glenda's cell again, and when that proved futile, she rang the office number once more.

"I'm sorry, she's still out, Ms. Hall," the assistant informed her.

"It's really urgent I speak to her, and she's not picking up her cell." Phoebe realized that she sounded like a child not getting her way.

"I'm sure she wouldn't mind me telling you," the assistant said. "She was going to pick up Brandon from school today and help him with his homework. From there she was heading over to a literary magazine fair they're holding on the quad this afternoon."

"All right, I'll try to catch up with her at the fair." Then Phoebe had an idea. "One more question. Do you know how I could find a list of all the school committees this term, and who's on them?"

"I'm not sure who would have access to that list. Dr. Johns, of course. And probably Dean Stockton."

Stockton was the last person in the world Phoebe wanted to ask.

As soon as she hung up, Phoebe realized she couldn't wait for the fair. She had to talk to Glenda *now*. She draped a coat over her shoulders, grabbed her purse, and headed for her car. Glenda would probably be back from Brandon's school by now and Phoebe planned to stop by the house. She would be interrupting mommy time, she knew, but she had to learn if Glenda had ever shared information about her past with anyone at Lyle. Phoebe had driven only a block toward Glenda's house when she was forced to flick on her windshield wipers because the drizzle had morphed into a light rain.

To Phoebe's surprise, the housekeeper didn't respond to her knock on the door. She tried again, and as she waited, she detected music playing inside—a jazz song. Someone was home and obviously couldn't hear her above the noise.

She pushed the front door open and called out hello. No one responded. The music seemed to be coming from the conservatory, and she followed it, like a thread. She reached the room and glanced around. There were speakers on a small table, the source of the jazz, but no one was in the room.

She glanced out the long windows, across the yard to the driveway. Glenda's car wasn't even there. Damn, Phoebe thought, Glenda must have shifted her plans. Phoebe backed out of the room and into the main hall, rushing to leave. As she took a step toward the front door, the landline in the house rang. She flinched. And then from just inside the living room, she heard a male voice answer hello. It was Mark. Phoebe froze in position.

"Yes, I understand," Mark said. "But never call me on this phone again, do you understand? I told you to use my cell."

Phoebe stayed still, holding her breath. It wouldn't be pretty to have Mark discover her presence, but at the same time, she was desperate to hear what he would say next.

"Of course, I told you that," he said after a few seconds. There was another long pause. She heard him clear his throat.

"I'll have it for you," he said crisply. "I said I would, and I will."

Oh, God, Phoebe thought. He was about to get off and possibly leave the room. She tiptoed to the front door and snuck outside, scrambled down the steps of the porch, and bolted to her car. Once inside she finally breathed and fired up the engine. Before pulling out into the street, she looked back at the house. To her chagrin, she saw the curtains of the living room part just an inch. Someone, most likely Mark, was peering outside.

Had he recognized her? If he had, he might guess she'd eavesdropped and would have another reason to keep her on his shit list. But what worried her even more were the words she'd overheard. Why wasn't the person supposed to call him on the landline? And what was it that Mark was supposed to produce?

She drove to campus and parked in the lot behind the student union. It was raining harder now, and her sweater sleeves and sling were soaked by the time she reached the front of the building. There were a few tables on the plaza draped with plastic coverings, but most, she realized, had obviously been dismantled because of the weather, and only a half dozen people now milled around. A dripping sign, written in script and propped against a chair, read, "Rain Date: Friday." Phoebe tried Glenda again on her cell, but she reached only voice mail. She waited for fifteen minutes under an overhang, thinking Glenda might still show, not knowing the fair had been canceled. Finally, after the last table was hauled off, Phoebe tramped back to her car. The ache in her elbow had returned full force.

Once home she popped two ibuprofen and made green tea, hoping to calm her jangly nerves. With the mug in one hand she circled through her rooms, hashing over her conversation with Jen. She *had* to find out what committee Lily had been on and who she'd fallen in love with. That could very well be the killer. But there were confusing aspects. How would Hutch have learned about the connection? And how did Trevor Harris's death fit into this scenario? Had Lily's lover killed him out of jealousy? But that *couldn't* be the case: it had sounded like Lily had fallen in love this fall after Trevor was clearly out of the picture. Phoebe grabbed her phone and dialed Jen's number.

"Is there any chance that Lily started the relationship with the older man when she was still with Trevor?" Phoebe asked when the girl picked up.

"No, it started this fall," Jen said. "And besides, she loved that guy Trevor. They were going to live together, and she was really upset when she thought he took off."

"So she never suspected something bad had happened to him?"

"No, because he'd been talking a lot about how fed up he was with Lyle and with being hassled here."

"Hassled?"

"About his grades. And by the campus cops. He told Lily they had it in for him."

*That* was interesting. Phoebe asked if Jen knew why, but the girl said she had no clue. Phoebe signed off, promising to call tomorrow.

It was dark out now, and foggy too, and the rooms seemed to be shrinking, pinning her in. She knew she had reason to be on edge, but the fading light wasn't helping. She dreaded the coming night and wished she'd never opened up that piece of cardboard. Why, she wondered, hadn't Glenda called her? And where was Duncan? Why the hell was no one getting back to her?

And then, it was as if she had conjured him up. She heard a knock at the front door, and when she spun around, she saw Duncan through the glass in the window.

"Hey," he said when she opened the door. His black trench glistened with water. "I got so crazed I never checked my phone, and when I heard your message, I decided to just hurry over."

"Oh, God," Phoebe said. "I'm just so glad you're here. There's something totally freaky going on."

As he stripped off his coat, she began to tell him about the tarot card.

"Let me play devil's advocate," Duncan said when she'd finished. "Couldn't it just be the Sixes leaving their own specific warning for you—that your fate is about to change?"

"Sure, I guess," Phoebe said, flinging her arms up. "But the more I think about it, the more it seems like too big of a coincidence. Fortuna always left the mark of the wheel. And there's a wheel right on the front of the card."

Duncan looked at her sympathetically, but she suspected he felt she was making much ado about nothing. "Even if someone *did* find out about Fortuna—let's say that Glenda mentioned it to someone—you shouldn't let it cause you any grief, Phoebe. What difference does it make if someone knows about your past?"

"What if it's *more* than that?" she blurted out. To her dismay, she heard her voice tremble as she realized something she hadn't considered before. "What if someone from Fortuna is here—at the school? I never knew who all of the members were."

"That seems unlikely. But even so, why be so afraid of them? They bullied you, but that's really it, right?"

"No," she said, her eyes welling with tears. "It was worse than that. Worse than I ever told you."

After her clothes were shredded, she finally confided in a teacher, who brought her to the headmistress. The woman had listened, nodded, expressed concern and said that the school would not only investigate but also reimburse her for some of the clothing. But at the same time the headmistress, with her too-pert nose in the air, had seemed unsympathetic, as if she'd been forced to discuss something that she found trivial, the problem of a student too wimpy to fight her own battles and take care of herself.

Later she thought about the choice of the word investigate. That word never suggested that the culprits in Fortuna—because surely it was them—would be brought to justice. And from what she knew, no one ever was.

But at least after that things were quiet. Spring came. She met a boy from a coed prep school nearby, and they had coffee twice in town. To her relief, life seemed normal again. Maybe, she thought, Fortuna had moved on to someone else.

On Easter weekend she stayed on campus to work— she had so much to do leading up to finals. The fact that the campus was nearly deserted was actually a relief to her. And then on Saturday night, as she was walking back to the dorm, the boys had grabbed her.

She never saw their faces. They came up behind her and threw a hood over her head. From the sound of them muttering to each other, she knew that there were three of them, and they weren't that old. They led her to a car and threw her in the back seat.

She thought she would be raped, and she was out of her mind with fear. But after a ten-minute drive they yanked her out of the car and forced her into some kind of crawl space. And then they sealed it shut.

She could barely breathe. It was cold and damp, and she thought she heard rats, scampering somewhere near her. Although she knew they must have driven away, she called out, again and again, to no avail. She tried to push, too, at what she thought was the opening, but she was too wedged in to create any force.

*For the next thirty-six hours, she just lay there in the total dark, weeping sometimes, wetting herself. She pretended her mother was next to her, telling her to hold on, to be strong. She knew people would start to look for her, but how would they ever guess she was in this place? She was certain that she was going to die.*

# 28

Duncan slipped his arm around Phoebe, careful of her bad arm, and led her to the couch, easing her onto one of the cushions.

"Tell me what happened," he said, sitting next to her.

She spilled out the whole story then—about the letters and the shredded clothes and then finally about being abducted and forced into the crawl space in the warehouse. She started to cry once but brushed the tears away.

"How did they finally find you?" Duncan asked. His expression was grim.

"It was partly because of Glenda," Phoebe said. "She came back from Brooklyn Sunday night, and when she couldn't find me, she reported it to the dorm mother.

The school alerted the police. On Monday morning, someone—one of the boys, they later thought—called from a phone booth with an anonymous tip about me in the warehouse and the police dug me out. I was in the hospital for a couple days. I thought of going back to school after that, but my mother wouldn't have it, and frankly, I was just too afraid. Needless to say, the school bent over backward to keep me from making a stink."

"I can't believe you went through that nightmare. And you're sure it was Fortuna who was behind your abduction?"

"Almost positive. I'd been falsely signed out of the dorm for the weekend, which is why the dorm mother initially had no reason to be alarmed—and it must have been Fortuna members who forged my signature. The boys, I've always assumed, were from the nearby coed prep school that we socialized with. I suspect the Fortuna members talked them into grabbing me, though my guess is that they never meant for it to get so out of hand."

"But why would they go to such an extreme to begin with?"

"I think because of a boy I'd started seeing," Phoebe said. "He went to that other prep school, and we'd had coffee a few times. I heard later that one of the

Fortuna girls was after him. She wanted to scare me off, apparently."

"And they never caught the boys who did it to you?"

"No. Nor the girls. The school made a show of trying to find out who the ringleaders were, but the daddies of the Fortuna girls were the ones who gave the big donations, so I doubt they tried very hard."

"Gosh, Phoebe," Duncan said. "I can only imagine how this Sixes nonsense has stirred up all the crap from the past."

On the one hand, Phoebe was glad she'd told him the story. She'd never even shared the full details with Alec. But now she felt even more churned up, knowing it was out in the open.

"Do you see what I mean now?" she implored. "I just keep wondering if someone from Fortuna is *here*, working with the Sixes."

"Tell me how I can help," he said.

She shook her head in despair. "I don't know. Maybe just food, for starters. I never ate today, and it's not helping."

He suggested ordering a pizza. After making the call, he asked if she'd mind if he took a shower. He'd been at the lab much of the afternoon, he told her, and needed to wash up. After Duncan headed upstairs, she opened a bottle of wine and poured a large glass. It's been twenty-five years, she thought, since Fortuna terrorized me, but I'm right back in that old place now, feeling undone again. She thought of Lily and Alexis and the other victims of the Sixes. She had to put a stop to what was happening here in Lyle.

A few minutes later, just as she heard the water start running in the shower, her cell phone rang. It was Glenda, finally calling back.

"Sorry to make you leave all those messages," Glenda said. "I ended up going to the local library with Brandon, and I had to turn off my phone."

"Have you *ever* mentioned Fortuna to anyone here at the college?" Phoebe demanded.

"Of course not. Why are you asking?"

She told Glenda about the tarot card.

"I don't believe it," Glenda said. "How can this be happening?"

"I wouldn't blame you, G, if you said something," Phoebe told her. "Maybe you mentioned it to someone when you talked about me coming to teach here, or when the whole Sixes business started up. It's not anything I ever insisted had to be kept secret."

"I've never breathed a word about it. Sure, you never told me it was supposed to be a secret, but since you always seemed to keep it private yourself, I did too.

Believe it or not, I've never even told Mark. After he met you, he asked why you'd left school, and I told him that you'd missed your mom too much."

"Well, someone's found out—or even worse, someone here was once a member and told the Sixes."

"Have you ever talked about it in an interview?"

"Never. And there was no press coverage of my abduction. The school made sure of that."

"We'll get to the bottom of this, Fee. I'm sure the cops are doing everything in their power to squeeze Blair and Gwen. It won't be long before we know who all the Sixes are, and then we can find out if there's really a connection to Fortuna."

Phoebe took another swig of wine. "Okay, it's just—you know. It's just making me crazy, that's all."

"I'm sure," Glenda said. "You called about something else, too. That committee Lily was on?"

"Right. I talked to someone who swears Blair and Gwen are being set up. She also says that Lily was in love with a faculty or administration member she met on a committee this fall. It sounds like they were having an affair—and that could be significant."

"I'm back in my office, and I can check now on my computer. Just give me a sec to find it."

Phoebe heard the sound of Glenda's phone being set down on the desk. As she waited, she realized she was holding her breath. Finally Glenda picked up the phone again.

"You're not going to believe this," Glenda said. "But then, maybe you will."

"*Who?*" Phoebe urged.

"Tom Stockton. It was a committee on campus life."

Phoebe inhaled sharply. It was the same committee Jen was on, though she'd nicely withheld this detail. "Damn, despite what you told me about him, I didn't see this one coming."

"You sure about this, Fee?"

"Not totally. But if it's true, he might be involved in the deaths. It could also explain why he's been so eager to promote the serial killer idea. It deflects all the attention away from him."

"Are you going to the cops about this?"

"Not yet. I want to check it out a bit more. And don't worry, I'll be careful." Her mind flashed back to her experience earlier in Glenda's house. "Tell me— how are things on *your* end?"

"For the time being, things seem relatively under control on campus, and I've managed to calm the board down—though I dread what will happen when more stuff starts leaking out about the Sixes. On the home front, it stinks. Mark has been out a lot lately, and he's always got these intricate excuses that seem rehearsed. I keep thinking about what my mother used to say: A liar's story is often just a little too pat."

In her mind Phoebe could see herself creeping down Glenda's front hallway, overhearing the ominous words that Mark had spoken. She needed to share with Glenda what she'd learned, but she didn't want to do it over the phone.

"Is there any chance I can see you soon?" Phoebe said. "I really want to catch up in person."

"Me too. There's a women's soccer game tomorrow at four. Can you meet me there?"

Phoebe promised she would.

"Are you going to be okay at home tonight?" Glenda asked.

"Yeah, Duncan's here."

There was a longer than usual pause.

"Okay, but remember you have a bed here whenever you need it," Glenda told her.

Phoebe thanked her and started to sign off. "Oh, wait," she said, remembering. "There's one other thing I heard. Someone mentioned to me that Trevor Harris was being hassled by Craig Ball before he died. Their word, not mine. Did you ever hear anything like that?"

"That's odd," Glenda said. "I don't recall Craig ever mentioning he'd had any issues with Trevor. And I don't like the word *hassle*. That's not the way we like to do business with students around here. Let me investigate, Fee."

After saying good-bye, Phoebe dropped the phone on the table and leaned back in the chair, considering the info she'd learned from Glenda. *Stockton*. Knowing that he had a predilection for college girls, it wasn't hard to imagine him falling for Lily. But it was tough to imagine it the other way around—what had that pretty, inquisitive girl seen in that pompous bore? And yet Phoebe knew Lily wasn't the girl she'd first imagined her to be. She'd apparently been up to her ears in dirty tricks.

So had Stockton thrown Lily into the river? If he was obsessed with her, he might have done it out of jealousy. Or rage, because he'd learned she'd first set out to exploit him. And when Hutch figured it out, Stockton showed up at his cabin and battered him to death. But how had Hutch learned the truth?

The situation, Phoebe realized, might be even sicker than Stockton killing a former lover. Maybe—if she was really going to push the envelope in her thinking—Stockton was the serial killer, drugging and drowning students. She'd seen him in Cat Tails. Perhaps he'd been there before. Was *he* the thirty- or forty-something man who had spoken to Wesley? Wesley had been at the school only two years, and might not even have been familiar with Stockton. She needed to show Wesley a picture of Stockton.

She heard the water shut off, and a few minutes later Duncan bounded down the stairs. His skin was dewy, and his wet hair was slicked back off his face. Later, after they slipped into bed, she reached out for him in the dark and ran her fingers deliberately along his chest and thighs.

"Are you sure?" he said softly. "I would love nothing more than to have sex with you, but is it okay with your injuries?"

"Well, if you think I'm waiting six weeks till this sling comes off, you're crazy."

She gave in to the sheer pleasure of his hands exploring her and the feel of him inside her. It was an utter relief to leave the world behind.

The next morning, she was first out of bed and had already put out a few provisions for breakfast by the time Duncan wandered into the kitchen.

"You seem like you're in a hurry," he said.

"There are a few things I must take care of," Phoebe said. "Are you ready for a piece of actually fun news?

"*Please.*"

She told him about her decision to babysit Ginger for a while.

Duncan smiled. "That's nice of you to do, Phoebe," he said. "It must be so tough for her, losing both her home and her master. Speaking of that, I wonder if we'll hear news of the case today. If the girls don't confess, they'll have to stand trial."

Phoebe had already decided she wasn't going to reveal specifics about Jen's visit—it wouldn't go down well with Duncan if he knew she was still poking around. But she wanted his take on one aspect.

"What if my first instinct about the murder was right? That Blair and Gwen didn't do it?" she asked.

Duncan, leaning against the sink, lowered his coffee cup, holding her eyes.

"Anything in particular inspiring this line of thinking?" he asked.

"Someone informed me yesterday that Lily was in love with a man—not a student—who works at Lyle. What if he was the one who killed Lily and then Hutch?"

"Who told you *that*?" he said.

"I can't say at the moment."

"For crying out loud, Phoebe," Duncan snapped. "Why can't you leave this all to the police? You keep putting yourself in danger."

She appreciated his concern, but she didn't need him telling her what to do—and certainly not in that tone.

"I'm looking for closure in this case, just like everyone else," Phoebe said firmly. "But I don't want closure based on a lie. The police may not have all the answers."

"I'm sorry I spoke to you like that," he said, sighing. "I'm just concerned about you."

She accepted his apology and began clearing the breakfast dishes. The next few moments were awkward and clunky. She could sense his mind churning and his mood darkening. But when he said good-bye a few minutes later, he seemed more like himself again.

"Why don't we go out to dinner tonight?" he said. "I've got a little cabin fever these days, and I'm sure you must too."

She agreed, and he kissed her good-bye. She locked the door behind him and peered out the window. As she watched him trip down her front steps, it was hard not to notice the sullen slump in his shoulders. She didn't like what had just happened.

Phoebe checked the time. She had a few hours until Hutch's nephew was due to arrive, and she intended to use the time to track down Stockton. She wanted to ask him about the committee and see what vibe she picked up from his answer. She called his office and was told he had back-to-back meetings this morning.

"It's fairly urgent," Phoebe said after identifying herself. "Can you tell me where he'll be at around ten?"

"Well, I'm not sure if—" And then, as if sensing she sounded silly withholding the information, the assistant volunteered that Stockton was presently at a meeting in the basement conference room of the library.

This time Phoebe walked the short distance to campus. The skies had cleared, but it was in the forties, with a stiff wind that made the flags on campus snap so hard they sounded as if they would tear in half. Students were bundled up today, some even in parkas. Since she was only able to drape her coat over her shoulders, Phoebe was shivering by the time she reached the library.

The woman at the library's front desk said she had no idea where Stockton's meeting was being held, but that there were several meeting rooms in the basement. Phoebe nearly flew down the stairs, worried about missing him. At this hour the basement level was nearly deserted, and as she searched along the corridors, she passed empty stacks, study carrels, and the glass-walled area that housed a collection of Revolutionary War–era letters, donated by an alumnus years ago.

Finally she heard a murmur of voices just ahead, and the echo of footsteps on the concrete floor. Two women turned a corner onto the corridor Phoebe was walking down.

"Good morning," Phoebe said. "You haven't seen Dean Stockton, have you?"

"We've just come from a meeting with him, actually," one said. "Make a left, and you'll find him farther down on the right."

Stockton was where they said he would be, slipping papers into a soft leather briefcase in the conference room. His camel topcoat and tartan scarf were still draped over one of the chairs. He turned at the sound of Phoebe entering the room.

"Well, well," he said, clearly surprised. "You're not someone I expected to see in the bowels of the library."

Phoebe smiled sweetly. She needed to keep this light, though she felt her heart skip a beat.

"I hope that's a compliment, Tom."

"Of course. Are you on the mend, by the way?"

"Yes, thanks for asking."

"I suspect it must be a bit like horseback riding. You'll want to get on again before it becomes too frightening of a prospect."

"I'm not following," Phoebe said, wondering what mind game he might be playing.

"Your bike. I heard you took a nasty spill."

"Oh . . . right."

"Now tell me what I can do for you," Stockton said. "Unless you're actually down here to read about hardships endured during the Revolution."

"I just have a quick question. I'm still trying to dig up information on the Sixes. They—"

"Why?" he asked, as he resumed stuffing his briefcase. "Aren't the police handling that now?"

"I'm just wrapping up what I was doing—and of course I'll inform the police of anything they need to know. Several days ago you mentioned that you'd organized a committee on quality of life on campus. Was Lily Mack on that committee?"

Stockton stopped his paper stuffing and looked up at her. "Why is that relevant?" he asked huffily.

"It's just a loose end I want to tie up."

"If you must ask, she *was* on it—but in name only. After the incident with the chairs, I invited her to join. She agreed, but never showed for any meetings." He grabbed his coat and scarf. "Now, if you'll excuse me, I have another meeting."

Was he telling the truth? Phoebe wondered as he strode from the room like someone headed to a world economic summit. It would explain why Jen hadn't mentioned Lily being on the committee. Of course, even if Lily hadn't attended any of the meetings, she'd been invited by Stockton to join. Jen may have simply been confused about how the two of them met. Or maybe Stockton *hadn't* been her love interest after all.

Phoebe made her way back along the corridor. She didn't pass another soul, and the only sound was her footsteps on the cement floor. Where *is* everyone? she thought anxiously. She felt suddenly claustrophobic being all alone below ground. She turned a corner and realized she'd gone the wrong way. Just get me the hell out of here, she thought. She quickly retraced her steps, nearly at a jog. When she finally located the stairwell, she took the steps two at a time.

Once outside, standing under the library's portico, Phoebe dug out her phone and tried Jen's number. The girl answered in a groggy voice, as if she was still in bed.

"Did you find something out?" Jen murmured after Phoebe identified herself.

"Not yet, but I have another question. You told me yesterday that Lily met the person she fell for on a committee this fall. But are you sure about that? Could she have met him under different circumstances?"

"Not this fall," the girl said, more coherently this time. "The committee was this past spring. That's when she met him. But she didn't really get the hots for him until this term—when she chose him for the fifth circle."

So then it *wasn't* Stockton. Phoebe signed off and immediately called Glenda's office. The assistant told her Dr. Johns was in meetings the entire morning.

"Is it possible for you to get a message to her?" Phoebe nearly pleaded. "Could you tell her I need some additional information. I need to know the committee Lily Mack was on during the *spring* term."

"I may be able to help you this time. I asked Dr. Johns how to access that information if I ever needed to find it again. Give me a moment, please."

Phoebe waited, watching as students began to surface on campus, like creatures emerging from their burrows after a storm.

"Okay, I've found it," the assistant said. "She was on a committee on animal testing."

"Who else was on it?" Phoebe asked quickly.

"Six, er, seven other students."

"But what *faculty* member?"

"Oh, let's see. Okay, here we go. It was Dr. Duncan Shaw."

## 29

I t felt as if someone had shoved Phoebe from behind full force, knocking the wind out of her.

"Um, okay," she said. "Anyone else? I mean, any other faculty on the committee?" Maybe Duncan hadn't been the only one.

Phoebe could sense the woman scanning the page on her computer. *Hurry up!* she wanted to scream.

"Just him, actually," the assistant said. "Can I help with anything else?"

"No, uh, no," Phoebe sputtered. "Thank you."

She dropped the phone in her purse. Her legs felt wobbly suddenly, and she leaned against the building for support. Two people leaving the library turned and checked her out, their eyes curious.

Had Duncan really had an affair with Lily? she wondered desperately. It just didn't fit. He seemed smart, mature, together, not the kind of guy who'd become entangled with a student and possibly jeopardize his standing at the college. And yet the truth was, she knew absolutely nothing about his personal life since his wife's death. Phoebe hadn't yet felt comfortable probing about that. She'd just assumed he'd dated very little since then, perhaps having a sexual fling or two. But then maybe that's exactly what Lily had been for him.

Of course, if she were to believe Jen, Lily had made the first move. As part of the fifth circle, her initial plan had been to seduce and exploit. Had Duncan discovered her original intent?

Whatever the case, Phoebe realized, an affair would certainly explain Duncan's behavior this morning—why he'd snapped at her when she'd raised the subject of Lily's love life.

But there was an even more awful question to consider: Had Duncan *murdered* Lily? She considered what she knew of him, as if she were spreading pages of notes on a table in front of her. He had stuck by his wife during her illness; he had good friends in his department; his students adored him. But even a good man could be pushed. There was that moody side of him, too, which might point to something dark—malevolent, even.

And one detail she couldn't ignore: he had seemed extremely interested in the murders, always pressing her for details. Was he just pumping me, she wondered, to make certain he knew as much as he could about the police investigation? Is that why he'd been so eager to check out Hutch's notes—to make sure there was nothing implicating him? He'd also pushed her to stop the research. Was that really because he feared her getting too close to the truth?

The whole notion was crushing. She'd had sex with Duncan; she *cared* about him. Was he really a murderer?

No, it couldn't be true, she told herself frantically. She caught a student looking at her and she realized she had been shaking her head back and forth.

She took a deep breath, trying to calm herself. What she needed to do, she could see, was to go someplace quiet, where she could think in peace. Her office. Clasping her coat closed with her good hand, she headed for Arthur Hall. As she rounded the corner of the library, she nearly collided with Pete Tobias. God, she thought, this is the freaking last thing I need right now—another face-to-face with Lucifer himself.

"Well, Phoebe Hall," he said. "I thought you might be avoiding me."

Be careful, she warned herself. Talking to him was like trying to skirt around a rattlesnake on a mountain trail. And she couldn't let him see how frazzled she felt at the moment.

"Shouldn't you be busy writing the retraction about me?" she asked.

He looked annoyed. "It's being posted today, actually," he said. "Of course, I think the real story turned out to be far more interesting than what we'd been led to believe was true. That students here decided to *frame* you. Why do you think anyone would want to do that?"

"Maybe they were mad because I don't grade on a curve," Phoebe snapped. "But I'll leave that for you to figure out, since you're such a good reporter."

He harrumphed. "I'll do that, then. By the way, I'm surprised you're not competing with me on the bigger story here."

"I'm not following."

"The ever-burgeoning body count in little old Lyle. It may not involve any of your celebrity crushes, but it's the kind of juicy story Phoebe Hall generally likes to get her hands on."

"Oh, I could never compete with you, Pete," she said. "Now if you'll excuse me, I need to be someplace."

Once inside her office, door closed, Phoebe collapsed at her desk and squeezed her eyes shut. She considered why Lily would have selected Duncan to seduce and exploit. She was a psych minor. She hadn't taken classes with him yet but perhaps she planned to next term.

But then she fell for him. And perhaps something went wrong. Was *Duncan* the mess Lily had referred to during her dash with Phoebe through the rain?

None of this meant, though, that he'd *killed* Lily. But what if he had? Phoebe thought. It meant he probably also killed Hutch. Was it Duncan who had chased her through the woods that night? she wondered miserably.

There was one thing she *could* see: how easy it would have been for Duncan to frame Blair. Thanks to Phoebe, he knew all about the Sixes and the house on Ash Street.

As she leaned back in her chair, trying to slow her breathing, a chilling thought shoved its way into Phoebe's brain: Lily and Trevor had drowned—and so had Duncan's wife.

There had to be a way to learn more. She needed to talk to Amanda again, she decided. Lily's roommate hadn't known much about the new guy in Lily's life, but asked some pointed questions, she might be able to cough up a detail. Phoebe called the girl's number and left a message on her voice mail.

She also left a message for Wesley. She wanted to obtain a better description of the man at the jukebox, the one who had seemed to intrigue Hutch so much.

Phoebe then tried to turn her attention to paperwork, but she felt nauseous, too crazed to concentrate. Everything seemed to be crushing in on her. She gathered her belongings together and locked up her office. As she turned around, she saw Jan Wait approaching her in the hall.

"Phoebe, hi, I hope you got my message. How *are* you?"

"Much better than on Monday," Phoebe said. "And I appreciate your call, Jan."

She wished there was some way to pump Jan for information about Duncan. She must know a fair amount about him because of his friendship with Miles. But she couldn't do it without shooting off a big red flare. She pictured Jan's reaction to a comment like, "I've been shacking up with Duncan—would you happen to know if he's a psychopathic murderer?"

"Is there anything I can do for you?" Jan asked. "You don't seem like a casserole kind of girl, but I'd be glad to drop one off if you could use it."

"That's sweet of you, but I'm managing pretty well now. It just takes some getting used to."

"I know. Miles broke his foot last year, and it turned into such a drag."

"How's his angina, by the way? Is he feeling better?"

"Angina? Why do you say that?"

"Oh, didn't he—"

"Miles doesn't have angina," Jan said.

It was the shove again, like someone ramming Phoebe between the shoulder blades. She fumbled for a reply.

"Um—oh, sorry. I'd heard a psych professor had an angina attack. For some reason I thought it was Miles. Well, look, I'd better run." There was a roaring sound in her ears, and she couldn't even think.

"You're sure you're okay?"

"Yes, yes, fine. I'll see you later."

She barely remembered the trip home. Her mind had scrambled over what she'd heard from Jan, trying to figure out what it meant. Duncan had clearly lied about Miles because he must have gone someplace else in those fifteen minutes. But *where*? Had *he* turned off the lights? To scare her off her research into the case?

Ten minutes after she reached home, Phoebe heard a dog yap outside and realized that Dan had arrived with Ginger. She swung open the door. Dan was tall—at least six-three—and he carried the tiny dog awkwardly against his body with one hand, as if he'd been forced to hold a woman's purse. The sight of the little dog overwhelmed Phoebe with both grief and relief.

Though Dan was sporting a beard, Phoebe thought she could see a little of Hutch in him. "Sorry to have to meet you under these circumstances," she told him.

"Same here," Dan said, stepping into the house. In his other hand Phoebe saw that he was carrying a large bag of dog supplies. He set the bag down and passed the chihuahua to Phoebe. As she took Ginger into her arms, she felt the dog's body suddenly soften.

"We couldn't get into my Uncle Ed's house, so everything's brand-new. Oh, and there's food in the bag. Any luck finding a home for her yet?"

"Not yet, but someone affiliated with the school is bound to want her." She could feel the dog's little snout pressed into her chest.

"She sure seems to like you," Dan said. "She never did seem very comfortable with me and my wife."

"Thank you," Phoebe said. "And again, I'm sorry for your loss."

As soon as he left, Phoebe pulled Ginger back and looked into her eyes. "You've had a tough time, haven't you, little girl?" Phoebe whispered to her. "I promise to take good care of you."

For the next few hours, she tried to acclimate Ginger to her new situation. She showed her around the house, filled the bowls with food and water, and took her for a walk up and down the street. But as much as Phoebe attempted to focus on Ginger, her thoughts were constantly torn back to Duncan, to the idea that he might be a killer.

She tried Wesley twice more but didn't reach him. She also called Jen Imbibio. She'd given the girl twenty-four hours to produce information, and it was time to confront her.

"Did you learn anything yet?" Phoebe asked when Jen answered.

"Uh, no. I just can't come right out and ask about the circles. I have to, you know, wait for the right moment."

"What about Fortuna?"

"Um, no, not yet. Not exactly."

Phoebe's heart skipped.

"Which *is* it, Jen?" Phoebe demanded. "Not yet or not exactly? Because not exactly suggests you found something."

"I don't have anything, you know, uh, specific. But I said something to the girl, the one in charge, and she got this kind of funny smile. Like she knew what I meant. But I can't be sure."

Phoebe fought to rein in her emotions.

"Did *you* find out anything?" Jen asked, filling the silence. "I mean, about the murder, that Blair didn't do it."

"I'm working on it, Jen," Phoebe said. "But it's a two-way street. I need some real answers from you, okay? I'll call you tomorrow, and I expect to hear something."

"Okay," the girl muttered.

Phoebe walked Ginger once more, trying to tamp down her mounting anxiety. When she returned, she called Duncan, knowing he'd now be at class. There was no way she could stay with him again until she figured out the truth.

"Hi, it's me," she said to his voice mail. "I'm sorry, but I have to bail tonight. Glenda needs me for something important, and I'm going to bunk down at her house. I'll—I'll talk to you tomorrow, okay?"

And then what do I say tomorrow, she wondered in despair, when I still don't have any answers?

At four she promised Ginger she would return shortly and, with her coat draped around her and a pashmina for extra warmth, she headed out on foot. She'd never been to the soccer field, but she knew where all the playing fields were—on the northern part of campus, west of the Grove and the science center. She entered the college through the western gate and walked north. Several of the playing fields were occupied—there were girls swinging hockey sticks on the one nearest to her, and football practice just beyond that. Farther down, she was pretty sure, was the soccer game—there was a fair number of people watching. Phoebe picked up her pace, eager to connect with Glenda. The ground was still soggy from the rain, and Phoebe felt her boots becoming damp. Though the pashmina helped her body stay warm, the wind was strong, and before long her face felt raw.

She spotted Glenda almost immediately along the sidelines of the field, towering above the crowd in her red coat. As Phoebe made her way in that direction, Glenda seemed to sense her presence and looked over. She waved and broke away from the people who'd congregated around her. As she reached Phoebe, her smile faded.

"What's happened now?" Glenda asked. She had obviously read Phoebe's face.

"The news just keeps getting better and better," Phoebe said. She spilled what she'd learned—that it was Duncan, not Tom, who'd been on the committee with Lily. Glenda flung her head back, grimacing.

"Oh, wow. You're sure?"

"That's the information in the computer. Of course, I have no proof they had an affair."

"Are you in love with him, Fee?"

Phoebe shrugged mournfully. "Not in love yet, fortunately," she said. "But in *like*, definitely. And it's not just that he might have had an affair with Lily. But what *else* might have happened."

The wind whipped Phoebe's hair in front of her face, and she yanked the strands away, tucking them behind her ears.

"I need to ask you a question, G," Phoebe said. "When I first told you about me and Duncan, you paused a beat. Why?"

Glenda looked off, gathering her words. The wind was playing havoc with her hair, too, and she smoothed it down distractedly with her hands.

"Not because I'd heard anything *bad* about him," she replied. "Of course I would have told you that. And look, the guy has a stellar reputation here. Not only do the kids like him, but he's published terrific papers. But when his wife was sick—well, there were rumors that his attention was diverted elsewhere."

"With a student?" Phoebe demanded.

"No," Glenda said. "Again, I would have told you something like that. I heard it was with someone in town. Look, people cheat every day, and maybe he just needed a way to cope with his wife's illness. But then there was the creepy way she died."

"You think he might have killed her?" Phoebe asked, her voice catching.

"Well, I didn't at the time. And I didn't five minutes ago. I just thought it was, like I said, creepy. But now you've got my mind racing."

"I feel like puking," Phoebe said.

"Should we tell the police?" Glenda asked.

"No," Phoebe said sharply. "Sorry—I just don't want to cast any suspicion on him with the cops until I have more information."

Behind them the crowd noise began to swell from a hum to a light roar and then finally jubilant cheering as a goal was obviously scored. Instinctively the two women turned their heads toward the field. As Phoebe's eyes ran over the scene, she saw that Rachel, the girl from her class, the one she spotted walking with Jen, was sitting on the players' bench.

"I'd better be getting back," Glenda said.

"That girl with the blond hair who's on the bench," Phoebe said. "Her name's Rachel Blunt. Do you know anything about her?"

"Just that she's out for a few days with an injury. Why?"

"She may be—look, I'll fill you in later. I'm still in information-gathering mode."

"Phoebe, please be careful."

"I will. Before I go, there's one more thing I need to tell you." Mentally Phoebe gritted her teeth and described her trip to Glenda's house yesterday, and what she'd overheard Mark say.

Glenda shook her head in disgust. "Do you think it was a woman?"

"If it was, he didn't seem all that friendly," Phoebe said. "I remember you told me that he once had that problem with online gambling. I've been wondering if that's what it is, that what he needed to deliver to the person was money."

"What a bastard. Of all the times for him to be pulling this."

Phoebe hugged Glenda with just her left arm. "I'll call you later. Let me know if I can do anything at all," she said.

Phoebe headed back toward West Gate, making slow progress over the sodden grass. She tried calling Wesley again. Still nothing. As she dropped her phone into her purse, she glanced around her. The other two playing fields were empty now, though far ahead of her she could see the football players trudging into the gym after practice. She was on the western edge of the Grove, and she realized that there was no one in the immediate vicinity. She pulled her pashmina around her and began to hurry.

When Phoebe stopped to catch her breath, she heard footsteps behind her and spun around. A man was coming towards her. He had on a dark jacket with a scarf obscuring the lower part of his face, but she knew the gait. It was Duncan. He's been following me, she thought. She froze for a moment, and then took a step awkwardly backward, unsure what to do.

"Phoebe, wait up," he called to her.

"What are you doing here?" she asked roughly.

"What am I *doing*?" he said. "I saw you at the game, and I wanted to catch up with you. Is something the matter? Why did you cancel tonight?"

"I thought I explained," Phoebe said. "I need to be with Glenda."

"No," he said, stepping closer. "Something's the matter, I can tell."

Phoebe glanced over his shoulder. Behind one of the dorms, a bunch of boys was tossing a Frisbee, calling out funny insults to each other as they played. She knew it wasn't smart to say anything, to confront Duncan, but she couldn't hold back.

"You lied to me," Phoebe blurted out. "You *knew* Lily, didn't you?"

Duncan said nothing for a moment and just looked at her, his eyes wary.

"All right," he said finally. "I *did* know her. But it's not what you think."

# 30

Phoebe had braced herself for the fact that Duncan had lied to her about knowing Lily, but the actual words still rocked her.

"Did you have an affair with her?" Phoebe said.

"No, of course not."

"*Really?*"

"You honestly think I had an affair with a student here?" Duncan said indignantly.

"Lily told at least one person that she was in love with a man she was on a committee with last spring."

Duncan pressed his lips together, as if holding the words back.

"Okay, something *did* happen," he said after a moment.

Phoebe's heart seemed to stop. She glanced over his shoulder again. The boys who'd been tossing the Frisbee had given up and drifted off.

"You slept with her?" Phoebe said.

"No, I told you I didn't," Duncan said. His anger was rising, and he swept a hand roughly through his hair. "But she seemed to have a crush on me, and it might have been partially my fault. I'd become friendly with her when we were on a committee in part because I knew she was a wreck about her boyfriend disappearing, but also because I liked that she was so passionate about animal rights. She came by my office a couple of times this term to continue the discussion. Then one day she called and asked me to grab a beer after class. I thought she was including other kids from the committee, but she was alone and I started to pick up this flirtatious undercurrent. So I backed off completely. Even if I'd been interested—and I *wasn't*—I would have never jeopardized my career here."

"And that's it?" Phoebe demanded.

He didn't say anything for a second, and she saw him take a breath.

"No," he said, "there's a bit more than that. About two weeks ago, I bumped into her at a farmer's market a few miles from here. It seemed odd to find her there, and later I realized she might have overheard me tell someone I was headed there on the weekend, and showed up on purpose. She asked if I wanted to have a cup of coffee with her. There were a few plastic tables set up. I felt backed into a corner, so I said yes. And as we were sitting there, she leaned over and kissed me—totally out of the blue."

He shook his head as if the memory still bugged him. Was it all an act? Phoebe wondered.

"I told her I was flattered," Duncan said, "but that I didn't believe in dating students. She apologized and said she was just confused about a bunch of things. I felt sorry for her—I could tell she was still troubled about the boyfriend and trying to sort things out. That was the last contact I had with her this semester—though I saw her a couple of times coming out of the science center. If I'm the man she told people about, I had no clue her feelings ran that deep."

"But why would you lie to me? Why tell me you didn't know her?"

"A student *drowns* in the river? A student I rebuffed romantically? That's not information I intended to broadcast on campus. I hadn't even told Miles."

He'd misled her so successfully before, she didn't know how to read whether this was the truth or not.

"Look, Phoebe," he said when she'd didn't reply. "That's why I acted like such a prick this morning when you mentioned her having an affair. Once you and I had become intimate, I was having second thoughts about withholding this information from you. I don't make a habit of lying."

"Is that right?" she said. "But you told me a lie just the other day. You said Miles had had an angina attack, but when I talked to Jan today, she claimed he doesn't have angina."

"Wait, you spoke to Jan?"

"I asked her if Miles was okay."

Duncan threw up his hands. "I should have told you. He hasn't admitted to Jan that he has it. He doesn't want to alarm her. If you don't believe me, call him."

He seemed frustrated with her. But that was what liars often did, she knew. They flipped things, becoming indignant with *you*.

"Then why tell me it was *Bruce* you were going to see?" she said.

"*What?*"

"You told me at first you were going upstairs to see Bruce."

"I misspoke, for God's sake. I work with both of them every day. Where are you going with this, Phoebe, anyway?"

"Well, there are these inconsistencies, but then I'm supposed to believe you when you say that there was really nothing between you and Lily. And then she ends up dead. And so does Hutch."

"Are you suggesting that I *did* something to her—that I *killed* her?"

Stop right there, Phoebe commanded herself. Don't go any further. But she couldn't contain herself.

"*Did* you?" she asked, her voice suddenly hoarse.

Duncan let his arms drop by his side and shook his head in dismay, his mouth pinched together.

"I don't believe you're doing this, Phoebe," he said. "I thought we had something together—something good."

He turned abruptly and traipsed off along the woods.

I guess that's it for us, Phoebe thought, regardless of what the truth is. I just ended everything.

She felt overwhelmed—by sadness and grief but also by anger that Duncan had lied to her, and by fear that everything he'd said just now had been lies as well. She wanted to believe him, but she was still nagged by doubt.

She waited a minute until Duncan was out of sight and then made her own way across campus. By the time she reached the gate, her head was pounding and her elbow ached unbearably.

She had just turned onto Hunter Street when her phone rang. Wesley, finally.

"What's going on?" he said, sounding agitated. "I got all these calls from you."

"I'm sorry about that," Phoebe said, sliding into the front seat. "I was just anxious to catch up with you."

"Is something the matter?"

"No, no. I just need your help. I want to get a bit more info from you about the man at the jukebox in Cat Tails."

"The man? Why does that matter anymore? They've arrested the girls who did it."

"Uh, maybe not. I'm having doubts that Blair and her friend are the killers."

"Whoa, really? And you think it was this man I talked to?"

"I don't know, but I just keep coming back to him. Is there any way you can meet me tonight? I can explain when I see you."

"Lemme think for a second," he said. "I'm still at work, and then I'm going out from here—but in the opposite direction from Lyle." There were a few seconds of silence. "Is there any way you could meet me here? It's about twenty, twenty-five minutes west of Lyle."

She didn't like the idea of driving all that way, especially because it would be completely dark soon, but she was desperate to meet with Wesley. In person she could take notes, prod him better. And even show him a picture.

"Okay," she said. "How late will you be there?"

"I was planning to leave in half an hour because I need to be at this other place. But if you hurry, I'll wait."

Phoebe was worried about how she would pull it off, but she didn't want to pass up the chance to see him. She scribbled down the address and signed off. Now she needed to hurry home, check on Ginger, and pick up her car. She also had to download a photo.

The little dog seemed overjoyed to see her and nearly leaped in her arms when she walked into the house. Phoebe took a few seconds to pet her and toss her one of the tiny treats from the package Dan had left. Next, with the clock ticking in her head, Phoebe pulled up the college Web site and downloaded the photo of Stockton. There was a remote chance, she thought, that once Lily had been spurned by Duncan—if that were really the case—she had moved on to Stockton, and the story had then morphed slightly in the telling.

Phoebe was in the car in less than ten minutes, but she was now behind schedule. She programmed the address into her GPS and pulled out of the driveway. Fortunately most of the trip turned out to be on back-country roads, and there was little traffic to contend with. As she drove, the misery she was feeling seemed to balloon with each mile. Her boots were soaked through from walking over soggy ground earlier, her elbow still ached, and her emotions were a battered mess. She *had* had something good with Duncan. And now it was over.

Wesley's feed company was at the edge of a small town called Springville, and Phoebe reached it fifteen minutes later than she'd promised. She prayed that Wesley was still waiting. As she pulled off the road into the parking lot, she saw a sign out front that read, "Closed," but there was one car still in the parking lot.

She stepped from her car into the cold. She was at the far right end of the large brick building, and peering through the twilight, she saw a stream running near the back. It was the one Wesley had mentioned, she realized, the one that once moved the paddle wheel that then turned the grist stones. In the air was the smell of something sweet but unidentifiable.

As she hurried toward the main door, she saw that she was actually looking at two buildings—the big old gristmill with a drive-through on one end—probably for trucks and vans making pickups—and a newer, less impressive structure on the far side that appeared to be devoted to the lawn care business. There was a light on just inside the main building, so she tried that door first. Entering, she spotted Wesley standing behind a counter in the two-story-high space, dressed in his standard-issue khaki pants, button-down shirt, and pullover. The smell she'd picked up outside was even stronger in here.

"Thanks so much for waiting," Phoebe told him. The front of the large room, she saw, had been set up as a store, with shelves of feed and supplies. It opened at the back onto an area with industrial-looking equipment and huge container bags. That was clearly where the feed was ground and bagged.

"Not a problem," Wesley said. "What'd you do to your arm?"

"Broke my elbow—but just a minor fracture."

He smoothed an eyebrow with his hand, a gesture she interpreted as impatience. He was being polite, but he was clearly eager to leave.

"This should only take a second," Phoebe said. "What's that smell, by the way?"

"Oh, that's probably the molasses you're smelling. We sweeten the animal feed with it. We have vats of it in the basement, and it's piped up to the back room."

As she drew a notebook from her purse, the store phone rang.

"Lemme just grab this, okay?" he said. "It's a guy calling back about a lawn issue."

Wesley answered, "Springville Feed Company," and ended up in a conversation about crabgrass. As he talked, Phoebe's eyes wandered over the space. In the middle of the first floor was an open area protected by a waist-high wooden fence; beyond it was the top of a large, weathered paddle wheel, at least twelve feet in diameter. She moved closer and stared down into a pit large enough to hold the wheel and several wooden gears. At one point the stream had run through there, she realized, making the wheel turn, but now it was totally dry.

Across the room she heard Wesley say good-bye, and she returned to where she'd been standing.

"Pretty interesting, isn't it?" he said, coming from behind the counter. "The water churned the paddle wheel around, and that moved the gears that in turn activated the grist stones." He pointed to an area to her left, and she swiveled her head in that direction. There was a large circular stone resting on the floor.

"Yes, fascinating," she said, though she hadn't a lick of interest at the moment. "Anyway, as I said on the phone, I'd love a better description of the man at the jukebox. You said he was in his late thirties, perhaps early forties, not dressed as a townie. Anything else you recall?"

Wesley slowly shook his head. "Not really," he said. "I mean, he seemed sure of himself, confident. That much I remember."

Phoebe pulled the photo of Stockton out of her purse. It was a long shot, but it was all she had.

"This wasn't the guy by any chance, was it?"

"He looks vaguely familiar, but no," Wesley said. "The guy I talked to was darker. Dark hair, dark eyes."

Phoebe stuffed the photo back in her purse and, after hesitating for a second, pulled out her phone. I can't believe I'm doing this, she thought.

"What about him?" she asked. She opened up the photo she had taken of Duncan in his kitchen last Friday.

"Oh, wow," Wesley said after a couple of seconds.

Phoebe caught her breath. "What?" she asked. It came out as barely a whisper.

"This is a professor from Lyle. I've seen him."

"What do you mean? He's the man you saw that night?"

"No, no, definitely not," Wesley said. He narrowed his gray eyes. "I just recognized him from school."

Thank God for small favors, Phoebe thought.

"So now you're thinking a guy did it, huh?" Wesley said as Phoebe dropped the phone back in her purse.

"Yes. Someone familiar with the area who knew about the Sixes and figured it would be easy to frame them. And very possibly someone connected to Lyle College. It might be the man you talked to that night, but maybe not. Can I ask you one more favor?"

"Is it going to take long?" Wesley asked. He sounded a little testy, as if he were starting to run out of patience.

"No, just a few minutes, I swear." She reached into her purse again and pulled out a copy of Hutch's notes.

"These are the notes Ed Hutchinson took after talking to you last fall. He told me that when he'd reread them, he'd found something significant in them, but he never had a chance to tell me what it was. Can you look and see if anything jumps out for you?"

Wesley shrugged his shoulders before he'd even looked but then glanced down and moved his eyes along the page.

"Sorry, nope," he said after not more than a cursory glance. "I mean, it's all just the stuff I told him."

"There must be something significant in the underlined parts," Phoebe said. "Mr. Hutchinson looked over a set of notes I took after *my* first meeting with you, and he highlighted the exact same things. It's uncanny, but the two sets of notes are almost identical. All the details are the same—nearly word for word. It's, well—"

And then, as she said the words, the truth seemed to charge into her brain, like someone flinging open a door and bursting into a room. The *same*. The two sets of notes were exactly the same. Every single detail given to Hutch had been repeated to her—*an entire year later*. Glenda's words from the other day echoed in her head: "A liar's story is often just a little too pat."

Phoebe now knew what Hutch had discovered through the notes. Wesley had made up the story. Because, she thought, without understanding the reason, Wesley was the killer.

She forced a smile, but she could feel how lopsided it was on her face. *Can he tell?* she wondered as terror mounted inside her. *Can he tell I just figured it out?*

"Well," she said feebly, "if nothing occurs to you, I'd better scoot and let you close up." She looked down, hoping he couldn't see her fear, and tucked the notes back into her purse. She saw that her fingers were trembling.

"Where're you headed?" he asked. When she forced herself to look back up at him, she saw that he'd slapped a smile on his own face, but it was ugly and mean.

"I thought I'd just stay in with a book tonight," she said. Fear had turned her voice into only a whisper. "Well, good night."

"You really think I'm going to let you leave now?"

She opened her mouth, but nothing came out.

"You know why I'm saying that, right?" he said. "I just saw you figure it out in your head. Or kind of, right?"

"I don't know what you mean," she said.

She started to turn around and aimed for the door, but he took a giant step with her and blocked her way.

"Don't make me fly into a rage, okay?" he said. His voice was different now, surly and low. "That's what Gramps did."

"I won't make you mad," she whispered. "I promise."

"That Gramps," he said, shaking his head back and forth as if someone had turned up the speed on him. "He thought he was so damn smart. Didn't that irritate the hell out of you?"

Humor him, she told herself. Until you can figure out what to do. "Did—did Hutch call you about the notes?"

"Well, I told you he called me—so I could make it seem like I'd shared the stuff about Blair. But he's too much of a busybody to just call." Wesley snickered. "He dropped by here last Saturday afternoon. I was outside the lawn care barn, and he pulled up in his truck. Took me a second to recognize him. Said he was sorry about not taking my case seriously before, and he was finally trying to follow up with me. He showed me the notes he'd taken, and then he whips out the notes from *you*. And all of a sudden he starts to go all Lenny Briscoe on me. He asks in this mocking way if I don't find it funny that every detail is the same. And then he says that when someone's telling the truth, they tend to forget certain details or recall them a bit differently. But liars often repeat it word for word because they've rehearsed it. The whole time he's not accusing me, just insinuating in this sly way, like he's the hotshot cop and I'm just some idiot.

"Then he tells me he's used the computer to check me out at school, and he's figured out that I was in a bunch of classes with Lily Mack."

"A bunch?" Phoebe recalled that Wesley had told her he was in *one*.

"I took three classes with that bitch. I was freaking in *love* with Lily. We were in a class together last fall, and we started sharing notes and having coffee together, that sort of thing. We had a connection, you know. But then she totally messes it up—she starts dating that flaming asshole, Trevor. I tried to make her see what a jerk he was, but she just didn't get it. So I made sure he was out of the picture and bided my time."

Even in her panic, Phoebe could see the pieces beginning to fit in her own mind.

"But before you killed Trevor, you decided to throw yourself into the river—so that his drowning would seem like part of a pattern?"

"Why not, right? I mean, there'd already been one drowning, and I'd read about these other cases on the Internet."

"How did you kill him?"

"It was so easy, it was kind of sick. I knew he hung out downtown, and one night at Cat Tails after I'd bided my time for a few months, I stood near him at the bar and put GHB in his drink. And then, after a while, I asked him if he wanted some weed. He was the kind of guy who called me Fathead behind my back, but he wouldn't turn down *that* kind of offer—plus he was pretty out of it by then. I told him to meet me in the parking lot by the river so no one would see us, and then I drove him up the road."

"Across from the Big Red Barn?"

"Yup. It was a piece of cake to just push him in."

"But then his body was never found."

"Yeah, I know. Can you believe that freaking luck? But it worked out in the end. Everybody thought he just took off. Which made him look like an even bigger asshole."

"But Lily still didn't want to date you."

"At first she was just too upset to do anything. I figured I'd just wait till she came back after the summer. But then we get together one day, and I finally tell her how I feel, and she says she never wants to be anything other than my fucking friend."

He twisted his mouth as he said the word *friend*, as if it filled him with disgust. Phoebe could barely look at him, but she knew she had to, had to keep him talking and calm.

"And then you killed Lily, too—because she didn't love you?"

"No," he snapped. "The problem was, she started to figure it out."

"Figure what out?"

"That I killed Trevor," he said, even fiercer now. "What the fuck else do you think?"

"Okay, I got it," Phoebe said. She commanded herself to breathe slowly, to fight her fear.

"I was still keeping tabs on her sometimes. I thought she might finally see what I could offer her, you know. I was watching her that night she went down to Cat Tails. I parked my car and went inside a few minutes later, like it was just a coincidence. I grabbed a beer and was hanging out near her, but trying not to crowd her. And then these guys came in who knew Trevor, who were around the night he disappeared, I guess, and she got upset once she started talking to them. She asked them about that night and if he gave any reason for wanting to just bail. And then out of the blue one of them looks over at me and goes, 'You talked to him a little bit that night, didn't you, Hines? Did he say anything to you?'

"Well, I guess that freaked her out. She finished her beer real quick and left. I drove up the street looking for her and convinced her to hop in my car so we could just talk. Of course, she wanted to know why I'd never told her about talking to Trevor, and I said it was because I hadn't wanted to upset her about what he'd confessed. I said he'd told me he didn't want to hurt her but he didn't love her and he just wanted to make a break for it."

Wesley was growing more and more agitated as he spoke, twisting his neck as if the shirt were choking him.

"I could see that she was becoming suspicious, that she knew a guy like Trevor wouldn't be confiding shit to me. I figured that she might go to the cops and they'd check my car and find that asshole's DNA in it or something. You know what's funny? There was a minute when I thought she was going to just bolt from the car and there was nothing I could do. But she was trying to figure out the truth—be the little investigator like you—and she kept talking to me. I had some coffee in a thermos, and I offered it to her while we were talking. I dropped the drug in the coffee and gave her a drink. She was totally passed out by the time I dumped her in the river."

Phoebe felt sick, seeing the image in her mind. At least Lily hadn't had to fight for her life in the dark, muddy water.

"And Hutch?" Phoebe asked. "He had to die, too?"

Wesley shook his head hard.

"I didn't know what to do about Gramps," he said. "After he left here, I was *crazy*. I knew he was going to probably go to the cops, and I needed to act fast. That stuff you told me about that stupid girl group was a total godsend. I planted all the stuff at the diner with you about Blair, and then I figured how I could set them up. And then I went to pay Gramps a visit. I wasn't sure I was going to kill him, but he didn't give me a choice."

He shook his head again.

"You want to do the right thing," he said. "But people just don't let you. Like Lily. She just wouldn't give me a chance."

He stared right at Phoebe. "And like you," he said.

"Bu—"

"You wouldn't back off. You kept snooping around. I tried to scare you by killing the lights in the science building that night. But even when they caught the girls, you wouldn't let it go."

He glanced off, as if in dismay. *Now!* Phoebe screamed to herself. She spun around and bolted toward the door. She'd only gone two steps before Wesley grabbed her fiercely by the hair and yanked her back. She yelped in pain.

"Where the fuck do you think you're going?" Wesley yelled. He was still behind her, and he coiled her hair roughly in his fist.

"Wesley, don't do this, please," she said. "You—you have a chance to stop it all now."

"And get caught?" He snickered. "Why would I want to do that?"

"They'll find out. I—I've told people. The man I'm seeing knows."

"I doubt it. I know who you've been seeing—the guy on your phone. Ten fucking minutes ago you thought *he* was the killer."

She started to struggle, trying to free herself from his grasp, but he yanked her hair even tighter. Then he drew his other hand back and punched her hard in the face. Her head snapped back. He let go of her hair, and she went crashing to the ground, landing on her broken elbow. It felt like someone had just lit a fire to her arm.

And then he had her by the hair again and was dragging her across the dusty floorboards.

"You're going to have to excuse me," Wesley said, panting. "But it's going to seem weird if I don't meet these people tonight. I'll have to deal with you later."

Finally he dropped her. She saw that she was against the wooden barrier that surrounded the pit. Was he going to tie her up and come back afterward? she wondered desperately. If he tied her up, she might have a chance to free herself.

But then he was hoisting her up, his thick arms under hers.

"No, Wesley, please," she pleaded. "Please, no."

She kicked at the barrier with both feet, but it was useless.

With one easy movement he raised her even higher. And then she was sailing through the air.

# 31

**B**efore she could even form a thought, the back of her body slammed into something hard. She heard a *thwack* sound as her shoulder blade made contact with the surface, and the wind rushed out of her. Then she was falling again, bounced from the first thing she'd struck. She hit the bottom of the pit seconds later, facedown, with her broken elbow driving into the ground. Pain blistered and then exploded through every inch of her.

She tried but couldn't even grab a breath. It felt as if a giant snake had circled her torso and begun to squeeze. But she was alive. Above her she knew Wesley must be watching, hoping she was dead.

After a minute she heard him move. There was a fast, scuffing sound of footsteps, gradually receding toward the front of the building. He's going now, she realized. Somehow she would try to escape. She opened her eyes just a little and peered through the dimness at the wall. Somewhere there must be toeholds that she could use to climb out.

And then all at once every light went out above her. She was lying in the pitch-black. No, no, please not this, Phoebe thought. It was as if she was in that dark space from years ago. But this time no one would ever come to rescue her.

Get a grip, she told herself.

Two minutes later, she detected the muffled sound of a car moving by. And then it was silent. Wesley would be doing everything in his power to get back as soon as he could. She knew she needed to hurry, to get the hell out *now*.

She commanded her brain to move her legs, but nothing happened. What if they're broken or paralyzed? she thought, terrified. But after a few tries she realized she could shift them. It was only her elbow that seemed truly damaged. The pain was searing now, like someone burning a hole through the bone with a blowtorch.

With her right hand, Phoebe tried to push her body up. When she'd managed to lift her torso a foot off the ground, she drew her right knee up under her abdomen for leverage. From there she slowly rolled over and pulled herself up into a sitting position. Then she struggled all the way up. As she reached a standing position, her right hand touched something oddly shaped and wooden in front of her. She had obviously landed by one of the gears to the right of the giant paddle wheel. She realized for the first time that she must have bounced off the paddle wheel on the way down. Though she'd smacked her back on it, the wheel had at least broken her fall, maybe saving her life.

Through the dark she inched forward, to the wall. She could feel her panic returning, something old and familiar, and she told herself to just breathe. With her good hand she began to search for any kind of exit or toehold or ladder, slowly moving around the perimeter of the pit. There *had* to be something like that, she thought; people must have once climbed in and out. But after a search all the way around, she'd found nothing.

*Think,* she told herself. What had Wesley said upstairs? Water turned the paddle wheel, which then turned the gears, which then turned the grist stones. But there was something else, something she remembered from her conversation with him in the diner. *The sluice gate.* It's where they let the water in.

She dropped to her knees and began to circumvent the pit again, but this time feeling lower along the wall, searching with her right hand for the old sluice gate. There would have to be two, she realized, one right behind the paddle wheel and another on the side directly opposite. But she was disoriented now, and wasn't sure where she was anymore.

Finally her hand felt something—a metal plate in the wall. She ran her hand roughly over it. On either side were two metal handles, clearly for raising the gate. She gave a tug to one of the handles with her right hand. Nothing happened. It might be welded in place, she realized, or stuck from years of disuse. She forced herself up into a standing position and tried again. This time it budged. She felt a surge of relief.

Hobbling to the other side of the gate, Phoebe tugged on the opposite handle. There. The gate inched up a bit more. Suddenly her feet were cold and she knew that water had begun to seep in—not gushing but steady, a slow-moving stream. Then she thought, What if the pit fills with water before I have a chance to fully lift the sluice gate?

Quickly she moved from side to side, hoisting the gate up an inch at a time on each side. The water was around her ankles now, icy cold. But finally the gate was raised enough to let a body through.

It wasn't going to be easy. She would be fighting the stream—and with only one arm to paddle with.

But she had no choice. Wesley would return and kill her.

Phoebe snagged a breath and plunged through the opening. Within seconds she was totally underwater, and the cold force hit her with a wallop. Water rushed up her nose. She struggled futilely to raise her head above the surface. Swim, she commanded herself. She kicked hard and scooped the water desperately with her right arm. Finally her boots scraped against something, and she realized they were dragging against the ground. With her lungs ready to burst, she shoved her head above water. She could see now. She was in the stream just to the right of the building, and above her the sky twinkled with stars. A sob of relief broke in her throat.

She crouched in the water, still gasping for breath, and peered through the darkness. She had begun to shiver. The security light on the end of the building illuminated the edge of the parking lot. Phoebe could see the outline of a single car in the lot—it was hers. Wesley's car was definitely gone.

But there was no point in trying to reach her own car. She didn't have her purse with her car key in it, and even if she did, she knew it would be risky to cross the lot—Wesley might come back at any moment. She turned and searched the area behind her with her eyes.

There was an embankment on this side of the stream that reached up to an area of ragged shrubbery. Phoebe staggered out of the stream, her wet clothes sucking at her body, and struggled up the embankment. Each step jarred her elbow, making her moan in pain.

As she reached the top, she realized that the small town of Springville was behind her, opposite the direction she was moving, but there were two houses ahead, each just off the road. One was dark, except for a bulb burning on the front porch, but lights were on throughout the other one. Phoebe stumbled toward it. She was shivering forcefully now, and her heart was beating hard from the effort of climbing. Water ran into her eyes. She reached up to wipe it from her face and smelled that it was actually blood.

As she neared the house, Phoebe could hear a TV going inside, and through the window she saw an older couple plopped on the couch, faces aimed at the TV and their expressions listless. She dragged herself up the steps of the porch and knocked hard on the door. You have to seem sane, she told herself. Or they will never let you in. Through the window she saw the shapes of both people rise from the couch and move toward the door, hesitant and uncertain.

"Who is it?" the man called without opening the door.

"I'm a teacher at Lyle College," Phoebe yelled through the door. "And someone tried to kill me. I need your help."

There was no reply, though behind the door she could hear the couple squabbling. Finally the door opened a crack, with the chain still in place. All she could see were two spiky white eyebrows.

"We'll call nine-one-one," a man's voice said. "Just wait on the porch there."

The road was just ten yards behind her, and Phoebe heard a car shoot by. When Wesley returned and saw the water in the pit, the first place he would look for Phoebe would be along the road.

"Please," Phoebe begged. "I'm afraid he'll find me out here. Can you let me in?"

She heard the woman tell the man no, but the man argued, and finally there was the sound of the chain bouncing against the doorframe. The door swung open, and the man ushered her inside. Phoebe stumbled into the hallway. The woman gasped in shock, and Phoebe sank slowly to the floor. She could see in the light that her left sleeve was soaked in blood.

The man commanded the woman to call 911 and then grab a blanket. He stooped to the floor, scanning Phoebe's body with his eyes.

"Your husband do this to you?" the man asked solemnly.

For a brief moment Phoebe felt like laughing. She was tempted to tell him, between chattering teeth, Yeah, we got into a domestic spat using a garden hose, but she knew she was lucky he'd let her in and she shouldn't rock the boat.

"No," she said, "not my husband."

A few minutes later the woman scurried back with the blanket and laid it over her. The shivering began to slowly subside. It took about fifteen minutes for the ambulance to arrive. Until then Phoebe lay in the hall, eyes closed, with the couple murmuring endlessly nearby. They never asked if she wanted to move to a chair or couch. As far as they know, Phoebe thought, I could be a lunatic. She kept wondering if Wesley had returned and would come banging on the door of the house, suspecting that's where she had escaped to.

Only when she was in the ambulance did she feel safe. She let her mind go nearly blank, except to think about the pain.

There seemed to be tons of people waiting when they reached the hospital, though their faces were mostly a blur. Phoebe guessed it was the same hospital she'd been taken to before. After she was lifted from the ambulance, she found the eyes of one of the nurses who now moved along the side of the stretcher.

"Please call Glenda Johns," Phoebe murmured, "at Lyle College."

*"Hey there,"* someone said. Phoebe forced her eyes open and squinted toward the voice. It was Glenda's.

"Hey," Phoebe muttered back.

"How do you feel, Fee?"

"Like hell. What's going on?"

"You remember that they operated on your elbow, right? It was shattered, and part of it was poking through your skin."

"Right," Phoebe said. She closed her eyes again, trying to wedge the memories free. She pictured herself being wheeled into the recovery room. A nurse comforting her. Then she remembered the water and plunging through it. And before that, being hurled into the pit.

"Wesley?" Phoebe whispered. "Did they catch him?"

"Yes, they nabbed him," Glenda said. "Craig says they're putting the pieces together."

At the mention of the detective's name, another memory shoved its way into Phoebe's brain: Michelson and a colleague—someone other than Huang this time—floating above her while she was still in the ER.

"What about Blair—and Gwen?" Phoebe asked.

"We've heard through their lawyers that they'll probably be released soon. I imagine the cops are waiting to be sure that Wesley is their guy."

"Wait—and *Ginger*," Phoebe said anxiously. "Has anyone been to my house?"

"Don't worry, I arranged for your lovely cleaning woman to let me in, and the dog's with us. Brandon hasn't let her out of his sight."

Phoebe tried to scooch herself up in bed without much success. Glenda located the button that automated the bed and raised the back.

"Don't overdo it, okay?" Glenda said. "By the way, the doctor said they ended up putting a pin in your elbow. The healing time's a bitch, but it should be as good as new eventually."

"I'm just lucky that I struck the paddle wheel first," Phoebe said. "That managed to break my fall. If I hadn't, I'd probably have broken my neck when I hit the ground."

"Do you feel up to telling me what happened?" Glenda asked.

Phoebe sketched out the basic details, and also filled in some blanks about Wesley. When she was finished. Glenda stroked her good arm.

"So is Wesley a serial killer, then?" Glenda asked. "Is that how you'd define him?"

"He probably didn't wake up each day with an urge to commit a horrific murder. But when someone got in his way—like Trevor—he killed without any regrets.

He's a sociopath, I'm sure—a Scott Peterson type who on the outside looks and acts like the boy next door but inside is hollow and emotionless."

"Did you ever have even a hint?"

"There was just one tiny moment. After I met him at the diner and he told me that Blair had actually been at Cat Tails the night he'd ended up in the river, something started nagging at me. But I could never put my finger on it. I think what bugged me deep down was how convenient it was for him to suddenly recall that Blair had been in the bar. He was starting to scramble a little, and I sensed it on some level.

"Of course, I could kick myself for missing the truth, but it's easy for guys like him to fool you," she added. A phrase Duncan had used surfaced in her mind. "They wear the mask of sanity. Like a few damn actors I've known."

Phoebe closed her eyes again. She felt woozy suddenly, as if she had just stepped close to the edge of a precipice and looked down.

"Do you want to go back to sleep?" Glenda asked.

"No," she said, opening her eyes again. "I feel like I've been sleeping for days, and I want to know what's going on. Talk to me. Is your job safe?"

"Don't know. The board isn't asking for my head yet. They certainly can't blame me for Wesley, but the Sixes are another story. They were formed during my tenure. As long as nothing else happens, I may be okay—which of course, will drive Stockton crazy because he seems to want me to fail."

"I'm so relieved, G."

"Oh, there's one piece of interesting news that I wanted to share. After I saw you at the soccer game, I went back to my office, and Val Porter paid me a visit. She had something to confess."

"Do tell."

"She said that last spring she'd engaged in some lip locking with a student—a female. They both had been drinking. This fall the young woman ended up in one of Val's classes, and she began to feel the tiniest bit of pressure from the girl. After you filled Tom in on the circles, he told Val about them, and she began to suspect that the girl was in the Sixes, and had targeted Val to be part of the girl's fifth circle. Val swears she never altered the girl's grade. But she was hysterical she might have jeopardized her job."

"That may explain why I heard her tossing her lunch in the ladies' room," Phoebe said. She looked off, thinking. "Do you think she's only telling you part of the story? I heard that Blair used to consult with someone, that there might be another person pulling the strings for the Sixes. Do you think it could have been

Val? It would make sense if you think about her interest in woman's empowerment."

Glenda shook her head slowly.

"I don't think so. Val seemed borderline hysterical to me."

"What about the girls in the Sixes?" Phoebe asked. "Are you putting names together?"

"We still can't establish for sure that anyone's a member—even Blair and Gwen. There's no proof. One of them is going to have to be willing to tattle."

"Damn. There's one girl who I may be able to put pressure on, but first I need to use her for something else."

"Leave that alone for now. You need to think about recovering. In fact, why don't I let you rest again? I can see you're sleepy."

"Okay, Mom."

"There's just one other thing I wanted to tell you. Duncan called me as soon as he heard the news about you."

"Really?" Phoebe said quietly.

"He told me that you two were no longer seeing each other, but he wanted to make sure you were all right. And he wanted me to tell you he'd asked about you."

Phoebe leaned her head back on the pillow, hesitating.

"Yeah, he didn't take too kindly to me insinuating that he might be a murderer. I guess that's not something you find in a *Cosmo* article on '50 Ways to Turn Your Man into a Mush Ball.'"

Glenda smiled wanly. "I'm sorry, Fee," she said. "Maybe it's for the best, though. After all, you won't be here forever. And now, I'll have to beg to even have you stay next term."

After Glenda had left, Phoebe forced herself to eat the soupy ice cream in the container on the tray. A nurse stopped in and checked her vital signs. Phoebe lay back ready to sleep, but she seemed too jumped up inside.

Wesley was in jail. She had nothing to fear from him now. But there wasn't really closure. The Sixes were still out there, unfettered. With Blair and Gwen back in the mix, they might gather strength again, wreaking havoc.

And somewhere on the campus, someone knew about Fortuna.

## 32

For the next few days Phoebe holed up at her house, trying to rest and eating food that Glenda or her housekeeper dropped off. Her story had made the local paper this time, which spawned coverage nearly everywhere. She was inundated with e-mails—from colleagues on campus as well as friends in Manhattan and L.A. She answered a few but didn't have the psychic energy for more than that. There were a ton of interview requests, too. Through her agent she said no to all of them for now, except the one from Peter Tobias. She didn't dignify his with a response.

A few times a day Phoebe took Ginger out for a walk, going a little bit farther on each trip. She felt so grateful to have the dog. She sensed that without Ginger curled on the couch beside her or trailing behind her in the house, she would have been swallowed alive by malaise. And there was nighttime Ginger to be grateful for, too. She turned out to be a brilliant little watchdog, who barked every time a leaf blew onto the porch. But even with Ginger keeping guard, Phoebe slept fitfully.

Late Monday night, Jan Wait phoned her, and when she saw the name, Phoebe made a quick decision not to let the call go to voice mail.

"Phoebe, you have to let me know if I can do anything," Jan said. "I'd drop off a ham, but I'm afraid you wouldn't eat it."

Phoebe laughed and assured Jan she would reach out if she needed anything.

"I should let you get back to resting," Jan said after they talked for a couple minutes about school matters. "But before I do, I want to apologize for making you sound like an idiot the other day. My darling husband has confessed to me that he *does* have angina."

So Duncan had told the truth about that, too. After Phoebe signed off, thoughts of him trampled through her brain. She'd done her best to keep him at bay—with only moderate success. She felt almost sick with regret, and yet she knew there was nothing she could do.

On Tuesday she e-mailed the students in her two classes, saying she would be back the next Monday but that in the meantime she wanted them to complete an assignment online by Friday. At the end of the e-mail she sent to Jen Imbibio, she added a short message: "We need to talk as soon as possible."

An hour later, there was a curt reply: "I wish I could, but I'm very busy right now."

"This can't wait," Phoebe replied. "Should I look for you in the cafeteria?"

That seemed to do the trick.

"No. I'll come to your house again."

The girl arrived the next morning, wearing tight jeans, a jean jacket, and a newsboy cap. She looked jaunty and smug today, her confidence temporarily restored. She obviously had no clue that the college was about to smoke out the Sixes.

"I'm disappointed I didn't hear from you," Phoebe said. "I took care of my end of the bargain. This was supposed to be a fair swap."

"I was going to get in touch," Jen said. "I really was. But then I heard you were in the hospital."

"Tell me what you found out about Fortuna."

The girl shrugged. "Nothing more. I did what you suggested to another member—told her I'd overheard you talking about the Sixes and Fortuna—and she just looked at me as if she had no *clue* what I was talking about."

"And the girl who's now in charge. She doesn't know anything?"

"I don't think so."

"And that's Rachel, right?" Phoebe said, making a guess.

"Yeah—" Jen caught herself. "How—? Look, I never said it was Rachel."

"What about the sixth circle? If they're supposedly setting you up in the outside world, how are they doing it?"

Jen bit her lip. "Um, I think it's about contacts or something."

"Please, Jen," Phoebe said curtly. "You don't expect me to believe that the Sixes suddenly turns into the Chamber of Commerce once people graduate, do you?"

The girl looked off to some distant spot across the room.

"They give you money, too, I think," she said quietly, looking back. "To help you get started."

*Money?* Phoebe thought, taken aback. "Where does it come from?" she asked.

"I don't know," Jen said. "I think there's some kind of benefactor, you know. It might be something like that."

Bullshit, Phoebe thought. But she sensed Jen truly didn't know.

Phoebe dismissed her. Afterward she sat at her kitchen table, thinking, perplexed by what she'd learned. She'd once heard that members of Skull and Bones were all given a lump sum of money to set them up for life. She had assumed it was only a legend. Perhaps it was a legend too that the Sixes rewarded members with cash, or a fake carrot held out to entice girls to join.

And if it *wasn't* a legend? The money surely couldn't come from anything good. She wondered what they might be up to. They thought nothing of having sex with guys and posting about it. Maybe they blackmailed people. But about what? Or, Phoebe thought, stretching, they made porn flicks. But wouldn't news of that have started to leak out? She had no clue how she would find out.

Sick to death of food deliveries, Phoebe made a meal for herself that night—just pasta with olive oil, garlic, and Parmesan, but it was heaven. She needed the fortification. As she leaned back on the sofa, finishing the meal and sipping a glass of wine, she made a plan for the next day. Seeing that Jen was a dead end, it was time to try a different approach.

She woke the next day feeling achy and sore and with a slight fever. She stayed in bed longer than she wanted. At around three she could feel herself rallying, and an hour later, she draped her coat over her shoulders and headed out on foot. She had found out earlier where Rachel lived—the student town houses directly across from the southern tip of campus.

Though she'd seen the town houses from a distance, she'd never been up close to them. There were twelve in a row. The school had built them to keep upperclassmen in student housing. They were all identical, though the one Rachel lived in had a blue bike locked to the front porch railing.

To Phoebe's dismay, she felt uneasy as she mounted the steps. She knew that once she confronted Rachel, there would be a ripple effect, and she had no idea what it would entail. And yet she couldn't let the Sixes paralyze her.

She knocked on the door and waited. There wasn't a sound. She had picked four o'clock, figuring Rachel might be back from her classes by then, but not yet at dinner. She rapped two more times, and still nothing. Unable to resist, she twisted the doorknob, and to her surprise it gave way in her hand. She pushed the door open and stepped inside. What the hell am I doing? she asked herself. But something other than good judgment seemed to be guiding her.

She was standing in a combination kitchen, dining, and living area, not much different from a dorm lounge.

There were a few dirty dishes scattered on the table, and an ironing board standing in the middle of the living space, with the iron flopped on one side.

From somewhere Phoebe thought she heard music playing, though she wasn't sure if it was coming from upstairs or from the hall that shot off to the right of the living area.

"Anyone home?" she called out.

Without warning, a girl appeared from the downstairs corridor. She was Asian and striking looking, dressed in a T-shirt and sweatpants that read "Lyle College" in faded letters across the front.

"Yes?" the girl asked, advancing into the room. She seemed deadpan except for the small crease that had just formed between her brows.

"I was looking for Rachel," Phoebe said. "Is she around?"

"She's at soccer practice," the girl said, as if anyone with a brain would know that.

That's right, Phoebe realized. She should have remembered.

"They make you go even if you're injured?"

"Oh, she was just out for a game."

"That's good. I'm Phoebe, by the way. You're . . . ?"

"Molly," she said after a split second. The girl clearly had her antennae up, wary of Phoebe's presence.

Phoebe bet this was the Molly that Jen Imbibio had exchanged the look with on Stockton's committee.

"Rachel's in one of my classes, and I wanted to stop by to give her a book to read," Phoebe fudged. "I haven't been in class this week."

"You can just leave it there," the girl said, pointing at the table with her chin. She scooped her long black hair distractedly into a ponytail and then immediately released it. As she raised her arms, Phoebe caught a glimpse of a ridged white brace around the girl's lower torso.

"Did you hurt yourself too?" Phoebe asked.

"I just pulled a muscle," the girl said, shrugging. "In gymnastics. The doctor said I have to stay out for a day or two."

Phoebe thought suddenly of the knee brace she'd seen in Blair and Gwen's hallway.

"Can they deal with injuries like that in the school infirmary?" Phoebe asked.

Molly scrunched her mouth up into a twisted pout. "No. You have to go off campus."

Phoebe glanced down at her own arm in the sling.

"I need someone myself—someone close to the school," she said. "I'd love the name of your doctor."

There was another hesitation. "Dr. Rossely," Molly finally said. "But he's very backed up, I hear."

"Okay," Phoebe said. There was something odd happening, she sensed. "That's Rachel's doctor, too, isn't it? I believe she mentioned him." Phoebe had no idea where she was going with the lie. But something had set off an alarm in her head.

"I guess," Molly said. Her eyes were wary now.

"Well, I'd better let you go," Phoebe said. "Have a nice night."

"You're not going to leave the book?" the girl said. It sounded like a challenge.

"You know, I think I'll wait and give it to her in person," Phoebe said. Funny, she thought. I've been forced to use one of Val Porter's old tricks.

The girl didn't see her out, but Phoebe could feel her eyes boring into her as she walked to the door and struggled to open it.

So what the hell is going on? Phoebe wondered as she walked home through the falling darkness. It could be pure coincidence that three seniors in the Sixes had injuries. After all, Alexis had said that most of the members were jocks—though that was interesting in itself. And there also had been that odd hesitation when Molly said her doctor's name, reluctance on her part, it seemed, to divulge the information.

Were they faking their injuries, Phoebe wondered, so that they'd be sidelined from games for some reason, maybe hurting the chances for victory the way athletes did in big-league sports where people waged bets on the outcome?

Phoebe found her phone, and after scoring a number for the only Dr. Rossely in Lyle—first name Todd—she called his office. She said she was recovering from an accident and wanted a second opinion. The receptionist said they would be able to squeeze her in at two tomorrow. So much for being all booked up. She felt a weird current pulsing through her: a mix of worry, anticipation, and recognition of something—but she didn't know what.

At home, she heated up the leftover pasta from the night before and dragged her duvet and pillow down to the couch, much to Ginger's confusion. But Phoebe had already decided that she would spend the night downstairs. She had stirred the pot with the Sixes again, and there was every chance they'd come calling once more. She needed to be where she could hear them if they tried to sneak in.

At ten Glenda called. "Sorry not to come by today," Glenda said.

"Well, your housekeeper dropped off a chicken pot pie for lunch, which was very yummy. I'm going to need liposuction by the time this is over."

"Dr. Carr mentioned you were doing some class work online. Don't push yourself, Fee, if you're not ready."

"No, I'm ready. In fact, I'm going stir-crazy. I know you're jammed up, but I'd love to see you some time. Don't get me wrong—Ginger is great. She's just not much of a conversationalist."

"Maybe Thursday. I have to go out of town tomorrow for a good chunk of the day."

"Where are you off to?"

"To see a donor who lives out of town. They need handholding through all of this mess."

"Okay," Phoebe said, though it seemed odd for Glenda to be leaving town for a day when the campus was in so much turmoil.

"There's one thing I want to bring you up to speed on," Glenda said. She let out a long, weary sigh. "It bugged me when you said that Trevor Harris had felt the campus cops were out to get him, and I decided to discreetly investigate. From what I can tell so far, it seems Ball's been shaking down certain students—pressuring them to make payments to him in exchange for not slapping them with charges for things like drugs or vandalism. No wonder campus drug use seems to be down."

"Oh, man," Phoebe said. Though she'd never cottoned to Ball, she hadn't seen this one coming. "I think I may have even spotted him in action. I came across him having a talk with the same male student twice, and he seemed sheepish about it."

"The bodies just keep piling up, don't they? I need you to go through the student handbooks and see if you can find that kid. But no one can know anything about this yet, okay? We're going to try a sting operation. Of course, this could be the proverbial straw that breaks the camel's back for me."

"G, I'm sorry. Let me know if I can help in any way."

She had planned to pick Glenda's brain about what she'd heard today regarding the doctor, but changed her mind. She would wait until she had more information. There was no point in upsetting Glenda any more than necessary.

She fell asleep at about ten thirty, a book still on her lap and Ginger curled between her legs. Sometime during the night, something roused her—as forcefully as if she'd been shaken awake. She shot up straight, confused. Both her back and her elbow hurt like hell, probably from being scrunched up on the couch. Was it pain that had woken her? Or something else? At her feet, Ginger remained motionless but emitted a long, steady growl.

"What is it?" Phoebe whispered urgently. She froze and listened. The dog stopped and then started again almost instantly, this time her growl laced with threat. Somewhere nearby there was something the dog didn't like. Phoebe searched with her hand to make sure her phone was within reach on the trunk next to the couch.

For a minute Phoebe detected nothing. But then, from outside a window along the side of the house, she thought she heard a sound. She strained to hear. It might have been nothing more than the creak of a tree branch in the wind. No other sound followed. For the next two hours Phoebe lay with her head against the armrest, listening. Around dawn she finally fell back to sleep. When the sun nudged her awake an hour later, Ginger crawled up toward her head and licked her face.

"You're such a good little doggie," Phoebe said. "What if you stayed with me forever?" Her words surprised her—she hadn't even sensed them in advance—but as soon as she spoke, she knew it was what she wanted to do.

Ginger licked her face again.

"I'll take that as a yes, okay?" Phoebe said.

She spent her morning reviewing the assignments that had begun to trickle in. But her mind kept returning to the appointment with Dr. Rossely that lay ahead. She wasn't sure why she felt so agitated about it. It all *means* something, she told herself. I'm just not yet sure what.

His office wasn't far from her, just two blocks south and one west in an area that was part residential, part business. There were a few older clapboard houses still on the street, but others had been torn down to make way for two-story office buildings like the one Rossely was in.

The space inside wasn't at all what she'd been expecting. Rather than some fussy or run-down-at-the-heels reception area, there was a spare, modern space with posters on the wall from exhibits of the Barnes Foundation. The two patients in the reception area never gave her a second glance, but the receptionist, a middle-aged woman dressed attractively in a pink satin blouse and pearl stud earrings, seemed to study her with recognition. Of course, Phoebe thought as she filled out the necessary forms. I'm a celeb around here now. I can't tell *them* I had a bad fall from a bike.

A nurse popped into reception about ten minutes later, called out Phoebe's name, and led her to an examining room. The doctor arrived shortly after that. He was around Phoebe's age, six-one, and more urbane than she was expecting. He had on a pair of fancy-looking frameless glasses, and he'd had his thinning hair trimmed into a buzz cut, a hip look she rarely saw in Lyle.

"Dr. Rossely," he said, shaking her hand. He practically oozed bedside manner. "My, you've had a busy week." So either he'd recognized her, too, or the receptionist had tipped him off.

"Oh, so I'm busted, then?" Phoebe said, smiling.

"I'd hardly say busted. You're a local star. It must have been some ordeal to go through."

"Yes, unfortunately it was. I'm a bit battered and bruised."

Rossely glanced down. "I see from your records that you were treated at Cranberry Med. Aren't you working with the doctors you had there?"

"By and large, yes," Phoebe said. "From what I can tell so far, they did a nice job repairing my elbow. But I'd like a second opinion on my right shoulder blade. It got whacked pretty bad and hurts like crazy. They told me it's only a bruise, and there's nothing they can do for it."

The words had sounded so forced and fake as she said them—it was as if she were doing a bad job performing in a high school play—and she wondered if he suspected that she was remolding the truth.

"And they didn't prescribe anything?"

"Tylenol with codeine. I tried it just for a few days."

"Well, let's take a look," he said. "In my opinion, there's always something that can be done. I don't like seeing people suffer needlessly."

He edged around the side of the examining table and opened the back of her gown. With a firm but careful touch, he probed the area with his fingers. Twice, she winced in pain. The part about her shoulder hurting hadn't been a lie.

"Sorry about that," Rossely said. "The area definitely seems inflamed. Let's get an X-ray and see if there's also swelling."

Rossely departed, and the nurse came back; she escorted Phoebe into another room for the X-ray. As Phoebe was led back to the examining room, she heard a buzz of activity coming from rooms up and down the corridor. Finally Rossely returned. He was holding an X-ray, and with one swift movement of his hand snapped it onto a light box mounted on the wall.

"Well, the good news is that there's no fracture," he said, smiling. "But as I said, there's definite inflammation, and that should be treated. Off the record, they should have paid more attention to this at Cranberry, but things get pretty crazy up there."

"Thank you," Phoebe said. Rossely opened her folder on the counter and jotted a few words down. Out of the corner of her eye she studied him. Though she found him unctuous, he certainly didn't look sinister in any way. Was this just some stupid wild goose chase on her part?

He swung around slowly, smiling.

"I also want to give you something for the pain," he said. "Pain's a funny thing. People often think they should tough it out and try to ignore it, but you can start a weird cycle that way. The pain almost feeds on itself, and then the cycle is hard to break. It's better to nip it in the bud."

"Of course, I did try the Tylenol with codeine," Phoebe said. "But I didn't feel it helped."

"This is much better," he said. "It's OxyContin. You should take two every twenty-four hours."

Instinctively, Phoebe's mouth parted in surprise. OxyContin, she knew, could be addictive. Hutch had even mentioned it going for $80 a pill on the black market.

"Is something the matter?" Rossely said, obviously noting her reaction.

"No, I was just wondering if it was safe. I've heard people sometimes have problems with it."

"It's safe if used correctly," Rossely said. He smiled tightly. "It's essential with any drug to follow the directions to a T. No more than two a day, as I said."

"Of course," Phoebe replied, realizing she'd ruffled his feathers a little. "And thank you. It's actually wonderful to have someone take my situation seriously."

Rossely lightened up again. "Good," he said. "That's what we're here for." He turned toward the counter and began to scribble the prescription. "I should see you again in a week."

"Will do," Phoebe said. As she slid down off the examining table, Rossely turned back around and handed her the prescription with long, slim fingers.

"By the way, do you mind my asking who recommended you?" he said. "You didn't note it on our form."

"A professor at the college who had heard your name. But I believe you treat several students from Lyle. Rachel Blunt?"

She saw the muscles of Rossely's face tighten.

"Rachel, yes." He seemed uncomfortable suddenly. Phoebe decided to go for broke.

"And Blair Usher, too," she said. "She had a sports injury as well."

"Forgive me, but I actually shouldn't be discussing patients with you," he said. Again, the tight smile, with lips as white as a clenched knuckle. "It's not only inappropriate, it's also against the law. I hope you understand."

"Of course," Phoebe said. "I'm sorry."

But she saw that she had clearly hit a nerve.

# 33

Phoebe wondered what it could possibly mean. She considered whether Rossely might be routinely prescribing OxyContin to student athletes, particularly those in the Sixes. Some of them may have become addicted to the drug—and that could be affecting their actions.

As soon as Phoebe was home, she called the campus health center. The person who answered the phone put her through to the nurse on duty.

"Is Dr. Todd Rossely someone on your list of recommended orthopedic experts?" Phoebe asked after identifying herself. She wanted to find out if the center referred students to Rossely, or if some of the Sixes had stumbled onto him on their own.

"Hmmm, I don't see him on the list," the nurse said. "But you could double-check with the director tomorrow."

Something was definitely off, Phoebe realized. Why would students go to a doctor not on the school's list?

As soon as she hung up, she called Glenda. She didn't answer her cell, and the automated message indicated she was out of range and a message couldn't be taken. She was obviously in a place with spotty service, but Phoebe had no idea where it was. Glenda, Phoebe realized, had been oddly vague about the donor she was going to see.

After dinner Phoebe tried again, with no luck. She then called Glenda's home number, but only the answering machine picked up.

"Glenda, call me the minute you get back, okay?" Phoebe said. "I'm taking Ginger for a walk, but I'll have my cell. There's a weird connection between a doctor in town and the Sixes, and I've got to figure out what it is. Is there anyone in health care services I can talk to?"

After she hung up, Phoebe put Ginger on the leash and locked the house. It was crisp out, but not the biting cold that had taken hold during the past few days. She'd been walking to the college and back with the dog, but tonight, when she reached the edge of the campus and started to turn back, Ginger tugged on her leash. The dog seemed eager to keep going, perhaps because the night was warmer than usual.

"Okay, okay," Phoebe said.

She wasn't far from the west gate to the college, the one that offered easy access to the playing fields. Phoebe walked with the dog up to the gate and entered the campus. She realized that Ginger would probably love a chance to scamper around on a little grass for a change. She let the dog lead her to the southern end of the fields, just to the left of the athletic center. There was a big workout center inside, and as she meandered with the dog, the door opened intermittently as students strolled in and out.

Phoebe tried to let her mind drift. She was eager for answers, but thinking so hard wasn't helping at the moment. Ginger seemed to relish being on the campus. She was sniffing at every single bush, leaf, and scrap of paper they passed. After a few minutes Phoebe realized that they'd wandered fairly far and were now at the edge of the baseball diamond, away from the light cast from the big windows of the athletic center. She took her eyes off the dog and looked round. There was no one else in sight. Dumb, she thought. How the hell did I let myself get up here alone in the dark?

"Let's go, princess," she said, tugging on Ginger's leash for her to shift directions. As Phoebe started to make a beeline back toward the athletic center, she heard the rustle of dried leaves off to her right. She spun in that direction. Suddenly a man stepped from behind one of the big maples. He was tall and wearing a long, dark coat that reached below his knees.

Phoebe's heart skipped. It's just someone from campus, she told herself, someone cutting through to reach the athletic center. And in a split second she saw she was right. It was Mark Johns. Ginger jumped a little in recognition. She was familiar with Mark, of course, from her stay at Glenda's.

"Hello, Mark," Phoebe said. Part of her was relieved it was him; another part felt awkward. The last time she'd talked to him was when he'd confronted her in the hall of his house. And then there was the dreadful experience of overhearing him on the phone as she crept down the hall of his house, practically on her belly.

"Hello, Phoebe," he said. His voice was cool, unfriendly. Clearly, Phoebe thought, he's as happy to see me, as I am to see him.

"How are you anyway?" she asked. She didn't know what else to say.

"Not so good, actually," he said.

"I'm sorry. I know what a tough time this has been."

"Oh, do you now?"

"Yes, Mark, I do," she said. Don't let this get hostile, she told herself. "I know it's been awful for Glenda and I'm sure it's been very hard on you as well."

"You know what *I* know, Phoebe?" he said. His voice sounded weird, even edgier than it had the day he'd chewed her out at his house. "What *I* know is that you just can't back off. You have to nose your way into *everything.*"

Oh boy, Phoebe thought. Glenda must have told him that Phoebe had overheard his phone call.

"I don't want to interfere in your marriage, Mark," Phoebe said. "I just want what's best for Glenda—and for you, too."

"What do you know about me anyway?" Mark said. "You've never had any damn sense of who I am."

"It's true we've never been close—but I care about you."

"Is that right?" he said. His tone was contemptuous. "You cared about me as I hauled my butt to wherever Glenda landed a hot new job, despite what it did to my *own* career? You cared about me as I had to play the president's wife, hugging the wall at those endless, go-dawful receptions? Funny, I never noticed you caring one freaking bit."

Phoebe knew at times that Mark might resent Glenda's success, but she'd never suspected his anger ran this deep.

"I'm sorry if I didn't seem attentive to you," Phoebe said. "I felt at times that you didn't like having me in Glenda's life. Look, maybe we could grab a cup of coffee this week and talk more about it?"

He shook his head and sighed angrily. "Oh, I'm afraid it's a little too late for coffee, Phoebe."

"You may feel it's too late to be friends with me," Phoebe said. "But it's not too late to save your marriage."

He let out a manic laugh that made her heart skip.

"Oh, now smart, sassy little Phoebe is going to play marriage counselor. Isn't that rich? No, Phoebe, I need you to come with me."

"Come with you?" Phoebe asked, startled. "*Where?*" She didn't like the way he was sounding or looking.

"You don't need to know where. I'm the boss tonight."

"No," Phoebe said. "I'm going home and you should do the same."

"Oh, nobody's going home right now," Mark said. He slipped his hand into the pocket of his coat and drew something out. At first she thought it was a tool of some kind, and then the light from the lamppost caught it: he was holding a gun. Phoebe felt her legs buckle in fear.

"Mark," Phoebe stammered. "What are you doing?"

"Like I told you, Phoebe. You need to come with me. Back over behind these trees. You and I have some unfinished business."

"Please, Mark," Phoebe said. She wondered desperately if there were people still coming out of the athletic center, someone she could shout to, but she didn't dare turn around. "I never meant to be disrespectful to you."

"It's not about respect right now. It's what I said before—you have to have your nose in every goddamn thing. I told Glenda she shouldn't have you look into Lily's disappearance, but oh no, it had to be Phoebe to the rescue. I always thought your little celebrity investigations were so pathetic, but wouldn't you know, you dug up a serial killer. Almost got yourself killed, just like that stupid girl, but somehow once again you survived."

"But why—why would you mind if I looked into Lily's death?" Phoebe asked. She took a breath, trying to calm herself.

"Because it just wasn't any of your business. And then you still couldn't stop, could you? You were out today, making more trouble."

*Today?* Frantically she wondered what he was talking about. She hadn't been out of the house—except for her trip to Rossely's. And she hadn't even had a chance to tell Glenda about that. But wait, she *had* told her, she suddenly realized. She'd left a message about it on Glenda's answering machine.

"Do you mean my trip to Dr. Rossely's?" Phoebe said. She was totally confused. She couldn't understand why Mark would care about that.

"Very good, Phoebe," Mark said. "Maybe you're a little smarter than I give you credit for."

"But what do you have to do with Rossely anyway?" My God, she suddenly realized, this might be about OxyContin. "You're not taking drugs, are you?"

"Oh, is *that* what you think?" he snapped. "That I'm just some kind of junkie? Is that why you went there? To check up on me?"

"No, it had nothing at all to do with you," Phoebe said. Don't push any buttons, she warned herself. "I found out that members of the Sixes are going to him. I'm wondering if some of them might be addicted to drugs he's giving them." Hutch's words echoed in her ears again: *Eighty dollars a pill.* "Or maybe—" she added, thinking out loud, "maybe they're getting prescriptions and *selling* the pills. On the black market." Was that the sixth circle, she suddenly wondered. *Dealing drugs?* "If Rossely's helping these girls deal drugs . . . ?"

"*Rossely?*" Mark said disdainfully. "You think *he's* in charge?"

He let out another exasperated sigh. "That's so typical of you, Phoebe—and Glenda too. I might be standing in the room, but you always assume someone *else* is in charge."

Then suddenly, she knew. "*You're* involved with the Sixes, aren't you?" she said. It can't be true, she told herself and yet she knew now that it was. She was in even graver danger than she'd realized.

"Ahh, you're finally catching on."

"But *why*, Mark? What could they possibly offer you?"

"Let your imagination run wild for a change, Phoebe," he said. "Or are you so used to spewing out the blabbering words of movie stars that you can't?"

Thoughts ricocheted in Phoebe's head. The fifth circle—*seduce and exploit*. The sense that Jen and Alexis both had that Blair was consulting with someone.

"Blair approached you, didn't she?" Phoebe said. "You had an affair with her."

"I hope you're not going to go all indignant on me for it, Phoebe. I *deserve* a woman who respects me."

"And did Blair cook up the drug scheme?"

"Blair? You think it was her idea? You love underestimating me."

"Mark, please," she said. He was becoming unhinged, but she had to keep him talking. Surely, at some point, people would pass by this part of campus, maybe even the campus police. "Whatever your reasons, you need to stop all this. If not for Glenda's sake, then for Brandon's. The Sixes are going to be exposed."

"Oh, that's right, you're on your little mission, aren't you? You just won't let go of the past."

"What do you mean *the past*?" Phoebe asked. She could feel something strange stirring in her, something beneath the fear.

"You've always had a hair up your ass about girls doing their thing. Your life would have been much less complicated if you'd just backed off years ago."

"You mean Fortuna, don't you?" Phoebe said, startled. "But Glenda said she'd never told you about Fortuna."

"Of course she told me," he said, cocking his head up. But Phoebe sensed he was lying.

"How do you really know about Fortuna?" Phoebe said. "Is there someone here, on campus, who was part of it?"

Mark said nothing. The gun jiggled slightly in his hand and Phoebe felt her knees buckle again. And then a thought rammed her brain, like an explosion.

"Omigod," Phoebe said. "When you were at school—you knew about Fortuna. You knew what happened to me."

Mark snickered. "Even back then, you were the girl who didn't know when she should just leave things fucking alone. You were just always asking for trouble."

The ground seemed to fall away beneath her.

"You were one of the boys, weren't you?" Phoebe said, nearly choking over her words. "One of the boys who buried me in the crawl space."

"Shut up, Phoebe," Mark said. "Just shut the fuck up."

She could see from his expression that she was right, though.

"Come on," he said, tightening his grip on the gun and pointing it straight at her. "Like I said, you need to come with—"

And then there was a rustling off to their right.

"Mark, put the gun down," someone shouted.

It was a woman's voice, coming from near the trees. They both looked up in surprise as Glenda burst into the halo of light from the lamppost.

"Go away, Glenda," Mark shouted. "What are you doing here?"

"You have to stop, Mark. If you kill Phoebe, what do you think that does to Brandon? Are you going to ruin his life, too?"

Mark began to flick the gun back and forth in his hand, like someone crazed. Suddenly he pointed it directly at his head.

"Mark, please no," Glenda called.

He took two steps backward and lowered the gun.

"Just so you know," he said hoarsely, "I was the one who called the police and told them where the crawl space was."

Then he pulled back his arm and hurled the gun toward the baseball diamond. A second later he took off running into the dark.

# 34

At just after seven on Friday night, as Phoebe was standing on her porch locking the front door, she heard a car pull up and instinctively she spun around. It was Glenda. Phoebe quickly crossed the yard to greet her.

"Hey," Phoebe said as Glenda stepped from the car. She was dressed in jeans and wearing almost zero makeup. Phoebe reached out and hugged Glenda with her good arm. "I'm so glad to see you."

"Did I catch you coming or going?" Glenda asked.

"Going. I was headed down to Tony's for dinner. Want to come?"

"I just never saw you as a Tony's girl. But, no, thanks. I need to get home and start organizing. I just dropped by to say hi."

"How was your trip? Phoebe asked. A week and a half ago, Glenda had resigned from the college and driven up to Boston with Brandon to visit former colleagues and figure out a strategy for herself.

"Okay," Glenda said. "I thought of jumping off the Prudential building a couple of times, but I guess I'm just not that morose of a chick. At least I got some decent advice while I was there."

"Are there people other than me who think you shouldn't have resigned?"

"I appreciate you having my back, Fee, but at some point resigning became a foregone conclusion. Do you remember how I took off that day, saying I was going to see a donor? I didn't want to lay too much on you at the time, but I actually drove to New York to talk to a lawyer about my situation. Even then he said that because of everything that had happened, I'd be lucky to keep my job, and when the truth about Mark came out, it was like I'd hit the third rail. Better to resign and avoid the extra trauma of being canned."

"So what's your plan from here?" Phoebe asked.

"I'm not sure. The good news, according to everybody I've spoken to, is that this may not be a career ender as far as academia goes. But I'll definitely have to look for a job lower down the ladder. Of course, it may be time to think of a career change. Or maybe *I'll* write a book—*My Life with a Dirty Rotten Liar.*"

"Have you learned any more about what happened with Mark?"

"Not much. It looks like he became involved with Blair last semester. I'm sure he thinks she made a play for him because he's just so gorgeous and charming, but I bet he was the person in power she targeted for that fifth circle you talked about. It also seems they cooked up the drug thing together. The Sixes were able to build their secret fund, and he was able to pay off his gambling debts. Apparently he's been at that again for a while."

"I never thought to ask you. How did you happen to come upon Mark and me that night?"

"As I was coming home from New York, I saw him jumping into his car. He must have just heard your voicemail message. He looked like a man on a serious mission, and I decided to follow him."

"How are you feeling about him right now?"

"He used young women at my college to deal drugs. He put me and Brandon at risk. He threatened you with a gun. Those aren't things I'll ever forgive. But I don't want to cut Brandon off from him."

"Does that mean you want to stay around here?"

"Not in the immediate vicinity. Kids are taunting Brandon at school, and I can't bear being near the college. I'm going to stay with my brother in New Jersey for a few weeks, just to get my bearings, and then I might look for a job in New York. There's a lot of opportunity there and it's close enough that Brandon can see Mark while he's still out on bail."

"Here's an idea, then," Phoebe said. "With the advance for my new book, I won't need to sublet my apartment after the first of the year, so why don't you and Brandon stay there for a while? And that way I can come and visit."

Glenda smiled and said it might be an offer she couldn't refuse.

"You need any help packing?" Phoebe asked.

"No, the school has graciously let me hire packers. Probably because they want to make sure I'm out in four days. It's going to be so humiliating when the moving truck pulls up."

"Trust me, Glenda. Your life isn't going to go according to your original plan, but it will be good again—sooner than you can imagine."

"Enough about me. How are you doing?"

"Almost mended. Any more updates on the Sixes? I've heard they've rounded more than a few of them up."

"Yeah. When Blair and Gwen were arrested the first time, the other members kept quiet. But now they're all worried about being swept up in the drug scandal, so they're coming forward and throwing each other under the bus."

"Wow, maybe I can finally toss out my night-light."

Glenda laughed. "That's not to say we'll root out all the bullying and meanness on campus. I'm afraid that's a sign of the times."

"But there'll always be the kids who rise above it, too. I was thinking the other day how this has all been so much about power. The Sixes wanted to exert their power over everyone else, just like Fortuna did. And the only way you fight them is to find some power in yourself. I was upset at first when I found out how en-trenched Lily was in the group, but she was compen-sating for a loss in her own life. And though she knew Blair would probably come after her, she did ultimately decide to break free."

"You were always afraid you didn't help her that day. But maybe something you said really did. Helped her find that power."

Phoebe shrugged. "I hope," she said. "But of course I'll never know."

After Glenda left, Phoebe drove down to Tony's. There was a parking spot directly in front of the build-ing on Bridge Street; as she stepped onto the sparkly sidewalk, Phoebe could smell the river in the crisp evening air. It had been just over a month since she'd stood there the night Lily had been reported missing, and yet in some ways it seemed like a year ago.

Taking a deep breath, she entered the restaurant. There were two guys at the bar tonight—a big, beefy dude at the very end, watching a ball game with his trucker hat tipped back on his head, and close to the door, Duncan Shaw. She knew he'd be there. She'd overheard Jan mention to someone that she and Miles were trying to lure Duncan out tonight, but he was having dinner alone at Tony's.

"Hello, Phoebe," he said when he turned and saw her. He looked startled. She'd set eyes on him only once since she'd been out of the hospital, from across the quad late one afternoon, but she was pretty sure he hadn't noticed her.

"Would—would you mind if I sat down for a minute?" she asked. There was a half-empty espresso cup in front of him, as well as the bill for dinner—with his credit card and the receipt lying on top. She had just managed to catch him.

"Sure, go ahead," he said neutrally. He scooted his stool over just a hair to make it easier for her to climb onto the one next to him. "Tony's off tonight, by the way. Family wedding this weekend."

"Actually, it wasn't him I was hoping to see," she said. "A spy told me you were going to be here."

"Ahh." He seemed to work the comment over in his mind. "How are you doing, anyway? I hope Glenda told you I called a couple of times to see how you were."

"Yes, she did, thanks," Phoebe said.

"It must have been awful," Duncan said, studying her. "I'm sure there were moments when you felt like you were reliving the nightmare you'd gone through in boarding school."

"Yes," she said softly. "Though maybe in the end that helped me. I had to drag it out in the open and finally try to deal with it."

"And did you? Find a way to deal with it?"

"I think so. Mostly by acknowledging how big an effect it really had on me. Not just the abduction and the day I spent trapped in the crawl space, but the months of being ostracized and bullied. For years I'd tried to put it behind me and pretend I hadn't allowed it to have any lasting impact. But that was a lie. Of course, I wish I could have seen the light without so many people being hurt at the same time."

"I heard that the board accepted Glenda's resignation. How's she doing?"

"It's been tough, but I know she won't let this undo her."

"I had the sense you weren't crazy about Mark. But did you ever suspect he might be capable of what he did?"

The news about Mark's involvement in a drug ring had been all over the campus and town. But only Phoebe and Glenda knew about his connection to Fortuna.

"I don't think Mark is inherently an evil person," Phoebe said quietly. "But Glenda's success ate at him more than I ever realized."

The bartender, who'd been in the back, moseyed over and scooped up Duncan's credit card. When he asked if Phoebe wanted anything, she ordered a glass of red wine.

"So with Glenda on her way out of Lyle, where does that leave you?" Duncan asked after the bartender had wandered off.

"I'm going to finish out the semester, of course, but I'm not going to teach next year. It would feel like a betrayal with Glenda gone."

"You'll head back to New York then?"

"Actually, I'm going to stick around town through the spring," she replied. "I've decided to write a book about what happened to me. Part true-crime story— I've always liked writers like Anne Rule and Bailey Weggins—but also part memoir."

"That's terrific," Duncan said. His response seemed genuine to her. "So no celebrity book then?"

"Nope. The Johnny Depps of the world can sleep a little easier. Actually, I think I've been sick of the whole celebrity genre longer than I realized. That may be why I wasn't paying enough attention to what the researcher on my last book was doing." Phoebe smiled. "Oh, and don't worry. The memoir part will focus mostly on what happened in boarding school. I won't be delving into any romantic details from my life now."

"Ahh, so my fifteen minutes of fame will have to be postponed," Duncan said. He smiled at her, but to her dismay he quickly signed the receipt and slipped his card into his wallet.

"I know you're just about to leave, so I won't hold you up," Phoebe said hurriedly. "But the reason I stopped by was to tell you how sorry I am about what I said to you that day by the Grove. It was awful, and I hope you can accept my apology."

Duncan looked off for a second, his deep brown eyes betraying no hint of how he would answer. He returned his gaze to her and shrugged. "Sure, why not?"

"That sounds a bit tentative," Phoebe said.

He exhaled a little, making a frustrated sound, and turned both hands palm side up.

"Well, it's not like you stepped on my *toe*, Phoebe. You suggested that I might have murdered Lily Mack. There's a bit more of an ouch factor with something like that."

She winced as he said the words. "I know," she said. "Again, I'm sorry. I—I'd begun to feel like everything was closing in on me then. And I just wasn't thinking straight."

Duncan's body seemed to relax. "Apology accepted, okay?"

"Thank you," she said.

He slid from the stool. Just behind him was a row of pegs, and he tugged his coat off one of them.

"Are you going to be okay getting back to campus?" he asked. She didn't allow herself to feel excited by the comment. The words suggested an invitation for a ride, but his tone had been totally perfunctory.

"Yes, I have my car," she said. "I'll have a bite to eat and then head home."

"Well, enjoy. Good night."

"Actually," Phoebe said as he turned to go, "there's one more thing I'd like to say. Do you have an extra minute?"

"Okay," he said after a second's hesitation. To her relief, he didn't appear annoyed. He leaned against the bar, looking at her.

"Like I said, I've had a chance to really think about my life lately," Phoebe said. "And I see now how much I always tended to hold back—you know—in personal situations. Maybe that's why I liked writing about celebrities—I could observe them and dig around about them, but I could keep my distance, too. My former boyfriend called recently and told me I suffered from a failure to get my feet wet emotionally."

Duncan didn't say anything, just studied her. She could tell he was wondering where she was going with all this. Phoebe grabbed another breath.

"That day by the woods, you told me that you thought we had something special, and I did, too," she said. "But at the same time I think I was looking for an excuse to pull back, and that's why I let myself doubt you. It was a stupid mistake, and I regret it terribly. I know you'll find this crazy—really crazy. But I'm hoping you'll give me another chance."

She saw his eyes widen. He hadn't seen this coming.

He took a deep breath, held it, and looked off toward the dining room, searching, she assumed, for a response.

"I—I just don't know what to say," he said. "It just seemed over that day."

"Don't tell me you're dating Val now," she said, trying to be playful. She cringed inside at her clunky attempt at humor, but Duncan actually chuckled.

"No," he said. "I'm not dating anyone. Believe it or not, this has been hard for me, too, Phoebe."

"I'm sorry I hurt you," Phoebe said. She felt a surge of guilt but at the same time wondered: if their split had really troubled him, there might still be something there. "You don't have to give me an answer tonight, but will you just think about what I asked?"

He held her eyes, parting his lips just a little.

"All right," he said after a couple of seconds. "I'll think about it."

He said good-bye and slipped out of the restaurant. The waiter finally returned with her wine. She took a long sip, set the glass down, and smiled. Duncan may not have given her an answer, but he'd done something that left her hopeful: he had nodded his head unconsciously when he'd spoken. And Phoebe knew—from so many years observing people while she interviewed them—that that was what people did when, without knowing it yet, they planned to say yes.

# Acknowledgments

S ome terrific people took time out of their demanding jobs to help me in the research for *The Sixes*, and I am very indebted to them: Jonathan Birbeck, Esq., chief deputy district attorney, Cumberland County, Pennsylvania; Cheryl Brown, associate vice chancellor, University of California at Davis; Barbara Butcher, chief of staff, New York City Medical Examiner; Dr. Chet Lerner, chief, Section of Infectious Diseases, New York Downtown Hospital; Dr. Mark Howell, psychotherapist; Dr. Jill Murray, psychotherapist and author; author Sheila Weller; Kenneth Wagner, Ph.D., CLM, water resources manager.

Thank you as well to Kathy Schneider for all her encouragement and support; Sandy Dijkstra for her awesome agenting; Sally Kim for being such a terrific editor; and Maya Ziv for her fabulous eleventh-hour guidance; and Rachel Elinsky for her continuous awesome work on the PR front.

# HARPER LUXE

## THE NEW LUXURY IN READING

We hope you enjoyed reading
our new, comfortable print size and found it
an experience you would like to repeat.

**Well — you're in luck!**

HarperLuxe offers the finest in fiction and
nonfiction books in this same larger print size and
paperback format. Light and easy to read, HarperLuxe
paperbacks are for book lovers who want to see
what they are reading without the strain.

For a full listing of titles and
new releases to come, please visit our website:

**www.HarperLuxe.com**

# HARPER LUXE